alternative medicine

ANDY EVANS

FIRST EDITION

www.andyevansfiction.com

author's note

This novel is a work of fiction. However, in my attempt to make the fantasy world feel more authentic, I have placed it in the real world of Dunedin, New Zealand, and, more specifically, in Dunedin Hospital. At the time of starting this novel, March 2017, I was a nurse employed at the Southern District Health Board, and it was a world I knew a little (Although, I have never worked in the Children's Ward, the Emergency Department, ICU, or many other locations used in this story). Where possible, I have tried to make the descriptions of these locations as accurate as possible; if details are inaccurate, such that it throws you out of the story, please accept my apologies.

The characters in this novel, unlike the locations, are fictitious. See the legal blurb on the copyright page.

I began work on this novel before the world experienced

the horrors, devastation, and far-reaching disruption of the global pandemic, COVID-19. How our lives have changed! While this story doesn't deal with a pandemic per se, it involves an infectious disease, the fictitious Lymphachela Virus. Since the pandemic, I have asked myself several times if I should continue with this story. Will anyone would want to read it? Certainly, in the light of New Zealand's response to COVID-19, I have tweaked certain scenes. Ultimately, the novel had reached enough critical mass that it was important to get it over the finish line. The editing process has been a long road indeed.

What you're about to embark on, Dear Reader, is a book about healing, about overcoming darkness and disease, about a doctor who realises his calling, and thus his ability to make a real difference, lies beyond the parameters of the medical professional.

A dark medical fantasy...

For Amy —

prologue

The woman passed beneath the streetlight on the corner of Great King Street and Hanover Street; her face, indeed much of her frame, concealed by shadows. Her breath swirled up into the crisp night air. Dressed in black, she was swift and silent. Hands clenching and unclenching, keeping the circulation moving, as the cold numbed the tips of her fingers. She turned, eyeing an empty Hanover Street. A solitary car drifted along on State Highway 1, barely slowing as it moved through the city and through traffic lights that favoured its passage.

Then the city was still again.

Too still.

When satisfied her movements were unobserved, the woman slipped across the road. Back into the shadows, keeping to those deepest and widest under the canopy of trees, and then hugging the wrought-iron fence which lined the hospital crèche.

She came at last to a fire exit on the southwest wall of the hospital, and here she paused.

Her pale fingers probed the door—its height, its width, undeterred that there was no exterior handle and nothing upon which to gain purchase.

The palm of her right hand slammed against the hard wooden exterior, right in the middle, where she guessed the release bar was located inside.

The noise boomed gunshot-like through the abandoned streets on this June night, threatening to disturb even the deepest slumber. The door, however, did not budge, not so much as an inch.

Again, her fingers probed the door, searching for something barely perceivable, less certain this time.

Her face remained downcast and obscured by shadow. The small adjacent retaining wall concealed her position. There were no security cameras on this side of the hospital; she'd already scoped out the perimeter several times.

Nevertheless, she glanced up and down Hanover Street, making sure she hadn't drawn unwanted attention. Nothing. Not even a breeze stirred. No signs of the trouble she'd felt earlier. The storefront of Henry's Beer, Wine and Spirits remained frozen under sepia tones on the opposite side of the street. The city continued its apparent slumber.

She struck the door again with her palm—harder, in a slightly lower position.

This time, while it made no less noise, the fire exit swung open, inviting her into the darkened interior.

With one last look up and down Hanover Street, she slipped into the hospital, pulling the door closed behind her.

Once inside, the woman followed a rabbit warren of corridors deep into the basement of the hospital. She moved cautiously, her eyes shifting back and forth, growing wider with apprehension. Her face and her neck were heavy with lines and folds, not only a sign of her age, but of the hardships she'd endured. Yet, she moved with the agility of a much younger woman. Hidden in her face, beyond the ravages of age and hardships, were the remnants of a long-forgotten beauty. Her hair, once black, was now brittle and mostly grey.

She came to a locker room opposite the main lift shaft. The locker room door was wedged open with a triangular block of wood, and a domestic's trolley was parked outside.

Surely, this was an opportunity? The Old Bastard showing her kindness for once?

The woman peered inside. The light in the locker room was on.

She entered. A thick fragrance hung in the air, floral and overpowering. In the far corner, somewhere behind a steep row of steel grey lockers, a shower was running, the water bubbling down some drain deep under the hospital's foundations. Muffled singing came from within. A woman's voice: Unselfconscious, holding a fair melody.

Skirting past the lockers, the woman tried each one. The majority did not budge, but she found one locker that opened. Inside hung a lilac uniform. She pulled it out, took it from its coat hanger, and held it to her chest. It was a couple of dress sizes too big, but passable. Even better, accompanying the uniform was a hospital ID badge on a lanyard, the Southern DHB logo embossed on the bottom. Typed on the badge was a name, then underneath, CLEANING SERVICES. There was a faded, pixilated photo which no one would recognise.

This was going a little *too* easy...

Removing her dark coat and her blouse, she slipped into the uniform. It was damp with sweat and cheap perfume, and slightly creased. She wrinkled her nose. She pulled on the pleated edges, trying to iron out the worst of the creases. It was more than a couple of sizes too big, but it would have to do.

The woman left the locker room, bundling her clothes into the skip on the domestic's trolley, then wheeling the trolley with her towards the Emergency Department.

The door said STAFF ONLY, but one swipe of the ID badge, and it opened for her. She held her breath, slowing. It was busier here, even at such an early hour. The lights all blazed. Several staff milled around the central Nurse's Station, although they seemed too busy to notice her. Many cubicles were occupied. Somewhere, behind one curtain, someone was whimpering in pain. A child, perhaps. The place was full of horrors. Horrors both major and minor. It was not by choice she came here.

The woman in the lilac uniform pushed her trolley into the department. The trick was to make it look like she belonged. *I'm here to clean house in the truest sense of the word*, she told herself, but that was an over-exaggeration. She'd come for David, and she'd be happy just to retrieve him and go back to her reclusive lifestyle.

Intuition drove her towards the Resus Bays. This is where the most acute patients came—the road traffic accidents, the coronary events, the aneurysms, the overdoses...

It was darker around Resus 2, as if one of the fluoros had failed. The air was thicker. And there was a terrible smell issuing from within. Something oily. Something that ought not to exist in any natural environment. This was no normal Seeper.

She knew David was inside.

Voices were coming from the other side of the curtain, and she wanted to enter immediately, but she waited, unsure how to proceed.

The curtain parted briefly and two ED nurses emerged, dressed in dark blue scrubs and walking straight towards her.

The woman turned and bowed her head.

"Where's the boy's father?" asked the first nurse.

"He said something about parking the car," said the other. "Why?"

The woman pretended to screw and unscrew the top on a bottle of cleaning solution. She willed herself to be invisible and the two nurses not to notice her.

"No reason," said the first nurse.

"Girl, keep your mind out of the gutter," said the other.

The woman held her breath.

"I like older men," said the first nurse as she passed by. "What's wrong with that? Especially when they're all worried and parental."

The second nurse laughed. "You're sick."

Neither nurse glanced in the woman's direction. They moved towards the Nurse's Station.

The woman exhaled a slow breath. She approached the cubicle, abandoning the cleaning trolley. There was a popping noise from inside, followed by a silence that felt too heavy. She glanced around the Emergency Department, making sure no one was following her movements. Again satisfied, she pulled the curtain across and stepped inside.

"David..." she whispered.

Moments later, the curtain billowed outwards as the woman was hurled from Resus 2.

"*Leave us!*" the thing in the cubicle roared. "*Your ministrations are fruitless!*"

And such was the force of the throw that she was lifted several metres across the corridor and crashed into one of the DynaMaps.

She braced for the impact, but when the pain hit, she was unprepared. It tore along her buttocks and down her left leg. She clenched her teeth, shut her mouth, but a small yelp escaped anyway.

The DynaMap at her back toppled, smacking the linoleum, its plastic casing cracking open, its inner circuitry exposed and spilling out.

She sat there, stunned.

This Seeper was like nothing she'd encountered before. She told herself she wasn't afraid, that she'd march back into Resus 2, even though she was clearly outmatched.

"We know you," it cursed. "*You cannot stop us!*"

She tried to regain her feet, but her left leg protested. A fresh jolt of pain stole her breath from her.

She was too late. She'd already drawn far too much attention. Several staff—nurses, doctors—were approaching. And, heading them all, was a large Security Guard with a fierce scowl and a belly that hung over his belt.

She scrambled to her feet and limped towards the exit. The oversized Security Guard was breathing down her neck. Heavy, heavy breaths. The smell of perspiration—hers, but mostly *his*—filled her nostrils. He, more than the others, seemed determined to catch her.

Please, God...

Reaching out, the Security Guard snagged the lanyard around the woman's neck. Her centre of gravity shifted rapidly backwards.

The lanyard cut into her throat. It took her breath mid-exhalation. She thought the strength in her legs might wilt away.

She was weary to her bones.

In pain.

God, so much pain.

And then the quick release mechanism on the lanyard broke, and she staggered forward once again, off-balance and awkward, but still moving towards the Ambulance Bay and into that chilly night.

part one

one

"Whatever I know, I owe solely to my assiduous reading of books of the ancients, to my desire to understand them and to appropriate this science; then I have added the observation and experience of my whole life."

Al-Zahrawi, page 67, 'The Healing Art'

I pushed the white trolley containing case notes, one wheel juddered, and fought against me.

It was my dubious pleasure every Monday morning, between 8.30am and 9.30am, to follow a living dinosaur named Dr Reginald O'Brien. Dr O'Brien, Paediatric Consultant. Where he led, I followed, struggling with the trolley and its squeaky wheel.

The Consultant was just over six feet, an inch or two

taller than me. His skin was pale, unless he got angry, when it would turn a blotchy red. It sagged in places, particularly around the jowls. He wore thin metal glasses, which did nothing to hide the lines along his brow or the severity of his eyes.

He paused outside Room 12. "This is..."

"Toby Harrison."

The innocuous smell of nebulised air lingered by the door.

The patient's name was written on a card outside the room, but Dr O'Brien shunned such readily available information. As Paediatric Registrar, it was my responsibility to remember such details, as though the ability to remember every patient's name was a direct indicator of my measure as a doctor.

"Toby... Toby..." Dr O'Brien reached for the trolley.

I passed him Toby's case notes. They were a hefty tome secured with a thick elastic band. This was volume three. Maybe I should have ordered the first two volumes from Medical Records as well?

While the Consultant unbound the notes, I summarised: "Toby's a twelve-year-old boy, brittle asthmatic. He presented with a marked wheeze three days ago." I lowered my voice. "Saturations were around 91 per cent. Very little air intake."

"And your management plan? Please tell me you have a plan?"

"I've prescribed regular nebulisers and a course of steroids."

"And?"

"Er... Magnesium... and I was thinking maybe CPAP/BiPAP."

"Hmmm." O'Brien rubbed his chin. "No, that's a bad idea. CPAP's never well tolerated in children. You should know that, Dr Newman."

I could think of no reply; nor did Dr O'Brien wait for one. He opened Toby's file, finding the most recent entry. Those stern eyes tracking back and forth as they scanned each line of my handwriting. "Well," he said, drawing out the suspense, "has the boy improved?"

"Come, see for yourself..."

Dr O'Brien's question was, of course, the million-dollar question, and I knew the answer the moment I turned the handle and opened the door. The curtains were across, and the room was gloomy. Toby was sitting on his bed, crouched over, having a nebuliser. For an instance, as my eyes adjusted to the low light, I imagined a large, amorphous mass leaning over the boy, crowding his space, making it near impossible for him to breathe. I blinked. Of course, there was nothing there.

The boy's uncle—Jim, John, something like that—slouched in an easy chair in the far corner. He was a chubby man, with greasy, thinning hair and a puck-marked face. He appeared to be asleep, but one eyelid flittered open.

The nebuliser gurgled. Toby fought for each breath. He was using most of the muscles in his neck, not to mention his auxiliary chest muscles, to get enough air. The smell of nebulised air permeated the room. Stray oxygen molecules collided, but none seemed to help Toby. The nebulising machine bubbled and churned regardless.

Dr O'Brien didn't follow me into the room, but stood in the doorway.

I went straight to Toby's bed and sat beside him. "Take it easy… that's right…" I placed my hand across Toby's shoulder. "I know it's easy to panic when you feel you can't get your breath… but you *can* breathe… you can… this medicine will expand your airways… do you feel it? And you *can* breathe…"

Toby's shoulders relaxed a little. Beneath the mask, which seemed too large for his face, I imagined the hint of a smile.

"There you go," I said, smiling back.

"How's he doin'?" asked Jim or John. His voice was deep and gravelly, precisely as I imagined it to sound. He now sat up in the easy chair, rubbing his eyes.

"He'll be just fine," I said. In terms of a long-term prognosis, this might not be strictly true, but in the short term, I was confident I was correct. I wasn't about to discuss Toby's long-term outlook at this precise moment.

I glanced up at Dr O'Brien. "Alright, Toby," I said. "How about I pop back a bit later when you're feeling better?"

Toby nodded.

Dr O'Brien and I stepped back into the bright, wide corridor and closed the door on Toby, his uncle and the gloom.

Dr O'Brien spoke, but only when he was sure that the door was closed and we were well out of earshot. "That was quite a performance in there," he said. "You're not doing yourself any favours, mind. That touchy-feely bedside manner. This is medicine not nursing, for God's sake. Scientific principles inform our practice."

"Sorry? What do you mean?"

"Getting too familiar with that kid," he said. "All that touchy-feeling dribble. You know as well as I do that his case is hopeless."

"How is it hopeless?"

"The boy's living a death sentence. Maybe not this episode, or the next, but soon. You've seen the X-rays, you've seen the scarring, you know as well as I do."

"I'm just trying to be optimistic."

"*Pha—!* It's not about optimism. You need to maintain Professional Detachment. That's what they always said back in the day, when I did my training."

Dr O'Brien, who had done his training back in the good old days of the Patriarchy, of cholera and flu epidemics, of children being seen and not heard, of corporal punishment... oh, and when prehistoric monsters walked the earth! I felt like I didn't need any advice from Dr O'Brien, resented the fact that he presumed to offer it, and yet deep down I feared he might be spot on.

Dr O'Brien was already moving along the corridor, towards the next patient, Toby Harrison already dismissed. A whiff of burnt toast drifted from the kitchenette.

I followed—pushing the trolley.

Around us, the Children's Ward was pure industry. A hundred separate conversations echoed along pumice-coloured corridors, fish-themed curtains were hauled around bed spaces, linen trolleys wheeled from one room to the next, a nurse hung a bag of intravenous antibiotics on a young boy in Room 5. Mornings were always the busiest, especially on a Monday. All things considered, it was probably the worst time for a ward round.

A clean, sterile smell filled the ward and quickly displaced any unpleasant odours.

The Consultant hovered by Room 3. "Who do we have here?"

I read the name card beside the door, then referred to my own scribbled notes. "This is Charlie O'Loughlin," I said. "She has chronic arthritis."

"And her progress?"

"Er, okay, I guess."

"Good."

"Did you want to see her?"

Dr O'Brien glanced down at his wristwatch. "No, we don't have time to see every single child and give them all a hug." Now he had a real bee in his bonnet. "Let's keep moving."

Unbelievable. I shook my head.

One patient that Dr O'Brien insisted on seeing was a nine-year-old girl named Serena Hopkins. Serena was dying from a rare haematological cancer called Megaloblastic Anaemia.

"Hello, Serena," I said, as we entered her room. "How're you feeling today?" The question was hypothetical, since I knew the answer with one glance. Serena's complexion was several shades too pale. Her hazel eyes were too large in her undernourished face and, overall, she was just too damn thin. My stomach churned and tensed. It was a wonder she had any fight left in her.

Serena's mother sat on the bed, braiding Serena's long brown hair. Her father sat in the chair beside her bed, reading a glossy magazine with a Lion on the cover and the title, *Authentic*.

Serena smiled. "Fine, thanks."

Mr Hopkins looked up from his magazine. He was an odd-looking man: a receding hairline, a large forehead with a sheen to it, and bug eyes. "Good morning, Dr O'Brien and Dr Newman."

Dr O'Brien and I both agreed it was a good morning, but Mr Hopkins wasn't finished. "God is good," he said. "He's looking after my Serena, like He always does. God is in the business of miracles, isn't that right?"

The question apparently wasn't addressed to me or Dr O'Brien, but to his wife and daughter.

"Amen," said Mrs Hopkins, demure and passive. "That He is!"

Serena merely nodded. Her eyelids drooped. She looked incredibly weary.

"Oh, what's wrong, Sugarplum?" Mr Hopkins asked, unimpressed by his daughter's lack of enthusiasm. "'Whoever shall confess that Jesus is the Son of God, God dwelleth in him, and he in God.'"

"Amen," said Mrs Hopkins. "Yes, and Amen."

Serena closed her eyes. "And what about girls, Dad? You said, 'God dwelleth in *him*'?"

"In girls too, of course, Sugarplum. God doesn't discriminate. God is Love."

Mrs Hopkins, perhaps sensing the stand-off between her husband and daughter, glanced at me, but couldn't hold the stare. "Do you believe in miracles, Dr Newman?"

I took my time answering. "I don't know," I said. "I think having a faith can be a wonderful thing. At its best, it can be truly inspiring."

"God uses believers and unbelievers alike," Mr Hopkins said. "I believe He uses doctors and nurses more than most, whether they acknowledge Him or not."

I didn't care for his tone or his insinuation. "Well, thank you." I turned back to Serena. "We'd like to repeat those blood tests again today, Serena. I've left a form with the Phlebotomist. Okay?"

"Okay."

Dr O'Brien was quiet in the background, which always made me a little anxious.

"The blood tests are known as markers," I said. "They tell us how well we're doing against this disease. When the results are in, I think we should all sit down and have a chat."

"God has already spoken," Mr Hopkins said, a little too defensively. "He has spoken many times through the Scriptures: '... by His stripes we are healed...' '... I have heard your prayer and seen your tears: I will heal you...' The Scriptures are overflowing with examples."

"Indeed," O'Brien said, and I saw his brow creasing and the colour filling out his cheeks. "All the same, let's wait for the bloods..."

"Thank you, doctor," said Mrs Hopkins. "And God bless."

"Yes," said Mr Hopkins. "God bless you both."

Dr O'Brien and I took the hint and left. Even without the blood tests, I knew the markers would only provide more damning evidence of disease progression. I saw it in Serena's eyes. I suspected she knew, too. Not only that, but I saw a ring of darkness that encircled her, although it could only be seen fleetingly and only in the periphery of my vision. I felt it. I knew it, in the same way I knew many things that it wasn't exactly possible to know.

Dr O'Brien waited until we were a long way down the corridor before he spoke again. "Wow, I've never seen denial like that before... Is that the sort of optimism you favour, Newman?"

"They're grieving," I suggested.

"They're bonkers. And it's not going to end well."

On that much, we at least agreed.

"I want you to sit down with them and spell out the prognosis. It's important they have realistic expectations going forward."

"I'm not sure if I feel ready to have that sort of conversation," I said. "I'm not sure if they're ready to hear it, either."

"It's part of your role, so get ready! You don't get to be the healthcare hero on this one, sorry. Occasionally, we have to break a few hearts and a few fantasies—God knows I've done my share over the years. The sooner, the better. Today is preferable."

"Well, I... I'm uncertain how to approach..."

"Simple. You sit them down, and you lay out the facts. We can't save everybody, unfortunately. Keep your personal feelings out of it. You're not here to win friends..."—He glanced at his watch again—"No time like the present..."

"What about the rest of the Ward Round?"

"I'll wait."

Of course, you'll wait, you old dinosaur. You'll wait and watch the junior doctor do all the jobs that you don't want to do. "I'll need to prepare. I can't just... I—"

Beep beep beep!

A series of mechanical shrieks came from my right hip, and a sickly vibration accompanied it. I tensed… then let myself relax. It was my pager.

Thank God!

I snapped the small black box with its LCD screen from its plastic casing and silenced the continuous beeps. I'd never imagined I'd actually be grateful for my pager going off.

I looked at Dr O'Brien, awaiting his approval.

"Very well," said Dr O'Brien. "If it's an emergency, go. Anything else: remind them you have Ward Round."

two

"When the Long Queen breathes her last breath, once the winter of two great wars has passed and a brief prosperity lulls Her kingdom, there shall arise a Great Scourge: it will fester in the outer islands, hidden from view, yet refining its wrath. Woe to those who feel this Scourge! Woe to the world if this Scourge is let loose and ne'er restrained!"

Ba'al Yimubn Ho, page 66, 'The Healing Art'

Five minutes later, I pulled back the curtain of Resus Two, only to be greeted by chaos.

ED staff, dressed in their blue scrubs, purple nitrile gloves and white plastic aprons, huddled around the centre of the Resus Bay, while other staff rushed around the periphery. Discarded packaging had been strewn over the bed space, the counter, and even the floor. Gloved hands gripped equipment, none of them idle. Oxygen and suction tubing was attached to the back wall, then coiled across the head of the bed. Kidney dishes were laden with needles and cannulas and blood tubes. The tang of sweat and blood hung in the air. There was another smell too, much harder to place: an oily smell. Worse still, a gloom filled the entire cubicle, thick, toxic, as if the fluorescent strips were struggling to provide enough wattage to even minimally light the space. The gloominess felt wrong, oppressive even. I didn't like that smell either. I'd been paged because I was the Paediatric Registrar, but suddenly, I felt like everything I knew (or thought I knew) had departed my brain. I felt old and very weary.

Amid all the chaos, the smell, the gloom, the subject of all this attention, was a teenage boy. His face was flushed a deep red. His arms flailed around, crashing into the cot sides. His eyes unfocused, his pupils blown out and enormous. "Stay away from me!" he yelled. "You're not a real doctor! Stay back!"

A heaviness filled my gut.

I took a deep breath. Although I didn't really want to, I stepped inside the cubicle.

The gloom enfolded me with claw-like fingers.

In the far corner, a man sat in a plastic chair. His body was trembling, his face deathly pale, his eyes down-turned, flitting across the floor.

Dr Mirza—the ED Registrar who'd paged me and saved me from the Ward Round—approached. He was a short, slender man, with immaculately groomed black hair. "Thank you for coming, Dr Newman," he said, then motioned towards the trolley bed. "This is David Layton. He's fourteen years old. He presented just after midnight with fever and delirium, then—at around 06:20hrs—his fever spiked further, to 39.5°C, and he developed a distinctive—"

The boy—David—screamed. "Keep him away from me! You're not real! *You're not fucking real!*"

The man in the plastic chair jumped to his feet, pushed past staff, and stood beside the bed. "David, it's okay, it's okay."

One nurse pulled at the man's shirt sleeve. "Mr Layton, please: If you don't sit down, we'll have to ask you to leave."

The man nodded. A grim smile graced his mouth, but spread no further. He returned to the plastic chair. His face etched with deep lines and haggard-looking. He cupped his head in both hands and quietly sobbed.

Meanwhile, David trembled on the emergency trolley and began hyperventilating.

I turned back to Dr Mirza.

"David has a generalised, or possibly quasi-dermatomal, skin rash. Actually, the distribution seems to follow the path of his major circulatory system. He's usually fit and well. No significant medical history."

I stepped closer to David. Something about the boy's

condition gave me a bad feeling. Something about the entire scenario didn't feel right. Viral infections that caused fever, even delirium, were not uncommon. Atypical rashes were commonplace in children, too. But both…?

David Layton was very unwell, and I sensed that if something wasn't done—the right thing—we could well lose him.

"David," I said, reaching for and taking the boy's hand in mine. "My name's Grant. I'm the doctor."

I wasn't expecting any reply, nor did I get one. The boy didn't pull his hand away, so I took that as a win.

"I want to talk to Dr Mirza here and your Dad, and then we'll see if we can help you. Okay?"

Again, no reply from David.

"Have we got IV access?" I asked Dr Mirza.

He nodded. One nurse pulled back the hospital bedsheet that covered David, revealing a cannula in David's left foot. They had reinforced it with several layers of Tegaderm. They really didn't want it to become dislodged.

"Good," I said. "And presumably you've taken all the routine bloods?"

"Yes," said Dr Mirza. "U&Es. FBC. The works."

"Blood gases?"

Dr Mirza nodded.

"Any hypoxia?"

"Evidence consistent with hyperventilation, nothing else."

"Any witnessed seizures?"

"No seizures."

"Paracetamol?"

"Rectally, about five, six minutes ago."

"Okay, good."

Something shifted in the room. A shadow. The flickering of an already feeble light. My initial impression was that David's father had approached the bed again, but this wasn't so.

Suddenly, David yanked his hand away. "Leave him alone!" he squealed, his eyes focusing on some unknown point just over my left shoulder. "Leave *us* alone! I'm not your fucking..." He paused, face reddening, struggling perhaps to find the word, then spat, "*... puppet!*"

"Do you want to give some midazolam?" Dr Mirza asked me. The question signalled a subtle change. Apparently, I was now the clinical lead.

"No," I said. Somehow, a sedative didn't seem like the right answer, not yet anyway. While more a gut feeling than the result of any specific rationale, I was no less convinced. "Wait, please. We need to learn a little more."

Some in the team bristled. They didn't approve of this decision, or my apparent indecisiveness, and I didn't have time to convince them otherwise. I approached the boy's father. He looked even more pale and wretched. There was life-saving equipment behind the plastic chair—the watchful eye of the defibrillator, endotracheal airways in every size, laryngoscopes ready for use—and, for one fleeting moment, I was convinced it was Mr Layton who needed that equipment more than his son. He looked very much like his heart had stopped beating, and he required urgent intervention.

"Mr Layton..." I resisted the urge to shake him or perform a sternal rub to check his level of consciousness. "Can we talk?"

His eyes remained fixed on the floor. "Can you help him, doctor?"

I wanted to avoid making any promises I couldn't keep. The truth was, I didn't know.

The Resus Bay seemed to close in further. The gloom became gloomier. That oily smell made me feel like I had something caught in my throat, or that I couldn't quite get my breath. "It would be extremely helpful if I could get a picture of how David is normally."

"Yes, yes, of course." Mr Layton lifted his eyes, finally looking into mine. "Call me Peter, please."

"When did this all start, Peter?"

"We were meant to go to the Edgar Centre yesterday afternoon, David likes to go to the Edge of the World expo and check out the Cosplay, but he'd taken himself to bed and when I went to his room, it was obvious he was crook."

"Obvious, how?"

"He was burning up," Peter said. "He was out of his mind and writhing around the bed."

"How is David's health normally? Does he have any history of illness? Any conditions that you know of?"

"No, nothing."

"What about vomiting and diarrhoea? Anything like that in the last few days?"

"Not that he mentioned to me."

"Good. And before becoming unwell this morning, did David complain about anything? Anything at all? A sore throat? Burning urine? Pain anywhere? Anything?"

"I don't—I can't think of anything..."

"This is helpful, thank you."

The BP cuff around David's upper arm gave a mechanical groan as it inflated. The ED staff were hovering, listening to my line of questioning and awaiting instruction.

David's hands pulled loose and began shaking the cot sides. "That's not your face! I see through you!" His eyes—intense, now with pinpoint pupils—tracked some visual hallucination in a slow arc around the Resus Bay. Two nurses restrained his arms. "Who are you? *Tell me!*"

One nurse muttered something about midazolam again, softly, under her breath.

Peter Layton's eyes were fixed on his son again. He rose from his chair, then reconsidered. I witnessed the light go out in his eyes. The sparkle. A wave of hopelessness crushed him anew. Everything was there to read in his eyes. The eyes being the windows to the soul.

"Pulse 138," called one of the staff. "BP is up, 165 over 110. Resps 30."

"Is David allergic to any medication?" I asked Peter. This question caused a stir among the staff, for such a question often preceded the administration of medication. They assumed I was ready to give the midazolam now.

Peter shook his head: no.

"What about foods—nuts, shellfish, that sort of thing?"

"No."

I turned to Dr Mirza. "Alright, let's give some midazolam." I still wasn't sure this was the right thing, but the hallucinations were clearly distressing for David and I figured, if nothing else, sedating him might buy us a little time to think of a better approach. "Let's start with five milligrams IV please."

Somewhere in the huddle of staff there was an exchange of control drug keys, and one person slipped away to fetch the medication.

Returning my attention to Peter, I asked, "Has David had all his immunisations at school?"

"Yes."

"And has all his schooling been here in New Zealand?"

"Yes. What do you think it is, Doctor...?" He searched for my name, but couldn't recall it, despite it being clearly written on my badge.

"Newman," I said. "And that's precisely what we're trying to find out." What I omitted to say was that I felt that his son's condition was perilous, and that some terrible intuition had left me with this impression. Whatever this infection was—I was certain it *was* an infection—I didn't like it. Somehow, I hid these feeling behind a veneer of professional detachment. Dr O'Brien would be so proud of me, if only he knew.

"Yes, yes, of course. Sorry."

"And do you keep good health, Peter?"

"Yes."

"And the boy's mother?"

"What?"

"Does she keep good health?"

"No, I mean... Her illness was very sudden."

I'd made a little faux pas apparently, which was perhaps not surprising given all the rapid-fire questions. Was David's mother dead? I knew I should probe further, find out what had killed the boy's mother and if it was relevant, but I didn't have the heart. Peter Layton already looked too fragile. "Oh, I'm sorry. I didn't mean to..."

Someone administered the midazolam.

"Get off me!" David kicked out with his left leg—the one with the cannula in. He reached forward and attempted to rip the device from his foot.

A couple of additional hands restrained him.

"Don't put me to sleep!" David said. On this occasion, he seemed to address the nursing staff directly. "I can't defend myself if... if I'm asleep! D-don't leave me here in the dark!

Please!" With great effort, he pushed those last few words out. "Don't leave me... with... *him!*"

David's eyelids fluttered.

"Pulse, 56... Resps, 12..."

There were other questions I wanted to ask Peter Layton, if only for thoroughness. What about David's grandparents? Were there any hereditary conditions? Did David take recreational drugs? Was he sexually active? These questions would have to wait.

David shifted onto his back and sank into the middle of the trolley bed. I thought, with all the midazolam flooding his system, that he was sound asleep. However, he still had some fight left. "No! Stay back!" he yelled suddenly, his eyes opening again. "You can't—! You're hurting me! I know what you are!" Several ED staff grappled with his flailing limbs, although the effort required was less now. "STAY BACK!" Stammering and slurring his words. "St-St—*Stoooooo*"

"Is he—? Is it a seizure?"

"Please, Peter..." I encouraged the boy's father back into his seat. "We're going to work out what's causing this. We will."

"Pulse, 77... Resps, 18..."

I wondered if I ought to phone Dr O'Brien, give him a heads-up. Maybe the old dinosaur might think of something I hadn't. That, after all, was the protocol. The shit was handed down the chain of command easily enough, but sometimes, on occasions such as this, the order was reversed, and it passed back up again. That's why Dr O'Brien was paid the big dollars.

"Pulse, 52... Resps, 9..."

"Airway adjuncts on standby."

"He's asleep and maintaining saturations."

No. I had had enough of Dr O'Brien already today. I would not call him. The crisis was averted... at least for now.

ED staff moved back from David's bed space, milling around the edges. Some tidied; some filled in paperwork retrospectively.

Peter Layton was rocking in his chair. "Thank you," he said, to no one in particular. "Thank you."

"We need to transfer David to the Children's Ward," I said. "I'll organise the bed. Thanks everyone. Good job."

I walked out of the cubicle, where the air felt fresher and lighter, but I still couldn't shake the feeling that David's condition was very dire and that the only thing we'd managed to do was apply a temporary Band-Aid.

three

"I see Pestilence coming, behold! I see its many eyes, its many teeth, its great and deadly shadow, and I stand in the gap, sword raised, waiting."

Trudy, the Surgeon of Truth, page 23, 'The Healing Art'

"Serena, may I talk with you and your parents...? Serena, we need to talk... Serena... there's never a good time for this, but I want to talk about your Megaloblastic Anaemia."

I wiped the dry, crusted pieces of sleep from my eyes. It had not been a good night at all. I had slept little, at least not that I remembered, and what sleep I got felt broken and filled with troubling thoughts. I knew I'd dreamt about David Layton's symptoms for sure, but I'd also dreamt about Serena Hopkins and breaking the bad news.

"I've been avoiding this topic for too long, and for that I'm sorry..."

No. No good. Don't apologise.

I stood before the bathroom mirror, rehearsing. At least, I guess that's what I was doing. My eyes were slightly bloodshot. My skin was pale and stretched. I couldn't even read my own facial expression.

Outside my flat, it was still dark, and a consistent rain fell onto the street and the pavement. There were another two hours before I needed to leave for work.

"Mr and Mrs Hopkins, I know you have your faith, I know you're believing for a miracle, but I have to tell you, as Serena's doctor, I have a more... cautious outlook."

No—too condescending.

"Your daughter isn't getting better; she's deteriorating and she's going to die."

No, no, no. Too abrupt; too confrontational.

"I'm not sure how to say this, except just to say it: Serena's disease is most likely going to kill her, and probably in the next six weeks."

I can't say that! No way!

"Listen..." (*Really? You're going to start a conversation like that with the word, 'Listen?'*). "... I do not know what it's like to have children, let alone face the prospect of that child getting sick and dying, but that's what's happening here."

Oh my God, that was truly awful.

"I have some terrible news, and I'm so, so sorry..."

Shit no!

If yesterday had been a bad day, I was certain today was going to surpass it. It was a feeling I had. Some days had a heaviness about them. As if in sympathy, the sky had filled with dark, brooding clouds as a major low pressure system moved in. Oh, today was going to be tough. As if I didn't have enough on my plate with David Layton and how to proceed with investigations and his treatment, now I was worried about talking with Serena Hopkins, too. I couldn't do it. I simply wasn't ready.

I opened the cupboard door in the bathroom. Inside was a row of medicine bottles: antihistamines, painkillers, antidepressants. I scanned each label, searching for the most appropriate one in my collection. Then I took the fluoxetine, popped one in my mouth, and washed it down with the dregs from my coffee mug. I grimaced. The coffee was bitter, the pill more so; both clawing at my throat as I swallowed.

The hospital cafeteria was abuzz with conversation, every table occupied, and lines of people backing up from both cash registers. Sugar-filled treats and fresh pastries were displayed behind heavily laden glass cabinets, the scent drifting far and wide. The morning tea rush was on.

Overhead, a steady rain pitter-pattered against the high glass ceiling, blurring the leaden sky from which it fell.

I spotted Dr Tim Butterfield and Dr Chong-Soo Lee and headed for their table, carrying a tray with a coffee and a slice of ginger crunch upon it. I was too heavy-handed placing the tray on the table, however, and some of my hot coffee splashed over the edge of its cup, soaking into the paper napkin. "Ah, shit!"

"Bad day?" Tim asked.

"Like a train wreck," I said. "You wouldn't believe it."

From my arrival at work I'd been busy, yo-yo-ing between the Children's Ward and Emergency Department, constantly having to readjust my priorities as my pager beeped and something new emerged that demanded my attention. I'd checked on David Layton, of course. He'd been given more midazolam overnight and was still heavily sedated. His temperature had spiked twice in the last 24 hours.

I still hadn't spoken with the Hopkins family.

"It's been non-stop," I summarised, then took a sip of my coffee. "I really need caffeine - stat. O'Brien's... well, O'Brien. And I've got this kid I'm worried about." I turned to Tim. "What about your day?"

"You know Medical." Tim had slicked back hair and an even slicker sense of fashion. He was from a new, but thankfully small, number of doctors who always insisted on wearing both a tie and a blazer. His clothes were always immaculately pressed, although I suspected someone else did the washing and ironing. "I live for the buzz." He chomped down on an over-sized white chocolate and raspberry muffin. "Adrenaline, that's my drug of choice these days. And the legal highs, of course: coffee, sugar and alcohol."

Chong frowned.

"How's your day, Chong?" I asked.

"Oncology's good, thanks. We've got a few poorlies at the moment, which is intense, but it's rewarding too." Chong wore a stethoscope around his neck and had several pens aligned in his shirt pocket. The shirt was about as formal as Chong got.

I took another sip of my coffee. "I envy you, Chong. It doesn't matter how busy you are, you never get flustered and you seem to love what you do."

"You do too!" Chong replied. He looked genuinely surprised at my suggestion that I didn't share his passion for medicine. I loved him for that defensiveness.

"No, I'm not sure I do anymore. I've spent too long putting out fires that I feel like I've lost my purpose and my drive."

"Putting out fires *is* modern medicine," Tim said, only half-joking.

"Well, maybe it shouldn't be!"

"I remember you at Med School," Chong said. He chewed on humus-dipped carrot sticks. He was possibly the healthiest guy I knew. He'd maintained a rigorous exercise and nutritional programme all the years I'd known him. "You practically lived in the Health Sciences building. I swear you got your own key cut."

I nibbled a piece of ginger crunch and took another sip of coffee. The slice was wonderful; the coffee average. "I feel tired all the time," I said. "Like I've been drained. Like I'm anaemic. This job isn't sustainable."

"You wait 'til you hit your thirties," Tim said.

"I'm serious, guys," I said. "I think medicine was the wrong career for me."

Tim lowered his coffee cup. "Nonsense!"

As more and more staff entered for their morning tea, the noise in the cafeteria increased. The coffee machines frothed and steamed. The cash register drawers opened and closed. Those staff who were finished wandered about with their trays in their hands, slopping dirty dishes into the hot, soapy water at the side of the room. There were boisterous farewells.

"You mentioned O'Brien," Chong said. "What's he done this time?"

It was getting harder to hear, so I felt assured of a certain confidentiality in our conversation. "There's a young girl on the ward," I said, leaning closer, lowering my voice. "She's palliative, only she doesn't understand that... and her parents, well, they definitely don't want to understand. O'Brien wants me to make them understand, but I don't think I can."

Chong spluttered on his carrot stick. He knew more

about the history with my mother than Tim did.

Tim said, "So you've graduated to the official O'Brien 'sink or swim' programme? Well done!"

"Not funny."

"What about the other thing?" asked Chong. I noted the concern in his eyes. "The kid you were worried about?"

"Oh yeah. That's been worrying me too. I admitted this boy yesterday morning—fever, delirium, this distinctive rash that appeared to follow all the major branches of his circulatory system."

"Okay... that's weird," Tim said.

"I know."

"So what is it?"

"Good question. I'm thinking something viral. We'll probably never know. The thing that really got me, though, was how much it scared me."

"How so?" Chong asked.

"Well, I was scared for the kid, what might happen to him. I was scared of his condition, too, the combination of symptoms and their severity. I was even scared just walking into the damn cubicle... the whole thing felt wrong. I can't really explain it."

"Mate, you're right," Tim said. "Sounds to me like you've been working too hard. Sounds like classic symptoms of over-tiredness. Maybe you need to book some annual leave and—"

"When can I take annual leave, Tim? I'm too busy."

"That's precisely why you need to," Chong said.

"It's not that easy," I said. "I don't think—"

Beep beep beep beeeppppppp!

My stomach lurched. My pager—again. I was convinced this would be bad news: something concerning David Layton, or maybe Serena. God, I hated this pager! In that moment, it was a symbol of everything that was wrong with my career.

Both Tim and Chong offered sympathetic smiles.

I stood and weaved my way between tables, chairs and people to a tiny recess where a phone was housed. I recognised the number, of course. It was one of the Children's Ward extensions. I was certain it must be about David. Maybe his chemical slumber had worn off and he was repeating his earlier performance, this time on the Children's Ward...

"Grant here."

One of the Children's Ward nurses spoke on the other end of the phone, but it was difficult to hear her over the loud conversation around me. I only caught two words: "Toby", something, something, "Home".

I strained. "What's that?"

The nurse repeated her message.

I still didn't hear her. I pressed the phone closer to my ear, blocking the other ear with a finger. My brow creased. "I'm sorry," I said. "Could you repeat that again, please?"

Finally, the nurse told me her message, enunciating each

syllable slowly, carefully. Words, sentences. Subject-verb-object. It was all there, not that any of it made sense.

"I'll come straight away," I promised.

I drifted back to the table, to my friends. I felt like all the colour must have drained from my face. My legs managed to carry me, but only just. If this was true, it changed everything. But it couldn't be true, could it?

Could it?

"What's up?" Chong asked.

"Is it your boy with the delirium and the rash?" asked Tim.

"No," I said. "It's Toby Harrison." I wouldn't ordinarily blubber out a patient's full name in the cafeteria like this, but I was in shock.

"Who?"

"Some kid on the Children's Ward. Patient of mine. Brittle asthmatic."

"It's tough when you lose one," Tim said. "It's one aspect of the job I don't think I'll ever get used to. They say death's a part of life, but—"

"No, no," I corrected. "Toby isn't dead. In fact, it's the opposite."

Tim and Chong both looked puzzled.

It didn't matter.

There wasn't time to explain. I was already moving towards the exit. My morning tea left there on the table, half-finished and still on its tray.

"I'm not staying," Toby was saying to his uncle. I still couldn't remember if it was Jim or John, but didn't like to ask him to repeat it. Toby wasn't in bed: he was up, dressed and stuffing his meagre belongings into a canvas bag. While he may have heard me enter Room 12, he didn't bother to turn and look. "I want to go home."

I closed the door after me, shutting out the low din from the rest of the ward.

"Ah, doctor," said Jim or John. "Maybe you can talk some sense into my boy."

"I'm not *your* boy!"

Toby's uncle offered his hand. "Newman, isn't it?" he said. "I'm Jim."

Jim, of course it was. I shook his hand. It was rough, calloused and firm. "Grant Newman, that's right."

"Thank you for all you've done for Toby."

"He didn't do shit," protested Toby.

"Toby!" said Uncle Jim. "Regardless, you've never looked this good in..."—he seemed to dredge through the past but came up blank—"... I don't know when..."

"I was healed. And *not* by him."

Toby's side room was on the southern side of the hospital and got very little sunlight at this time of the morning. Although recently painted, the walls appeared drab, the plastic panels already scuffed and tired. There was a lived-in smell. Stale air, dirty clothes, body odour, all proving stronger than the underlying detergent. Despite this, something had occurred here in this room. Something had changed. I felt it.

"I've read about cases like this," I said, somewhat breathless from running up the stairs. "We prefer the term 'spontaneous remission' rather than 'healing' but, hey, that's just semantics."

"Fuck semantics. I want to get out of here."

"Toby, language!"

Toby finally turned around. The difference was startling, even amongst all the drabness. He was no longer this pale kid, all ribs and auxiliary muscles, with a cyanotic blue tinge to his lips.

Toby spoke to his uncle. "Stop acting like you're my dad." His voice was remarkably clear now that he wasn't fighting for each breath. His face was flushed with colour, vitality and, most startling of all, anger. His hair, his teeth, even his eyes, all looked healthier. "You're my uncle. I don't have to do anything you say."

I knew then that Toby's asthma had gone... which, of course, was impossible. Asthma didn't go into remission. It couldn't. It was a chronic lung problem. The best you could hope for was establishing good symptom control. Every doctor knows this.

The sparkle in Toby's eyes told a different truth.

"Listen, Toby," I said. "I think it's great that you've been healed. I do. However, I think it's important that we verify the healing."

"Verify, how?"

"Just a few tests."

"No. No more tests. I'm sick of all the tests. My whole life's been a series of tests."

"Please," I said. "This is important. I'd be remiss if I let you walk out the door without checking you over properly. For all we know, the effects of the... of this... might be temporary... and your breathing might deteriorate again."

"You can't stop me from leaving."

I nodded. "You're correct. But I was hoping to appeal to your better judgement. What's another hour, right?"

Uncle Jim drew closer to his nephew. "Maybe you should stay, Toby."

"Maybe *you* should stay!" Toby snapped back. He had finished packing his bag and transferred it onto the bed. He turned to me once more. "I know I'm healed. I don't need to prove it to anyone — not you and not him."

"Tell me how this happened, Toby," I said.

Toby sat on the bed next to his bag. He looked down at his feet.

"Tell him, Toby!"

Toby took a sip of water from the glass on the bedside table. "She did it. The woman." His voice was slower, more cautious. "She was in my room last night and she touched me..." — he pointed to the centre of his chest — "... right here — and —"

"Who touched you?"

"Dunno." He took another sip of water. "I thought she was crazy. She was real intense. But the minute she touched me, said 'Release him and face me', I felt the burning inside my lungs and I knew she'd done something."

A healing implied a healer, but I hadn't made that connection - until now. "When was this? What time?"

"I don't know. Two a.m.. Maybe three."

"What was this woman doing in your room, anyway? Was she one of the night staff?"

"No, I don't think so," Toby said, looking up. "She wasn't wearing a uniform." He must have noticed the concerned glance I shared with his uncle. "I know, random!"

"Can you describe her?"

"Nah, not really. It was too dark."

This sounded bad. A strange woman visiting a teenage boy in his hospital bed during the night, scaring him, *touching* him. "Alright, Toby, I need you to tell me exactly what happened. What this woman did."

Toby took another drink, swallowing hard. "She woke me up. I heard her moving around the bed... then she was talking to someone. She was angry."

Were it not for Toby's healthy, well-perfused skin colour, I would have sworn that such talk was confusion resulting from hypoxia. "Who was she talking to?"

"Dunno. I hid under the blankets and told her to leave, said I'd scream or press the Emergency Button if she didn't."

"Then what happened?"

"She said, 'That's gratitude for you' and she just kept moving around the bed, like she was trying to corner something. She kept hissing and saying, 'Come back here!' in this intense voice. She wasn't talking to me anymore, though."

"But who was she speaking to? Did you see anyone else in the room?"

"No one."

"And then what?"

"I remember something else! More weirdness! Going back to before she touched me, I remember she said, 'Who touched you? Who's looking after you?' and 'Whose are these fingerprints?' What else...? Oh yeah, then she asked, 'Why did they touch you and yet not heal you?' then *she* touched *me*, like I said. I felt something happening immediately, but it took a few hours before the sickness completely left my body."

"You mean asthma?"

"Obviously."

"Toby, there's no cure for asthma."

There was defiance in Toby's eyes. "I don't have asthma anymore, see?" The boy took a deep breath to demonstrate how clear his lungs were, held it, then, after what would have previously been an impossible pause, released his breath. "I'm healed," he said, and smiled.

I genuinely liked that smile: it was warm and sincere. I liked the health to which that smile attested more, even if I couldn't explain this remission.

"This Healer," I said. "What else can you tell me about her? Anything might be helpful."

"Helpful? Helpful to who? What you gonna do? Hunt her down and bore her to death with all your questions? Or will you tell her that healing, or 'spontaneous remission', doesn't exist? 'Cos I know it does. What more proof do you need?" Toby Harrison had done all the cooperating he was prepared to do. "Can I go now?"

I watched him and his Uncle Jim leave, but not before I'd got Uncle Jim, who was registered as Toby's legal guardian, to sign a Disclaimer Form. Toby's leaving was against my advice and, if anything should happen to him, I would not be held responsible.

Jenny Epps was in the Clean Utility.

I swiped my hospital ID to enter—*Bleep-bleep... click*—and pushed on the door.

Jenny took a bottle of medication down from one shelf, carefully matching it against MedChart on the laptop. She barely reached five feet in height, which made it awkward for her to wield the laptop and the high trolley upon which it sat.

"Hi Jenny."

"Hi." Her voice was warm and friendly, although she was concentrating on her task and I wasn't sure if this was the best time for my questions. I enjoyed Jenny's company. She was fun and easygoing.

She unscrewed the lid of the white container, tipping the bottle in such a way that only one round white pill slid out and landed inside the lid.

"Could I have a word?" I asked.

"Sure, what's up?"

Jenny had been a nurse on the Children's Ward for at least as long as I'd been there, and probably a lot longer. While some of the nursing staff were transitory, not Jenny. The Children's Ward wouldn't be quite the same if she were ever to leave. Her hearty laughter. Her bubbly personality.

I liked Jenny. Liked how she looked: her smooth skin, her rosy cheeks, her dark, flowing hair so onerously tied back, the swell of her breasts under her tunic. I liked how she was upbeat and often lifted others with her presence. For one of such a small stature, her laughter was loud and contagious. There was a lot to like. Sometimes, however, I felt we could be more than friends, but I'd never pursued this beyond idle fantasy. There was a connection between us, one I valued but didn't fully understand, one I didn't want to spoil. Romantic relationships with work colleagues were tenuous ground in my experience.

"I wanted to ask you about Toby Harrison..."

She stopped. She turned and looked at me. "If you're asking me what happened, I can't explain it." She chased the pill from the lid into a plastic medicine cup. "There's no way he should be walking around, much less going home."

I nodded. "Did you see anything?"

"I just saw him leave."

That wasn't what I meant.

The Clean Utility had shelves on four sides, where boxes and bottles of medicines in assorted sizes had been carefully arranged in categories. The room was austere, spotlessly clean, a testament to 'efficiency' or 'lean thinking' or whatever the latest term was. The stainless steel workbench glistened under the fluorescent lights; a flatpack of trusty V-Wipes sitting nearby, freshly used. A medicinal pine scent permeated the room. Beneath the workbench, intravenous fluids in 100ml, 500ml and 1000ml bags had been stacked according to their electrolyte percentages. In the far corner, space had been allocated for the blood glucose monitor and a couple of DynaMaps.

I tried a different tack. "Have you seen any suspicious characters?"

"Suspicious?" Jenny asked. She turned from the laptop and the workbench again, giving me her full attention. "Suspicious... how?"

"Toby claims a mysterious woman came to him in the night, touched him and healed him."

The corners of Jenny's lips twitched and curled. She smirked, and in a moment I was sure I'd hear her laughter. "Isn't that every teenage boy's fantasy?"

My cheeks flushed. "Usually they come dressed in nurse's uniforms too," I said. "But Toby didn't think this woman was a nurse."

Jenny's smile faded. Her brow creased. "You're serious?"

"Yeah."

"No," she said. "I didn't see anyone, but if there is some Healer at large that's not such a bad thing. It could be a good thing, right?"

She was right and, in my eagerness to find answers, I hadn't actually thought of it that way. "If it's legitimate, yes, it's amazing."

She replaced a medicine bottle on the shelf and grabbed another. She paused. A pause that lasted too long. The medication forgotten. "Can I make an observation, Grant?" she said finally.

She fixed her eyes upon me. Her gaze was deep. And suddenly I wasn't sure I wanted to hear her observation. What if she possessed the ability to see within me and expose my thoughts and emotions? Once more, the heat rose into my cheeks. "Okay..." I said.

"You look tired," she said, her eyes softening. "Is everything alright?"

"I'm fine," I said, making light of her concern, even as I was touched by its genuineness. "Isn't tiredness an occupational hazard?"

"It shouldn't be," she said. "Us health workers ought to know better."

"Agreed."

She smiled. I smiled. Then I left the Clean Utility.

The next person I saw was Pastor Ari Dixon, the Hospital Chaplain. He was leaning against the Nurse's Station as I approached. He wore a dark black shirt, open at the collar, and matching black-frame glasses. When he smiled, it lit up his entire face and his pristine white teeth were striking. I knew him a little, well enough to make conversation, so I said, "Excuse me, Chaplain. May I ask you something?"

"Certainly."

Without my asking, the Chaplain led me a little away from the Nurse's Station, to the quieter back corridor where we could talk with greater confidentiality. He did this with such grace, such economy of movement, that he'd obviously anticipated I was going to ask him some curly question, or he was regularly asked deep, philosophical questions.

We stood beside the red and white arrest trolley, which was stored in a small recess in the corridor.

The back corridor was on the south side of the hospital, such that it was tangibly cooler and darker. Dust clawed at my nose and throat. This side of the corridor obviously got less attention from the cleaning staff.

"I wanted to ask you about healing," I said. "Do you think God—the Christian God—is still in the business of healing? In your professional opinion, that is."

Pastor Ari didn't look like a typical Chaplain. He was tall, handsome and in his late thirties. The man took great pride in his appearance, from the way he styled his hair to his fashion choices. Everything was in its proper place. Not one hair had strayed. He was popular, witty, charming, and seemed like a genuinely nice person. Almost too nice. "Put it like this," he said, after a considered pause. "I wouldn't be here if I didn't believe that."

"What do you mean?"

"I may not be medical staff," he said, "but my job is no less important. People need hope. God is in the business of hope."

"But what about healing?" I asked. "Healing specifically."

Pastor Ari smiled at me. "I believe God uses skilled doctors and nurses to do His healings."

"But what about laying hands on the sick—you know, like Jesus used to do in those Bible stories? Do you think that happens today?"

A shadow passed over the Chaplain's face. "There are people who claim to have ministries like that," he said, rubbing the back of his neck. "I'm not sure how scriptural these claims are. I have seen nothing to sway me. Most are manipulators and charlatans."

"But do you think—at least hypothetically—that, sometimes, it might be possible?"

"I don't know, Grant. I certainly don't have the monopoly on God's truth. If He wanted to imbue someone with His power, to heal the sick... well, that's His sovereign right, I guess. Would I have an issue with it? You bet."

"Really? Why?"

"For starters, I'd want to know why He didn't give me that gift."

"I guess..."

"Can you imagine how it'd feel — stretching out your hand, touching someone, seeing their sickness depart — *Boom!* — seeing them made well...?"

"So you haven't been wandering around the hospital late at night, dressed as a woman, healing the sick, then?"

This time more than a shadow passed over the Chaplain's face. A frown darkened his features. "I'm sorry?"

"Excuse my humour, Pastor." I could feel my cheeks burning. "Another occupational hazard."

Pastor Ari smiled, although it was a tight-lipped smile. He didn't understand the reference, which meant he clearly hadn't heard about Toby.

I said, "There was a boy on this ward, a really bad asthmatic, but he discharged himself about an hour ago. He claims a mysterious woman visited him last night, and that she healed him."

"Oh."

"Yeah."

"And were you able to confirm this healing?"

"No, unfortunately not. This boy has had a lot of time in hospital over the years and he wasn't inclined to spend any longer here."

"That's a shame."

"I know. But certainly subjectively, he looked like he'd been on the receiving-end of a miracle. It was quite incredible."

"And did he claim God—"

That's as far as Pastor Ari got.

Hurried footsteps filled the corridor, rumbling like approaching thunder.

We both turned in their direction. The pastor's words stopped mid-sentence, the point he was about to make lost forever.

Clinical Nurse Manager Helen Tooms came striding around the corner with the Nursing Director. CNM Tooms was a woman of slight build, yet extremely imposing. Her hair, her make-up, was always immaculate. Her eyeliner and her lipstick painted in dark, almost gothic tones. Foundation covered the lines and cracks in her face and made her mood impossible to gauge. She was dressed in a dark suit that hid her amorphous frame.

The Nursing Director, in comparison, looked rather ordinary next to CNM Tooms and lacked any natural authority. She wore a neutral-coloured dress and blazer.

While she technically outranked Tooms, most people might mistakenly interpret the power play the other way around.

"Gentlemen," CNM Tooms said, her eyes glacial, a smile that bore more resemblance to a sneer. She passed us like some cold draught, then she and the Nursing Director withdrew into her office, which was along the back corridor.

"What were you saying?" I asked the Chaplain. We both understood that our conversation couldn't continue as before. CNM Tooms had that effect.

"I can't remember."

I lowered my voice. "If you see anyone or hear anything, will you let me know?"

"Definitely."

I thanked the Chaplain and returned to my desk.

I sat there looking over Toby's case notes. I took the disclaimer form that Toby's uncle had signed and fastened it into the back of volume three. Then I turned the pages to where I'd been writing, but hadn't finished. I documented how Toby had refused all recommended diagnostic tests, tests that would have given objective proof of his claims.

I wavered, unsure how to finish my entry.

Finally, at the bottom of the page, in a place usually reserved for the physician's working diagnosis, I scribbled SPONTANEOUS REMISSION, then added a question mark.

A woman's voice behind me: "Excuse me."

The voice came from the gloom, along the same corridor where the Chaplain and I had spoken several hours ago. Her voice was soft and restrained.

I turned.

She seemed to emerge from the wall itself, as if from some secret recess. She was five-five, maybe five-six. Of slight build. I'd put her age at around sixty years old, possibly a little younger. She didn't look like she'd aged all that well. Her face was tired, the wrinkles cut so deep they appeared like scars. Her hair flowed long and dark, although as she moved further into the light, I saw it was more grey than black. She was limping. Her left leg apparently injured. She kept glancing over her shoulder, though, as if at any moment she might take flight.

Without asking permission, she took both my hands in hers, and studied them. "Healing hands," she said. Her hands were warm. "I knew it! 'One will know another'—just like it says in 'The Healing Art'".

I should have understood who she was with the comment 'healing hands', but I was slow. "I'm sorry," I said, pulling my hands back, thinking this woman was just some random lunatic. "Do I know you? Is there something in particular you want?"

"You can help me."

I wasn't sure if this was a request or simply a statement. "How?"

She reached for my ID badge and pulled it closer, staring at the faded image taken back when I'd started at the DHB. "Dr Grant Newman," she read. "Paediatric Registrar."

Who was this woman? Was she dangerous? "How about you start by telling me who *you* are? I might be more inclined to help if—"

"I'm Audrey," she said. "Beyond that: trust me—the less you know, the better."

"Then why on earth should I help you?"

"Because you're a Healer like me. 'A sharp implement'."

What? She was the Healer? *Really?* The one I'd been investigating most of the day. She seemed too softly spoken to be the same aggressor Toby had described, and yet.... A solitary laugh slipped from my mouth. I hadn't meant to laugh. Whoever she was, she had inside information, information that I wanted and simultaneously rejected. And what was that other bit about me? What the fuck? "I'm a doctor," I said, a little defensively. "I practice medical science. Whatever you do... I'm not sure I even believe in... in healing."

Voices boomed along the corridor, approaching. Footsteps accompanied the voices.

"We don't have time," she said, backing away, then finally turning and running. "But we'll speak again... soon."

"Wait!"

Too late. She'd already taken the Fire Exit, and I heard her retreating down the concrete stairwell.

four

"Man is a microcosm, or a little world, because he is an extract from all the stars and planets of the whole firmament, from the earth and the elements; and so he is their quintessence."

Paracelsus, page 111, 'The Healing Art'

"David, hi! I'm Grant, one of the Paediatric doctors. How are you feeling?"

David Layton's fever had broken in the early hours of Wednesday morning. I got the news from the nurse when I got to work and I went to visit him immediately.

"Good." David was sitting on his bed, freshly starched hospital sheets draped over his legs. He was a handsome kid, especially now whatever illness had brought him into the hospital had loosened its grip. His hair was a thick, long brown, which wouldn't have looked out of place in the 1970s. He was pale skinned, freckled, and a real intelligence shone in his blue eyes.

The room was dark and grey. The light was inadequate.

I went to the window. Outside, the clouds had descended, shrouding neighbouring buildings in a stony grey gloom, so that they loomed from the drizzle like the large floating hulls in some ship's graveyard.

"Actually," he corrected, "I feel groggy. And my whole body is aching like crazy."

I turned from the window and back to David, nodding. "I'm sure you do. You gave us quite a scare. Right, well, let's see what we can do to make you feel better." His half-eaten breakfast sat on the tray before him. It pleased me he felt well enough to eat, although his appetite obviously hadn't fully returned. "How much have you had to drink? Are you thirsty?"

David nodded. "Really thirsty."

"Okay, well, plenty of fluids for you then, young man. You'll have lost a lot of fluid with running such a high temperature and we need to replace them." I noted intravenous fluids were still chugging through the Baxter pump next to the bed, infusing the remains of a litre of saline into the cannula in David's foot. "It's good if you can take stuff orally, too."

"Dad just went to get me a fruit juice."

"That's good. In the meantime..." I slid the water jug

across his bedside table. "Now, tell me about your pain: If you had to score it between 0 and 10, where would it be?"

"Seven, maybe eight."

"I'll give you some painkillers," I said. "It'll be much quicker if we give it intravenously."

David smiled.

I excused myself and went to find the nurse with the drug keys. We signed some morphine out of the Control Drug cupboard in the Dispensary. She drew this up, along with some metoclopramide, and placed both syringes in a cardboard pulp kidney dish, which I took back to David's room.

I approached the easy chair next to David's bed, presumably where his father had been sitting. "May I?"

"Certainly."

I sat down. "I'd like to ask you a few questions, David, if you're feeling up to it."

"Sure, okay."

I paused the Baxter pump. I leaned over and piggy-backed the syringe containing the metoclopramide to the IV line. "What symptoms did you get at first? And when did they begin?" I pushed the drum of the first syringe nice and slow.

"Well, that's the weird thing," he said. "I haven't felt exactly right for a few weeks."

"A few weeks?"

"Yeah. Weird, eh?"

"That is unusual. It suggests that whatever this is — and I suspect it's a viral infection — it must have a very long incubation period."

A whiff of lavender hung in the air. It was a clean smell. A good smell. A smell which hopefully signified the eradication of germs from every surface. Beneath it, however, perhaps more memory, that oily smell, the one I'd smelt in the ED, lingered. This smell made me uneasy.

"There's something else," David said.

Once the metoclopramide was given, I withdrew that syringe and started with the morphine. "Yes?"

"Well, I think it's related, but when I was crook, I... I... that's when I saw the boy. Wow! Whatever you're giving me, it feels *goood.*"

"That's morphine," I said. "What boy?"

"This k-kid. He looked half starved, you know... His clothes were more like rags and he was filthy... And he had a runny nose. Like, it was streaming continually, and he kept sniffing and snorting."

David's pupils were constricting, and I decided that that was enough morphine for now. "You think you contracted the virus from this boy?"

"Not exactly. It's just that the day I started feeling funny, well, that's when I noticed the boy following me."

"A coincidence, surely?"

"I thought so at first, but now I'm not so sure. I kept seeing this boy, over the last few weeks, and again on

Monday morning in the Emergency Department, with the other man, the doctor, and I just... I don't know... he's linked to my illness somehow. But that was a hallucination, right? They both were, weren't they?"

I wondered if David had any psychiatric history. I also wondered if I ought to wait for Peter Layton to return before we went any further along this particular road. "Well, it is common enough to see and hear things when you've got a really high temperature, but it rarely starts weeks before." Then, throwing caution to the wind, I asked, "What did this boy look like exactly?"

"He looked like something out of a Charles Dickens novel (We read 'Oliver Twist' in Year Seven). He was all skin and bones, a hollowed out face and this deep hunger in his eyes..."

"What school do you go to?"

"Logan Park."

"And did he speak, this boy?"

"No, never. When I tried to speak with him, he'd always run away."

"And the first time you saw him was...?"

"I was sitting on the school bus by the window. I saw the boy on the pavement. Only he looked so out of place, so unhappy, and he was looking right at me, his eyes tracking me as the bus pulled away from the curb."

"Okay. Any other symptoms at this stage? Feeling hot or cold? Shivery?"

"Yeah, I felt freezing."

"It is possible you spiked a temperature, then. That might explain why you were hallucinating — assuming, that is, the boy was a hallucination."

"It gets weirder," he said. "The next time I saw him was maybe a week later, and he was sitting up in the bleachers at Moana Pool when we were having our swimming tournament."

"And where were you?"

"In the pool. I'd just completed my heat, and I was catching my breath. Only I looked over and I saw him there, sitting all by himself. And again he's looking at me. Staring, really. I mightn't have noticed if he wasn't being so obvious about it. He had this hacking cough, too. The kind that draws attention to itself."

"And did you feel unwell that day?"

"No, I felt great. I'd just smashed my PB."

"So, no fever?"

"No. Definitely not. I'd had a bit of rash a few days before, but it had disappeared by then. I remember being slightly worried leading up to the tournament; didn't want to be in just my togs with this rash, you know."

I nodded. "So isn't the most likely explanation that this boy is real and not a hallucination?"

Beep beep! Beep beep!

My pager. I located the mute button on the front and pressed it. It wasn't a fast page; it wasn't urgent. Whoever it was, I'm sure they could wait a few minutes. I was far more interested in David's story.

"Sorry about that," I said. "Please, continue."

"There are two reasons the boy can't be real:" David looked exhausted suddenly, like he'd benefit from a good week of deep sleep. There were sizeable shadows under his eyes. "First, no one else seems to see him, and second, no one can move like he does."

"Like what?"

"He just disappears," David said. "The next time I saw him was in the Meridian Mall. He was going up one escalator, and I was coming down another, and there he was, watching me. He coughed into his right hand, then smeared that hand all over the handrail. 'What do you want?' I yelled across at him, 'Who are you?' The boy didn't answer. He never does. He just stared back at me. Stared me out. Beneath his tattered clothes, his ribs moved in and out. He looked so... so awful that I turned away. Only when I looked again, he was gone. Vanished. In the middle of the escalator! There was no way he could have made it to the top of the escalator, not with all those people around him. No one moves that quickly. Where did he go? Did he jump? Of course, I checked out most of the shops and even the parking building, but I didn't see him anywhere. That's why I think the boy might actually be in my head."

What I didn't mention to David was that this didn't sound like fever-induced hallucination, but something more serious. Perhaps some kind of pathogen-induced psychosis. I felt that familiar fear clawing inside me, and wondered once again if this disease, whatever it was, was something really sinister. I also wondered if it had finished with David or if we'd see a subsequent relapse. The room still felt too dark and too grey. "You mentioned something about another man, a doctor?"

"Yes. I didn't see him at first, it was just the boy. But as this went on, I realised the boy was working with the doctor... or maybe the doctor was using this boy somehow. I'm not sure. Anyhow, he's this older man dressed in a white doctor's coat, although I don't think he's a real doctor. Just like the boy, he too looked out of place, out of time even, and the two of them seemed to have this really strange relationship."

"Oh, how so?"

"Well, I saw them both on Sunday evening. They were standing at the front of my house, in the flower bed, and they were both watching me. The boy was standing in front of the older man, the Man in the White Coat, and the Man in the White Coat was massaging his shoulders. While the boy was mostly just staring at me — I stood there in my bedroom window, looking at them both, watching *them* watching *me* — he looked mildly uncomfortable about the doctor touching him in this way. And then I saw the weirdest thing. I saw the doctor grab something from the boy's hair: a flea, or head lice, or something, and then the doctor just pops it in his mouth real casual, like. It was like monkeys do — you know, grooming one another. Made me wanna chunder. And that's when I started feeling all hot and cold and my arms and legs started aching.

"I tried to catch them, I ran outside (I say run, but it's hard to run when you're coming down with something and all your energy's spent). It was useless: they'd gone, if they'd ever been there. Later that night... well, I can't remember much. I remember the crunch of gravel on our driveway as they stretchered me into the ambulance, and this red and blue light washing over me. I remember Dad being there beside me, holding my hand and feeling like I was heading to this place of safety and everything would be okay there. Of course, that all changed when we actually got to the Emergency Department."

"Why's that?"

"Because *they* were right there with me in the cubicle: the boy and that creepy doctor."

It was at that point that Peter Layton returned, holding a magazine and a bottle of squeezed orange juice. "Hello, Dr Newman," he said. "Doesn't David look so much better? I can't thank you enough for everything you've done." He deposited the items he was holding on David's bedside table, then offered his hand.

I stood and offered mine, and we shook. Although technically David looked better, I didn't think he looked good. Naturally, I kept that to myself.

Someone tapped on my shoulder as I left David's room. A hard, bony finger, even through the fabric of my shirt. "Ah, Dr Newman, there you are!"

I turned around slowly. CNM Tooms stood before me in the corridor, her cold, predatory eyes piercing mine.

"Yes, I was just chatting with David."

She circled me. Even though she was much smaller than me, it felt threatening. "You must've been there for quite some time..."

"David is much improved," I said. "I took the opportunity to ask him some questions. Get a bit of history."

"And your pager doesn't work in David's room?"

"I didn't think it was urgent."

"You wouldn't know if it's urgent without answering it," she spat. "I have this expectation that when you get paged, you answer in a timely manner."

We both headed towards the Nurse's Station. I wanted nothing except to escape, but she wasn't finished with me yet. "Well, I'm here now. What do you want?"

"I noticed there were a few loose ends from Monday's ward round — discharge summaries, mostly, an outstanding script. I don't want you to leave today without completing them."

"*You're serious?* You give me the big lecture on answering my pager and it's over paperwork?"

"Paperwork is part of your role, doctor."

"Yes, but it's hardly urgent!"

Tooms sneered. "Is that so?"

Jenny was sitting inside the Nurse's Station and heard our conversation (it would be hard not to). She offered me a small smile and rolled her eyes, but was careful not to let Tooms see. Jenny was always a welcome sight. Her smile could lift my mood, but at this precise moment I could ill afford to relax my guard or to become distracted.

"Well," CNM Tooms said, perhaps sensing my waning interest. "We'll see if Dr O'Brien shares your opinion, shall we?"

I had to walk away... otherwise, I might have said something I'd regret.

Probably two or three minutes later, as I pushed through the double doors of the Children's Ward, the Old Dinosaur rang me on my mobile.

"Newman," he said. "I've been thinking about that girl, the one with Megaloblastic Anaemia. Have you spoken to the family yet?"

Why did it feel like everybody was checking up on me, making sure I was doing my job properly? Had Tooms already made good on her threat and spoken to him? Was O'Brien's phone call a pretence for something else, or was I being paranoid?

I wasn't sure how to answer, except with the truth. "No. I haven't had the chance yet—"

"Why not?" he growled, but before I could come up with a response, he'd hung up.

While there were probably a hundred things I ought to have been doing, I no longer cared: I needed to get away and cool off.

I wandered the hospital's many corridors, passing row after row of windows. Outside, the mist cloaked everything, clinging to every surface with its oppressive grip. The cold, damp air pressed against the windowpanes. This weather system was here for at least another four days, according to the weather forecast.

I paced, not really knowing where I was going, only that I needed some time out.

My footsteps slapped the polished, grey linoleum.

My heart drummed in my chest.

The corridor widened into a room filled with medical antiquities, with display cases on either side. I'd passed through here a thousand times before, usually in a hurry, and never really took in the display.

I paused now.

I took a breath.

I forced myself to slow down and think calmly.

The hospital shared this slightly morbid collection with Otago University's School of Medicine. Behind the glass, protected from time and gathering dust, lay many implements, looking like the devices of torture: blades, forceps, clamps, scissors, and more. There were vintage commodes and urinals crafted from fine porcelain, primitive breathing machines and Amputation Knives, more like swords than knives, their edges eroded, evidence perhaps of the limbs they'd hacked off in years gone by. Hanging over them, on the wall, an oil painting of some distinguished doctor and humanitarian I'd never heard of, with heavy eyebrows and a dour facial expression.

Surely this great man, whoever he was, must have known his share of struggles? Could he have foreseen the struggle of the modern doctor? If so, what advice might he give?

These artefacts attested to the long, sometimes rocky, medical heritage here in Dunedin. The hard fought gains of pioneering medical men and women. The breakthroughs. The steady advancements. A proud tradition.

In a small, perhaps insignificant way, I was a part of that tradition, too. I'd achieved the academic standards of the University, I'd survived my house officer years relatively unscathed and I continued to refine my clinical skills through long, arduous hours of work.

I would not let Tooms or Dr O'Brien jeopardise my career. No way.

I met Chong for lunch in the cafeteria. This was around 12.30pm. The place was bustling as it always did around this time of day: the steady rise of voices, laughter, the clatter of cutlery, the scraping of chair legs.

I was eating comfort food: sausage and chips. Chong, of course, had gone with the healthier option: sushi, spicy mayo sauce and a side of mixed salad.

"How's that kid you were worried about?" Chong asked when he'd finished a mouthful. "The one with the fever, the rash and the delirium. The one you mentioned yesterday."

"David?"

"You didn't mention his name."

"He's much better," I said, chewing and swallowing. "His fever broke overnight. I was able to chat with him this morning." I relayed to Chong a shortened version of David's story, including the snotty-nosed kid and the creepy doctor.

Chong gripped his stethoscope and re-positioned it around his neck. "Fever-induced hallucinations?"

"Probably. He reckons this started a few weeks ago. He believes these two individuals are connected to his illness."

"You're still worried about this boy, aren't you?" Chong asked. "Is there any objective reason you should be, besides his continual insistence on imaginary figures?"

The hint of a smell—a burning smell—wafted out of the adjoining kitchen.

"No, just a feeling."

I told Chong about my run in with Tooms and Dr O'Brien's phone call, and like a good mate, he listened. I asked Chong about his day. When we'd done whinging (actually, the whinging was mostly me), we changed subjects. I probably should have told Chong about my encounter with Audrey, but I didn't. Instead, I remembered the time back in Med School when Tim and I had smoked marijuana, and how I'd made the mistake of telling Chong. Not only had Chong convinced himself that we would both flunk Medical School and descend into the life of hardened drug users, he'd stopped speaking to both of us for almost an entire week. The encounter with Audrey felt similarly taboo, like it too might offend Chong's sensibilities, so I held that part back. Later, of course, that decision would come back to bite me.

The rest of the afternoon was busy. Besides finishing up the paperwork that Tooms expected of me, I had a couple of admissions come through the Emergency Department and several reviews on the Children's Ward itself.

When I finally stepped outside of the hospital, it was 8pm. It had been dark for over three hours. The weather remained cold, wet, and miserable. The street lights on Great King Street cast the world in a blurry, sepia tone.

"Dr Newman?" Audrey stepped out from the shadows. She had been hiding behind one of the concrete pillars to the right of the Main Entrance.

"How's your leg?" I asked, noting that she did not appear to be limping anymore.

"Good," she said. "I heal quickly."

I didn't want to have a lengthy conversation. I was tired

and my feet throbbed. "I'm just on my way home," I said, hoping this would convey my exhaustion.

Audrey did not seem to pick up on my prompt. "How's your patient doing - David Layton?" She stepped closer. Her hair was wet and bedraggled. Her eyes were intense. "I only ask because I'm not permitted to visit."

"Are you family?"

"You'll have to watch the boy closely," she said. "His condition is quite... unusual. Have you sensed anything odd?"

"Like what?"

"Healers sense things," she said, but did not elaborate.

I had sensed things when it came to David Layton, and with other children too, but I thought of it as my 'medical intuition' rather than any power I might possess. "What did you do to Toby Harrison?" I asked. "Some sort of trick? Because the boy claims you healed him... and..."

"It's not a trick," she said. "Like I said, the less you know, the better." She paused, then: "Why did you become a doctor, Dr Newman?"

"What is this?" I asked. "You ask me lots of questions and expect answers, yet when I ask you something, you refuse to answer. And please call me Grant."

"There isn't much time, Grant. A major upheaval is happening in the hospital. Strange movements. Whispers I don't care for. I need you to be my eyes."

"Right now, all I need is to get home and get some rest.

There's always something 'major' happening in this hospital, trust me. Anyone who works here knows that." Yeah, that was true enough; so why did Audrey's comments rattle me? "I would like to talk to you some more about Toby, though. Will I see you again?"

Audrey's eyes glistened. They seemed to pin me to the spot for a moment, preventing me from moving. And then she blinked. Finally, she sighed. "Possibly." Then added, "Although not if I can avoid it."

five

"I fear there will come a day, hopefully long after my demise, when antibiotics will no longer assist us. They have given us a brief reprieve, but not sufficient to make me and my kind redundant."

Dr Joseph Heltzmann, page 209, 'The Healing Art'

On Thursday morning, I sat at my desk on the Children's Ward, which was in a small alcove next to the Nurse's Station. Here, a chair, a computer and a phone had been set up for my professional use. I hadn't scaled the heights far enough to merit my own office.

"Here, read this," Audrey said, suddenly appearing before me, rocking back and forth, back and forth, from her heels to the balls of her feet, then handing me a well-worn paperback. She wore baggy grey track pants and a thick black overcoat. Her long grey hair was untamed and crazy. "This'll tell you everything you need to know."

"What is it?" I asked.

"Think of it as a training manual, of sorts. A collection of writings about healing the sick, written by a very diverse group of healers over many centuries." The book was unassuming, unattractive even, with its light brown cover. The booked was titled 'The Healing Art', but no author was identified. Flicking through the pages, no one author was named on the interior title page either. There was a Table of Contents, however, with each chapter written by different authors. A long list of them, although, at a cursory glance, they were not names I recognised.

I rested the book on my desk. "I'm busy right now," I said, hoping I'd come across as assertive rather than rude. "I have to prep for the Paeds Meeting."

I returned my gaze to the computer screen, although in the periphery of my vision, Audrey continued to rock back and forth, back and forth, in this slow rhythm of hers. Finally, she said, "I'm sorry. We got off to a poor start. I... I'm not good with people..."

I didn't have time for this. "Why are you here, Audrey?"

"I told you—"

"Oh, you need me to be 'your eyes', right?"

"Well, it's more than that—"

"Let me tell you what I see," I said. "I see a woman that looks scared, jumpy—"

She blushed. "There's this fat Security Guard who's relentless—"

"Let me finish. For all I know, she might use drugs and be having many delusional thoughts. In fact,"—I placed my left hand on the phone—"the only reason I haven't already rung Security is because I was curious about how you faked Toby Harrison's healing."

"It wasn't fake. I'm a Healer and so are you!"

I lifted the handset and typed in the Emergency Number: 777. I lifted the phone to my ear.

"Don't!" she said. "I healed someone else last night. A guy on the Respiratory Ward."

The dial tone rang once, twice.

"Who? Which ward?"

Audrey glanced up and down the corridor. "I don't know his name. I think the ward was 7A."

The phone line clicked and an Operator spoke. "What is the nature of your emergency?"

"Please," Audrey said to me. "I need your help. Check out the guy on the Respiratory Ward. Please."

On the phone, the Operator re-phrased her question, "Hello? Is this an emergency?"

"Sorry," I said. "I've rung the wrong number." I hung up the phone.

I sucked in a deep breath.

Audrey stood before me, no longer rocking, jaw flexed and her face stretched. Only her eyes betrayed any emotion; they moist with tears, glistening under the ceiling lights.

"Alright," I said. "I've got a mate who works on 7A. I'll speak to him."—I saw the concern flash across her face—"*Discreetly*. I'll look at the evidence. But even if it is compelling, I'm making no promises."

A large rimu table was the centrepiece of the Paediatric Conference Room, which was otherwise a plain and uninspiring space. Around this table sat a variety of health professionals: Occupational Therapists, Physiotherapists, Play Therapists, a Lactation Consultant, two Social Workers, the Child Protection Officer, various nursing staff, including CNM Tooms. Most people kept to their own professional group; God forbid there'd be any interdisciplinary cross-pollination of ideas! Conversation was friendly, but not too friendly. A mixture of accents and jargon bounced between the four walls, but it was muted: never too loud, never overpowering.

Dr O'Brien sat at the head of the table. "Okay, Dr Newman, over to you. Who's first on the list?"

A hush settled across the room.

I looked down at my unfinished list. The text was too small and swam before my eyes. The array of case notes splayed over the table were little help either, suddenly forbidding now that all eyes were scrutinising me. My throat was painfully dry. My water a little too far away; yes, I could stretch out and reach it, but it would betray the shaking of my hands. I wasn't even sure I could speak. "Good morning, everyone," I managed, forcing my nerves to settle. "Well, I wonder if we could break with tradition and discuss a patient named David Layton...?"

"No," said Dr O'Brien. "Let's stick to alphabetical order, please."

"It's just—"

"Alphabetical order."

I took a deep breath. "The first patient is Lilly Anderson. She's thirteen years old... Sh-She presented with acute vomiting and diarrhoea... She has a twelve month—no, eighteen-month—history of the same. Intermittent, of course... and naturally she was dehydrated... I, er... sorry, I don't remember which day she was admitted."

"Last Wednesday," Tooms said, a smile stretching the skin of her face and her wrinkles opening like great fissures. Oh, she was enjoying watching me squirm.

"Yes, of course. Her... Her..." The room was too hot. I couldn't breathe. I pulled at my shirt collar. My tie felt like it was strangling me.

"Are you okay, Dr Newman? Do you need some more water?"

"No, I'm fine. Thanks."

"What were her U&Es on admission?" Dr O'Brien asked.

For a moment, I couldn't recall what U&Es meant, which was ridiculous. When I remembered and when I tried to drag the answer from my brain, it wasn't there; it didn't exist. "No... Sorry... I don't know..."

But this wasn't good enough. Dr O'Brien was very dogmatic about how each patient was to be presented by the Registrar at these meetings. There was to be no deviation and no mistakes. I was expected to know each child on the ward, whether I had admitted them or not, and to have memorised all the pertinent information. There were no excuses.

"Her bloods, Dr Newman? Was she hyponatremic? Hypocalcaemic?"

"Oh... er, no, not really. Well, mildly, I suppose. The locum who admitted her felt it was prudent to admit for observation."

"I see," Dr O'Brien said. "And what about her latest U&Es? Have they improved?"

"Marginally. They got a little worse over the weekend, I think. But now they're improving."

"You don't seem sure? Do you want to check the notes?"

This was a trick question, of course. If I did actually consult the case notes, I might as well admit I hadn't done the prep. "I... er... no, I don't need to."

"You're sure?"

"Yes."

The Paediatric Meeting had been established many years ago on the pretext of better multidisciplinary communication and collective problem solving, but there was another, darker function. That purpose was to showcase Dr O'Brien's dominance, to show that he, the Consultant, was at the top of the food chain. How Dr O'Brien liked to impress with medical terminology! It was a performance. He loved to dazzle the audience with the sheer depth of his knowledge. However, he didn't tolerate fools or laziness. One meeting might expose the best and the worst in the man; from a deep wealth of knowledge and experience to an obnoxious, intolerant bully.

Silence.

Except the churning of the heat pump pushing out warm, stifling air.

They knew, just as I knew, that a storm was brewing. And Dr O'Brien's temper was the stuff of legends.

Dr O'Brien glared. A deep fury barely contained within his eyes. He pushed the metal-rimmed glasses back across his nose. "It seems to me, Dr Newman, that you've come to our meeting without doing your job. This despite being given time specifically to prepare. Is that a fair assessment?"

"No, I... I thought I'd done enough..."

"You 'thought you'd done enough'? Well, clearly, doctor, that's *not* the case. Why else would you be stumbling over the very first patient? I expect better of you, Dr Newman."

"Sorry."

I hated the Paediatric Meetings. I always had. Dr O'Brien was so old school and, frankly, it often felt more like an exercise in humiliation rather than a practice that might actually help me become a better doctor.

I felt the heat rising up my face, but I couldn't stop it.

"Hmmm. Well, you leave me with a difficult decision," Dr O'Brien said. "Do we proceed with the meeting or postpone it? If we proceed, it could be a very long meeting judging by your efforts so far. Lots of flapping through the case notes, trying to find information that ought to be at your fingertips. Doesn't sound particularly pleasant, does it, Dr Newman?"

"No."

"And it's damn right disrespectful for the rest of the team, all of whom are busy people."

"Yes, true, but—"

Dr O'Brien pushed on, addressing the entire room. A measured tone, so perfectly fucking reasonable. "That's why I insist on these things," he said. "I know you think I'm an old fuddy-duddy. I *know*." He turned back to me. "Maybe you'd like to explain to me and the rest of the team why you're not prepared, Dr Newman?"

I wondered when this humiliation was going to end. "To be fair, I thought I *had* prepared." This wasn't strictly true.

"To be fair… the evidence is to the contrary."

Evidence? What was he talking about? "I have no excuse." What a complete bastard! "I'm very sorry."

"Ah, but that's not strictly true, is it, Dr Newman?"

"Sorry?"

"Maybe you'd like to tell the rest of the team what you spent most of yesterday doing? You were preoccupied, were you not? Your focus was elsewhere."

"Sorry, I don't follow." Of course, I followed. I looked over at Tooms, who met my stare evenly. The bitch was enjoying this. She must have gotten wind of my investigations into Toby's spontaneous remission, and spilled her guts to Dr O'Brien.

Dr O'Brien continued, now in full flow. "Isn't it true, Dr Newman, that you've spent most of your time over the last twenty-four hours investigating a certain...—I'm not sure what to call it?—... *incident*."

"You mean Toby's spontaneous remission?"

"*Indeed!*"

"My curiosity was piqued, but I didn't neglect my job."

"For anyone who doesn't know," said Dr O'Brien. "Dr Newman here believes that Toby Harrison was healed of his asthma. He has left the boundaries of medical science, medical *fact*, and veered into... (again, I'm lost for words) ... science *fiction*." He reached across the table, sliding over a set of notes.

I could smell my fear, thick and pungent. "Actually, I was trying to debunk Toby's healing... or at least explain it in scientific terms." I wasn't sure this was precisely the truth, not in my heart of hearts.

Dr O'Brien raised the notes above his head, then

slammed them full force onto the wooden table. Several people jumped in fright. One person gasped.

They were Toby Harrison's notes.

"You wrote 'spontaneous remission' in the boy's notes! Thus lending it credibility."

I had written 'spontaneous remission', that was true, but I'd added a question mark afterwards. *That* question mark was the all-important punctuation mark. "I didn't mean—

"If you must pursue these investigations," Dr O'Brien said, "And ruin a fine medical career, then do so in your own time in the future. Is that clear?"

"Perfectly clear."

The meeting was postponed. It had lasted barely fifteen minutes.

I needed coffee, the strongest coffee I could find. Ten minutes later and I was still shaking. I stood in the queue before the Dispensary.

Perhaps I should apologise to Dr O'Brien? Perhaps it was the least I could do?

No... Dr O'Brien was many things, but gracious wasn't one of them. It'd probably only make things worse, make me look weak and pathetic. Yes, I'd been slack. I'd allowed Audrey to distract me, but it was hardly the unforgivable sin, and it certainly didn't warrant public humiliation.

Or perhaps I should just ignore what had happened at the meeting. Dr O'Brien was a bully. However much I wanted to stand up to this on principle alone, sometimes it was wisdom to accept your limitations, to accept there was nothing you could do. Bullying was endemic in the hospital according to some staff, and I was but one man. Ignore it, move on.

I edged a few steps forward as the queue progressed.

The ground floor was a hub of activity. Orderlies pushed patients in wheelchairs. Staff, patients and visitors all converged upon this large grey expanse of carpet, the low ceiling amplifying their chatter. A receptionist stood behind the main desk, giving directions. Someone else—a volunteer—manned the St John's Information Desk, looking older than many of the patients she was helping. People, people, people. They sat in or around the Whānau Room, or stood reading signs, or they queued by one of several lifts.

The hospital was always busy.

Dispensary staff in their black t-shirts responded to the demand; sumps emptied and re-packed with fresh coffee ground, mammoth machines steaming and gurgling. The glorious aroma of real coffee spilling from the shop front.

The third and best option, I decided, was to quit medicine entirely. I was no doctor. I was fooling no one. How many times this week alone had I demonstrated that?

Oh, there was the rent and the bills. There was my never-ending student loan. Five years at Medical School hadn't been cheap. Not to mention the overwhelming sense of failure I'd experience if I turned my back on all those years of hard work and commitment. And yet...

Could I just walk away? Was it that simple? If my heart wasn't in it anymore — and I really wasn't sure — then why remain in a profession that no longer fit me?

People traipsed in from the street: Damp coats, wet leather shoes, saturated umbrellas.

My iPhone rang. I eased it from my trouser pocket, glancing at the caller ID. It was my father. Perfect. Could this day get any worse? I raised the phone to my ear. "What do you want?"

"I had a patient who DNA'd," my father said. "So I had a little time. It's been a while. Thought I'd schedule a little father-son time."

I stepped out of the queue and walked to the side of the lobby, where there were fewer people and more chance of hearing. "You mean check on me? Like some asset in your portfolio?"

"Don't be ridiculous!"

"Did Dr O'Brien just speak to you?"

"No, why would he?"

"Never mind." Did I really think I could quit medicine? My relationship with my father was tenuous, but without medicine there'd be nothing, no common bond.

"So?"

"So what?"

"How are you?"

What would he say if he knew I was entertaining throwing away all those years of training? There was no way I could quit. Not now, not ever. This was my life now. "I'm fine father. Busy, you know. Always busy."

"Good, good. Well, I won't keep you."

"Sure. Right. Okay, father."

I hung up.

I returned to the back of the queue. I needed that coffee more than ever. It was at times like these that I really missed my mum. I could talk to mum and she'd always listen. She would have known exactly what I ought to do.

six

"The student will be a sharp implement, a sword wet with blood; the student will surpass the mentor, for he is born not of fury, but of compassion."

Trudy, the Surgeon of Truth, page 17, 'The Healing Art'

Later that day, I had lunch with Tim and Chong in the Staff Cafeteria. The place was packed. A rising chatter filled the room.

Overhead, a fine rain continued to fall upon the glass ceiling.

"How's your day?" I asked Tim. Today's blazer was a burgundy colour. I paused, trying to make my next question seem casual. "Any unusual occurrences on 7A today?"

Tim's hands stopped moving, his knife and fork poised

halfway between his plate and his mouth. He stared at me. "How did you know?"

This would be my opportunity to tell both my friends about the various conversations I'd had with Audrey, but I didn't. "The rumour mill," I said, the lie coming far too easily. "There are no secrets in this hospital."

"One of my patients claims an angel visited him and that she healed him. His name's Paul Swartz."

"Interesting..."

"Hey, what happened to that kid the other day? You know, the one you said was the 'opposite of dying'? What was that all about?"

"Oh, you mean Toby?" I waved a hand. "That was nothing."

"Yeah. Well, the interesting thing about Paul Swartz — while I don't necessarily accept the notion of angels — the healing itself is pretty damn convincing."

"Can I meet him?" I asked.

"Really?" It was Chong's turn to look surprised. "I thought you found any patient over the age of sixteen fundamentally objectionable? Aren't you worried Tim might lure you over to the dark side of adult medicine?"

"Not at all," I said. "I'll stick with my children, thanks. All the same, this guy's been touched by an angel and I want to meet him."

"Sure," said Tim. "Paul's agreed to stay while we run some diagnostics. How about later this afternoon?"

"How about now?"

"What? Right now?" Tim looked down at his plate, at food that might go uneaten. "Can't I at least finish my lunch?"

Tim brought up Paul Swartz's X-ray images on his computer. There were many images, the last taken only three days ago, and possibly the worst. They showed advanced lung hyperinflation, a flattened diaphragm, a narrow heart and a massive amount of consolidation in both lower lobes, all of which were consistent with pneumonia on a background of COPD. Like large white nimbus clouds gathering above his abdomen, about to unleash a storm; brooding, menacing, obscuring many anatomical landmarks.

I stepped back from Tim's desk and shook my head. "She healed *that?*" An excitement whirred in my gut and I felt suddenly more animated.

Tim nodded. "It certainly looks convincing."

This patient, unlike Toby Harrison, had agreed to stay for tests. I could validate this healing. "I have to meet this guy."

From his desk, Tim led me through Ward 7A to one of the four-bedded bays. As best as I could tell, the ward was identical in layout to the rest of the wards in the old ward block — the sluice, the treatment room, the linen cupboard, a storeroom, everything where I'd expect it to be. The two-tone green walls, with tired, flaking paint. A glossy posters listing patients' rights and responsibilities. The noises differed from my ward: the coughs gruffer; the voices deeper. A foreboding permeated the corridors and rooms; the absence of joy, a sense of waiting, of a slow, collective suffocation. No amount of detergent could eradicate the astringent odours of fear and despair that hung in the air like some spiritual darkness.

I didn't do adults, no thank you. The weight in this ward was almost unbearable. I was glad I'd specialised in Paeds.

Paul Swartz was on the left-hand side of the bay, sat in a chair, looking out of the window. He was dressed in a striped shirt and grey trousers. His bed was made as if it had never been slept in.

"Excuse me, Mr Swartz," Tim said. "This is my colleague, Dr Grant Newman. I wonder if you'd mind telling him what you told me this morning?"

Paul Swartz turned towards us. His face was aged with long, hard wrinkles, much more than his fifty-eight years. His hair was grey and receding. In his eyes, there was a terrible knowledge and a hint of some deeper emotion. This man had looked long and hard into the jaws of death, lingered there until it had become an accepted reality, but now something had changed. He acknowledged Tim and me. Here was a man who'd been traumatised by illness, yet I saw no obvious symptoms of the illness itself.

Tim drew the curtains around the bed space. It was a

futile exercise. They offered the illusion of privacy, even though Paul Swartz's three neighbours could hear everything.

What would Paul say?

"I thought I was dreaming at first," Paul said. He had a thick South African accent. "Only I don't sleep all that well. Going to sleep always comes with a certain anxiety when you can't breathe. A dread. I especially don't sleep when I'm in this place." His eyes circled, indicating either this room, or the ward, or maybe the entire hospital. "You know, strange bed, strange place. It took me a while to get my pillows and the back rest right. I can't—I mean, I *couldn't*—lie too flat." Paul looked at me. "It felt like I'd only just drifted off to sleep when I heard someone moving about just where you're standing now. At first, I thought it was one of the nurses."

"It wasn't?" I asked.

"No."

"How can you be sure?"

"When you've been in hospital as long as I have, you get to know the nurses. Even the agency nurses. If this woman was a nurse, she wasn't dressed like one and I hadn't seen her before."

"Did you get a good look at this woman?"

"Oh, yes."

"What did she look like?"

"She was beautiful," Paul said. "Her skin was flawless. She had this long, silvery hair. A few curls. Her eyes were piercing. I'll never forget those eyes. I think she scared the sickness out of me. She was wearing a black top and black pants. All black, you know, like the rugby team. Or like she was trying to dampen down her light."

This wasn't a description of Audrey. Paul Swartz was making this stuff up, or at least exaggerating. He was hyping his story up. I frowned. "And approximately what time did she visit you?"

"I know exactly," Paul said. "'Cause I looked at my watch just after she spoke to me. It was 2.15am."

"What did she say?"

"I asked her who she was," Paul explained. "She just shushed me and said, 'I'm an angel'. Then she touched me and said the words, 'Release him and face me'. Such powerful words! And me, touched by an angel. Incredible, eh?"

Why would Audrey say this? I would ask her the next time I saw her.

Tim was right. The subjective evidence for healing was compelling. From a casual glance there seemed to be no trace of any chronic lung disease in Paul Swartz: it had gone, but perhaps there were some lingering cerebral effects from all those years of hypoxia. "And you're sure of your description?" I asked. "I mean, it would've been pretty dark at 2.15am."

Paul locked eyes with me. "She had this inner glow... And her face! Oh my Lord!"

I grabbed the DynaMap from the other side of Paul's bed and wheeled it towards him. I picked up the sats probe and offered it to one of Paul Swartz's fingers. "Do you mind?"

"Not at all."

I placed the probe on Paul's left index finger.

It took a few seconds for the readout to register. The red numbers flashing—... 98%... 99%...—before finally settling on a reading of 99%.

Incredible. I took the probe off Paul's finger and placed it on my own. My saturations were only 97%.

How could Paul have better sats than me? It was surely not possible. The man may be certifiable, but he wasn't hypoxic.

"So why did she choose you as opposed to the other men in the room?" I asked.

Paul exhaled slowly. "That I don't know," he said. "You see... I had this coming to me. I deserved it, you understand. Smoked heavy since I was in my teens. Abused my body. I haven't been a good person, not at all. Selfish. Made a lot of mistakes in my life; took the people who loved me for granted." He paused, looking doleful. "The last thing I expected was a kindness like this. God's grace."

"You believe God did this?" I asked.

"Absolutely, I do."

"She could've healed me!" shouted one guy in the bed bay. He tried to say something else, but deteriorated into a coughing fit instead. "*Bah!*" he said at last, his coughing subsiding.

I lowered my voice. "From my point of view, it would be very helpful if we could verify your healing. I know this may well feel like an inconvenience, but—"

"What've you got in mind?" asked Paul.

"Another chest X-ray."

"Fine. When?"

"No time like the present." I looked across at Tim, who stood there, tight-lipped and nearly impossible to read. "Give me five minutes to phone an Orderly. Tim, would you order the X-ray please?"

Tim nodded.

"I don't need an Orderly," Paul said. "I can walk."

"It's six floors down," I said. "And the lifts are on the other side of the hospital."

"I don't need the lift. The stairs will be fine. You have stairs, don't you?"

"You're joking, right?"

Paul Swartz wasn't joking. A few minutes later, we took the stairs down towards the X-ray Department. All the stairwells were next to the lift shafts, there in the event of a major fire and the need for evacuation. They were fashioned from concrete, minimally lit and cramped. It was cooler in the stairwell too, a welcome escape from the stifling heat of the wards. Not only did Paul walk down six flights of stairs, he set a cracking pace, one which I struggled to match. Two pairs of shoes striking each step, the sound booming within the confined space, echoing up, up, up and down, down, down.

Through a heavy lead-lined door, the X-ray room was dimly lit. A muted hum came from the air conditioning vents. In the centre of the room was the X-ray table with a thin, neat mattress. Above, the X-ray generator hung on an articulated arm.

The Radiographer asked Paul to remove his shirt and then to stand against the wall.

Meanwhile, I stood behind a lead-lined screen next to the console. I observed the radiographer position Paul within the X-ray field. She asked him his full name and date of birth, checking these details against his patient bracelet and the computer-generated request form Tim had sent through. Everything was done by the book.

When she was satisfied, the Radiographer joined me behind the screen. "Alright, Paul. Deep breath... and hold...." She pressed a button. A sign illuminated over the door: X-RAYS: DO NOT ENTER WHEN LIGHT IS ON. A long, loud warning beep was emitted as the image was captured. "... and relax."

Soon this image appeared on the console screen, showing what I already knew: that Paul Swartz no longer had any trace of Chronic Obstructive Pulmonary Disease.

"That can't be right," I heard the Radiographer say as she

wandered back into the imaging room, but I didn't bother to explain.

It was right.

Impossible, yes, but it was right.

I was busy that afternoon, looping between ED and the Children's Ward. My pager was silent for no longer than twenty minutes at a time. For once, I found the busyness good and the distractions welcome, for they kept me from dwelling on what was troubling me.

Paul Swartz had been healed. I had objective evidence to support this.

Toby Harrison had most probably been healed, too.

Audrey's claims, it would seem, were legitimate.

I, however, thought about my mother:

The door to Mum's room was slightly ajar. I lingered just outside, unsure. It was dark inside. She'd got the curtains drawn. I pushed the door—just a little. I leaned in. I strained to see my mother in the gloom...

I thought about what might have happened if Audrey had been around when my mother was sick and dying of cancer. Maybe, *maybe*, Audrey could have healed her. Of course, there was no cure for cancer. Treatment options got better and better, but there was no cure. Then again, there was no cure for asthma or COPD either, but that hadn't prevented Audrey, had it?

But the thing that troubled me most of all were Audrey's words to me: *You're a Healer too*. How could this be true and yet I'd been unaware of it? Surely, she meant this in a generalist sense: as in, you're a doctor, so you're a healer. Just like the Chaplain had said, "God uses skilled doctors and nurses to do His healings".

The alternative was too awful to contemplate, and I tried to push the idea from my mind, with little success. *If* I was a Healer like Audrey, then I had possessed the power to heal my mother but, simply because I was unaware of it, I hadn't done so. In effect, my mother had died needlessly and I, in my failure to use my power, was largely responsible.

My pager beeped—again.

I headed towards the nearest phone, but as I did, I decided I would talk to Audrey at the next opportunity and find out exactly what she meant.

That evening, lying in my bed, I leafed through the pages of 'The Healing Art'. It was an odd little book. Beyond its plain brown cover, it lacked many features of a bona fide paperback. There was no author or editor named, either on the cover or in the front matter, rather each chapter had been attributed to an individual "healer". Neither was there a publication date, a publisher, an ISBN or a copyright declaration. There was no stated affiliation with a University, learning or religious institution. The book's spine looked professional enough, as though Audrey had collected these pages herself, but sent them away somewhere to be properly bound. The book possessed the usual printing press smells —paper, ink, glue—but also older, more evocative smells: dust, damp, sweat, even a trace of dried blood.

I hadn't heard of most of the "healers", probably because they were alternative practitioners. There was the short chapter written by Yeshua of Nazareth. I'd love to get Pastor Dixon's take on that one. One chapter was attributed to Asclepius, which was familiar somehow. I checked Google on my phone. Turns out Asclepius was the Greco-Roman god of medicine, the son of Apollo. The chapter was written in archaic language, but I doubted any god, real or fictitious, would have the time to contribute a chapter to some obscure book on healing.

I found the passage Audrey had referenced on page 17. It was attributed to Trudy, the so-called Surgeon of Truth, who seemed to have written a couple of chapters in the book.

It read:

Healing hands will leave their mark, even as sickness is expelled. One healer shall know another. And one shall train another, student and mentor.

The student will be a sharp implement, a sword wet with blood; the student will surpass his mentor, for he is born not of fury, but of compassion. Wherefore, the wise man must cast aside his former wisdom, for it shall be purged in the School of War, and all that remains is the sword.

I closed the page. This was cryptic garbage! Nonsense riddles! I didn't believe anyone could see into the future, much less *my* future, and the deliberate use of vague terms and metaphors, while it might have impressed readers years ago, wasn't so persuasive on a modern audience.

Yet Audrey revered this book and its text. And Audrey, using this knowledge, had healed Toby Harrison and Paul Swartz.

I opened the book again.

I skimmed through several pages, but the narrative became more and more bizarre; one chapter read like a horror novel, with graphic descriptions of monsters called Seepers. These, I think, were a metaphor for disease and the disease process. There was a section about some ritual. There was even reference to some kind of parallel dimension called the Sablosphere. None of it gained any traction in my brain. My eyelids grew heavy and, several times, I'd switched off and my eyes had closed over. I pressed on, determined to understand this strange book and to find the answers I needed.

At some point I fell asleep, my bedside light still on. It was not a deep nor restful sleep.

seven

"What sense would it make or what would it benefit a physician if he discovered the origin of the diseases but could not cure or alleviate them?"

Paracelsus, page 112, 'The Healing Art'

The following morning, as I trudged through the Hospital's Main Foyer, I saw Audrey across the room. She appeared to be looking for me. However, when she noticed me looking in her direction, she lowered her head, shifted a little, and tried to mingle with the crowd.

I wasn't in the mood for Audrey's games.

I pushed forward.

Moving around and between us were people with slouched shoulders and weary faces, wrapped up in jackets as they came in from the cold. People herded through the foyer. These people were here because they had to be—most of them, like me, were beginning their shifts.

Overheard conversations seemed dreary, barely registering a note of excitement or enthusiasm, drab like the walls and the carpet, or like the inclement weather outside.

Wafting from the Dispensary, a strong coffee smell attempted to lift the mood.

"Are you avoiding me?" I asked Audrey, levelling with her, although, admittedly, I had five or six inches of height advantage.

"No," she said, taking a half step backward.

"Why did you try to hide?"

"I wasn't hiding. I was mingling."

This was snowballing into an argument and wouldn't achieve anything positive. I stopped myself. Audrey's eyes were hard, her entire posture defensive, the lines on her face etched by the unforgiving ceiling lights. She wore a black woollen polar neck and dark grey stretch pants. I paused. When I was sure I could keep my voice calm, I said, "I need to talk to you."

"Not here."

"Then where?"

She pointed. "Over there." She led me towards the St John Information Desk. Next to the desk, a door led into a stairwell. This was a tight, square-shaped space cut from concrete, its steps rising up and up, each level with its own carefully curated artwork to distinguish it from the other levels.

"What is it?" she asked, pulling the door through to the foyer closed.

"You said I was a Healer. A Healer too. What did you mean?"

"I think it's pretty obvious what I meant." She kept her voice low, and it was further muted by the concrete walls and floors.

"Are you suggesting I can heal the sick like you can?"

"Ah, so I'm not some fake?"

I clenched the wooden balustrade. "Answer the question."

"There's a price, Grant. A heavy price. It was wrong of me to involve you in my problems. It was selfish."

"If I am a Healer, I need you to show me how."

"Did you read that book?"

I nodded. "Some. It made little sense."

"It makes more sense once you see *them*."

Okay... I didn't trust Audrey, not really. I wanted to. What I did trust was the healings she'd performed, on Toby and especially on Paul. She wasn't some fake. However, that did not mean she wasn't a strange or even deranged person. And what exactly was her agenda? Despite my reservations, I was compelled to ask, "*Them?*"

"Did you read page 35? About the ritual?"

I shook my head. "Okay, what ritual? If there's a ritual to make me a healer, can we, like, perform it now?"

"No."

"Why not?"

"I've already explained why."

This was getting nowhere. I changed tack. "Why did you tell Paul Swartz you were an angel?"

"Sometimes it's easier to tell people what they expect to hear. I don't have the time or the patience to explain everything to everyone."

"You don't know that," I said, hoping to challenge her thinking without pushing her too far. "How'd you know you're not making assumptions?"

It was her turn to pause. Her nostrils flared, and she stared at me. "I'm protecting you," she said at last. "You know that, don't you? You seem like a pretty nice guy, one of the good doctors, and the last thing I want is to screw up your life and your career."

"If I've got this gift, this healing ability, like you suggest, perhaps that's not your decision to make." I thought I might lose her, that she might simply take flight, and I'd never have this opportunity ever again.

"Be careful what you wish for. Once you lose your complacent eyes..."

"What if I became a doctor because I'm really a Healer? What if that's what I'm meant to do and the practice of medicine is a poor second? And what if I can achieve more good as a Healer?"

She sighed, seeming to genuinely weigh up my request. "Well, it would be very helpful. It might re-stack the odds."

She took a step closer. Her face, deep with shadows, was haggard. "Close your eyes," she instructed, raising her hands to my face. Then she pressed both her thumbs onto my eyelids with considerable force, so hard that the murky red behind my eyelids exploded into black stars.

I backed into the balustrade. Patterns whirled before me. "Woa! Easy there!"

Audrey ignored me and kept pushing and pushing. Finally, she was done. "Open your eyes," she said. "Do you see anything different?"

Slowly, I opened my eyes. I stared through the window back into the foyer, where I saw people ambling about. "Like what?"

Audrey sighed. "You'll know when you see them. Let's try again."

Again she instructed me to close my eyes and again she pressed her thumbs hard against my eyelids and pushed, as if her goal was to pop one of my eyeballs.

"Now do you see?" she asked when it was over.

Again, I looked out at the foyer through that small, square window. I saw nothing that was different or out of the ordinary. Just the steady flow of people entering the hospital, dispersing into the various corridors that led from there. "I don't know what you're talking about. What'm I meant to see?"

Audrey shook her head. She approached me once again, and this time I stepped back and stumbled on a step.

"Do you trust me?"

I nearly blurted out the truth, but instead I cracked a joke: "*I'm* the doctor. That's what I'm supposed to say."

The joke fell flat.

"Do you want this or not?"

I got back to my feet. "How am I meant to see anything when my eyes are so sore?"

"Your eyes perceive alright," she said, "it's the brain's interpretation that's standing in the way", and before I reacted, she was pressing her thumbs against my eyelids once more.

It occurred to me how bizarre it would look if anyone were to walk in on this little ritual. Would they view it as an assault? An act of passion? What? Yet even as I fought the urge to laugh (a natural reaction when someone invades your personal space), I realised, or glimpsed at any rate, that this ritual was serious business and potentially life-changing.

This time she pressed so hard I wanted to yell. I could feel the pressure building up inside my skull, and I felt certain that at any moment one (or both) of my eyeballs would actually succumb to the pressure.

"Do you see?" she said at last, releasing her grip.

I opened my eyes; I looked into the foyer, and—

Oh my God, suddenly there were a lot more people in the foyer. Strangers. People who cast larger-than-life shadows. People that rode on the backs of others. People who sneered and had sharp teeth and an ugliness that defied the natural symmetry of the human face.

I realised, of course, that these additional people weren't really people at all. It seemed they lived all around the hospital and perhaps beyond it. They were accustomed to being unseen by human eyes—for many walked with a swagger or a sense of great arrogance. Yet I saw them now, just as Audrey did, and there was no way to un-see them.

Suddenly, I knew what Audrey was talking about.

"Shit!"

The vomit rose in my throat, and the only thought I had was: I must get to the nearest toilet before I spew. The trouble being the nearest toilet meant crossing the foyer and mingling with... with *them*.

I didn't care.

I bolted through the door and into the suddenly crowded foyer. I sprinted for the toilets, even as I bobbed and weaved between all those that looked like they'd spilled out of a freak show.

I made it to the toilet—just. I plunged inside the cubicle; the vomit rising up and pouring from my mouth in thick chunks.

It came with such gusto and, for a moment, I was certain that it would not stop, that I would suffocate on the contents of my stomach.

When I was done, I leaned against the off-white porcelain, gasping. Finally, I sat back on the damp floor of the toilet stall. My eyes were blurry with tears and my nose was streaming and it felt like something—a piece of carrot, maybe—was lodged in one of my nostrils.

Audrey stood at the doorway of the stall. "You okay?"

"What do you think?"

"I think the ritual worked," she said. "Your eyes aren't complacent any longer." She paused a moment, then added, "Sorry."

"What the fuck are those things?" My stomach heaved again, flipped, and then decided it wouldn't eject my stomach lining as well. "Are they demons? How can they...?"

"Not exactly. They're Seepers. They're responsible for all diseases you've ever studied and lots that you can't even imagine."

I reached up and flushed the toilet.

This is what madness must be like. Sitting on the floor of the men's toilet discussing some other-worldly creatures that couldn't exist, and yet did exist. Audrey had done something weird to my eyes. The cold, tiled floor was not the most comfortable seat. A numbness spread through my buttocks even as the dampness worked its way into my bones, yet I had no desire to leave. The cistern refilled with water. Even the lingering urine smell, which permeated the entire space, wasn't enough to make me move.

Audrey stood against the doorway to the stall, peering down at me, shaking her head. "Sorry," she repeated.

Once again, if anyone were to enter, I wondered how they'd interpret what was happening.

"How do you live with this knowledge?" I asked.

"I haven't done so well. No..."

"So what's the plan? Heal the entire world? How many Seepers are there, anyway?"

"That's a good approach if you want to get yourself killed."

"A little too ambitious?"

Audrey gave no response.

"I can't un-see them, can I?"

She shook her head. She had her hair tied back in a simple ponytail, and it shook too. "No, you can't. And I get it. I went through all this myself. You'll probably hate me—"

The taste of bile lingered in my mouth. "I—"

Beep beep beep beeepppp!

My pager, its discordant noise ripping me from this reality back to some kind of normality where I had a job and responsibilities. I unclipped it from my belt and studied the LCD screen, a feeling not dissimilar to motion sickness washing over me. It read: EXT 5689.

The Children's Ward.

"I can't answer this," I said, looking down at the black plastic box in my hand. "I can't."

Audrey led me by the hand, back through the foyer and to the nearest phone. One was on the far wall next to the Southern Communities Laboratories. I knew this without looking, for I'd used it frequently.

"Keep your eyes open," Audrey said. "You're drawing too much attention."

As she pulled me along, I opened my eyes and looked around the room. We were surrounded by so many of these weird creatures, most of them vaguely human-like, at least in appearance, although they didn't act like humans. Their sole purpose seemed to be to inflict pain. One creature was hammering on the head of its victim, a man in his early sixties, who sat in the corner and looked like the weight of the world was upon him. Another creature clambered across the floor on all fours, taking bites out of passers-by seemingly at random. A third creature poked its victim in the eyes. A fourth rode on the back of a young, weary-looking woman.

"Eyes forward," Audrey said. "Don't look at them. Keep looking at me."

But it was hard not to look at them. Their cruelty, the

sadism they found in hurting their victims, it was like nothing I'd witnessed before.

"Keep your eyes *here*," said Audrey, taking my head in her hands and pointing it towards hers. She lowered her voice and spoke barely above a whisper. "If you stare, they'll know you can see them. Trust me: we don't want that."

What would happen if they knew? Whatever the answer, I didn't want to know, so I tried to push such thoughts from my mind.

We reached the phone. Audrey picked up the headset and passed it to me. "Go on," she said. "Phone the number."

I shook my head. "How can I act like—?"

"You'll adapt."

I wedged the handset between my head and shoulders and, with trembling hands, typed in the number on the keypad.

It rang twice and then I got through to Trish, one of the nurses on the Children's Ward.

"Grant," Trish said. "Thanks for calling back. It's David Layton." A stab of dread. I'd always felt that David's improvement was temporary. "He's crashed. We need you to come right away."

There were so many questions I wanted to ask, but now wasn't the time. "Yes," I said. "I'm a couple of minutes away." I replaced the receiver.

"What is it?" asked Audrey.

"I have to get back to the ward."

I'd almost forgotten the Seepers that populated the hospital. My professional persona, with its way of facing emergencies, had briefly taken charge.

Audrey broke my bubble. "Remember: Don't stare. Things are going to be a lot different now. You're going to see the perpetrators of disease, but you need to avoid prolonged eye contact."

I nodded. I suddenly felt very vulnerable, dread pooling in my stomach. "You're not coming with me, are you?"

"No," she said. "I'm reluctant to come into the Children's Ward anymore. It's too risky. The Seeper there knows me."

We navigated through the now-strange terrain of the hospital, Audrey leading the way. There were Seepers all around us, more familiar with the building than me, more entrenched than I thought possible. I knew nothing, it seemed. Absolutely nothing. And everything that I'd thought I knew had suddenly forsaken me.

Audrey came as far as the lifts. Her parting words were: "Whatever you see—the man or the monster—do not engage it! That's not a battle you're going to win."

I met David's 'Creepy Doctor', the Man in the White Coat, when I entered David's room, Room 18, and found him sprawled over David's bed. His hair was silver grey and his coat, unbuttoned, billowed out on either side of him. The way he lay across the bed obscured David from my view: it looked like he was intent on smothering the boy! There was also two nurses in the room. However, they didn't seem to object to this behaviour, so I assumed my initial impression was wrong.

I lunged forward to pull him off, but something restrained me, some instinct. *Don't touch!*

The Man in the White Coat rose from the bed in a slow, calculated manner. He lifted both hands in the air. He looked like some eccentric medical professor about to expound on some finer point of anatomy. His jaw shifted from side to side, as if it were uncomfortable somehow, making his teeth grind.

I glimpsed David's face, yet I barely recognised it.

My eyes were fixed on this unfamiliar and unorthodox doctor. Why had he climbed upon David's bed like this? According to the message, David had 'crashed', so how was this going to help? Was this some hybrid form of CPR?

"David went downhill about twenty minutes ago," one nurse said, but it was like she was speaking from another room.

I could only stare at the doctor on the bed. He had extraordinarily long fingers. As I continued to watch, captivated, the fingers of his right hand formed a triangular wedge. Suddenly, he plunged his right hand down into David's abdomen just below the xiphisternum.

David shot up in the bed, his mouth open, winded, unable to draw in a breath.

This was my first proper look at David. Oh my God, what a change! His entire face was swollen, many of his features were buried beneath sacs of fluid. His eyes were sunken within inflated sockets. His lips were puckered and misshapen.

A sudden memory overwhelmed me:

The door to Mum's room was slightly ajar. I lingered just outside, unsure. It was dark inside. She'd got the curtains drawn. I pushed the door—just a little. I leaned in. I strained to see my mother in the gloom...

A tingling arose in my stomach and I felt like I might vomit. I swallowed the queasiness back, even as I pushed the memory away. This wasn't the time. This wasn't about me.

David's rash was back, linking then obliterating the boy's freckles. It had erupted into pus-filled boils that further maligned his features. Nor did the swelling stop at his face. It extended to his arms and torso. His arms were elephantine.

David tried to raise his arms, to defend himself, but he lacked even the basic strength to master them and they dropped back onto the mattress. The boils littered his arms too.

The Man in the White Coat jumped from the bed, causing the entire frame to creak. He was an older man. His face was slender and lined with deep grooves. There was a twinkle in the depths of his eyes. He smiled, his teeth white and perfectly aligned, then he rounded the bed to approach from the far side.

"No," David gasped. It was such a weak, pathetic sound. He twisted and tried to turn away from the Man in the White Coat, but every movement seemed uncomfortable. He rattled one of the cot sides with his heavy arm.

One nurse stepped forward, perhaps to protect him from harming himself or ripping the IV from his foot. "Easy there, David."

I stepped forward, too.

"What should we do, Grant?" asked the other nurse. I think her name was Sandy. Where her colleague had rushed to David's side, she remained at this side of the room. Neither seemed phased by the unconventional behaviour of this strange doctor.

I didn't understand the question. My only thought was that someone ought to phone Security. "Sorry?"

"What should we do?"

The Man in the White Coat stabbed one of his impossibly long fingers at David's face, popping one boil.

David screamed.

"Stop it!" I yelled.

That was the moment I realised the Man in the White Coat was another one of Audrey's Seepers. Neither of the nurses could see him, not like I could, not like David could.

With another finger, the Man in the White Coat continued to prod more boils until the lower half of David's face oozed purulent yellow pus. Only this time he—it—was watching me and measuring my reaction.

I turned from his gaze quickly.

Sandy's brow was furrowed. "Dr Newman?"

"Sorry," I said. "It's been a tough morning."

Sandy looked far from convinced, however, as if she were questioning my sanity.

The oily smell was thick in the room, the one I'd first smelt in the Emergency Department. Cloying. Sticking to the pores of the skin like something that might never wash off. Somehow I understood that this smell emanated from this thing (What had Audrey said? "Whatever you see in there, the man or the monster, do not engage it!").

"Tell me what happened?" I asked, trying my best only to look at David, but not at this creature.

The other nurse piped up. "He crashed about twenty minutes ago. The swelling... the skin lesions... they came out of nowhere."

"Obs?"

"BP 150/100. Pulse irregular and around 110. Sats have dropped to 93%"

"*Shit!*" This was bad. David had nasal prongs on for supplementary oxygen, although it looked like he might tear them off his face at any moment. He needed high flow oxygen. "Any fever?"

"Slightly, 37.9 degrees Celsius."

The Man in the White Coat turned away from me and

back to David. It stuck its nails in David's bloated abdomen and ripped four lines in his flesh.

David howled. Both his arms crashed into the cot sides. Blood and pus pooled over his abdomen, then dripped down onto the sheet.

"What the hell—?"

"*Jesus!*"

I felt cold inside, and yet a bead of sweat slid down my forehead. I was simultaneously hot and cold. I didn't know how to fight such a creature and, if it suspected that I could actually see it (which I was certain it must), who knew what danger I might be in? "Call Dr O'Brien," I managed. I was way out of my depth. I knew so little about these creatures: their strengths, their weaknesses. I wasn't capable of objectively assessing David from a clinical point of view; all my training and knowledge had been relegated or simply departed my brain.

Sandy slipped out of the room.

The Man in the White Coat raised his left arm, ready to strike the boy again.

David recoiled, his eyes popping open. "Get him away from me! Don't let him hurt me!"

"He's delirious," the remaining nurse said.

No, he wasn't. He might wish for delirium. Delirium might be favourable. If our positions were reversed, David and I, I might wish for the refuge of delirium too. And if this nurse could see what we saw, if her complacent eyes were suddenly opened, she'd never say such a thing.

Of course, I said nothing.

O'Brien arrived with a great bluster. His thinning hair was untamed, his skin blotchy, the lines and curves of his face deep and angry. He immediately went to David's bedside, virtually pushing me out of the way. Even the Man in the White Coat paused for a moment to consider the new arrival.

"What the hell's happening here, Newman?" O'Brien barked.

"I...I—er..." I truly could not come up with a half-coherent answer. All my effort was going into avoiding eye contact with the Seeper in the room. I studied the wooden laminate floor, or the pumice-coloured walls, or the red Emergency button, or the oxygen and suction ports. I was certain my cover was blown.

"He crashed about half an hour ago," offered the nurse.

"So why am I only finding out now?"

Again, a dark memory of my mother returned:

The door to Mum's room was slightly ajar. I lingered just outside, unsure. It was dark inside. She'd got the curtains drawn. I pushed the door—just a little. I leaned in. I strained to see my mother in the gloom...

David screamed.

The creature ran one of its long fingers down David's abdomen, its nails splitting open the boy's skin like an over-ripe peach.

"*Jesus, Newman!* Don't just stand there! Do something." O'Brien cupped his hand over David's brow, then frowned. "What's causing this oedema?"

The cause of the oedema was sprawled over the bed next to David. I watched it in my peripheral vision as it reared up once again. It's white coat covering David's lower half like some great shroud. Of course, I couldn't tell O'Brien any of this. "I don't know."

The creature lowered its head. I thought it might bite a chunk out of David's stomach, but it worked its jaw up and down, up and down, until it had produced a sizeable ball of saliva in its mouth. I watched then in horror—I couldn't help but watch—as this dripped in a long, thick white string down into David's stomach wounds. The creature produced a strange pop, popping noise, not from its mouth but from somewhere inside its skull.

David screamed some more.

"So, *hypothesise*. How're we going to treat this?"

"Prophylactic antibiotics?"

O'Brien exhaled loudly. "Prophylactic? Infection is the *least* of our concerns right now." His face reddened. "Where's this oedema coming from?"

I could see the cause, unlike any of my colleagues in the room, but I could not explain the mechanism of disease in a way that would be acceptable to the Old Dinosaur. "I still maintain this disease has an infective cause. Possibly a virus."

O'Brien shook his head. "Then your antibiotics aren't prophylactic, are they?"

He was right. "No," I conceded, "you're right." I just wasn't thinking straight. Worse, I could feel panic rising inside me. My arms and legs wouldn't stop shaking.

"So your treatment options are...? *Think!*"

The Man in the White Coat stopped torturing David and turned in my direction, awaiting my reply too. In medicine, we treated people's conditions blindly much of the time, albeit with educated guesses based on the presentation of symptoms and the empirical evidence before us. Only now I was no longer blind. Now the perpetrator of this disease was looking right back at me, daring me to say something that might betray this knowledge. As much as I wanted to help David and say something that might impress my Consultant, I could not take the risk.

"C'mon, man, think!"

My throat dried up. If I said anything too specific, the Man in the White Coat would know I could see it. I said nothing. I couldn't speak.

After a long pause, the Man in the White Coat returned its attention to David. It kneaded the boy's abdomen, making the oedema that was trapped under the skin wobble.

"We need to treat the oedema," O'Brien said at last, his cold eyes gazing at me. "Come on! We need steroids, we need diuretics, we need analgesia (Please, someone get this poor boy some morphine), we need anti-pyretics. And then, yes, maybe after that, some prophylactic antibiotics." O'Brien sighed. "I think maybe you ought to go back to your textbooks, Dr Newman."

The nurses mobilised.

The Man in the White Coat jumped from David's bed and stood before O'Brien, hissing. It circled O'Brien, apparently to see if it could intimidate him.

O'Brien, of course, was none the wiser. He continued to bark his orders.

Sandy passed me a medication chart, and I prescribed everything O'Brien wanted, unable to tell if these were sound clinical decisions or not. I was happy just to be given a job, something to take my attention away from the Man in the White Coat.

Finally, the creature retreated to the corner of the room, and sat on the laminate floor, but it had a malignant smile smeared over its face.

David settled and appeared to sleep.

"Okay," O'Brien declared. "That's better. We'll let the boy sleep." This wasn't a victory, rather an impasse. The way the Man in the White Coat flexed and stretched its limbs, and breathed loudly, I knew it hadn't finished its torment, even without looking directly. David would be attacked and would deteriorate again, but for the time being, at least we'd be able to tell his father he was "stable". I never liked that word. It always felt too vague.

O'Brien and I wandered from David's room. Peter Layton was waiting in the corridor outside. I was grateful that O'Brien spoke to him, for I wasn't sure I could, and I certainly didn't feel able to offer anything close to hope or reassurance.

I couldn't stop trembling. I was an emotional, psychological, and physical wreck. All I could think about were Seepers: Would I round the next corner and see one or even an entire group? If so, how would I mask my emotions? How much longer could I keep up this pretence? I wanted only to get out of the hospital until I could speak to Audrey again.

"Everything okay?" O'Brien asked as we got a little further along the corridor. There was little warmth in his voice.

I saw no benefit in lying. "No, I'm not feeling so good," I said. "I think maybe I ought to take the rest of the day off..."

O'Brien stopped, considering my request. "Yes, well, I think it might be best if I let you go." It was in his voice, in every word he uttered: Disappointment, in me as a person and as a medical practitioner.

"Thank you."

"You're not on duty over the weekend, are you?"

"No."

"Just as well," O'Brien said, and walked away.

eight

"I know nothing, or certainly next to nothing. All I can say, with any degree of certainty, is that the world was not created to entertain suffering as it does."

Father Morris Hughes, page 211, 'The Healing Art'

I spent the weekend in my flat with the curtains closed, trying to come to terms with events of the last week. Sometimes I peeked out at the street below, expecting to see *them* walking around in the daylight hours. I lay in my bed, huddled under my duvet, but sleep only came fleetingly and was haunted by dark dreams. I checked and re-checked that my front door was locked and all the windows were latched. What if they knew I could see *them* and paid me a visit?

What was it Audrey had called them? Seepers.

None of this made any sense, unless I'd suffered a complete psychotic break, unless Audrey had somehow infected me with her delusions. Deep down I knew they were real, however, as much as I wished they weren't. I'd seen with my own eyes the carnage these creatures worked upon my patients. I was a man of Science, but now I had to reconcile a very different narrative...

Mostly I moped around the flat in my pyjamas. I saw no reason to get dressed, no reason to wash or to shave. I ate junk food: tinned fruit, one dollar white bread, packets of chippies, instant noodles. There were more nutritious options in the supermarket down the street, but the thought of venturing outside was too much. I tried watching the TV, but found nothing that could distract me. Reading was the same, my mind refusing to engage.

I was bored and restless, which I've never coped well with. I liked to be busy. If left alone with too many of my own thoughts, they nearly always turned to my mother and the way she'd died. That was the last thing I wanted to dwell on, especially now that I knew that her death, like so many others, may have been preventable.

What did Breast Cancer *look* like? Did it wear a human face as it stalked the population for its next victim? And if I could've recognised it back then, would I have been able to save my mother?

I revisited what had happened with David, how O'Brien

and I had tried to stabilise him. For me, this had been intolerable. I had had to feign scientific deduction as I countered everything the Seeper threw at the boy. I had had to avoid staring or doing anything that might betray the fact I had knowledge of and could see this creature. All of this while repressing the scream rising up from inside me.

Was this what medicine would be like from now on? If so, surely my career was over. How could I return to ward rounds and the daily tasks of the Registrar? Or how could I look at a sick child when I also saw the creature responsible for attacking that child? Could I look and do nothing, or next to nothing? And what would happen if I tried to tackle one of these Seepers directly, beside people's misconceptions and the likely loss of my medical registration?

I didn't know.

I wanted to talk to Audrey, but had no way to get in touch with her.

I dwelled and mused and brooded and contemplated all these things. The hour grew late, but I barely noticed. Saturday rolled into Sunday. I forgot about food and even sleep. Yes, the knowledge of Seepers was new, but I'd been fighting them for the entirety of my medical career without even knowing it. It was personal too; they'd taken my mother from me! Maybe there was some way to use this knowledge and leverage it against them. Surely, the least I could do was learn some new fighting skills?

On Sunday evening I realised I could not stay in my flat

forever, thinking about death and disease and slowly losing my grasp on reality. I could phone in sick, but I only had finite sick leave, and there were only so many excuses I could offer my employer to explain why I wasn't at work. And there was much work to be done.

I would return to the hospital tomorrow.

nine

"Although Alchemy has now fallen into contempt, and is even considered a thing of the past, the physician should not be influenced by such judgements."

Paracelsus, page 112, 'The Healing Art'.

I remember my first day as House Officer stepping into Dunedin hospital, Tim and Chong beside me, all of us looking decidedly green around the gills. I remember how anxious we'd all felt. Everything was new, and five years at University and numerous placements had done little to prepare us for the responsibility we would shoulder.

Returning to work on Monday morning felt very similar. There was a heaviness in my gut.

The main foyer was crowded, as it always was at this time of day. I expected to see Seepers everywhere, but at a casual glance, I couldn't see any. Just people. Normal people. Many of them my colleagues. Dressed in winter coats and carrying wet umbrellas.

I paused next to a table and some stools opposite the Dispensary, and scanned the people in the foyer more closely. The smell of freshly brewed coffee assaulted my nostrils.

There were no Seepers.

Had I imagined everything? Perhaps the whole theory that this was some kind of psychotic break, albeit a temporary one, was correct? Certainly I was stressed, it was a constant with my work, but I didn't think this alone could explain it.

One of the Children's Ward nurses, Brenda, walked past. She must have been coming off the night shift. She waved at me, and I realised I must have been staring into space.

"Hi, Brenda."

I moved towards the elevators, still searching for Seepers, only trying to be less conspicuous. I stood by the elevator with a couple of other regular people. One of them pressed the button to summon the lift. We waited. The lift arrived, and the doors pinged open. Stood in the middle of the lift, and the first to exit, was a huge Seeper. It had impossibly wide shoulders, bulbous eyes and a misshapen head, like some medical experiment gone wrong.

I gasped. My jaw dropped. As the creature pushed its way through the elevator doorway, I can't explain why it didn't notice my expression.

It didn't even slow.

It staggered towards Gynae outpatients and the STD clinic.

The Seepers were real, after all. There were far fewer of them than I'd seen on Friday, like many had left or were going to greater lengths to hide. Either way, I didn't like it. It was all wrong. Like Audrey said, something was 'going down', but what, I didn't know.

Riding up in the elevator, my pulse was racing in both wrists, and my stomach was churning.

O'Brien arrived at 8.30am and we started the Ward Round. He didn't bother to ask how I was feeling. I grabbed the white trolley and followed him.

I expected to see Seepers all around the Children's Ward, but, if they were present at all, they were hiding. That is, until we came to David Layton's room.

There were two Seepers in David's side room—The Man in the White Coat, who stood in the corner, watching, and the Snotty-nosed boy, the one David had described, who was kneeling at the foot of David's bed. The oily smell was there too.

David lay rigid on his bed, his arms and neck and stomach heavy with fluid, reminding me of my mother before she had died. Peter Layton kept vigil at his bedside and looked up as we entered.

"How is he?" I asked.

Peter shook his head.

The room was uncomfortably crowded, although only David and I saw all who were present, and with David it was hopefully between bouts of delirium. I was tempted to look at the Man in the White Coat, to see his reaction to our arrival, but didn't.

O'Brien shuffled past me and stood at the foot of the bed, nearly toppling the Snotty-nosed boy without even realising.

The Snotty-nosed boy scampered beneath the bed. His clothes were bedraggled, just like David had said, and he continually wiped at his nose with filthy hands, then smeared the mucus over his clothes, over the floor, over the metal frame of the bed. As I looked down, his legs disappeared under the bed.

O'Brien grabbed the obs chart clipped onto the end of the bed and examined it. He was wearing a pale blue shirt and a loud red tie; the latter standing out against his pale features, but acting like a barometer to measure his anger. "Hmmmm," he said. "There's improvement since Friday, but not exactly the result we were hoping for." O'Brien addressed Peter. "Has your son spoken to you much over the last 24 hours?"

Peter shook his head again. "A little, yes, but most of the things he said made little sense."

"That's the fever," O'Brien said.

Peter smiled sadly. "I wish David wasn't so... tormented."

"We can give another sedative," O'Brien said, although even he seemed to falter, perhaps realising that this wasn't much of a solution.

I kept my eyes pinned on David and Peter, even as the Man in the White Coat moved about in the corner of my eye and the Snotty-nosed boy made noises beneath the bed.

"What ails you, boy?" the Man in the White Coat asked suddenly. For an instant I thought he—it—was addressing me, that it had somehow climbed up the wall and was speaking down from the ceiling. In fact, it was addressing the boy under the bed.

"I like dust," said the boy, who wasn't really a boy at all. "It reminds me of all the germs that the cleaners miss." The boy laughed, a loud laugh, full of mirth. His laugh turned into a cough. The cough was the deep, hacking variety that ordinarily would have worried me.

"Arise!" the Man in the White Coat said. "Or you'll miss the real artistry."

O'Brien was explaining to Peter Layton how viral infections were tricky, and how secondary bacterial infections often resulted when the body's immune system could not overcome the infection immediately. Peter nodded. I don't know how much information he was actually absorbing.

David's eyes fluttered open. "What time is it?" he croaked between swollen and cracked lips.

Peter glanced down at his wristwatch. "It's 8:45am, David," he said. "It's Monday. The doctors are here to see you."

"No more doctors..."

"He doesn't mean that," Peter said, looking at O'Brien and me. "It's the fever speaking."

"That's okay, Mr Layton," O'Brien said. "No offence taken, is there, Dr Newman?"

"None at all."

"I take offence!" said the Man in the White Coat, edging closer to the bed. "This one does not appreciate the great lengths we have taken or, indeed, the privilege bestowed upon him."

I shivered.

"We're here to help, David," O'Brien offered.

With his bloated limbs, David attempted to push himself back up the bed. "No! *No, please!*"

"This doctor is impotent," the Man in the White Coat said, standing shoulder to shoulder with O'Brien at the foot of David's bed. The Man in the White Coat seemed corporeal enough, even from the edge of my vision. What would happen if it pushed O'Brien out of the way? "He is old and foolish," continued the Man in the White Coat. "We shall fill his ageing frame with all manner of creative diseases. Only *we* can help you."

"You're not here to help me," David said, his voice hitching up a few notes. "You're trying to kill me!"

"Nonsense," O'Brien said, a little too defensively.

"Nonsense," the Man in the White Coat echoed. "Killing is humdrum. We are the Masters of Syringes, Tourniquets and other delights!"

From beneath the bed, the Snotty-nosed boy snickered.

David swiped at the air with his oedematous hands and arms, as if engaged in a physical battle with the Seepers in his room. His flesh was heavy and shifted unnaturally. His skin had a translucent quality, such that I could make out his veins and arteries.

The same, repeating memory slammed into me:

The door to Mum's room was slightly ajar. I lingered just outside, unsure. It was dark inside. She'd got the curtains drawn. I pushed the door—just a little. I leaned in. I strained to see my mother in the gloom...

I blinked, snapping out of my reverie. I forced myself to approach David's bed. I knew I couldn't say too much, not until I'd learnt to navigate this situation better, but needing to contribute something. I leaned closer, despite the oedema, and looked David in the eyes. "David, listen to me. This is Dr Newman. Grant. Remember me?" I reached out my hand and steadied David's shoulder. The flesh under the boy's hospital gown quivered. "Whatever you see or hear, whatever it is, ignore it. I want you to listen to Dr O'Brien and me. We're *real* doctors. We're doing everything we can to help you. You've been very sick."

"The whole hospital is crawling with monsters," David said. "They're everywhere."

"Ignore them."

"Don't reinforce his hallucinations," O'Brien said.

"You're going to get better," I said. "It's going to be okay."

"On the contrary!" the Man in the White Coat said. " All you'll know is despair. Your doctors are imbeciles who know nothing of our designs. You're under our control, completely and undeniably."

David groaned and pulled away from my grip. "Leave me alone."

"We will measure your human limit," the Man in the White Coat said, pulling the edges of his white coat together. "With great care and patience. Then our entertainment will begin."

"Come on," O'Brien said, looking at me. "We'd better continue the Ward Round." He turned to Peter. "I'll send in one of the nurses with a sedative."

Peter nodded.

We left the room to a chorus of scoffing from the Man in the White Coat and the Snotty-nosed boy, whose pale face and gaunt cheeks emerged from under the bed. I didn't want to leave, and yet I wasn't sure how long I could stay and remain composed. Poor David. These Seepers hadn't finished their torment. I would be called back soon enough. Rather than being some passive witness, however, what I needed was to work out an effective defence against these creatures.

I needed Audrey's help.

We reclaimed the white trolley and continued along the back corridor. I noticed O'Brien glancing at his watch. We'd taken a lot longer than expected with David, and now he'd no doubt be looking to cut corners so he could finish on time.

The last patient was Serena Hopkins. I looked through the window into Room 8, and there she was lying on the bed with her parents on either side. There was a Seeper on the bed with her, curled up next to her on the mattress. While it looked mostly human—its face, its torso—it had strange protrusions for hands which had latched onto Serena's body: one to her spine and one between her legs.

I recoiled with disgust.

But that wasn't the worst thing. The look on Serena's face was the worst part. She was looking back at me; her face washed with pain, but it was the anger in her eyes that got to me the most. The anger was directed at *me*. For my omissions. I should have told her the truth about her diagnosis.

I looked away.

"Did you speak with Serena?" O'Brien asked.

"No."

"Well," said O'Brien, offering a humourless smile. "The truth is, we can't always help everyone, however much we might want to." He didn't peer through the window into Serena's room. "Kids get sick. Sometimes kids are going to die. That's reality."

With that, the old dinosaur walked away, and the Ward Round was over.

ten

"There are no incurable diseases — only the lack of will. There are no worthless herbs — only the lack of knowledge."

Ibn Sina, page 180, 'The Healing Art'

"Your Healer," said Chong over the phone. "She's back."

I was sitting at my desk in the Children's Ward. "That has to be good, doesn't it? Where was she this time?"

"That's the part you're not going to like."

My stomach muscles clenched. I consciously relaxed them. I pressed my mobile closer to my ear. "How's that?"

"It was on 8C," said Chong.

My stomach knotted.

"The patient's name is Fiona Peters," Chong continued. "Until this morning, she had stage 3 breast cancer."

I swallowed.

"Will you come?" Chong asked.

I couldn't speak.

"Grant?"

Fifteen minutes later, I passed over the threshold of Ward 8C and walked inside. The last time I'd been here was when my mother was admitted after her very last cycle of chemotherapy. The ward had changed little. The same colour scheme, the same drab, slightly dated decor, the scuffed and battered walls which had collided with too many hospital beds over the years.

My chest tightened. I could no longer breathe as easily, like something had partially blocked my airway.

I remembered how gaunt my mother had been, how tired she'd looked. Her skin had been flaking, her lips chapped, but there was no sign of the lymphoedema at that stage. I remembered all the lines and tubes that had been stuck into her body and that terrible, terrible hopelessness. She was dehydrated and neutropenic, they said. Her neutrophils were so minimal they'd had to do a manual count. The Oncologist said that any more chemo would kill her and immediately discontinued all future treatments. That was mid-October. She was dead by November.

No doubt there'd be Seepers on this ward that were

related to the one that had killed my mother. How might *they* appear? Would they resemble the thing that was killing Serena Hopkins in the Children's Ward? Would I see them ingesting their victims?

I wasn't ready for that.

Chong approached along the main corridor. "Grant! Over here."

Just the sight of my friend lifted my mood and expelled much of my anxiety. He led me past the Nurse's Station, to the back corridor, where the Isolation Rooms were located. It was quieter here.

I knew this corridor and these rooms all too well.

"Where's the patient?" I asked.

Chong smiled. "Before I introduce you to Fiona Peters, I wanted to have a quick chat." His smile became slightly mischievous. "She's what you might call 'something of a character...'"

"You don't find her healing credible?"

"I didn't say that. It's just..."

"What?"

"Miss Peters claims your Healer sexually molested her..."

That was certainly different.

"... the healing — if that's what we're dealing with here — seems almost secondary to her. She intends to take her complaint to the highest level. Can you believe that? I assumed you'd want to talk to her, so I've arranged for a nurse to act as a chaperone."

"Good idea," I said.

In terms of Seepers, however, I hadn't spotted even one.

Fiona Peters was reclining in a La-Z-Boy chair next to her bed in a four-bedded bay. She wore a navy-and-white striped top and a patterned bandana with a pink fabric flower on one side. On her left arm, moving along the forearm, was a silver wristwatch, a hospital bracelet and an intravenous cannula. Next to the chair, a Baxter pump was attached to a drip stand. A half-finished bag of fluids was wound through it, yet the pump had been switched off.

"This is Dr Newman," Chong said. "He'd like to ask you a few questions, if that's okay?"

"Have you come to feel my breasts, too?" Fiona Peters asked. "Why the hell not? Everyone else has."

I felt heat rising in my face. My God, all these years of medicine, of examining patients in intimate places, and I was still a prude. I was very pleased to have Chong and a chaperone present.

Chong drew the pale blue curtains around the bed space, then moved aside, standing next to the washbasin. The nurse remained in the background, not speaking, merely a witness to any impropriety. I was unsure how to approach Fiona Peters.

"Well?" said Fiona. "What'd you wanna ask? I'm not hanging around here all day."

"No, of course. Well, I wonder if you could begin by telling me what happened."

"*Again?*"

"Please, if you wouldn't mind? I've been following this Healer. I'm trying to get a profile of her."

"Healer? Is that what you call her? I think 'pervert' would be a more appropriate word."

"Did she heal you or not?" I shouldn't have spoken like this. It was unprofessional, but this woman was certifiable.

Fiona shrugged, then gestured towards Chong. "Like I said to your friend here, the way she touched me was all wrong. And yes, she *might* have healed me, but she also *took* something from me. I felt it. Strangest thing I've ever felt."

"What did she take?" I asked. "Besides the cancer." With all the nervous energy, I could feel my patience slipping.

"It's hard to say. All I know is she violated me somehow. I know that makes little sense. She was so aggressive. It was so... wrong."

"And how did you come to meet this woman?"

Fiona Peters tutted and rolled her eyes. She was clearly disgruntled at having to recount the entire story again. "I met her just outside the Whānau Room," she said. "I couldn't sleep. I often sit there and read a magazine or watch the city lights."

"What time was this?" I asked.

"2:30am or thereabouts. Anyway, I saw this woman, and I wondered who the heck she was. I hadn't seen her before. She wasn't one of the staff. And she looked too healthy to be a patient. I wondered why in hell she was wandering the Oncology Ward at this hour."

"Did you get a good look at her?"

"Of course I did! She was up close and personal."

"Can you describe her?"

"Let me see," Fiona said, pausing a moment. "She was my height. Five-four, five-five. Perhaps a little taller. Her hair was mostly grey and was just long enough to cover her ears. She was real pale, but not in a dying-of-cancer sort of way. She had this lurid lipstick. I reckon she'd easily be in her late sixties. Old enough to, you know... I didn't think her libido would be that strong."

Again, I felt a flush spread across my cheeks.

"And she just stood there," Fiona said. "She was staring at my breasts. Didn't try to hide it. Not subtle. I haven't got anything against them, but—"

"*Them?*"

"Lesbians," Fiona said solemnly. "Each to their own, I say. I expect them to keep their passions under control, though. I mean, it isn't decent."

"Did she speak to you?"

"I spoke to her," Fiona said. "Probably because I felt so awkward. I told her I was due to have a mastectomy next week. I tried to make a joke of it, you know. Told her I'd be

Lob-sided Fee because... because I'd be all uneven." Fiona leaned to the right to illustrate. "Since she was looking at my breasts, I figured I might as well talk about them."

"What did she say?"

"She said that she saw something on my left breast—that's the one that had the cancer."

"Did she say what she saw?"

"No."

"Had you told her it was the left breast that had the malignancy?"

"I don't think so, no."

I paused. I looked across at Chong, but couldn't read his facial expression. He turned one of his pens round and round in his hand. I looked at the nurse too, but her impartiality didn't falter. I wasn't sure I wanted to continue this conversation, but I knew I must. For completeness. "So, what happened then?"

"She starts saying stuff like 'I can heal you' and 'Let me get the cancer'."

"And what did you think?"

"I didn't know what to think, to be honest. I think at first I thought I was dreaming or something. Then I thought that maybe this was some cheap trick to get me to lift my top and expose myself."

"Did she ask you to undress?"

Fiona pondered the question. "No," she said at last. "Not in so many words."

"But she touched you — touched your breasts — right?"

"Yes."

"So, how did that come about?"

"Well, I guess I thought it was worth a shot."

"Sorry?"

"The healing. I wanted to see if she could actually do it. She looked the business. You know, like maybe she could do it, if anyone could."

"So you" — I searched for the right words and decided that Fiona's own words were the safest — "'exposed yourself'? Then what happened?"

"I asked her if she liked what she saw? It's just the way I am. I shoot my mouth off when I'm nervous."

"I see. And what did she say?"

"She said 'no'. Real blunt like that. No, she did not like what she saw. Of course, I was offended. I've always thought of my breasts as one of my best assets. That's why I was so upset about the mastectomy."

"But she meant the cancer, didn't she?"

"Yes, I suppose."

"Is it possible there wasn't a sexual motive?"

"You weren't there," Fiona said. "You didn't see or feel the way she touched me. Her words, 'Release her and face me'. It made me all funny inside. Sent weird sensations through me." Fiona shuddered. "First I was hot, then cold, then hot again. I felt the cancer in my breast shifting. Cancer can't move like that, can it?"

I didn't answer. I still hadn't seen a solitary Seeper in this ward.

"Then she approached me again, said something about there being one more, that I was blocking her, something like that. I warned her, 'Touch me again and I'll scream!' I wouldn't have done it, not really, but I was feeling weird. *Jesus.* So, she just turned and left. Didn't say another word — not to me, anyway — just turned and ran back along the corridor. But I heard her muttering stuff, stuff like 'Come back here now!' and 'Face me and die!' only she wasn't speaking to me anymore."

"Who was she speaking to?"

"I don't know. I didn't see anyone else."

This part of the story bore a startling resemblance to Toby Harrison's. Audrey would have been addressing the Cancer directly. Once again, I wondered what Breast Cancer might look like? "Anything else you remember?"

"Not really," Fiona said. "I felt very peculiar. I returned to my room, to my bed. I thought I was going to faint."

"And when did you know you were healed?"

"Late-morning, when I woke up. I slept for nine straight hours. I haven't slept this long since I was a teenager. And when I woke up, I was different. I knew the cancer had gone. Every last malignant cell. All of it."

"That must've felt good?"

"Yes... and no. I still felt the physical memory of her

touch. Like this invisible imprint that she'd left behind on my skin. A reminder of her violation."

Violation? She used that word again. What an unusual reaction!

"If you wouldn't mind submitting to a staging scan, so we can verify..."

"Sure." Fiona scowled. "Why not?"

I looked over at Chong. He nodded. I turned back to Fiona. "Thank you for your time, Mrs Peters."

"*Miss*."

"*Miss* Peters. Yes, thank you."

Fifteen minutes after leaving 8C, I received a page from the Triage Nurse in ED. "Can you come now?" she asked, her voice tense over the phone line. "We've got a twelve-year-old boy just brought in by ambulance. He's in bad shape. I believe you might know him."

"Who?"

"Name's Toby Harrison."

The strength drained away from my body. I had not been expecting to hear Toby's name, at least not so soon. "On my way," I said, my voice falling. I didn't relish the prospect of picking up the pieces of Toby's ill health. I didn't particularly wish to see the Seeper that was responsible for making Toby's life so miserable from such an early age. And why had Audrey's healing failed? What did this mean?

As I hurried to ED, I went through a mental checklist for the management of acute exacerbation of asthma.

Once in ED, I was directed to Resus Three. I pulled back the curtain. ED staff were scrambling within. Toby was lying on the bed, but I knew immediately this wasn't an asthma attack.

He was delirious. He was thrashing about on the trolley, hitting out at the cot sides. There was blood everywhere—on the sheets, on his clothes—where Toby had scratched the tops off boils, boils which were upon his neck, his forearms and the lower parts of his legs. His body was grossly oedematous. All the health he'd regained when Audrey healed him; all of it had been stolen again.

My jaw dropped.

The same memory, unbidden, came rushing back:

The door to Mum's room was slightly ajar. I lingered just outside, unsure. It was dark inside. She'd got the curtains drawn. I pushed the door—just a little. I leaned in. I strained to see my mother in the gloom...

Not only had I stopped in my tracks, I was back-pedalling out of the cubicle. These were the same symptoms I'd seen in David Layton! An oily smell caught in my nose and throat and I couldn't draw a breath.

Oh my God! This was bad. This was terrible.

My gut churned, a wave of nausea rising inside me.

That's when I noticed the Man in the White Coat sat next to the defibrillator. Calm, smiling, rubbing his hands together as he oversaw his handiwork. He'd struck down David and now he'd targeted Toby. This was a second case, but what was the connection?

"Good," said one of the ED nurses, addressing me. "Over here."

I took my time putting on gloves and a gown, trying to gather my thoughts, averting my eyes from the thing in the corner of the cubicle.

It took almost an hour and a half to stabilise Toby Harrison. I'd wanted to avoid midazolam, if possible, but the Man in the White Coat in the Resus Bay made clear-thinking difficult. I tried to focus on Toby, on the work. The Man in the White Coat did not interfere with my efforts, preferring to watch from the sidelines. He'd already done his damage—for now. In the end, midazolam proved the best option, giving Toby some respite. I arranged for his transfer to the Children's Ward, then left promptly. As I climbed the stairs back to the first floor, I bumped into Audrey. How long had she been loitering in the stairwell? Was she waiting for me? The light was mostly even in the stairwell, and yet she'd somehow found a more shadowy area.

"Where've you been?" she asked. There was an edge to her voice, which I was in no mood for.

"I had days off."

"*Days off?*" The edge became edgier. "This isn't a Monday

to Friday gig. These creatures never take breaks. They're at work night and day."

My hand went down to the polished surface of the wooden balustrade. I took a deep breath. I barely knew Audrey, so why did she think she could lecture me? "Oh wait," I said, trying my best to keep my voice controlled. "You perform some weird shit on me, on my eyes—"

"You asked me to."

"True... but you still buggered off and left me. So please don't tell me I can't have days off. I needed to process all this stuff, and you didn't exactly stick around to help me."

"Sorry." She bowed her head. Her hair contained many strands of grey. "I wanted to. It's just..."

"Anyway, that creature, that Seeper, the main one, I had a strange encounter with it this morning in David's room."

"David *Layton*?"

"Yeah. So the Seeper brought a friend with it. And then, this afternoon, I've just come from ED, where I've readmitted Toby Harrison (remember him?) and I find it there too. Toby's got the same symptoms as David."

"*Bastard!*"

"To tell you the truth, when I heard Toby was back, I thought the whole healing thing might be a hoax."

Audrey shook her head. "This Seeper is getting stronger. It could be the Scourge—"

"Honestly, just doing my job seems... impossible, given... everything. And I'm worried about David and Toby."

"Me too."

I doubted that. Her response seemed glib. I glared at Audrey, suddenly annoyed. "Why would *you* care?"

She matched my stare, her eyes fierce and suddenly full of pain. Tears glistening even in the muted light. "I care because David *is* my son, and you and me are the only two people who can save him."

eleven

"I have witnessed the fabric of the world torn asunder, great cracks appearing upon the wall; further, I have perceived the Seeps bleeding into this, our world; a great, malignant horde of them, pushing forth from the Sablosphere like tormenting hornets, even as time itself was unwound."

Garri, The Great Angekok, p 77, 'The Healing Art'

The following morning, I forgot my ID badge and headed back to my locker to retrieve it. I walked along the corridor on the Lower Ground Floor, deep in the bowels of the hospital, and somehow I got disorientated. I walked and walked. This was not the way to the locker room. Something compelled me to keep walking, however, like a rat pressed into a narrow tunnel scurrying on and on forever. The substantial weight of the hospital over my head, floor upon floor, layer upon layer of concrete, entombing me.

The corridor was much longer than I remembered, stretching before me into some unseeable, unknowable future.

This was definitely *not* the way to the locker room.

Something bad lay ahead of me.

Something terrible.

The light cast everything in a pale green monotone. My shoes clicked on the linoleum. I walked past several open doors—to plant rooms and such places, but these were none of my business and I kept moving. I was *compelled* to keep moving. Abandoned medical equipment littered either side of the corridor, draped in dust sheets. An antiquated anaesthetic machine: how long ago had this been decommissioned?

On and on. Still, the corridor stretched before me, drawing me, drawing me to...

Something...

The lights went out. The whole corridor plunged into total darkness, deep and thick.

I stopped. Unsure of what to do.

My heart was hammering. I couldn't breathe and I thought I might die from suffocation, the weight of the hospital bearing down on me, but then I found air. One breath. Then a second. And a third.

One fluorescent strip came back to life—weak, muted, flickering. And then some others. The path ahead was gradually illuminated, but now it flickered before me: on... off... on... off...

I walked a little faster, feeling very uneasy. What lay before me? Something dark and terrible just around the next corner in this impossibly long corridor. I didn't want to see, never, and yet I pressed on.

Lights on... lights off... lights on...

A morbid curiosity drove me. I had to know what it was. Even as my skin crawled and a trace of cold slithered down my spine. And, as unpleasant as it might be, perhaps my very survival depended on seeing what lay just around the next corner.

I knew this corridor; I walked it almost daily. It had never been this long before, somehow stretched in space and time. I ought to know what lay ahead, and yet I simply couldn't recall what it was.

The corner loomed before me.

Lights off... lights on... lights off... lights on...

I stepped around the corner... and there was more corridor stretching before me. Only now I remembered where this corridor led: to the Morgue. All paths led to the Morgue. My breathing was far too loud, my heart thundered in my chest, and yet trembling legs carried me forward.

There was a curtain drawn across the width of the corridor. The curtain meant one thing: The Orderlies used it to seal off the corridor when they wheeled the dead on gurneys from the small service lift and into the Morgue.

What was beyond that curtain now?

I didn't want to look, and yet I had to. With fumbling fingers, I pulled that thick drape aside and saw—

The Morgue door was wide open. The dead were piled up inside, so many that they spilled out into the corridor.

I stood there, mouth open.

Many of these corpses had been dead for some time. They were twisted and rigid. Their necks were black and bloated, the chunky limbs finally shedding all that excess fluid, great pools of it oozing over the floor. Dead eyes, life long extinguished. Pallid skin, no longer resembling anything human, but glossy, plastic, peeling away.

These people had died from the same disease that afflicted David and Toby. These were the Man in the White Coat's victims.

The Morgue was overflowing. A mountain of bodies piled inside, filling every available cubic metre of space. Body on body on body, carelessly cast one upon another, limbs intertwined in the loveless embrace of death and desecration. Clouds of flies buzzed around them, so loud it was like a scream, as they lay their larva among the congealing flesh. Elsewhere, the decay was more advanced: maggots had already hatched, squirming and revelling in the dissolving tissue.

The smell assaulted me. I couldn't stop my body from

purging what remained in my stomach. I puked everywhere: On the linoleum, on my shoes. A chunk of vomitus lodging itself in one nostril. The bitterness lingering in my mouth.

Wiping tears from my eyes, I saw all the bodies piled before me, piled up and up and up, and back and back and back. As far as I could see. They ceased to be individuals, these cadavers, but had somehow merged into one—a seething, gelatinous mess. And among this misshapen mess I saw items that offended: a woman's hand, dainty, perfectly intact, an engagement ring glistening on the third finger; an eyeball, floating in molten flesh; long, golden locks of hair attached to a skull with no skin upon it, the skin having been eaten by stomach acid that had leeched from a neighbour's torso.

"There shall be no space for the suffering we have wrought," a voice said, cold and alien. "Your Morgue will overflow and still the bodies will pile up..."

I turned to raise my objection, and—

I awoke with a jolt, my body covered in sweat and my heart pounding in my chest.

I was in my flat.

I looked at my alarm clock. I had forty-five minutes to get ready for work.

When I arrived at the Children's Ward, my nightmare still unsettled me. Was it just a bad dream or something more ominous, such as a prediction of the future, or an extension of the powers Audrey had bestowed upon me?

The ward was quiet. I saw no Seepers.

Along the back corridor, I heard laughter from Serena Hopkins' room. That was strange, especially given the poor prognosis that O'Brien had spelt out so recently. Yet Serena, her father and mother were all laughing. Had they all lapsed back into denial so soon?

I approached cautiously, unsure if I would be welcome or not. I knocked, then pushed open the door and stepped inside Room 8.

Serena still sat on her bed, but had a lot more colour than I'd seen in her for a long time. "Dr Newman," she said, and she seemed genuinely pleased to see me, her face widening into a smile. "I've had some wonderful news."

"Oh?"

"God has performed a miracle!" Mr Hopkins announced, seemingly unable to contain his excitement and stealing his daughter's thunder. Through the window, the sun had finally relegated all the rain clouds that had persisted for so long. While the weather might be more optimistic, the optimism in the room felt wrong.

"Really?"

Serena nodded. Her eyes shone. "I had a visitor overnight," she said. "He came to me in my dream, and—"

"He?"

"That's right. A doctor. He was wearing one of those white lab coats."

The Man in the White Coat? But that made no sense. "I see. And what did he do?"

Mrs Hopkins sat in a grey plastic chair in the room's corner in an almost prayerful position. "You don't believe what my daughter's saying, do you, Dr Newman? You don't believe God can show his favour like this?"

"You'd be surprised what I believe," I said. "At the same time,"—I turned back to Serena—"You've been very unwell for a long time, Serena, so I think a little caution is warranted."

Mr Hopkins said, "Caution or unbelief?" His eyes were wide and his forehead was particularly shiny.

"*Caution*," I said. "Now tell me more about this doctor? Does he have a name?"

"No, he never gave his name," Serena said. "Or if he did, I don't remember it. In fact, most of what happened has disappeared into a haze, and I only really remember what I told my parents when I first woke up."

"Which is?"

"The doctor asked me why I put up with such a 'diseased disease', when I was so young and had so much potential. He used other words—*bigger* words—but that's what he meant. I definitely remember him saying 'diseased disease' because I thought that's a pretty funny thing to say."

I scanned the room and even glanced under the bed. There was no sign of the Seeper, the one I'd seen yesterday, with its strange protrusions. "What did you say?"

"I said, 'please, sir, if you know how to free me, then tell me. I've been sick so long I can't remember anything else'. He said, 'We have long waited for this moment. Behold! The strong will overthrow the weak. See?' At that point, my whole body was filled with this bright, bright light and I felt the cancer being burnt from several places throughout my body. I felt the tumours burning, this incredible pain, but then the pain disappeared. The darkness lifted. I felt life fill my body once more. I breathed in and out. 'Is this what you want, Serena Hopkins?' the doctor asked. 'I feel great,' I said. 'That is excellent. We will adjourn now, but later we shall talk again.' Then he was gone, and that must have been when I woke up. Now I've dreamed many times of being healed, but never of anything that felt so real. I just knew this was no ordinary dream; Dad said it was a visitation."

"By whom?"

"By God, of course. Or at least one of his angels."

"You're not the first person I've heard talk of angels," I said, but this was worlds apart from Paul Swartz's angel, and it made me very uneasy.

"Well, maybe there's something in it, Dr Newman," Mr Hopkins suggested. "The truth may not be popular or easy, but it should be spoken, should it not? 'The truth will set us free'."

"'Jesus is the same yesterday, today and tomorrow'," Mrs Hopkins chimed in.

"We always knew that God would raise up our daughter," Mr Hopkins said. "We've held our faith and now our faith has been rewarded."

"So what happens now?" I asked, although I feared I knew the answer already.

"We'll be leaving," Mr Hopkins said. "No point in taking up a perfectly good hospital bed, not when there are other children out there who might need it. Sometimes God moves sovereignly and, when He does, isn't it just a thing to behold?"

I said nothing. Irrespective of my views on God, there seemed little point in arguing with Mr Hopkins or his family. They had their beliefs; I had mine. To me, what had happened here had little to do with the sovereign power of God. As I left, I thought — or, at least, imagined I did — that I caught the slightest whiff of that oily smell, and dread nudged its way back into my gut again.

I needed to talk to Audrey.

Shortly afterwards, I was called to the Emergency Department. A fourteen-month-old boy had presented there with what I assumed was Bronchiectasis.

When I pulled back the curtain in his cubicle, the Seeper

that shared the cot with the infant surprised me. It was like a weird cross between a rat and a chimpanzee, with completely white fur and red bulbous eyes, lined with thick capillaries. It had attached itself to the infant's left nipple and suckled there. The child squealed and sat uncomfortably in the cot's corner.

Both the child and the Seeper looked up as I entered. The Seeper quickly dismissed me and went back to its suckling.

"Where is this boy's mother or father?" I asked the ED nurses who'd led me to the cubicle.

The nurse shrugged. "She couldn't stay. Something about other children in the car and taking them to a friend's place. Said she'd be back as soon as she could."

I nodded. I approached the crying infant and spoke gently. "That's alright, we'll look after you..."

"Jamie," the nurse finished.

"We'll look after you, Jamie."

Jamie didn't look convinced. How could one so young have such caution?

I reached into the cot and picked up Jamie. As I lifted him into my arms, the Seeper became dislodged from his nipple and dropped to the floor with a thick slap. A jolt of coldness passed through me. I shuddered. "That's better," I said, thrown, yet keeping my eyes only on the child. "You just wanted someone to hold you."

The boy brightened. The tears ebbed away.

Meanwhile, the Seeper lumbered into the corner of the cubicle, where it hissed and snarled. While I tried not to look in its direction, it had an impressive array of teeth, capable of considerable damage, I'm sure.

I kept rocking Jamie, and he relaxed.

Maybe if I kept hold of him, this creature wouldn't harm him again? A superficial assessment would suggest that separating the two had had a remarkable effect on him. There were no chest crackles or lip cyanosis, things which I'd usually associate with a child unwell with Bronchiectasis.

On closer inspection, I recognised Jamie. This was not the first time he'd been to ED with breathing problems, despite his young age.

I'd never seen the creature who'd caused his disease before. Many doctors assumed diseases like Bronchiectasis were solely the result of environmental factors—poverty or cold, damp houses—but this clearly wasn't the whole picture.

Nor, it seemed, did all Seepers have human forms.

My pager beeped. I jumped and Jamie startled. "Sorry about that, little man."

I couldn't place Jamie back in the cot, not with the Seeper eyeing him greedily and advancing. I couldn't leave him alone, not to answer my pager.

Equally, my pager might be important. No, it was more than that: I had a feeling, some intuition, and *knew* it was.

I glanced back out at the rest of the Department. The

place was loud and busy, and, unlike other areas of the hospital, I wasn't sure everyone I saw was human. What staff I did see were far too preoccupied with the sick to help me.

So I kept hold of the child and carried him with me to the Nurse's Station and the nearest phone.

The pager showed one of the Children's Ward extensions.

"It's David Layton," I was informed by one of the Children's Ward staff over the phone. "He's taken a turn for the worse. Can you come now?"

I was fighting enemies on several fronts, without a clue what I was doing...

I looked down at Jamie cradled in my arms. "I'm caught up in ED right now," I said. "Can it wait?"

A protracted pause. "Well..."

"I'll be there as soon as I can," I promised. It was the best I could do under the circumstances. A bit like Jamie's mother.

I ignored my intuitions at my peril.

Looking round the Emergency Department again, there was really no one who was able to relieve me. I thought about taking Jamie to the ward with me, but you couldn't simply uplift an infant from what was supposed to be a place of safety, especially not to fit around your own work schedule. It violated so many hospital protocols. What if Jamie's mother returned and couldn't find her son? The ED staff were all so busy, I couldn't even reliably leave a message for her.

I returned to the cubicle. I rocked Jamie and soon he fell asleep.

The Seeper was still in the corner, not sleeping, but at least quiet, happy to bide its time until I was gone.

Ten minutes passed.

Fifteen minutes.

Finally, a Health Care Assistant popped her head into the cubicle and asked if I was okay.

I seized the opportunity. "I need you to look after this child," I said, nodding towards Jamie. "As much as you might want to put him back in the cot, you mustn't. And you must not leave him."

The Assistant frowned.

"The diagnosis here is quite tricky," I lied. "It's imperative that you hold this child and keep holding him, at least until I return, or the child's mother does. If you don't, I fear the child will regress quickly."

Her frown lightened, but didn't disappear entirely.

"I need to go to the Children's Ward," I continued. "But I'll be back as soon as I can to admit this boy."

The Assistant nodded.

When it came to first impressions, I'd learned to trust my gut. This woman appeared trustworthy enough. She was human, and she seemed motivated by kindness. So I left Jamie in her care and rushed back to the Children's Ward.

When I arrived at Room 18, David's room, it was empty. I was too late.

I found Jenny sitting in the Nurse's Station, typing notes into the computer, a mug of coffee next to the keyboard. "Where's David?" I asked.

She looked up. Her skin was flawless, even under the uncomplimentary lights. Her cheeks blossomed. "ICU."

"That bad?"

Oh, but I knew it would be...

She nodded. A pain expression crossed her forehead. "O'Brien sorted the transfer. David was... not good."

"Shit!"

Jenny smiled, seeming to read my thoughts. "O'Brien seemed pretty pissed."

David was in bad shape. His arms, his legs, his neck, his torso, pretty much everywhere, were swollen. He lay on the bed like some cast sheep, struggling to breathe. On closer inspection, David's skin had taken an almost translucent quality, and many of the veins in his forehead and his hands were visible; thin, blue lines swimming like eels in a transparent sea.

Memories resurfaced:

The door to Mum's room was slightly ajar. I lingered just outside, unsure. It was dark inside. She'd got the curtains drawn. I pushed the door—just a little. I leaned in. I strained to see my mother in the gloom...

I snapped out of my reverie.

David's eyes opened, his eyes seeming to focus on me, and, for a moment, I thought he might open his mouth and scream, his anguish filling all of the ICU. He raised his hand a little, but it proved too heavy, and he dropped it back to his side.

"David..." I said. "I'm sorry..."

Around his bed, there was the debris of the acutely unwell patient: strewn sterile packing, the caps off needles, spilt blood and saline, unused syringes.

Bruises tracked along David's pale, bloated arms, the site of several failed cannulation attempts. Finally, a central line had been thrust into the boy's right jugular, then hastily stitched, pulling the bloated flesh over itself. A small dribble of blood pooled beneath the Tegaderm dressing. O'Brien had stopped short of intubating the boy, which, given his respiratory effort, seemed like an oversight. I was hardly in a position to criticise, however. David was my patient, and I hadn't been there to advocate for him.

The Man in the White Coat suddenly stood at the foot of David's bed, although the curtains around the bed space remained undisturbed. He held up an Intraosseous Needle between the thumb and first finger of his right hand. It had been ripped from its sterile packaging. "*Look!*" he said to David. "Isn't this magnificent?"

David's eyes widened, then closed tightly. He tried to

articulate something, but no sound came from his mouth, except for fast breaths.

“The purity of these instruments!” the Man in the White Coat continued. “The precision! Sharp, such that they easily divide human skin. In the fullness of time, *you* will understand everything.”

The Seeper turned his attention to me. His face tightening, the skin stretching into a snarl. “And this one—this doctor—” He spat the word. The cord along his neck bulged. “He would save you, David. Can such a pathetic creature achieve anything of meaning? He is beyond pathetic.”

I realised I was holding my breath. Slowly and deliberately, I pushed my breath out. I’d forgotten that I wasn’t meant to stare. I forced myself to look away. I even made a show of checking the sats probe on David’s fingers and the electrocardiography leads on his chest. As soon as it seemed reasonable, I fled David’s bed space and the ICU.

On my way down to the Children’s Ward, I stopped in the toilets to vomit.

That evening I picked up ‘The Healing Art’ again, and while I now understood that the text was intended as a literal guidebook for Healers, most of its meaning was still hidden from me.

twelve

"These foul creatures have crawled from the Sablosphere and, for all I know, it is to the Sablosphere that they will be banished hereafter."

Tym-U-mah, The Alchemist, page 133, 'The Healing Art'

The following morning, I was sitting at my desk on the Children's Ward when Pastor Ari approached me. "May I have a word?"

Something in his tone alarmed me. "Sure."

"I'm not well," he said, his voice quivering. "Only I don't think it's anything traditional medicine can help with."

I leaned closer and lowered my voice. "What the problem?"

He, too, lowered his voice to a mere whisper. "I've got

motor neurone disease." For once, his hair wasn't perfectly gelled back. There was a smudge on one lens of his glasses. Even his shirt looked creased, as if this were the second consecutive day he had worn it.

"*What—?* Are you sure?" There was no cure for motor neurone disease. It was a death sentence, often slow and protracted. Traditional medicine could only offer symptom control, and even that was hit and miss.

"Yes," he said. "That's what the guy told me. I have medium to advanced symptoms already. I Googled it."

"*Whoa, whoa, whoa!*" I raised my hands. "You *Googled* it? What guy?"

The Chaplain kept his voice low and even. "There was this guy who came running through the chapel a few days ago."

"And he told you you had motor neurone disease? How the hell would he know?"

"He gave it to me," Pastor Ari said. "Said it was his 'parting gift'."

"And you believed him?" On one level, the gullibility of the Chaplain astonished me. On another, deeper level, however, I knew that everything he was telling me was correct. It *felt* right.

"Not at first. I looked it up. Motor Neurone isn't contagious. In fact, they're not really sure how someone comes to develop it."

"Precisely."

"But when the symptoms came..."

"They could be psychosomatic," I said, although there was no real conviction in my voice and I think Pastor Ari could tell. "Someone manipulative plants a thought at just the right moment. Perhaps you're feeling a little down or vulnerable."

"Grant, I *know* and I think you do, too."

"Without the evidence of EMG or nerve conduction studies... I don't think you should jump to any conclusions."

"If you saw this guy..." Pastor Ari appeared to diminish in stature, backing away into the corridor. Suddenly I missed the Chaplain's smile more than ever.

"What did he look like?"

"He was tall, angular and awkward. And the way he moved... if anyone could be the physical representation of Motor Neurone disease, it was him. I know that sounds dramatic, but the way he looked at me, that cruel little smile. He blew in my face and he touched my lips with his index finger, like he wanted me to keep some dirty little secret. I've never believed in demons before, thought they were metaphorical, but this guy..."

"None of that means—"

"I'm well aware of how this sounds, Grant. The last two nights I've gone to bed and been overwhelmed with worry. When I slept, it was short-lived, the weight of nightmares dragging me down further. I tried prayer, but God has been silent. I know none of this is rational, and I can't explain it, but I *know*. I know. I thought you might be open to this... *unusual* presentation and, if you find this Healer, maybe you could ask her to help me."

"I'll do that."

The Man in the White Coat sat on David's chest, its knees pressed into the mattress and its coat flowing down on either side of the boy like a surgical drape. In its mouth, it clenched a fluid-filled syringe, with a long needle extending from the end, its tip glistening in the overhead lights of the Intensive Care Unit. The smell of oil, or something similar, lingered, polluting the air throughout.

David struggled beneath the weight, but his struggles were entirely in vain.

I stood there, watching, not wanting to see, yet unable to turn my eyes away.

David's oedematous limbs stirred memories in me:

The door to Mum's room was slightly ajar. I lingered just outside, unsure. It was dark inside. She'd got the curtains drawn. I pushed the door—just a little. I leaned in. I strained to see my mother in the gloom...

David murmured, bringing me back to the present.

The Man in the White Coat was performing some kind of bizarre surgery. It had attached several tourniquets to David's limbs, making already bloated arms and legs much more exaggerated. The procedure involved piercing the needle into these engorged areas, drawing off what looked like lymphatic fluid, and then injecting it subcutaneously elsewhere, like David's face and genitals.

How much of this bizarre attack did David register? He'd spiked another temperature about an hour ago and hopefully delirium hid him from the worst of his pain and suffering. Yet in his sunken eyes I imagined I read terror.

The ICU staff had given a further dose of midazolam, at my behest. They did not remove the Man in White Coat's tourniquets; they did not appear to see them at all. Would the midazolam even enter David's wider blood stream?

I felt torn about the midazolam. David's heart rate still danced around 130 beats per minutes on the attached heart monitor. His resps were too fast, short and shallow, hardly surprising given the weight upon his chest. These were not the vital signs of a teenage boy entering a state of sedation, but the adrenaline-flooded nightmare of the chemically restrained. I remembered how he'd begged us not to sedate him that morning in ED. Yet I felt I had to do something. Maybe it was given more for my benefit and the staff of ICU?

The Man in the White Coat thrust the needle under David's skin, depressed the plunger on the syringe, injecting more lymphatic fluid, this time into David's left temple area.

David's skin bulged further.

He moaned with pain. He tried to lift his enormous arms,

but the Man in the White Coat had them firmly pinned down.

I couldn't watch any longer. I fled from ICU and stood in the corridor outside, hands on my knees, fighting a wave of nausea. I couldn't continue like this. I was no longer a capable physician. How was I meant to think critically when I was confronted with the horrors of the Seepers at every turn?

My pager emitted a series of shrill beeps. *Beep beep beep!*

I groaned inwardly. More bad news, no doubt. Another crisis. Another fire to extinguish. And more damning evidence of my incompetence, my powerlessness.

I stumbled along the corridor. I rounded the corner and found the nearest phone, next to the lifts. The page was from the Children's Ward. Toby Harrison had deteriorated.

I summoned the lift. Somewhere deep in the shaft, cables shuddered and churned. I waited. When the door opened, I was pleased to find the carriage empty: no people and no Seepers. If the Seeper with wide shoulders, bulbous eyes and a misshapen head had been inside, I might have simply run away screaming.

I stepped into the lift and pressed the button for the first floor. The lift descended. Another wave of nausea gripped me. Was it a sudden onset of vertigo? I closed my eyes. When I opened them, the lift had changed. The interior walls were all leaning inwards, lines and corners that ought to be straight and perpendicular had become warped. I pressed my hands against the wall to check if it was still real, still solid.

The surface was cool, but it was real enough.

Was I getting sick too? Had the Man in the White Coat somehow infected me with the same disease he'd given David and Toby?

Overhead, cables continued to grind and the distant motor droned. How could such a twisted carriage continue to move down the shaft? Surely some catastrophic mechanical failure was imminent?

When the lift eased to a stop on the first floor and the door pinged open, I wasted no time exiting.

I power-walked along the corridor towards the Children's Ward.

When I set eyes upon Toby, I was shocked. The resemblance to David was uncanny: the same fever-induced delirium and nonsensical speech (Toby was ranting about strange patterns throughout the ward and entities that lived inside the walls), the same bloated limbs and torso—

The door to Mum's room was slightly ajar. I lingered just outside, unsure. It was dark inside. She'd got the curtains drawn. I pushed the door—just a little. I leaned in. I strained to see my mother in the gloom...

—the same boils, the same rash and the same open sores along a distended abdomen. It was the same disease process, a disease somehow engineered by the Man in the White Coat. But the most shocking thing was that the creator itself, the Man in the White Coat, had beaten me to the Children's Ward. It stood next to Toby with its needle and syringe and its weird tourniquets. Still, it wore its human face: the aged doctor with an even smile and silver-grey hair.

"We need to transfer Toby to ICU," I told the staff, and I hurried to the Nurse's Station to make the necessary phone calls.

Later, when I returned to the ICU to visit David and Toby, I was relieved that the Man in the White Coat was no longer straddling David. He/it sat in a chair on the opposite side of the bed to Peter Layton, a perverse parody of the vigil the boy's father kept. David was finally settled, although there remained nothing I could do and very little hope I could offer the boy's father.

Across the unit, lying on the next bed and divided by a thin curtain, Toby Harrison was a different story. The Man in the White Coat tightened one of its tourniquets around his left arm, then slapped the arm vigorously to make the veins protrude. Toby wriggled in the bed, but couldn't escape.

I looked back at David's bed space. The Man in the White Coat was still sat there. And it was Toby's bed space too *at the same time*. There were two of them! White Coats *plural!* The oily smell had only intensified, and it made my stomach turn.

My God!

I tried not to stare, or to make it obvious that I could see them, but there were two, and they both had identical faces and wore identical clothes. This Seeper had a double or a twin or something.

Thick dread twisted tentacles around my gut.

I'd taken the Hippocratic Oath at the end of Med School, not because it was compulsory, but because I believed in its principles and obligations. Where were these principles and obligations now? I had lost my way. Suddenly I was powerless and, being powerless, my ethical principles didn't seem to count for much. I wanted to help David and Toby, but I didn't know how. I was frustrated, physically repulsed, and, for reasons I didn't quite understand, couldn't stop thinking about my mother's death.

I slipped out of the ICU before the White Coats, or Peter Layton, or any of the staff noticed me.

I was the worst doctor.

Audrey sought me out in the Children's Ward later that afternoon. "How's David?" she asked, a disembodied voice that came from behind me and echoed through the corridor. I turned. She was leaning against the wall, glancing up and down the corridor. "And how's that other boy? I see he's been moved somewhere."

I was sitting at my desk working on Discharge Summaries. "David and Toby are both in ICU," I said.

Audrey stepped from the shadows. "I can't get anywhere near Critical Care." She had a stooped posture and kept clasping her hands together. "Visiting numbers are limited and Peter's always there. And there's Security too. That fat Security Guard."

"There's another reason not to visit," I said.

Audrey stiffened. "Oh?"

"That Seeper, the one that's attacking David, turns out there's two of them."

"*What?*"

"*Two* Men in White Coats," I repeated. "One for David, one for Toby. They're like identical twins."

"I don't know what it means," Audrey said, "but don't make the mistake of attributing human relationships to these creatures. Some of them may look human, but that's not their true form."

"What is their true form?"

Audrey shrugged, then ignored my question entirely. "So, how's David?"

"Settled, for now. But I'm not sure for how long."

Audrey rubbed at her forehead. When she spoke, she clenched her jaw and her voice sounded muffled and tense. "It's happening," she said. "I can feel it. Things are... shifting. The things foretold in 'The Healing Art' are being fulfilled. You believe me, don't you?"

I nodded. "I've seen stuff, yeah."

"Such as...?"

I was amused that Audrey expected me to answer all her questions, yet dismissed mine. "Well, yesterday one of my patients, a girl named Serena, claimed to be healed of Megaloblastic Anaemia. I'm assuming this wasn't your handiwork?"

Audrey shook her head.

"She claims a doctor visited her in a dream and dispelled the sickness. When she woke up, it was a reality."

Audrey inhaled a little too rapidly.

"It didn't feel quite right to me either, but all healings are essentially good, aren't they?"

"No, not always."

"How can someone being healed not be good? Are you suggesting that the healings *you* do are good but, if someone else does them, they're *not?*"

"It's about intention."

I didn't really understand.

"You're a Healer, I'm a Healer," she said, "and I know of one more, but she's immature in her gifting and wouldn't be able to pull off something of this level. If there was anyone else, I would have picked up the fingerprints by now." Audrey slid down the wall, her knees bending nimbly. "I've heard rumours of other healings in the hospital and the community, but I suspect it's Seeper power play."

"Power play? Do you mean there's some kind of political hierarchy among Seepers?"

Audrey shrugged. "Possibly. My goal is to kill them, not stand around asking questions."

I wanted to explain that taking the time to understand an enemy could lead to a more effective way of killing them. This, after all, was the entire point of my medical training, even if I hadn't realised it at the time. I held the words back. Audrey often spoke abruptly, or spoke with no censorship, as though she was un-practiced in social interactions. I wasn't offended. She was worried about her son. "The Hospital Chaplain approached me this morning," I said, remembering my encounter and also my promise. "He claimed that a man blew in his face and touched his lips and gave him Motor Neurone Disease. This man (who I assume was a Seeper) said it was a 'parting gift'. Is that even possible?"

"*Shit!*"

I gasped. "Seepers have *that* sort of power?"

"I think the rats are abandoning the ship," Audrey said, moving towards the exit. "I need to find out why."

"Please tell me you're going to hang around," I blurted, before she could escape. "That I'll have some way to contact you, you know, if things turn bad."

"I'll seek you out," she said with a weak smile, pausing in the doorway for a moment. "If I seem elusive, I'm sorry, I'm not much of a team player and Security are proving... difficult."

thirteen

"The true war is Occult: It lies between Heaven and Earth. Our enemy afflicts the body and the mind, yet hides in plain sight. Do not be deceived and do not be fearful. For a warrior shall rise in every age; one who will sweep back the tide of decay, touching the hearts of men and restoring their bodies and minds."

Jinn the Healer, page 200, 'The Healing Art'

On Thursday morning, I got to the Paediatric Conference Room early. I'd done my prep for the Paediatric Meeting and felt ready for anything O'Brien might throw at me. Seepers or not, I wanted to prove I had what it took to be a good doctor.

A couple of physios stood outside in the corridor while the room itself was in darkness.

A bad feeling crept into my gut. "What's up?"

"Lighting issue," said one.

I entered the Conference Room and felt for the light switch on the left-hand wall. I flicked the switch. Nothing. I flicked it the other way. One of the ceiling fluoros flickered to life, illuminating the boardroom table and the bare walls, but then the light stuttered and failed and darkness reclaimed the space.

"Odd," I said. "Has anyone done a BEIMS form?"

"Yes."

More staff were arriving for the meeting.

I stared back into the darkness, flipping the light switch back and forth several times. Once a few of the fluoros ignited, but this was short-lived. The best I could manage was all four strips flickering and giving off a sickly half-light. This only lasted for ten or fifteen seconds, then there was complete darkness. And in that darkness, I imagined movement that wasn't there: the walls bending and warping, amorphous shapes descending from the ceiling, the floor buckling and rising to greet this new reality.

"Is the meeting going to be postponed again?" someone asked.

"There's a sparky on the way," said another.

I turned back just in time to see O'Brien puffing along the corridor. His face was red, his brow covered in a light sweat. He considered the entire group, offering the briefest smile, but then those reptilian eyes fixed on me. "What's going on here, Newman?"

"Faulty lights," I said. "Apparently, there's someone on the way to fix them."

O'Brien sighed. "I don't have time for this."

"Maybe we could find another room?"

O'Brien's left shoe drummed on the floor. "Everywhere will be booked... No, I'm sorry, we've got no choice but to can the meeting."

There were murmurs and grumbles from the multidisciplinary team. Heads nodded. One of the O.T.'s rolled her eyes. No one voiced any alternatives.

"What about the Colquhoun Theatre?" I suggested.

"You needn't pretend to be disappointed," O'Brien said. "We both know your heart's not in medicine anymore."

I retreated from the Children's Ward, O'Brien's comments still stinging. I hated myself for being so dependent on his validation. What did it matter what the Old Dinosaur thought of me?

I had some extra time on my hands. I wondered what I might do with it, besides grab a coffee, but when I bumped into Audrey in the stairwell, I knew immediately. I led her down to the Ground Floor.

"Where are we going?" she enquired.

"I've got a problem I'm hoping you can take care of," I said. "I gave someone my word."

She followed, although it seemed with some reluctance.

The Chapel was quiet and still. The air felt clean, filtered from imperfections, the stained glass adding a splash of warmth and colour to the room. A thick curtain, the carpet and the wooden beams across the ceiling all soaked up sound, banishing the rest of the hospital with its stress, its troubles and its busyness. The pews stretched out before us in a gentle arc, divided in two by a walkway through the middle.

Pastor Ari was sitting in one pew off to the far side. I didn't see him at first, not until he rose to his feet. He approached, staggering along the aisle. I hardly recognised him. He had removed his glasses. Tears streaked his cheeks in long tracks. His sunny disposition was gone, consumed by darkness, by thunderstorms and night time. A terrible knowledge danced in his eyes, and more than tears threatened to rise from their depths.

"Ari," I said. "This is Audrey. She's the Healer. You asked..."

Ari shook his head and approached Audrey. "Yes," he said. "You have no idea what this means to me."

Audrey's arms tensed at her side. "Grant said something about someone leaving you a 'parting gift'."

"That's right," said Pastor Dixon. "That's what the man

told me, only I don't think he was a man. I think he was some sort of demon."

"Do you *believe* I can heal you?"

A hush fell over the chapel. An awkwardness. At the front of the room, slightly off-centre, a plain wooden cross was fixed to a wall of white panels.

"I believe it's worth a try," Pastor Dixon replied finally, and then, turning to me, added, "There's not a lot of other options from what I understand."

"You didn't answer my question, though," Audrey said. Her confrontational tone shocked me. She glared at the Chaplain, lips pressed flat. "I've healed three people," she said. "Is that enough for you?"

Pastor Ari shrugged. "That's three more than me."

"What if that were trickery?" Audrey pushed. Had I have known she was going to take this approach, I never would have brought her here. "What if I'm some fraud? I mean, I'm not a pastor, or a minister, or anything. How do you know I'm qualified?"

The Chaplain looked from me back to Audrey. "Are you a fraud?"

"You tell me."

"Now I'm not sure what to believe..."

Audrey turned to me, her wrinkles prominent, her eyes filled with sadness. "I can't help this man. He doubts me. I'm his stumbling block, that and his religious beliefs. I try to read him, but he's a closed book. His religion has closed his mind and blocked the passage. I've got nothing against Chaplains, or religion per se, but,"—Audrey looked directly at Pastor Ari—"your calling was never to this. You do a disservice to those who *are* called to be chaplains."

Was Audrey being deliberately offensive or did she possess incredible insight into the depths of the Chaplain's inner being? "Isn't it worth a try?"

"No point," she said. "Without openness, without some sense of belief, I have nothing to offer." She turned back to the Chaplain. "Even Jesus—arguably the greatest of all Healers—couldn't perform miracles when he came to unbelieving towns and villages."

"Are *you* comparing yourself to the Saviour?" the Chaplain asked, and suddenly there was a tone in his voice, an edge, an aggression I'd never heard in him before and which I didn't much care for. His brow furrowed. "I've heard everything now! Unbelievable! You're actually putting yourself *on the same level* as Jesus!" I'd never heard Pastor Dixon even raise his voice. The anger transformed his entire face, just as his smile usually did, only it distorted it, robbing him of much of his good looks.

"Come on, Grant," said Audrey. "This is a waste of our time."

She turned and left.

I wasn't sure what had just happened here, except that it felt awkward and wrong. I looked at the Chaplain, shrugged and followed Audrey.

Later that afternoon, while I was sitting in the ICU overseeing David and Toby's treatment, I got a bad feeling. It wasn't merely the presence of the White Coats, which, of course, no one else could see, or their continued attacks on my two patients, but something else. I remembered my morgue nightmare: *something terrible was coming.* I felt it in my gut, a weight that sat there like undigested food. When I inhaled, my breath was too sharp. All my nerves were jangling. Every time I looked down at my hands, whether holding a pen or a stethoscope, I noticed they were trembling.

The Intensive Care Unit was suddenly suffocating, the walls too imposing, and the entire space horribly claustrophobic. I had to leave... and not just because the White Coats had free rein with David and Toby, not just because I was feeling powerless and clueless.

Because of this feeling.

I bolted for the exit. The air in the corridor outside immediately felt cleaner and cooler. The oily smell was instantly removed.

I didn't know where I was going; I followed my nose and my instincts.

I came to the lifts... and I kept walking. I wasn't keen to ride another lift, not after what had happened yesterday.

I took the adjacent stairs. I pounded down the concrete

steps, holding the wooden balustrade, not trusting my footing.

Audrey was climbing the stairs, the sound of her rushing feet masked by my own. We met around the third floor. "Good," she said, upon spying me. "I was looking for you."

That didn't sound good. Audrey didn't seek people out to exchange pleasantries. "What's wrong?"

"I've just spent the last half an hour in the Emergency Department," she said. "The girl you told me about with the Haematological Condition, the one who got healed in a dream, well, she's back and she's got the same disease as David and that other boy. The Man in the White Coat—well, *one* of them—is with her right now."

"What?" I said. "That's impossible."

"I've just seen him," Audrey said. "*It*, I mean *it*. I couldn't get too close, but I'd recognise that Seeper anywhere."

"But they're *both* in ICU. I've literally just come from there."

Audrey folded her arms over her stomach. She spoke in a quiet voice, "I need to figure out their agenda. If this is the Scourge—"

But I already knew their agenda, or some part of it, and it did little to help the bad feeling I had. "Isn't it obvious?"

"What?"

"This creature is replicating itself like a virus does. Whatever it's giving these children, it's contagious. It's starting an epidemic."

"There's *three* of them?"

I nodded. "There's going to be a lot more if we don't stop them."

Audrey sighed. Her body seemed to deflate. "That's impossible. Even fighting one, I... it was incredibly strong."

"They'll only get stronger. We can't afford to waste time."

"And what are you suggesting we do?"

"For starters, we need to be wearing PPE. We need to stop the spread—"

"This is not your typical infection."

"I realise that—"

A series of beeps came from my hip. I tilted my pager so I could see the screen and who'd paged me. Sure enough, it was the Emergency Department.

fourteen

"Science without experience does not bring much confidence."

Ambroise Paré, page 202, 'The Healing Art'

"Dr O'Brien, I wanted to talk to you about David Layton, Toby Harrison and Serena Hopkins." This was on Friday morning. I'd walked over to O'Brien's Office in the Clinical Services Building. The CSB building was much quieter compared to the ward block, its gloomy and inefficient corridors, hodgepodge doors and whispering walls.

I leaned against the door frame. O'Brien's office space was so cramped there was literally nowhere else to stand.

"Yes."

"I think the disease is viral."

O'Brien nodded. "Reasonable." He leaned back in his

office chair, resting his hands behind his head. His eyes studied me. His desk was littered with medical documents, his computer keyboard half buried beneath them.

"And I'm worried about how it's spreading."

"You've initiated full PPE precautions," he said. "That's a sensible measure, at least until we know what we're dealing with."

O'Brien was sparing with his praise, but now wasn't the time to soak up this compliment. "Yes," I agreed. A wiser man might have left it there, but not me. "I think it might be more infectious than we think."

His demeanour changed. His blood broiled and his face reddened. "Based on *what?*" he asked, an irritation lacing his voice. He sat up in his chair, which squeaked under his weight. He pushed his glasses back along the bridge of his nose. "Three cases in how many days? That's hardly cause for alarm."

O'Brien's office was musty and in need of some fresh air. Dust motes swirled in the sunlight that angled through the window.

"What if it has a more ambitious agenda?"

"We're talking about a virus, right? Your personification of this pathogen isn't helping your argument. How could you possibly know that? A feeling? Something in your water? This isn't more of your touchy-feely healer bullshit, is it?"

I ignored the slight. "I think we need to consider the possibility this virus could become an epidemic."

O'Brien grimaced, as if he'd tasted something unpleasant. I thought he might let rip at me, but he restrained himself. "Nonsense."

"We still don't know exactly what it is. What if it spreads and we can't stop it?"

"Don't be dramatic," O'Brien said. He shifted forward in his chair and began re-positioning papers on his desk. "There are better minds than yours and mine working on the problem. We need to keep our focus on the patients under our care." His message was clear: End of discussion, meeting over.

"Of course."

I found 'Virology' later that afternoon. The door was a pale cream colour with no windows. It was an unassuming door in a quiet corridor on the third floor of the Clinical Services Building surrounded by other, equally unassuming doors: 'Microbiology', 'Haematology', 'Serology' and 'ICT'.

I knocked and entered.

Inside, sat on a swivel chair, was a bearded man in a white lab coat. "Hello," he said in a booming voice, turning in my direction. He had messy hair. His shirt buttons didn't align. His workspace, unlike O'Brien's, was incredibly sparse. The office had large windows and was filled with sunlight. On the back bench, there were centrifuges and other machines, which I knew little about. In the corner, a glass cabinet which was full of many virology tubes.

“Hello,” I said. “I’m Grant. I’m the Paediatric Reg.”

“Hello, Grant. I’m Dr Brienbeer. Thomas. I’m one of the Microbiologists.” Brienbeer smiled at me. It was a warm smile. “How can I help you?”

“I’ve got three patients who’ve presented with viral symptoms and, based on the collection of symptoms, I believe it’s the same virus.”

Brienbeer’s eyes glistened. He nodded. “A scientist with a hypothesis. I like that.”

O’Brien had responded positively at first, before quickly dismissing me and my theories. I felt more hopeful about Brienbeer. “Now, in each case, we’ve sent Virology swabs, and I think we’re dealing with a new virus.”

Brienbeer jumped up from his chair, suddenly animated. “A new virus? Really?”

“I’ve seen nothing like it,” I said. “The symptoms: Fever, delirium, massive oedema. The thing is, I don’t know if anyone in the lab is connecting these three cases. You’ll have done PCR, Immunology, the usual, but has anyone looked at this virus under the microscope?”

“Do you have their NHIs?”

I brought a folded piece of paper from my breast pocket, unfolded it, and read. “Alpha, Bravo, Alpha, 5683... Lima, Mike, Zulu, 1212... and Yankee, Oscar, Echo, 9990...”

Brienbeer scribbled down the hospital numbers on a

small notepad. "I'll review the samples under the microscope myself," he said. "If I see anything of concern, I'll let you know. You're using appropriate infection control measures, I assume?"

"Absolutely. But we've only just introduced them."

Brienbeer smiled again. "Very good."

I thanked him and I left, feeling somewhat reassured. That had been easy and was in stark contrast to O'Brien's reaction. Brienbeer had treated me with respect and professional courtesy, highlighting just how lacking this was in my consultant.

fifteen

"Not all men can see as I, nor would I wish it upon them. I see the underneath. I see the cause. How then shall I respond?"

Mond XI, page 99, 'The Healing Art'

Generally, I don't mind working weekends. They're usually quieter and the Old Dinosaur isn't around to question my clinical judgments. The pace was usually slower, which was always welcome. I even imagined that I might find time to counter the White Coats, to work out how to fight them or at least arrest the spread of their mysterious disease. Approaching the hospital, I tried to ignore the heaviness I felt in my gut.

"Did you hear about Jenny?" Sandy asked the moment I

walked onto the Children's Ward. She was leaning against the Nurse's Station, a peculiar look upon her face.

A bad feeling rose in my gut.

"Admitted last night," Sandy said, her eyes heavy and downcast. And yet those eyes twinkled. In her urge to tell her story, she'd forgotten that Jenny was a friend and colleague. Sandy had the juiciest scoop and was determined to milk it for all it was worth.

"Admitted with *what?*"

Deep down, I knew the answer before it came.

"That infection," Sandy said, "The same one infecting the children—David, Toby, Serena. We should've been wearing protective gear much earlier, I reckon."

If this was a dig at me, I ignored it. "Which ward is she on?" An urgency gripped me, and I no longer cared for Sandy and her gossip.

"8 Med. In an isolation room."

I took the stairs up to the 8th floor. I went immediately to the Reception Desk and spoke to one of the Administrative staff. "Hi, I'm Grant Newman. Can you tell me about Jenny Epps, please? She's a close friend of mine." My heart and my respiratory rates were both too fast and a sour taste, like off-ripe grapefruits, rose into my mouth.

"I'm afraid I can't give you any details," she said. "Patient privacy."

"But I'm *staff*," I said, a little too loud. "I work with Jenny."

"Then I'm sure you're aware of the hospital policy."

I was overheating, and it was more than the climbing of stairs. I had to concentrate to keep my voice low and steady. "Can you at least tell me she's going to be okay...?" It was a stupid thing to ask anyone. This was the sort of question I was used to fending off from worried parents.

The Receptionist smiled, a wide and condescending smile. "Jenny's in Room 3." She gestured in the general direction. "Jenny's in isolation. You're welcome to see her, but you can't enter the room, for reasons I'm sure you can appreciate, Grant Newman. Beyond that, I understand her mother will come in this afternoon. She might be willing to talk to you about Jenny's condition, since you're a friend."

"Thank you."

I hurried around to Room 3. There was extra signage all around the door: FULL ISOLATION PRECAUTIONS, DROPLET AND CONTACT PRECAUTIONS and DO NOT ENTER: SPEAK TO NURSING STAFF. I peered in through the glass window. The room was perfunctory: its walls cold, its floor sparse, its sole window had a film of dust. Jenny lay on the bed and, even from this distance, she looked noticeably paler and worn out. She swam in an over-sized hospital gown. Her hair looked depleted, as though all its nutrients had been diverted into Jenny's core to sustain her. It lay wet and bedraggled down her face. Meanwhile, her face was puffy and her arms were swollen, the latter reminding me of my mother's lymphoedema.

I gasped. A chill ran through me. This was very bad. I was

so used to seeing Jenny in her nurse's uniform, healthy and vivacious, her warm smile and her quiet professionalism.

Jenny spotted me and managed to lift her arm and wave.

I waved back.

Jenny's swollen fingers crawled over her bedside table, a motion which looked extremely painful and difficult, and tried to grip her mobile phone. Finally, having snagged it, she looked over at me.

I was so transfixed by the dramatic change in Jenny's appearance; it took me a moment to realise her meaning: She wanted me to call her.

I took my iPhone from my pocket, found her number and rang it.

Jenny's voice was hoarse when she eventually answered. "Hello, Grant."

"Hi. How're you doing? Sorry, dumb question."

"I've been better," she said, a faint smile fluttering across her puffy cheeks. "This thing's really knocked the stuffing out of me."

"I'm sorry." If I hadn't been so distracted by the Men in White Coats, maybe I would have seen this virus was contagious sooner. "Is there anything you need? Anything I can do?"

She shook her head. "Having a visitor is nice. A friendly face." She smiled. "I feel a bit like a leper in here."

"You're *not* a leper."

"Am I going to get like Toby and David?" she asked, her

voice trembling and cracking. "Like Serena? Am I going to die?"

My legs went weak beneath me, and it took a great deal of effort to simply stay upright. "Of course you're *not going to die!*" I protested, but I had over-promised and I knew it. I could not guarantee that Jenny would survive this any more than I had been able to guarantee my mother would survive her cancer. The lie had come so easily. Had I learnt nothing?

Jenny, at least, seemed comforted by my words, by my protest.

That's when the Man in the White Coat—*one* of them, at least—rose from behind Jenny's bed and smiled at me. It had the same silver-grey hair and too-perfect smile. It looked directly at me, as if it knew that I could see it. Fear and dread coiled around my gut and squeezed tight.

"Well," I said, struggling to keep any sense of composure. "I better go. They might notice my absence in the Children's Ward. Don't want to give Tooms any more reason to dislike me."

Jenny smiled. A small smile, but a smile nonetheless. "Will you visit again tomorrow?"

"Every day, until you're better."

"That sounds good."

Jenny waved at me. Merely lifting her arm obviously pained her. The Man in the White Coat also waved with its long fingers.

I turned and left the ward as quickly as I could.

"We need to do something about these Men in White Coats!" I said to Audrey later that morning. She stood beside my desk on the Children's Ward, glancing up and down the back corridor. She hadn't come to the ward in a while, and perhaps only visited now because David and Toby, and therefore the White Coats, were in the ICU. "Aren't we meant to be healers?"

"Yes, but no," she said. "You're not ready. I—"

"So we're just going to let them multiply? If we can't stop them, surely we can slow them down?"

"I won't be responsible for your death... or worse. I've already engaged one of these creatures last week and it threw me out of the cubicle like I was some petty annoyance. I'm not keen to repeat the mistake, at least not until you're up to speed."

"Alright, so *get* me up to speed."

"That's why I came," she said. "I want you to bring one of your patients to me so I can heal them. See one, do one, teach one: that's the best way to learn. That Chaplain doesn't count."

"Which patient?"

"Pick one. Someone who's going to be open to the possibility of healing. Perhaps a child with a long-term condition. One with parents who aren't likely to ask too many questions or complain."

"Presumably not David, Toby, Serena or Jenny?"

Audrey glanced along the corridor. "Jenny?"

"Never mind."

I decided on Charlie O'Loughlin. She was a thirteen-year-old girl with juvenile arthritis. She'd been in the Children's Ward for nearly two months. Despite the obvious pain each time she moved, I'd never once heard her complain. Her mother would visit when she could, but not too frequently. I understood Charlie had younger siblings who needed looking after too.

Charlie was sitting on her bed in Room 3. She had long, mousy brown hair and was yet to lose the pre-pubescent fat in her face. I kept my voice low. "How are you, Charlie?" I asked, approaching her bed.

"Yeah, alright."

"I have something to ask you," I said. "It's a bit of a strange request, and I won't be in the least bit offended if you say no."

This piqued her interest. She leaned closer to me, sensing that this was going to be a secretive conversation. A flicker of concern crossed her eyes. The slightest frown creased her brow. Was I about to say something inappropriate? "What is it?"

Was this appropriate? Was I playing favourites? Picking one person as more worthy to receive than another? Healing, though. That was something entirely different... "I want you to meet a woman," I said. "A friend of mine."

"Who is she?" Charlie asked, and again her brow darkened.

The room suddenly seemed smaller, its walls thinner, the privacy of our conversation no longer assured. "She's a Healer, and she wants to rid you of your arthritis forever."

"*If only!*" Charlie said, with a little laugh. The laugh soon dried up in her throat. She looked at me again, this time without a trace of humour. "You're not joking, are you?"

"No."

"She can really do this?"

"Yes," I said. "I've seen others she's healed."

Charlie took a moment to think, then replied simply, "Okay."

I helped Charlie into a wheelchair and pushed her to the Whānau Room. It had large windows, a grey carpeted floor and a handful of easy chairs. Audrey was waiting there for us. The Whānau Room would be our impromptu clinic room.

"This is Charlie," I told Audrey as I parked the wheelchair. "She has—"

"No," said Audrey. "I don't need you to tell me her diagnosis. You're still so caught up in your medical way of thinking, rather than using your senses, using your *eyes*."

I shrugged at Charlie: that was me put in my place.

Charlie giggled nervously. In her eyes, however, I noticed a rising alarm.

"It's alright, Charlie," Audrey said. "I'm here to help you."

Audrey crouched before the girl. "If you're willing, I want you to take my hands?"

Charlie offered both her hands. "Sure."

Audrey took her hands in her own. She closed her eyes as if she were receiving some sort of divine communication. She frowned. Then her eyes opened again. "It's in all your joints," she said at last. "Horrible! How long has it been there?"

"Since I was nine."

"Too long," Audrey said, then sighed. "Are you feeling brave, Charlie? Shall we begin?"

Charlie glanced sideways at me, then back at Audrey. "Yes... okay."

Audrey's entire demeanour changed then. She was no longer addressing the thirteen-year-old girl, but rather her eyes burned *through* Charlie, *inside* Charlie. The sudden animosity hardened the lines across her face. "You know who I am, don't you?"

Charlie flinched and tried pulling back her hands.

Audrey held on tight, her knuckles white. "Think you can torment her? Think I don't know exactly what you're doing?" Audrey inhaled, pitched forward, and yelled, "*Release her and face me!*"

Charlie's body convulsed.

My God, what had I done? This was worse than Pastor Dixon. This had been a mistake...

"You have to push," Audrey said, seeming to address me, her eyes flicking in my direction. I did not know what she was talking about, but it snapped me from my absence of mind. "It comes from the heart and not the head."

"Huh?"

"As per 'The Healing Art'."

Charlie jerked and danced, and then these movements suddenly ceased. A slender, gaunt-looking child climbed out of her. No, not really a child at all. This was Charlie's arthritis. A Seeper. Such a pale, pathetically skinny thing: its bones brittle, its movement erratic. Its mouth dropped open, like it was gulping in mouthfuls of air, readjusting to the atmosphere after years of dwelling *inside* this girl. It lunged forward and almost collapsed under its own weight.

The creature stood in the middle of the Whānau Room, its eyes scanning the ceiling and the walls, then looking out of the large windows with longing.

Audrey held this strange creature.

"You're nothing," it hissed. "Al Nihil will crush you. Al Nihil will crush us all."

"No," Audrey said. "*I'm* the one who will crush *you*."

The creature tried to pull from Audrey's grip. A wretched, albino child, only with weird flesh, almost ethereal, like a shadow within a shadow.

Audrey closed her eyes, concentrated.

The Seeper struggled against Audrey's grip, but with no success. Its skin becoming more translucent. Its face changed, anger and aggression giving way to fear. There was something pitiful in its struggle, for it was clearly outmatched by Audrey now it was exposed. I ought not to have felt any pity, given the suffering it had inflicted on Charlie all these years, and yet the final image, its last facial expression, was a good facsimile of terror. Eyes wide. Shaking. Rasping breaths. Then the creature faded from existence. Gone.

"You killed it?" I asked Audrey. It was a question and yet it came out more like an accusation.

Audrey opened her eyes, gave me a strange, disapproving look, but said nothing.

Charlie was on her feet and crying. I hadn't even noticed her rise from her wheelchair.

I rushed to her side, thinking that she might fall. "Are you alright, Charlie?"

Charlie was flexing her arms in front of her, moving them back and forth freely with no pain. "I'm so happy," she said. "I'm... I'm..."

Audrey approached Charlie, too. "You're free," she said, a smile cracking across her face. Audrey side-glanced at me.

"Thank you," said Charlie, and fresh tears ran down her cheeks. "Thank you, *thank you.*" She looked at me. "*Both* of you."

I suddenly felt very emotional and fought back tears of my own.

"Your suffering wasn't right," Audrey said. "It wasn't fair. This disease was an intruder, an affront." She turned to me again, this time her voice softening. "The healing comes from the heart, *through* empathy, which is through sight and touch."

I didn't know what she meant, but I nodded. Apparently, this was an instruction for my benefit.

Audrey took Charlie's hand. "One last thing."

"What's that?" Charlie asked.

"You mustn't tell anyone about this. Don't mention Grant, or me, or this meeting. If we are to continue our work, we must work in secret."

"But *how* do I explain this?" Charlie said, joyously flexing her arms again and then lifting each leg in turn. "What'll I say to mum?"

"Anything you like," Audrey said. "Make something up. Say it was the remarkable care you received on the Children's Ward. Say it was luck, or God, or the right combination of medicine. Say anything you like, just don't mention us."

Charlie nodded. "Okay."

The healing of Charlie O'Loughlin gave me a much-needed lift. Not only had I witnessed Audrey at work, but she seemed open to the idea of training me in her Healing Art. The only thing that bothered me was Audrey killing the Seeper. I'm not saying it didn't deserve to die, but the scientist in me at least wanted to understand why such a creature existed in the first place.

As a Paediatric Registrar, I was well placed. While the fundamentals of medicine seemed to have little effect on this virus, or the White Coats, it was useful to have ready access to all the relevant clinical areas. I could observe those who were sick and, if one of them deteriorated, I could sound the alarm. In effect, I was the watchman.

Of course, this didn't mean I wasn't impatient. If I was a Healer, why wasn't I healing?

I visited the ICU to check on David and Toby. Both had spiked temperatures during the night but were currently afebrile. David still had a good deal of swelling around his body and Toby, while less swollen, had a nasty rash. Both were sleeping.

Two White Coats sat in the ICU but, for the time being at least, they had stopped toying with my patients.

I was pleased that all the staff were dressed in PPE gear, as per my instructions.

After ICU I went to the Children's Ward. I checked on Serena. They had placed her in one of the negative-pressure rooms. She had the fever, the swollen limbs and torso, and was clearly feeling very sorry for herself. The Megaloblastic Anaemia hadn't made her look this unwell, and I could only guess how bad she was feeling. She didn't appear to notice me standing at the window.

The Man in the White Coat sat in the chair beside her bed, eyes closed, seemingly in some sort of meditation. The room reeked of oil... or something that had been allowed to fester for millions of years beneath the earth. At least the creature was keeping its hands off Serena—for now. I wondered if I ought to transfer her to ICU as a precaution. If she followed the same pattern as David and Toby, this would only be a matter of time.

My pager beeped. It was Dr Brienbeer. "Have you linked the three cases I told you about?" I asked over the phone. I resisted the urge to tell him about Jenny, a fourth case.

"Come and see."

When I entered the lab Brienbeer was stooped over an electron microscope. It comprised of a large white cylinder, a pair of eyepieces at the base and a networked computer. Brienbeer rose, turned and smiled at me. "Grant, come over here. I want to show you what this virus looks like."

I weaved my way between benches and stood next to Brienbeer. He gestured for me to look through the eyepieces. I leaned over and pressed my eyes into the cups.

"Turn this handle to adjust the focus, if you need to."

Actually, the image I saw was already in perfect focus. What I saw looked far too complex to be a single organism. This was the offending virus. It looked a little like an armoured tadpole. It had a thick tail with a barbed end. Any comparison to a tadpole ended when you considered the other end: This virus appeared to have a mouth, and in its mouth what looked to be rows and rows of teeth. The teeth were barbed. Although the whole organism was far too small to be seen by anything other than an electron microscope, it was chilling nonetheless. "*Shit!*" Of course, it was more than a virus, more than a microbiological threat, it had a metaphysical dimension which I couldn't understand. "*Shit! Shit!*"

"I'm calling it Lymphachela," Brienbeer said. "I've always wanted to name a virus and this one's like nothing I've seen or studied."

"Just remember who told you about it," I quipped. "Personally, I think Newman's Virus has a nice ring to it."

Brienbeer seemed unsure how to take my humour. He chose to avoid the issue entirely, and instead explained how he'd come about the name—a mixture of 'lymph' because it appeared to primarily attach itself to the lymphatic system and '-chela' from the Latin for "crab-like" or "claw". The name seemed fitting enough.

"All three cases you told me about have this same virus," Brienbeer said. "Our system had already flagged one case, but you've bought us time by connecting the dots. Thank you."

"There's a fourth case," I said. "She's a nurse on the Children's Ward. A friend of mine."

"I'm sorry."

"What is the potential for this virus to keep spreading?"

Brienbeer nodded. "It's not contained, clearly. It's too early to predict its growth trajectory. I think it's vital we get a handle on it or we could well be dealing with a new epidemic."

I couldn't help but hear a certain excitement in Brienbeer's voice, despite the seriousness of the threat. As a microbiologist a new virus like this was a career highlight. "What do we do?"

"Everyone with the virus is isolated, right?"

"Right."

"Good. Hopefully that's enough to stop it in its tracks."

I thought about the White Coats, about the perverse pleasure they took in torturing their victims and how they seemed to move around the hospital at will, and I doubted these measures would suffice. "And if it's not enough?"

"We pass it up the chain of command: The CEO, the Medical Officer of Health, even the Ministry. They'll all need to know about the Lymphachela Virus."

"Let's hope it doesn't come to that," I said.

"Agreed."

That night, I decided not to read 'The Healing Art'. It would not aid my sleep. Despite this, one line kept repeating through my mind, a line I hadn't been able to shake:

"... the Student will surpass the Mentor, for he is born not of fury, but of compassion."

Who was I to question Audrey? How many people had I healed exactly? What wealth of experience did I have? Still I wondered, Was there a better way to heal? Was Audrey's aggression a strength or a weakness? And what did this particular passage mean?

sixteen

"Complacency affects the eyes, mostly. Oh, that I might return to my ignorance!"

Worsel Olrichen, page 89, 'The Healing Art'

Lilly Anderson had been a problem since her admission last week. All the tests I'd ordered had come back inconclusive. I couldn't explain why she had an eighteen-month history of diarrhoea and vomiting and I'd had little success treating it. While some days were better than others, most days she vomited at least once or twice. Her bowels were extremely erratic too, something that might be seen in Crohn's disease or Colitis, but Lilly's colonoscopy had come back as surprisingly normal. A healthy gut.

Lilly was a very private girl. If I didn't ask her specific

questions about her symptoms, I doubt she'd even report them.

I looked for a Seeper who might be the culprit, but saw none.

On Sunday, Lilly had several bouts of vomiting. I'd given her fluids and antiemetics to settle the symptoms, but all I'd done was take the edge off them a little. I was stuck. Lilly was steadily losing weight, something she could seldom afford to do. She didn't have much weight to begin with.

So I thought of Lilly when Audrey approached me about someone else to heal. Today, of course, it was going to be *my* turn.

"How are you feeling now?" I asked Lilly, returning to her room.

"Not too bad."

The way she refused to look me in the eye: she wasn't telling me everything. "Are you telling me the truth?"

Lilly paused. "Mostly."

I smiled. "I want to help you, Lilly. I can't do that if you're not being entirely truthful with me."

"No one can help me."

There was a depth to Lilly that I couldn't fathom. Secrets, mysteries, something. More than mere self-deprecation, she suffered from a chronic lack of confidence, too. "Lilly, I wonder if you'd be keen to try a different approach to treating you?"

"Sure, why not?"

"I want you to meet a friend of mine. She's a Healer. As you know—"

Lilly's eyes bulged. "Are you *allowed* to recommend healers?"

"No, not really," I said. "But she's proved very perceptive, better than our blood tests and scans, and I only offer the invitation to you because you looked so wretched this morning. If you're not interested—"

"I didn't say I wasn't interested," she said. "And I'm not trying to make trouble for you."

"That's a relief," I lied. The fact she understood that suggesting such an option was outside of my scope of practice and could land me in serious trouble made me feel extremely vulnerable.

"It's just my dad gets very touchy about different doctors. I've had a few negative experiences over the months..."

She did not elaborate further, and yet all sorts of alarm bells began ringing in my head. I hadn't considered Lilly's father and whether he was likely to visit today. I wished I could retract the offer and pick someone else. "Well, I don't want you to get into trouble with your father."

"That's alright," Lilly said. "My father isn't due in for another hour. When can I meet your Healer?"

I paused, still unsure. There really was no turning back. "How does now sound?"

"Perfect."

I took Lilly to meet Audrey in an office along the back

corridor of the Children's Ward. Lilly walked gingerly, clutching her stomach with one hand and a vomit container in the other. She was frighteningly pale.

Audrey was waiting inside the office, sitting on a revolving chair. "Who do we have here?" she asked.

"I'm Lilly."

"Come on in, Lilly. My name's Audrey. I assume Grant's told you what I do."

Lilly nodded.

"Grant here is a Healer too," Audrey said. "How do you feel about being healed?"

"Okay."

"Just *okay*?"

"Good, I guess."

"*Good?*" Audrey pushed. "Can I ask how long you've been sick?"

"About eighteen months," Lilly said.

"And what happened eighteen months ago?"

Lilly glanced sideways at me, then turned back to Audrey. "That's what we were hoping *you* could tell us."

"I know what ails you," Audrey said.

I knew at that moment that I would not be healing Lilly Anderson, Audrey would. So much for see one, do one, teach one. Whatever this was, it was way out of my league. Audrey had taken the reins and, even though I didn't know why, I was relieved.

"I saw *it* the moment you walked into the room," Audrey

continued. "Trust me, it would be progress if you would admit the catalyst for all this."

Lilly looked shocked. A hint of colour bloomed in her cheeks. "You mean...?"

Audrey nodded.

"I'm not telling anyone about that!" she said. "That's a dirty, shameful thing. *No.*"

This was all going wrong. I would be in so much trouble. There was the very real possibility I could lose my job.

Oh God...

That's when the Seeper slivered out of Lilly's body: it had a multitude of hands. Although it now stood at Lilly's side, shivering violently, distinctive from its host, it still kept its hands on *her* — hands across her mouth, hands on her groin, hands cupped over her breasts and over her ears. It was skinny and pale, much like Lilly, with a suggestion of internal organs visible through its skin. It was such an odd thing to be stood, trembling, in an office with a steel grey filing cabinet, a corner desk, a computer and the usual hospital stationary.

"You have to learn to talk about this," Audrey said to Lilly, ignoring the Seeper entirely. "The person who abuses you might tell you you can't, that you must never talk, but that's a lie. He'll continue to get away with what he's doing if you keep his secrets."

"It's *my* fault," Lilly said, and she sobbed. "I brought it on myself."

"There are other children who've been abused by the

very adults who are supposed to take care of them," Audrey said. "And many of them will say the same thing. But ask yourself, how can that possibly be true?"

"I'm a dirty slut."

"No, you're a beautiful girl and I never want to hear you call yourself a 'slut'. You are *not* a slut. *Never.*"

Lilly's tears ran readily. Her whole body was shaking, not unlike the Seeper that still held her in its grip. Suddenly, she broke free from its grip and launched herself into Audrey's arms. Unlike Fiona Peters, Lilly had broken free from whatever abuse she'd endured. Audrey embraced her and rocked her gently.

The Seeper took a step toward Lilly and Audrey. This was its last mistake. Even while hugging Lilly, Audrey's right hand grabbed one of the creature's many arms and squeezed. The struggle was brief. Shock, then pain, spreading over its face. Then, just like Charlie's Seeper yesterday, it faded from view and was gone. It didn't utter even one word of angst or protest.

"We will not let your father touch you again," Audrey said, although how she knew Lilly's father was the abuser, I do not know. "We're going to help you," Audrey continued.

I said, "I'm going to speak to some people and we'll put protection around you, Lilly."

Lilly nodded, her face still buried in Audrey's chest.

I had many questions: The most prominent one being, how did the act of a human—in this case, Lilly's father—give a Seeper access to its victim? What was the connection between sexual abuse and emotional trauma and a physical disease process? I wanted to interrogate the Seeper and find answers, but Audrey had slammed shut that door of opportunity. I asked no questions, of course. It wasn't appropriate. I didn't want to do anything that might jeopardise Audrey training me. So, instead, I excused myself and went to my desk to make the arrangements. I phoned the Emergency Social Worker, who walked me through the process. Among other measures, we would transfer Lilly to another ward and intercept her father on his next visit.

Afterwards, I visited Jenny on 8Med, just as I had promised, and while Jenny seemed eager to talk, I said nothing about what had occurred with Lilly Anderson.

seventeen

"There is no healing by committee. Healing is, and must always be, a secret art. We are servants of God, yet we tread the night and the secret highways between man's fear and his greatest need."

Yellow Dagger, page 150, 'The Healing Art'

I arrived at the Children's Ward at 08:30hrs on Monday morning. I was due to start on a stretch of nights later, but unfortunately, that didn't excuse me from the Monday ward round. Penelope, our Receptionist, sat at her desk ('Welcome Kia Ora' written across it), but I saw no one else. There were no nurses at the Nurse's Station, and no sign of Dr O'Brien. The white trolley was parked up. It was wrong, all wrong, and it gave me a very bad feeling.

"Morning." I rubbed my hands together, warming them after the frost outside.

Penelope mumbled some reply, but didn't raise her eye from her computer monitor. She looked bad tempered and testy. Her cheeks and her forehead looked like forming thunderheads.

"Where is everyone?" I asked.

She raised her eyebrows. "They've all gone to that meeting, haven't they?" Her eyes remained on the screen.

"Meeting?"

"Yeah," she said. "'Bout that new virus. Typical. We're all gonna die, but some of us have to stay and man the bloody shop floor."

After learning this meeting was in the Colquhoun Theatre, I thanked her and left. I'd already missed the opportunity for a lie in, so I thought I'd try to crash the meeting. I was curious what they might say about the Lymphachela Virus.

The Colquhoun Theatre was a large, semi-circled room with tiered seating, blending a mix of styles and eras in its decor. Its high ceiling and fluorescent strips made it a convenient, high-tech lecture theatre, while its wood-panelled walls and the large oil paintings of luminaries were a reminder of the hospital's proud medical history and tradition.

I took a seat in the third row. The room was filling quickly. A handful of latecomers continued to file in.

The room's acoustics carried nervous chatter, pushed like dust particles from the air conditioning, circulating through the entire room, round and round and round.

I looked for Tim or Chong, but saw neither.

Dr O'Brien was sat in the front row, no doubt pissed off that the ward round had had to be postponed. Across the other side of the theatre, I spotted Tooms, giving me daggers. She was sitting with another Clinical Nurse Manager.

The heat was stifling. I was already overheating in my shirt and pants. The thick leather seat sweating against my back.

The first speaker was Dr Adam Kobayashi, the Medical Officer for Health. A tall, lean man, balding, with thin spectacles, keen eyes and a chiselled face. He stood behind the lectern and leaned into the microphone. "Alright everyone. Let's begin, shall we? I'd like to thank you all for making this hastily called meeting..."

Most of the Senior Management team was present and had been allocated seating in the front row of the auditorium. A show of solidarity, whether or not it existed.

"... I'm sure you'll agree that, in light of circumstances, we need to mobilise quickly. Our aim is to give you all the information we currently have on this virus, as well as talk you through our evolving response. There'll be time for questions at the end..."

A few murmurs of disapproval from the crowd.

Dr Kobayashi raised his hands. "... this is a highly emotive subject for all of us, and fears run high. I know, I know, so please, *please* don't interrupt the presentation... There'll be plenty of time for questions at the end..."

Grumbles.

Dr Kobayashi cleared his throat. "First, then: the virus. It's known as the Lymphachela Virus. This is a name coined by Dr Brienbeer, one of our microbiology team. Now, unfortunately, Dr Brienbeer has resigned his position..." —*What?* When had Brienbeer resigned? I spoke to him two days ago, and he said nothing about resigning—"... so he couldn't be here today to explain his findings, but we have this image from his computer..."

A data projector shone the image onto the front of the auditorium. It was the same image I'd seen under the electron microscope, only this time blown up so that it spread across almost the entire width of the auditorium.

Around the room, there were gasps of surprise and shock.

Dr Kobayashi continued, "The virus attaches itself to a person's immune system. It's aggressive, and once it attaches itself, it's very difficult to dislodge. We believe it enters the human body via the Lymphatic System, although the precise mechanism is unknown. The symptoms include massive oedema, pain and delirium. The virus seems to disarm the patient's immune system, then attacks the internal organs...

We're not sure how it spreads, how contagious it is, what the duration of illness is likely to be, or indeed if we can cure it. We have three confirmed cases on the Children's Ward, and one additional staff member. We'd like that to be the limit.

"Now I know the word's been bandied around the rumour mill, so let's talk about it: Does this virus have the potential to become an epidemic or even a pandemic? *Any* new virus has that potential, and this one's no exception, although we think that is highly unlikely. That being said, we don't plan to underestimate this virus. For that reason, today I've notified the Ministry of Health of our status. We hope the three children and one adult who are sick with this virus respond quickly to treatment. Now we all have a part to play in this, so I'd like to hand you over to Mr Fontaine to talk us through what is an appropriate response... thank you..."

Dr Kobayashi sat down.

That was it? That was the sum total of knowledge of this virus? Nausea twirled my stomach. Bile tickled the back of my throat. My sense of unease hitched up a few more notches. While I hadn't expected Dr Kobayashi to talk about any metaphysical aspects of this virus, I thought there might be some insight into its unique microbiology. Not 'we're not sure how it spreads, how contagious it is, what the duration of illness is likely to be, or indeed if it can be cured'. My God, was he trying to incite complete hopelessness? The hospital was fucked! *We're all fucked!* Is that why Brienbeer quit?

Michael Fontaine was the Southern DHB CEO. He stood

and approached the lectern. He was chubby, broad-shouldered and much shorter than I remembered. He had one of those faces which was instantly recognisable, perhaps because of his recent appearance on a poster enthusing about the seasonal flu vaccination. "Thank you, Dr Kobayashi," he said. "First and foremost, I'd like to appeal to each of you as professionals to not only continue to do the fantastic work that you all do, but to go about it in a calm, considered way. Panic serves no one. Let us process the facts —as they become known—and respond in the manner in which we've all been trained.

"I can promise you that your safety, staff safety, is paramount. For this reason, today I've ordered extra quantities of PPE gear, which will be readily available in all clinical areas and, in particular, those front-line areas like the Emergency Department and the Medical Assessment Unit. PPE gear will be worn by all staff in the Children's Ward, naturally, and we will take all measures to keep the four known cases isolated."

Someone heckled. "What measures?"

The CEO's cheeks flushed. "All those affected are in side rooms (and have been in side rooms since their admissions with this virus or, in the case of the staff member, since we became aware of their symptoms) and these rooms have capacity for negative pressure. That and the use of PPE, rigorous hand washing..."

The whole theatre creaked with tension. Would those gathered begin stamping their feet? Would they riot?

"Now there's bound to be intense public interest," Mr Fontaine continued. "That's unavoidable, I'm afraid. I would ask, however, that you don't speak with the media at this stage. We will prepare a response for the media in due course, but it's not our number one priority. Staff safety is. As for the identities of those three children, I remind you you are all bound by confidentiality clauses. Please don't mention their names, not even to your spouses or your nearest family."

More murmuring. A deeper unrest.

Once again, the message was brief, lacking any real substance. Essentially, there were three main points: Keep calm; we're getting more PPE gear; and don't talk to the media. The CEO then invited the audience to ask their questions, and both he and Dr Kobayashi did their best to provide answers.

"What assurances can the Medical Officer of Health (or the CEO, for that matter), give that we haven't already been exposed to this virus? What's the incubation period?"

"Do we have the right to stay at home if we feel the risks are too great?"

Michael Fontaine started talking about personal and professional responsibility, before jeers and booing drowned him out. The noise level rose sharply, booming through the theatre to a menacing crescendo.

Someone behind me yelled, "Yeah, Mr Fontaine, and how is your nice, clean office up at the Wakari site?"

Another round of jeers followed. Elsewhere, nervous chatter, more fervent than before.

"What if the virus spreads? What then?"

"Is it true Dr Brienbeer fled Dunedin?"

The room temperature climbed. There were too many bodies in close proximity, and not enough cool, fresh air. The reek of perspiration clawed at my nostrils.

"Why can't the infected be taken elsewhere?"

Eventually, before the crowd descended into an angry mob, the meeting was adjourned, with the promise of a second meeting in the next day or two.

As most people stood and filed out of their rows, I remained seated. I didn't know what to do. I felt compelled to warn someone in authority of the real dangers we faced, but how could I do this credibly? How could I talk about Seepers, or the Men in White Coats, when most people didn't see them and would swiftly discredit me?

What difference would the Ministry of Health make? The official response had been knee jerk, lacked any real depth, and was more about spin than scientific knowledge.

An alternative approach was needed.

As I left the auditorium, my plan was to make my way to the on-call room and try to force myself to get a couple of hours of sleep.

There was still a bottleneck around the two exits. Again, I

looked for Tim and Chong, but didn't see them. Much of the boisterousness from the meeting carried out beyond the auditorium and into the corridor.

Someone tapped my right shoulder. "A word, please, Dr Newman."

I span around.

CNM Tooms stood there, entirely too close for my comfort, her eyes considering me like I was some insect she was about to exterminate. Her hair was more dark orange than auburn, the fringe perfectly horizontal in a neat bob.

"Sorry?"

"I'd like a word with you," she repeated.

We both stepped to one side, allowing the remaining people behind us to pass by unhindered.

Once the auditorium had quietened a little, Tooms said, "So I've heard about what you got up to at the weekend. "

"You have? And what is that?"

"Please don't tell me you're going to deny it?"

"If I knew what *it* was, then I'd know whether or not to deny it."

Tooms pursed her lips, her skin pale and taut. "Very well. You want me to spell it out? How about the practising of alternative medicine?"

"Is this the modern equivalent of being accused of witchcraft?" I smiled at my quip, but felt no genuine humour.

"This is potentially a very serious breach of your scope of practice."

That wiped the smile off my face. Whatever I said next, I would have to choose my words carefully. "And who told you this?"

"That's not important."

"On the contrary," I said. "If I'm being accused of something, I'd like to know who my accuser is."

"Tell me about Lilly Anderson," she said, seeming to change tack. "I find it quite incredible that a restraining order is in place against her father so swiftly. There must have been very compelling evidence. *How* did you come by such evidence?"

"Lilly told me."

"Unlikely."

"Is it my abilities you doubt, or that Lilly might want to break free from an abusive father?"

"You had help," she said, glowering, the light dancing in her eyes against an impenetrable darkness. "*I know you did!*"

"I would have thought you'd be happy that an intervention has happened and an innocent girl is no longer living in an abusive situation."

"You think you're so smart, don't you?"

"I've answered your questions," I said, "but if you're only here to insult me, then I've got other places to be."

And before she had time to compose a reply, I walked out of the auditorium.

eighteen

"It is always darkest in the third watch of the night,
when the veil between life and death is thinnest."
Hugo the Younger, page 177, 'The Healing Art'

Beep beep beep beeeppppppp!

The noise repeated, over and over and over, familiar yet unfamiliar, dragging me from forgotten dreams. I shivered, deep in my bones, as if caught in some dark tide, the undertow threatening to reveal some waking nightmare, a reality I was hopelessly unprepared for.

I fumbled for the alarm clock... but it wasn't there. It wasn't my alarm clock, no. It was my pager, damn it.

Panic spiked my veins. A tightness squeezed my chest.

Then I remembered this wasn't my flat, but the on-call room. *I* was on-call.

What time was it?

I pulled my wrist from under the covers and studied my watch.

02:03hrs.

Beep beep beeeepppp!

There was something odd about the noise my pager was making—it was more urgent, more piercing.

It took me a moment to realise it was a *fast* page, meaning it was urgent.

Yes, I really was on-call tonight.

David...?

Toby...?

Pulled back my bedsheets, standing, disorientated, searching for the light switch, flicking it on. The light stung my eyes. The on-call room was essentially a small box. A phone on the wall. A single bed. A bedside table and a lamp. An ugly brown carpet that was unravelling.

David!

Toby!

I grabbed my pager, flipping it over to the display. It was ICU. I couldn't shake the ominous feeling. Fingers trembling, I rang the extension. Both David Layton and Toby Harrison had deteriorated, I was told.

"On my way."

I bumped into Audrey in the stairwell on my way to the ICU. We exchanged glances. "David and Toby have deteriorated," I gasped, taking two steps at a time.

"I *felt* them," she said, "I *felt* David," and she followed me.

We ran together. Audrey was far more agile than me at climbing stairs. Fitter, too.

A small gathering of staff huddled in the corridor outside the unit. From their body language, it seemed they'd closed ranks, speaking in hushed tones with some urgency.

One nurse, a spokesperson, approached me. "Dr Newman, good! There's a bit of a situation—" Her eyes darted across at Audrey. "Who's this?"

"She's with me," I replied. There was no time for explanations. "I was told both David and Toby had deteriorated. Which one deteriorated first?"

My stomach churned.

"Hard to say," said the nurse. "It seemed pretty much simultaneous. We've been working in two separate teams. We have cleared the other beds."

I nodded. "What are their obs like?"

A high-pitched scream came from within the ICU. It built to such fierceness that I wondered how any human being could survive, what must surely be, devastating pain. I had seen pain, but this... I was pretty sure it was David's scream, although I couldn't be sure.

Audrey rushed towards the entry.

"*No!*" said the nurse. "You can't go in there without PPE!"

Audrey ignored the small table where boxes of gloves, gowns and N95 masks had been stowed. She ran straight inside the ICU.

Another staff member turned to me. "Who was that? You know she'll have to quarantine?"

"Right now," I said, "my main concern is working out which patient is the most acute, which one needs help first."

"The quieter one," another offered.

It was decided, then. I'd start with Toby. Unlike Audrey, I didn't want to take any chance with this virus. I had seen that sucker under the microscope, so I took a moment to don some PPE gear. It had been a while since I'd worn such gear, and I'm not sure I put everything on in the precise order. All the while, that twisting sense of dread lay heavy in my gut.

I stepped into ICU and steered left towards Toby's bed. All the curtains had been pulled around, dramatically reducing the light and space. Hands trembling, a sweat spiking my brow, I pulled back the curtain.

Toby wasn't alone.

I knew he wouldn't be.

There was a nurse at his side, fully kitted out in PPE, but her role was observational: for all the help she was rendering to Toby, she might have well not been there.

One of the White Coats was there too, lying on Toby's bed. Even through the mask, the oily smell assaulted my nostrils.

Toby's entire body had ballooned. He was red-faced and

looked wretched. He leaned to his right side like a cast sheep, unable to right its position. His breathing was laboured and, worse, I saw a telltale tinge of blue around his lips.

The White Coat held a strange implement, halfway between a pair of barbecue tongues and a surgical blade, and had somehow burrowed into the back of Toby's neck. A slow trickle of Toby's blood oozed from the hole, pooling over the white linen. With each twist and turn of this implement, Toby's body would jerk and he'd moan with pain. Had it exposed the boy's spinal cord?

Much like the nurse next to me, I didn't know what to do. I simply stared through my visor. Not a single constructive thought would spark. My mind was blank, at least until the memory emerged:

The door to Mum's room was slightly ajar. I lingered just outside, unsure. It was dark inside. She'd got the curtains drawn. I pushed the door—just a little. I leaned in. I strained to see my mother in the gloom...

I pushed the memory away: *no!*

From David's bed space, there came a loud thud, which caused the entire floor to flex beneath me. Next, there was a rattling of what sounded like cot-sides, the shearing of something metal and the spilling of many small particles over the floor. Another thud. Then a third. Audrey cried out. That got me moving.

I pushed aside the curtain, just in time to see another

White Coat pinning Audrey up against the wall, in between the oxygen, the suction and the monitor.

Audrey's eyes bulged. She fought and kicked and tried to extricate herself, all to no avail. The White Coat was too strong.

Suddenly, it dropped her back to the floor, but its grip on her neck remained.

On instinct, I ran forward, and I grabbed the back of the Seeper's coat and I pulled as quickly and as hard as I could.

It stumbled backwards, but even as it did so, it turned its head and glared at me. There was hatred in those eyes, a hatred that ran deep, but I also saw surprise. My strategy had worked. It released Audrey as it fell, and she came crashing down to the floor. A floor which was littered with blood tubes, packets of alcohol/clorhex swabs, and unopened IV cannulas.

The Seeper wasn't done—not with David, not with Audrey and, now, not with me. It smiled. A horrible, twisted, sadistic expression. Its dark eyes twinkled at me. "How dare you interfere!"

It lunged at me.

Audrey was faster. She pushed me out of its way. I skidded along the floor, landing roughly against the twisted metal tubing at the foot of David's bed.

In retaliation, the creature scooped Audrey up and flung her across the room.

She landed hard, smashing into one of the drip stands,

toppling it, then somehow becoming entangled in the curtains, pulling them clean off their railings.

I could look straight through into Toby's bed space.

I didn't like what I saw. The first White Coat was murdering Toby. In fact, seeing both White Coats, seeing both boys, Toby's need was greater.

I staggered towards Toby's bed and told the stunned-looking nurse, "*Go! Get help! Quickly! Get O'Brien! Get the crash team!*"

Behind her visor, I saw her processing things. She looked at me, then at Audrey, then at the curtain which lay on the floor and the rest of the carnage; then she looked at the two patients, Toby and David, before finally running towards the exit. I wasn't sure if she would actually summon any meaningful help or if she was panicking.

I looked down at Toby. The White Coat had embedded its weird instrument further into the boy's neck, twisting and jiggling it.

If there was some medical intervention to offer, my over-stressed brain couldn't summon it. A direct approach was best. I lunged forward, grabbing the White Coat's hands and wrestling them, and the instrument, away from Toby.

The White Coat flicked me off, like I was little more than an annoying fly buzzing around. Its strength was frightening.

Once again, I skidded over the floor, this time whacking my thigh against the cot side of Toby's bed.

Meanwhile, the White Coat continued its precision work,

pulling on individual nerves, which made Toby's left leg jerk beneath the bedsheets.

The boy grunted and gasped. His eyes, even through a fog of delirium, bulged in terror.

Again, I ran at the White Coat, grabbing one of its arms, pulling it away and clinging on with all the strength I had left. That oily smell poured from its skin.

"Feeble creature," it said, looking down at me.

It tried to shake me off, but this time I held firm.

I shut my eyes and focused on holding tight. If I held the creature's arm, maybe this would minimise the harm it was inflicting on Toby.

To my right, Audrey struggled against the other White Coat. Equipment was hurled across the unit, there were crashes and bangs, followed by grunts and hisses and a scream. I wanted to help her, but something tightened around my wrist. The grip was so intense it seared into my flesh. Next my feet were lifted clean off the floor and I dangled there, in mid-air, feeling like my shoulder joint might pop from its socket.

I opened my eyes.

The White Coat pressed its face up against my visor. "Do you wish to share this boy's fate, puny man? Would you like the Tonsil Guillotine inserted posteriorly?"

I sucked in my breath and I closed my eyes again, the creature's proximity and intense gaze too unsettling. My brain scrambled to think, to focus. There was a subtext to what the creature said. Something buried beneath its words. Fear. Was it possible that it was just as afraid of me as I was of it? There was only one reason I could see these creatures when others couldn't. Audrey was right: I was a Healer; and if I was a Healer, then I was a threat.

So, I *pushed*. At least I tried to. I allowed myself to dwell on the situation, on David and Toby, on the pain I was in, on this cursed creature... and I *pushed*. I tried to imitate what Audrey had done to Charlie and Lilly and let whatever power I had come from the centre of my chest. From the emotional epicentre.

I must have got something right, because the Seeper dropped me like I was suddenly too hot.

I hit the floor hard. I slumped.

The creature towered over me. "You are powerless to stop us."

I said nothing. I couldn't. I was in too much pain—my wrists, my legs, my hip and, most recently, my back. I may be easily injured, at least compared with this Seeper, but I wasn't a puny man. I had hurt it. This truth was etched on the White Coat's face, a rare and sudden uncertainty in its eyes. A seldom-exposed frailty. It was true, then: I was a Healer. This was how to exercise my power.

To my right, Audrey screamed. The scream was so shrill, so pained, that both the White Coat and I turned in her direction.

Audrey embraced the broken body of her son. David was

motionless, his bloated flesh drained, his eyes glazed over. The other White Coat stood over them both, shaking its hands and puffing out its chest. It had had its fill. It had taken its prize.

There was no time to process what I saw. Toby's White Coat kicked me, targeting my injured hip.

I yelped.

I skidded across the floor.

"So there is *another* Healer," it said, stepping closer. "We thought before we saw you looking. Didn't your mentor teach you it's rude to stare?"

I slid across the floor. I had to get to David. I had to help Audrey. They were the focus now. I'd been wrong: David was the sicker of the two boys. I tried to regain my feet, but the pain stopped me cold, my body simply refusing to comply.

"What the hell's happening here?" I knew the voice. I recognised the tone.

I turned to see O'Brien stood behind me, at the foot of Toby's bed, kitted out in a yellow gown, gloves, a face mask, most of his face obscured behind a half-misted visor, but his outrage tangible.

Other members of the team stood behind O'Brien, also kitted in full PPE.

They surveyed the scene.

And then they filed into the room, a cohesive team of doctors and nurses, and they went to Toby and to David, checking vital signs and assessing status.

A pair of gloved hands grabbed me by the upper arms, lifting me, ready or not, to my feet. "Come with me," a gruff voice said from behind a mask and visor. It was one of the Security Guards. There was no arguing. I wasn't sure my legs would support me, but he manhandled me towards the exit, regardless.

Another Security Guard, a man almost as wide as he was tall, wrestled with Audrey, trying to prize her from David, but she fought back. Her cries became more anguished. Finally, the Fat Security Guard pried her away.

David's body lay on the floor. A nurse felt his neck for the carotid artery... then shook her head at one of her colleagues. David was dead. His skin looked so cold. The nurse didn't attempt CPR. It was a futile exercise, apparently.

The Security Guard pulled me towards the exit.

"This hospital is *ours*," the Seeper gloated. It looked across at its double, then lowered its eyes to me, smiling, "You and your puny friend aren't welcome in our house!" And then it simply walked through one of the internal walls of the ICU, as if there was no physical barrier whatsoever. It could be both physical *and* ethereal.

Most staff worked on Toby and, based on their quiet urgency and their body language, I knew things weren't looking good. Of course, they couldn't see the White Coat still attached to Toby's neck.

It was too late to say anything, or help. They whisked me out of the ICU and into the corridor.

Audrey was being held there by the fat Security Guard and, whenever he relaxed his grip, even for a second, she attempted to break free. "Hold still!" he barked.

O'Brien approached me. "You have some explaining to do." There was rage in his voice, moderately diminished by the PPE gear he wore. He turned to Audrey. "You *both* do."

While technically he hadn't asked a question, I couldn't think of anything to say, not one word.

Why wasn't he in the ICU trying to help Toby?

He looked down at me, using all his height against me. "*You'll never work in this hospital again, Newman!*"

I nodded, and then I lowered my head. How could I explain the things I had seen, much less the actions I'd taken? O'Brien would never understand. He'd spent decades within the medical model that he'd never comprehend any alternative view.

I would take my punishment, whatever it might be. If that meant never working in the hospital again, so be it. I had only wanted to help the children in my care—David, Toby, the others. My conscience was clear.

"This will go before a tribunal," he said.

I was bruised and battered, my hands shaking from spent adrenaline, my mouth dry. I was afraid, terrified even, but not of O'Brien. Nothing O'Brien could threaten me with compared to the White Coats.

If the White Coats weren't stopped....

Suddenly, Audrey broke free and ran back into the ICU.

"*Stop her!*" O'Brien yelled

The fat Security guard pursued her, "Come back here, you slippery bitch!" A few moments later, Audrey was wrestled back out into the corridor by this large man. O'Brien approached her. "The children in there are potentially infectious and yet you walk in without PPE gear. Why?"

"Do you really think your mask and gown can protect you? You have no idea what you're dealing with!"

Even behind the protective gear, I observed O'Brien's grin. "And you do, I suppose?"

"Get this ape to un-hand me," Audrey said, once again trying to pull from the Security Guard's restraining hands. "Leave me to my work. If I can only —"

"I don't think so."

I thought things couldn't get any worse for Audrey, but then Peter Layton came bounding along the corridor, his arms raised, constricted as they were pushed into the sleeves of a protective gown. A nurse trailed him, policing the wearing of PPE gear, even as she fastened the gown at Peter's back. Peter wasn't interested in PPE gear, however. He'd spied his ex-wife. "*What's she doing here?*" he asked, a distinct chill in his voice, even through his mask. "She's not meant to get within one hundred metres of David."

Audrey looked tired. Her eyes were sunken in their sockets and her skin had paled. "What does any of that matter now?" she muttered.

"Oh, it matters! It matters a great—" Finally Peter Layton seemed to interpret the terrible truth in his ex-wife words, for he stopped mid-flow. "David...? *How's David?*"

O'Brien took this as his cue. "Please, Mr Layton, I need you to sit down."

Peter Layton was having nothing of the sort. "*No, no no! That can't be right!*"

The Security Guard shuffled next to me. He flexed his shoulders, preparing for a potential confrontation and the need to intervene. Beads of sweat stood out on his forehead. He was still breathless, his breathing not sounding the healthiest.

O'Brien turned to me. "I think you've done enough damage here, Newman," he said. Behind his mask and visor, his face had erupted with multiple red blotches. "I suggest you get the hell out of this hospital. *Your career's over!* And if I so much as catch you in the building again, so help me God, you'll be sorry..." He fixed Audrey with a stare, considering her, unsure perhaps how to categorise her. "... *and take this quack with you!*"

So, they marched Audrey and I along the corridor, to the jolting sounds of Peter Layton's sobs. Deep, grating sobs.

I didn't have the heart to look back.

My entire body felt numb.

part two

nineteen

"The pit is bottomless, the descent impossibly steep. Beyond the light of day, I cannot describe even half the horrors writhing down there."

Hyu , page 11, 'The Healing Art'

I opened my eyes slowly.

Grey green light filtered through thin curtains. This wasn't my flat. It wasn't the on-call room. I was lying on someone's couch, in someone's lounge, but I didn't recall whose. The cold air bit at my uncovered skin. It flowed from behind the curtains, making me wonder if the window had been left open or the glass was missing. The room seemed to lack even the most basic of heating. Everywhere was full; boxes, newspapers, books, furniture buried beneath stuff, more stuff covering that stuff, a hoarder's paradise. At some point, a small bird must have got inside and generously opened its bowels. The bird poo, now dried, still clung to the room's contents. Apparently, no one had thought to clean it away. The room, from what I could make out, was a throwback from the 1980s, with floral-patterned wallpaper in an advanced state of peeling. The curtains were equally dated. A thin layer of dust coated every surface. Dust motes swirled in the air, caught in the early light. I coughed: a wet, hacking cough. Yet my mouth was horribly dry. A strange feathery taste coated my tongue. And I needed to pee. I *really* needed to pee.

I pulled back the heavy, coarse wool blankets, which prickled the skin of my hands, neck and face. I had no recollection of covering myself with these, so who did? Yesterday's clothes, my trousers and my shirt, clung to me, sticky and creased. The cold air assaulted me, falling upon me like knives or teeth. I didn't care, the pressure in my bladder was too great, and I rose from my temporary bed.

Big mistake!

My head was thick and somewhere in my brain drums were pounding, building ominously into the mother of all hangovers. The room blurred and span slowly clockwise.

I lay back down, resting my head on the pillow. I remembered a bottle of Fireball Cinnamon Whisky. I remembered an empty bottle, even. And although I never drank spirits, it seemed this time I'd made an exception, my sluggish brain scrambling to piece together the gory details.

What had started as a quick drink of condolence had quickly got out of hand. I remembered who I'd been drinking with: Audrey. There were other details too, unformed, dancing just out of my reach.

I groaned.

The room still turned, little by little, tilted at a weird angle. Perhaps it was the earth's rotation, I didn't know. The soft springs collapsed under my weight. I lay there, gasping. My stomach lurched. For one horrible moment, I thought I might vomit all over the nasty green carpet, and my vomit might remain there indefinitely, or at least until it rotted through the floorboards or attracted hungry vermin. I squeezed my eyes shut. The room only span faster. I opened them again. Littered on the floor beside the coffee table were the broken remains of my pager. The battery compartment had been pulled off, the LCD screen and plastic casing cracked, and its inner circuitry smashed and exposed.

"Shit!"

It was safe to assume it would never bother me again. That's right, my medical career was over...

As much as I wanted to lie there, my bladder was going to burst if I didn't find the toilet soon. I swung my legs around and sat upon the edge of the couch, trying to work up the courage to stand again. My head was throbbing in sickening waves, like the worst case of motion sickness ever. My vision swam and, much to my alarm, black floaters danced before me.

I blinked them away.

Taking a deep breath, I pushed up from the couch. The room had finally stopped turning, but it swayed. I staggered towards the nearest door, weaving in-between boxes of non-perishables. One box was filled with no-frill Wheat Biscuits. Another with jumbo packets of Harraway's Rolled Oats. There were bulk loads of toilet paper, the cheap stuff I remembered from my student days. There were large plastic containers filled with what looked like water. There were several unmarked white bags, one ripped on the top corner, revealing tea bags inside. Nasty, cheap tea bags, like the ones they stock at the Hospital Cafeteria. No wonder I preferred coffee. I walked past a large wooden bookshelf, which strained under the weight of badly stacked books.

Where was the damn toilet?

I twisted the door handle and opened the door. I didn't know where I was going, and didn't particularly want to wander around some stranger's house, but there was no other choice. I stumbled down the hallway, using one wall to steady myself. The rest of the house was worse than the lounge—holes in the plasterboard, stained carpets, dirt and grime. I wondered how it was possible for someone to live like this.

The toilet was the second door I tried. It was squeezed into one corner of the bathroom, next to an off-cream vanity and a heated towel rail with a severed power cable. The bathroom had dust-covered venetian blinds and wallpaper which extended to the edge of the bath. Heavy foliage crowded the bathroom window from the outside, branches scraping against the glass, restricting what light entered the room.

I swayed forward. I stood before the toilet bowl, legs shoulder width apart, penis in hand, and relieved myself.

The urine flowed out in a long, glorious torrent. It was darker and stronger smelling than usual.

When I was done, I zipped up my fly and flushed the toilet. The pipes shuddered inside the wall. The toilet bowl wasn't the cleanest. There was a yellow tide mark on the porcelain, as if urine had been allowed to sit there and stagnate. It was much like my medical career. That too had been flushed down the toilet, why, just last night, but all those years couldn't simply be washed away. They too would leave a deep, memorable stain.

What exactly had happened? What had seemed so clear last night, suddenly didn't make any kind of sense.

I shivered and I coughed. My throat, my whole mouth, were horribly parched. I wobbled out of the bathroom, back along the hallway, trying other doors as I went. The kitchen was the third door on the right. I walked in and almost fell over a box of Value Dry Pasta Spirals. A large box with enough pasta stockpiled to feed someone for an entire year. There were other boxes too, taking much of the available floor space. The bench tops were a dark green laminate, the cabinets were pine. The sink was stacked with dirty dishes, including two glasses, the whisky still coating the bottom, and the discarded one litre bottle. The harsh smell of whisky took me by surprise and flipped my entire stomach.

I held my breath. I swallowed hard, trying to control my rising gorge.

I turned away from the sink.

Thankfully, the rest of the bench tops were reasonably clear. If they'd been littered with long abandoned plates, the food scraps having gone rancid, this might have been enough to tip my stomach over the edge.

When the nausea had finally passed, I found a clean glass in one cupboard and filled it with water from the cold tap. I drank greedily. I needed to rehydrate. My stomach lurched in greeting and, for the third time that morning, the thought I might lose the contents of my stomach became a real possibility.

I closed my eyes—again.

I waited, this time half leaning over the sink.

I prayed, not that I believed in God. Still, I prayed that if I could survive this, if the things I couldn't quite remember from last night turned out to be entirely unsubstantiated, then I would never, ever touch spirits again for the rest of my life.

My stomach growled, gurgled, squealed, moaned and then finally settled.

Opening my eyes, relieved, I made my way back along the hallway and into the lounge. I stood in the doorway for a moment, looking at all the clutter, at the boxes and the chaos. There was no TV, I noticed. No music system, no heating. Except for the books, there was nothing in the room to offer any form of entertainment. A clunky old Windows PC sat on a small desk in the far corner, perhaps offering the possibility of an internet connection.

I turned to the bookshelf. I hoped I'd learn a lot about my host from the books they'd collected, the books they'd read, the books they'd chosen to display, the mere fact that they placed an emphasis on books. I scanned the titles. Most of the books were religious books, which made my heart sink. There were several versions of The Holy Bible, the Torah and the Koran. There were a few rather heavy looking theology books, biblical concordances, texts on various languages, specifically Hebrew, Greek, Latin and Arabic. There were several copies of 'The Healing Art'.

The entirety of the bottom shelf was designated for Nursing Textbooks, among them 'Legal Aspects of Nursing', 'An Encyclopaedia of Modern Nursing' and 'Tortora and Derrickson / Principle of Anatomy and Physiology: 15th Edition'.

Moving around the various obstacles, I returned to the couch and pulled open the curtains. Twisted vines and dark green leaves filled the window frame. The glass was cracked in the bottom left pane. A small piece had become dislodged, allowing frigid air to pour inside. It felt as though the whole house was slowly being claimed by vegetation and that, one day, it would disappear completely into the city's green belt like some enchanted castle in a fairytale.

"Did you flush the toilet?" a woman's voice croaked.

I turned gingerly.

Audrey stood in the doorway. My host. David's mother. Her eyes were bloodshot, probably much like my own. Her hair was knotted and bedraggled. She looked far older than I remembered, her skin dry and flaking. If I felt rough, it was fair to say she looked dramatically worse. She seemed to consider me like some unwanted memory, like something she wished she could bury forever.

My own memories came crashing back, breaking through my throbbing brain and the poorly constructed walls of excess alcohol. I remembered I'd been on-call last night. I remembered being fast paged and rushing back to the ICU, where I had to decide which boy to prioritise—Toby or David. As it happened, it didn't matter either way. We'd done all we could, all we could think of, but it had ultimately been in vain. David had crashed. David had died, killed by the White Coat, or by complications of the Lymphachela Virus (in medical speak). Toby had crashed, too. He was probably dead as well, although I didn't know for sure. There was that terrible confrontation with Peter Layton and then we'd been escorted off the ward by Security.

Leaving the hospital had come with a sense of finality. I knew that I was a failure. A miserable excuse of a human being, who wasn't cut out to be a doctor. I had left with

Audrey, since taking care of her seemed like the least I could do given what had happened to her son.

We'd emerged out of the hospital in the low, pre-dawn light. A heavy drizzle fell, soaking everything, the bricks and the pavement, surprisingly wetting. The wind had fallen away. The entire city sulked, fully immersed in the low-lying gloom.

Audrey walked quickly, and I had struggled to keep to her pace with all my aches and pains. For the longest time neither of us spoke, words seeming so inadequate under the circumstances. We'd begun the ascent of Pitt Street in silence, our faces pressed against the savage weather, clothes drenched and dripping. Still, she set this terrifying pace. "Sorry about David," I'd said, my breathing laboured between my clenched teeth. "You did everything you could. You couldn't.... He was a nice kid..."

She nodded. That was it. No other response. And she'd kept walking.

There were lots of other questions that I'd wanted to ask, but I wasn't sure that I should. She was broken. She grieved for a son she'd never really known. She had the power to heal, but she hadn't been able to save him, just as *I* hadn't been able to save him. As terrible as I felt, I couldn't begin to imagine what she must be feeling.

I followed her. She led the way. Perhaps, I reasoned, if I followed her long enough, there would be a more appropriate time to ask my questions. Either way, it was my duty to follow her, I decided, even if it blurred some perceived professional boundaries. What did those boundaries matter now? My career was over. That was all I knew.

The house was located on the dog-leg of a section and was nestled against a thick bank of trees that formed part of the city's green belt. The gravel driveway was easy to miss as you snaked your way up Corrie Street. Even if you stumbled upon the driveway, there was still no guarantee you'd find the house, which was buried behind wild hedgerows, overgrown trees and a mass of undergrowth that had reached monstrous proportions. There was no obvious entry point. Audrey knew the way, though, and pushed her way through the bushes. I followed. Rainwater dripped down from the leaves and branches, finding the gap between my neck and my shirt collar, the one place which, until then, had remained dry. I shuddered.

We emerged to a couple of tiled steps and a porch roof over a red-brick house. The front door was a dark blue with an old-fashioned brass doorknob. The paint was peeling badly. Some creeper had grown along the door's surface, its fingers trying to pry the panes of glass from the stained-glass window. Once this would have been one of Dunedin's premium properties, before it had been left to this sad ruination.

Audrey fished a key from her pocket. The door had swollen in the jam but she opened it with a hard shove.

"Is this where you live?" I'd asked, trying to hide the surprise from my voice.

"Yes."

"Okay."

"Okay."

"*Are you okay?*"

She considered the question for a long time, then shrugged. "Is there another choice?"

I hadn't been convinced. I lingered on the doorstep, unsure of what I could do about the situation.

"I need a drink," she said. "Are you just going to stand there?"

I wasn't sure which was worse, the rooms of endless clutter or the dank, musty smell that rushed to greet me. Both had overwhelmed me as I'd stepped over the threshold. I wasn't sure where to look or where to walk. I followed Audrey into the lounge, where she cleared a space for me on the couch. She'd brought me a towel so I could dry my hair and dab dry my clothing, although she hadn't offered any dry clothes. My skin had broken out in fresh goosebumps, but she'd brought me a generous glass of whisky, and that soon put a fire in my belly. Soon I forgot the cold. I forgot my damp clothes. Soon I matched my host glass for glass, my head spinning and all my woes temporarily forgotten. Audrey seemed to handle her liquor with far more dignity than me, and I wondered if, for her, this was a regular occurrence. I found, in that moment at least, that I didn't really care. Eventually, when the bottle had run dry, she'd taken herself off to bed. And I'd fallen into a drunken sleep on the couch.

Now, seeing her stood in the doorway, those haunted eyes and embittered face, I felt the need to apologise again. "I'm sorry about David." I really felt I ought to acknowledge David's death.

"Did you flush the toilet?"

"Yes. *Why?*"

"Did you have a crap?"

What strange conversations were exchanged between fellow healers? "No. Just a wee."

"Then there's no need to flush the toilet. It's very wasteful. I'm trying to conserve water."

Okay... right...

Once again, I puzzled over the large containers of water in the lounge. Being this close to the City Centre, the house would almost certainly be on the town water supply, so what possible reason might she have for conserving water? I let the question slide. "I'm sorry."

"Anyway, what do you want? Why are you *still* here?

Just like that, my welcome was revoked.

I searched for some sort of reply. I glanced down at the broken pager again. It was DHB property and, for the life of me, I couldn't recall how it had been broken like this. I wondered if they'd ever ask for it back.

Suddenly I remembered how the pager had broken. I

remembered how I'd joked about it while we'd been drinking. "This little box, small as it may be, is ruining my life," I'd said. "I'm a dog and this is my leash. This little gadget." Then I'd placed the pager on the floor, lifted the edge of the coffee table and let it drop. The leg, and the sheer weight of the timber, had pulverised the plastic device. It had been the heaviest thing I could find. For good measure, I'd repeated the procedure a few more times. "There," I'd announced at last. "Silence. Peace and quiet." Audrey had laughed, but was she really laughing with me? Were we really drinking together or two people drinking separately? For me, however, this had been a moment of unusual clarity, in spite of the strange pull of the alcohol on my neurones. For eight years, I'd trained to be a doctor. *Eight years!* Six years in medical school. Two years working in Paediatrics. I'd become a Registrar earlier that year, reaching a stage in my career where I thought I actually knew a thing or two, that I was finally consolidating my learning, but in reality my entire paradigm, the whole medical model, was incorrect, as was evidenced by the woman drinking neat whisky opposite me and the healings she'd performed single-handedly. Now that was funny. That was worth raising a glass to!

"Well?" she asked, now standing in the same lounge where only a few hours ago we'd consumed an entire bottle of whisky. She was sober now, it seemed. Her guard was well and truly raised.

"I want you to train me," I said, and when I said it I knew it was the truth.

She laughed then. Cold, embittered, humourless. It was certainly not the response that I had hoped for.

The next day, Wednesday, my phone rang. It was Tim Butterfield. His voice sounded slightly odd, distant somehow, as if he were phoning from another country rather than less than a mile down the road.

"How're you, Grant?"

"I'm good," I said, although we both knew that wasn't true.

"You're weren't at your flat," he said.

I wasn't ready to share my whereabouts just yet, even with one of my closest friends. It was safer on a number of levels if I didn't tell anyone, although I was touched Tim had been around to my flat.

I wondered what he'd heard about the events of Monday night. What rumours were circulating?

I didn't like to ask.

"Chong's pissed with you," he said finally, with a great sigh, as if speaking these few words had taken great effort. "He reckons you've sided with your Healer over him. Says you've turned your back on your mates."

"And what do you say?"

"I told Chong to zip it. I said there was bound to be an explanation and, as mates, we ought to give you the benefit of the doubt."

"That's appreciated."

Tim waited, perhaps hoping that I might elaborate on my version of events, but I wasn't ready to go there. I wasn't sure I fully understood events. I was still coming to terms with everything I'd lost. If I was a Healer, like Audrey, what did this actually mean? Audrey seemed to tolerate my staying here, although she was lost in grief and unwilling to talk things through.

"You're sure you're okay?" Tim asked.

"Yeah," I said. "I need a bit of time to process my thoughts, that's all."

"Fair enough, mate." That was all he was going to get from me. He said goodbye and hung up.

My phone rang again the next day, around lunchtime. I had just eaten a very-average tinned corned beef sandwich, using ingredients I'd scrounged from Audrey's kitchen and helped myself to. I dabbed the mayonnaise from my mouth. The mayonnaise had made it palatable.

It was my father. I sighed. Wasn't it nice to be so popular? I waited a few seconds, unsure whether to take the call. Finally, I swiped my finger across the screen and lifted the phone to my ear. "Hello," I said, trying to hide the sudden quiver from my voice.

"You're all over the newspaper, you know," my father said. "And on National Radio! Do you have any idea how *I* feel? *My son quits medicine and I find out through the bloody ODT!*"

"It must be awful for you!"

"Don't you take that sarcastic tone with me. I'm your father. *What's going on?*"

"I'm not sure what's going on."

"But presumably you have some plan?"

Audrey's lounge seemed to oppose the idea of any plans. The layers of dust, the deep shadows, the engrained clutter, even the bowing bookshelf and the way the books had been haphazardly stacked: none of these things spoke of intention or purpose. "No plan. Nothing."

"I can talk to Dr O'Brien, smooth the rough edges, ask him—"

"No, don't. I'm not going back."

"But... I don't understand..."

"It's not necessary to understand everything. There are many things we don't understand, but that's okay."

"This is about this virus," my father said. "A terrible thing. Terrible. It's got a lot of people worried."

"No, this is about *me*."

"You've been working too hard. Take a break. Get away. Anything, but for God's sake, *don't throw away your entire career!*"

"It's *your* career, father, not *mine*."

"I don't understand..."

"Sorry about—" The call cut out. The battery on my phone had died. "... that."

I asked Audrey if her computer worked and if she had an internet connection. She shrugged, saying that she hadn't used it in some time. After I removed some of the clutter, brushed dust off the keyboard, I discovered there was an ethernet cable attached.

I pressed the power button and Windows XP booted. I could hear the computer's hard drives grinding. Finally, the outdated wallpaper, the gentle curve of some grassy slope, flicked onto the monitor.

I clicked on Internet Explorer and went to the Radio New Zealand website, where they had a link to a news audio feed. The speakers inside the monitor crackled and hissed, but I heard well enough:

"*... A serious viral outbreak continues to rage in Dunedin Hospital, the Southern DHB has confirmed. There are sixteen reported cases, including two fatalities..."

David was the first fatality. Toby was most likely the second. What about Jenny? Or Serena? And there were now sixteen cases! My God! That can't be right! My theory about this being an epidemic was coming true.

Suddenly I needed a coffee.

I leaned closer to the computer.

"... *The virus has been dubbed the 'Lymphachela Virus'. The symptoms include a high temperature; confusion; and swelling, especially about the arms and legs. Anyone in the Otago region with these symptoms is urged to report straight to the hospital—to Dunedin Emergency Department—rather than seeking help from their GP. A special triage facility has been set up to assess and treat those infected. The Ministry of Health has stopped short of declaring this outbreak an epidemic, but say they will continue to monitor the situation closely. We will keep you up-to-date on any developments...*"

Had I really thought I could rest here and pretend this virus wasn't happening? Did I actually believe that I could simply turn away from my medical calling and ignore all the suffering? If true, I really was that miserable excuse of a human being!

"*In related news, a Paediatric doctor has gone missing following the deaths of two teenagers in his care at Dunedin hospital...*"

I gasped.

My hands trembling, touching my parted lips.

"... *Dr Grant Newman, who was on-call on the Children's Ward on Monday evening, abandoned his post shortly after their deaths, which are believed to be the two fatalities from the Lymphachela Virus. And while the Coroner was quick to rule out death by misadventure, the Communications Officer for the DHB told media that the hospital will launch an Internal Investigation. Colleagues state they are very concerned for Dr Newman's well-being. Mrs Helen Tooms, Clinical Nurse Manager on the Children's Ward, made this statement:"*—Suddenly Tooms' icy inflections blurted from the speaker, sounding sincere, but it was a lie—*"'Grant, we're all worried about you: please get in touch.'"*

"Fuck you!" I yelled at the computer.

"In other news, the IRD has issued a mass—"

Audrey leaned over, grabbed the mouse and stopped the audio feed.

"*Sixteen cases!*" I got to my feet and paced the room, although all the clutter prevented me from striding out. "Three days ago there were, like... four cases. *We have to do something!*"

Audrey's eyes followed me. Hard, inscrutable. "No, not yet. You're not anywhere near ready."

I skirted past a box filled with Homebrand Peach Halves in Syrup. "I need to get back to work." I moved towards the lounge doorway... the hallway... the front door...

"You don't have a job anymore, remember?" she said. "And what precisely do you plan to do, Grant, besides getting yourself killed?"

I stopped. I returned to the lounge and stood in the doorway. "I can't just sit here, spinning my wheels, pretending—"

"*No!*" she said. "It's too dangerous. You're just getting started. You don't know these Seepers or how to fight them."

"So, *tell me!* How do we fight it? *Start* my training."

"When you're ready..."

"Sixteen people have this virus! It's not hanging around waiting for the right time. We need to act *now*."

"I said *no*. Screw this up, you die! I won't... I can't..." Audrey's eyes studied me, trying to read me and my resolve. Beyond the burst capillaries, her eyes were a deep emerald green. In her youth, she must have been a very beautiful woman, before age had played such a cruel hand. "Why do you want to be a Healer, Grant?" she asked.

The question threw me off guard. It had been her who had approached me about my gifting, after all. "I want to help people..."

She laughed. A hard, cynical kind of laugh. "I used to think that, too."

On Friday morning, I had to escape Audrey's house. I couldn't stand to be holed up inside any longer. I needed a walk and some fresh air. I needed thinking space. I kept away from the City Centre and the main thorough-fares, sticking to the Green Belt instead. I didn't want to risk people recognising me.

The sun was shining, which was a welcome change. The

birds chirped in the trees, flitting from one branch to the next.

One woman was walking her dog. I saw no one else.

It was hard to believe that just down the hill, the hospital was being over-run by unseen creatures who'd unleashed a deadly virus. How many White Coats would there be now?

I stopped, inhaling deeply. The air was cool and fresh. It felt good as it poured into my lungs. But my heart was beating too fast, and it had nothing to do with the brisk pace I'd set.

I was kidding no one, least of all myself.

I had a job to do… so why wasn't I doing it? Why wasn't Audrey training me for it like she'd promised?

I risked returning to my flat, if only to pick up a few things: toiletries, some fresh clothes, the charger for my phone, a selection of medications, which I transferred from the bathroom cupboard into my medication bag. That was all. I didn't linger there. I was careful not to be seen. The whole place was one big reminder of my former life, the life I'd now lost. I didn't want to stay there.

Then I began the long trek back to Audrey's house.

On Saturday I got another phone call from Tim. "I just wanted to tell you that that patient of yours—Serena—passed away earlier this morning."

He said it just like that. No softening of the blow. No building up to the bad news. He simply blurted it out, with no regard for how I might feel. I figured I deserved as much.

The shock hit me like a kick in the gut. "How?"

"Lymphachela," he said, and there was this massive subtext in his voice, but he held it all under the surface. "I thought you'd want to know."

"Yes, thank you," I said.

"Where are you, mate?" he asked. He coughed and must have tried to muffle the sound with his hand. "It'd be best all round if you stopped hiding. People are worried." That was it. Message delivered. Tim hung up on me. Maybe Tim was worried; maybe not. I was clearly testing our friendship to its limit. I got the distinct impression there was something else he wasn't telling me.

Yet another bad feeling.

On Sunday afternoon, I read on my phone how the Ministry of Health had employed a military cordon around Dunedin hospital in an effort "to protect the people of Otago". There were numerous comments on the news feed: it was a gross violation of civil liberties; the Council should be sacked for letting this happen on their watch; calls for the Health Minister and the Prime Minister to both resign; someone trying to organise a protest rally outside the hospital; explicit suggestions of what the Director General of Health might wish to insert in various anatomical structures around his person; as well as other colourful, if nonsensical, remarks that reflected the general anger.

"Too little, too late," Audrey said, when I shared the news. She took a sip of red wine. She'd been drinking a lot in recent days. With that bit of wisdom delivered, she retreated to her bedroom.

All of which did little to settle my unease.

twenty

"Don't take too many pills! Not only will you rattle as you lumber down the high street, but your wallet will be poorer. An abundance of pills saved no one's life."

Dr Joseph Heltzmann, page 209, 'The Healing Art'

Monday morning. The usual dread that woke me on Monday mornings was absent. A dread that stemmed from facing a ward round with Dr O'Brien, and accompanying these thoughts a gnawing unease or actual nausea. I didn't miss these feelings. I felt weightless, lying there on the couch, as if anything I might do today could be effortless. A light day.

Soft morning sunlight filtered through the lounge curtains and fell over the coarse fabric of the blankets.

"I... I think I've done something stupid," Audrey said, appearing in the lounge doorway, leaning against the wooden frame, almost as if she needed its structure to support her weight. Her face had withered further, ageing overnight, her hair knotted like a home for strange birds. Her voice wavered with uncertainty. That hard exterior, the one she always portrayed to the world, had somehow been stripped away and underneath there was a vulnerability.

I stared at her. The lightness evaporated. "What did you do?"

"I've taken some pills. I didn't mean to."

I thought of my medicine collection—the essential ones, the prn ones, the ones I kept for emergencies. She wasn't referring to my medicine collection, though. "Pills? *What pills?*"

"Panadol."

Something in her tone alarmed me, but I didn't want to over-react. In my gut, that old feeling of dread eased itself back in. "Do you have a headache?" I asked. "Is that why you took...?"

"No," she said. "What I mean is, I took *a lot* of them."

I jumped to my feet, finding that I wasn't weightless after all. The blankets slid from me, messy folds curving across the couch and the floor. "A lot? How many's *a lot*?"

"All of them. The whole packet."

"*When?* How long ago?"

"Just now."

Fuck!

I raced past the coffee table and stood at her side. "Show me the packet." My mind tried to assess the situation... the potential damage. It was racing from one thought to the next. Supermarkets and pharmacies wouldn't dispense more than twenty-four 500mg tablets of paracetamol at a time, precisely because of the devastating effects of even a moderate overdose. The liver couldn't metabolise them. Too large a dose and it simply failed. What followed was a slow, painful death as a cascade of internal organs shut down, one after another. I had seen the effects first hand in ED once as a trainee intern and never wanted to see that again.

She led me through the clutter, carefully and wordlessly, until we reached her bedroom. On her bed, there were two silver foil strips next to an empty paracetamol box. Both strips were empty.

"You took *both*?" I had to be certain. "And they were both full?"

Audrey nodded. Her face was puffy. Her eyes were red and glistened.

Twenty-four tablets. That was a total dose of 12 grams. More than enough to kill her... if I didn't act quickly. "You need to induce vomiting. *Now*."

"*What?* Stick my fingers down my throat?" There was something else, besides vulnerability, in her voice: fear.

"Yes."

"I c-can't!"

"You must. Do it *now*. If you don't, I will."

I followed her into the bathroom, where she kneeled and leaned over the toilet bowl. She thrust two fingers deep into her mouth. She gagged, but no vomit came. She turned aside; her face twisted in repulsion, strings of spittle hanging from her chin. Again she plunged her fingers into her mouth, this time going deeper. She retched. Her neck distended as a thick, yellowy, porridge-like slop forced its way up through her oesophagus. It wasn't enough, though. There was no sign of the pills in the toilet bowl.

"Keep going."

The next time she used just her index finger, pushing and angling it towards the back of her throat, then gagging, gagging as a whole quantity of half-digested white pills rushed from her mouth and slopped into the toilet water.

She gasped for breath, then spat the foul, acidic taste from her mouth. Beads of sweat laced her brow.

"Good," I said. "Now do it again... please. Just to be sure."

She turned to look up at me, her eyes red and teary. "You're serious?" Her hands grabbed the toilet seat so tight that her knuckles turned white.

"Deadly serious. If you don't, we're going to ED."

She obliged. This time bringing up a series of vomit, bile and probably a fair amount of her stomach lining. There were no more pills, however, which was a reassuring sign.

"Good," I said. "I think that's done it. How're you feeling?"

She dragged herself away from the toilet and leaned against the bath. "Like shit. My throat's raw."

"Do you mind, on this occasion, if I flush the toilet?"

Her face was dry and shrivelled, but the smallest smile curled the side of her mouth. "Please, be my guest."

I leaned over and twisted the lever, watching as Audrey's stomach content gurgled down the drain. "I'll grab you a glass of water." I turned, I was about to leave the bathroom, when I reconsidered. "I'm assuming that you don't have any more paracetamol?"

"You don't have to worry."

"Alright," I said. I believed her. It looked like genuine remorse on her face. I went to the kitchen to get her a glass, then poured some water from one container in the lounge.

When I returned, I found her lying on her bed and I placed the glass of water on the bedside table.

"Thanks." She sat up and took a sip. "Oooh... that's good."

"You're welcome."

"It's quite nice having my own personal doctor."

"I'm no doctor."

"Nonsense," she said, taking another sip. "You're compassionate, like all the best doctors."

twenty one

"Let me state it plainly: the push is the deepening of the capacity, such that it influences another living soul. The capacity cannot be stolen nor will it prosper, except where it has been freely received."

Pim Pusher, page 7, 'The Healing Art'

That afternoon, I took Audrey a mug of coffee. She motioned for me to sit on the chair next to her bed. I did so. "It isn't easy dealing with the reality of Seepers," she said, and I knew she was ready to talk, that things were on her mind.

Her face was old and lined, the skin tough and full of blemishes, yet there was a kindness that sparkled in her eyes.

"I've been a recluse since I first saw them," she continued.

"Why? What happened?"

"His name was Eric Bernard Charles," she said. "I still

remember that. Bernie, for short. He was the victim. A resident at Orabone House. I was working there as a RN. He used to be a well-respected family lawyer in Dunedin before he retired and got too old and frail to live at home anymore. He kept his humour, though. That's why a lot of staff—myself included—had a soft spot for Bernie. Certainly, he didn't deserve what happened."

I pushed my glasses up my nose.

"It was awful. A fiasco, really. A massive stroke. That's the official cause of death, according to the Coroner.

"This was my second attempt at nursing. After I got back on my feet. After my illness. I didn't have the confidence to work in a hospital anymore, but I figured a Rest Home would be easier. Less stressful. Did I get that wrong! I'd been in the job... six weeks, maybe seven. I'd done one of those refresher courses where you practise checking people's blood pressures and programming Baxter pumps. The practical skills. And I was finally feeling that my career was getting back on track when I saw the trail on the carpet leading past Agnes Bonguard's office and up the stairs."

I leaned forward. "Trail?"

"It was slime. A trail of slime. A thick, creamy goo. Trouble was, none of the other staff saw it."

"How'd you know?"

"A couple of girls had walked right through it and hadn't noticed. One had it caked all over her All Birds and was merrily distributing the stuff through into the TV lounge and the dining room. She was quite oblivious. It had a particular smell, too. Really nasty. It wasn't something you'd just ignore, it's just they didn't have the Sensitivity like I did."

"Sensitivity?"

"Yeah. Sensitivity. Getting your eyes. Losing the Complacency. All mean the same thing. It's what happened to *you* when we performed the ritual."

"But how did it happen to you? Had someone done the ritual to you?"

"No," Audrey said. "Not all Healers come via the ritual. In my case, the Sensitivity came out of my post-natal depression. Of course, I didn't realise that at the time. I hadn't discovered 'The Healing Art' yet." She sighed. "I think there are several ways it can happen—based on what I've read (always assuming the Old Bastard has allotted you to that gift). Sorry, that's the way it is. We're all special snowflakes, but we're not all Healers."

"Old Bastard?"

"Sorry, you'll have to excuse my humour. That's my nickname for God. The Good Lord. Anyway, some people, like me, get their eyes when they've hit rock bottom and, in their brokenness, they discover an empathy for the world around them.

"So I followed the trail and it lead to Bernie's room. The slime was more abundant just outside his room, and the smell... well, it was somewhere between burnt rubber and over-boiled cabbage, although even that's not quite accurate.

"The smell was worse again when I pushed open the door to Bernie's room... but I stopped caring when I saw what was inside."

I drew in my breath.

"It was feeding on Bernie's brains. It was leaning over the top of his La-Z-Boy chair and merrily sucking out the contents of his skull through a large proboscis. The trail of slime led all the way to its tail, where a big puddle of the stuff was being continuously secreted. Bernie, meanwhile, was slumped in the chair, his legs twitching and jerking.

"I just stared at this thing, this creature, for the longest time. I'm not sure what I thought. It was monstrous, an oversized slug, or perhaps a little like one of those elephant seals. It's flesh grey and black, all mottled. The thing which passed for a head, hideous! With huge bulbous eyes, a face riddled with lumps and bumps like tumours, the proboscis protruding from the lower portion! And it just kept on feeding as if it didn't care that I, Bernie's nurse, was standing there watching. This struck me as incredibly arrogant... and was probably the thing that spurred me into action. I didn't realise until later that it wasn't accustomed to being seen by human eyes.

"I charged into the room and I pushed this thing off Bernie with all my strength. Only problem was it was attached to Bernie. *It* fell... but it took Bernie and me with it, too. The La-Z-Boy toppled over and our combined weight obliterated its one armrest. We all went sprawling over the floor. Leather ripped. Wood splintered. A glass lampshade smashed, the glass fragments raining down on us.

"The creature leapt up again, snarling at me, finally aware that I could see it. It rose on its tail, threatening, as tall as it was wide. An ugly, obese thing. Bernie's blood was on its snout and dribbled down onto the puckered layers of flab that formed its chin. It expelled a loud, moist breath, spittle and blood flying in the air.

"I got to my feet, my whole body stiff and unyielding. There were pieces of glass stuck in both palms. I was shaking with fear and rage and emotional exhaustion.

"Poor Bernie, meanwhile, remained on the floor, groaning with pain. He appeared to be completely paralysed on the left side of his body. I tried to help him up, or at least drag him to safety, but the creature charged me.

"Well, I went down again. This time, the creature was on top of me. We rolled over the floor, destroying a coffee table, a magazine rack and Bernie's reading glasses. The creature was in a frenzy. Its alien eyes seemed to pin me to the spot. It used its sheer weight to keep me there, to push the air from my lungs and slowly crush me. I fought back, but I didn't have the strength. It understood it was superior. It chuckled—a thick, wet chuckle. Victory dawning in its strange eyes.

"And right next to us, also on the floor, unable to help me or even himself, was Bernie. I don't know if he had any rational thoughts left in his mind or if this thing had robbed them all. For Bernie's sake, I hoped his mind was entirely gone, that he didn't have to make sense of what was happening right before him. I certainly couldn't make sense of it. Even now, I still struggle.

"I freed my bloody left hand, brought it round and planted it in the creature's mishmash face... and I *pushed*, only it wasn't so much a physical push, but something that came from deep inside me. And that's when the power came.

"The creature recoiled as though I'd electrocuted it. That whole face changed. It was hurt and uncertain. These were new experiences for it. The balance of power had suddenly shifted in my favour. It turned out I had fire in my hands.

"I brought up my right hand too, so I had both gripping its face, and I *pushed* again.

"The creature screamed in pain and fear and rage... and that's when the door to Bernie's room swung open and the rest of the staff from Orabone stood there, staring at us, trying to make sense of what they saw. The only problem was they couldn't see the Seeper! What they saw was Bernie and me sprawled on the floor, Bernie's chair toppled, and a lot of wreckage. Well, you can understand how that might look, right?"

I nodded.

"They were like a lynch mob and they practically frog-marched me to Agnes Bonguard's office. This seems to be a reoccurring theme in my life. Agnes was the Matron and a very stern woman. When she heard what the other staff told her, she got mad. This was the worst case of Elder Abuse that she'd ever heard of. This was a police matter and, if she had her way, I'd get prison time for what I'd done.

"I tried to explain that I needed to get back to Bernie's room, but she forbid it. 'You'll stay right there until the police arrive, young lady' she said, and became my self-appointed guard to make sure that's exactly what I did. Bernie died a short time after that (This was according to the Coroner's Report). The creature finished its meal in peace, unchallenged. I assumed, having eaten its full, that it would slink back into whatever pit of hell it had come from, but I was wrong. These creatures mostly work alone and, it turns out, they take interruptions very personally.

"The police took me down to the Central Police Station on Great King Street for questioning. Actually, I think it was more for my protection. I knew I couldn't say anything about the creature, and I had a hard time trying to explain the circumstances. I made up some story about Bernie being a big man, and how I was helping him up from the chair when he must have had a stroke. How he'd slumped down, and I'd tried my best to prevent him from dropping to the floor, but couldn't. How we'd both fallen hard. How furniture had broken in the process. I don't think they believed me, but since the evidence against me was circumstantial at best, they didn't press any charges. What they did was lodge a formal complaint against me with the Nursing Council. I knew when they said that that I'd never work as a nurse again, and I was right about that much. They removed me from the register following a tribunal, which I didn't even bother to attend.

"It was late by the time I'd finished with the police, so they agreed to drop me off outside my front door (only this was my Mum's house then and I was staying there temporarily, because that's what you do when your marriage fails, right?).

"When I turned the key, I knew something was wrong. Yes, it was late, but the house was too quiet. Some curtains were still open. There was an absence of cooking smells. And some other things were off too, little things, but collectively they became larger than the sum of their parts. Suddenly, I didn't care if I woke Mum up. I raced around the house, turning on all the lights, calling out, '*Mum! Mum!*'

"I found Mum slumped against one cupboard in the laundry. She was cold and her limbs were rigid. I couldn't even reposition her to make her look more comfortable. She'd been dead for at least a couple of hours. The right side of her face was all drooped, the same as Bernie's had been. Saliva had pooled on that side of her mouth and slowly bubbled and slid down her chin.

"I *knew* who had killed her. I don't know how it found out where we lived, but it did. That information was on my file. I'd hurt it... and it had hurt me right back. Mum was..." Audrey sighed, but didn't finish her sentence.

I was familiar with the pain of losing a mother. "I'm very sorry."

"After that, I stayed in the house, mostly. I had the Sensitivity, but God I didn't want it! I saw Seepers everywhere. In all shapes and sizes. They dribbled and snarled as they made their way up the escalators at the Meridian Mall... or they wore their human masks and mingled among the crowds at the Farmer's Market down by the Railway Station... or they were an oppressive force that hung over the city, much worse than any Scotch Mist. It's worse at night. It's like they know we're more vulnerable then. But the very worst place, the place I never wanted to set foot inside again, was the hospital. The place was crawling with them. Wall-to-wall horrors. Inflicting their victims with pain and misery; with all manner of sicknesses. Literally killing us.

"It was too much, so I stayed in Mum's house. Only with Mum being dead, it became *my* house. I found there was very little reason to venture outside if you don't want to. You can even order your groceries, and most of the things you need, online. In fact, I wouldn't have left at all if David hadn't fallen ill."

Peter Layton had said that David's mother wasn't 'involved' anymore. "*How* did you hear?"

She raised her eyes heavenward. "The Old Bastard told me, of course. We talk every day, Him and me."

"I see." I didn't. I was an atheist.

"Of course, He's gone all silent on me now. Sometimes, most times even, He's not a great one for chatting."

"You can always talk to me," I said. "I may not be omnipresent, but I'll gladly listen."

"Thanks," she said. "And, of course, you're welcome to stay as long as you like. What I'm trying to say, Grant, is that I'm hardly the best role model. None of this Seeper shit is straightforward and it's taken me years to realise just how much I'm *not* dealing with it all. You've only just got your eyes. I reckon you need to go easy on yourself."

I nodded, wondering if Audrey would ever train me in the Healing Art.

A little later that afternoon, my iPhone rang, jolting me from my thoughts. I no longer kept it in my pocket, but had left it on the floor next to the couch.

It was Chong ringing.

"Chong, hi..." I answered. "How are you?" I immediately had a bad feeling. A spike of dread.

"Not so good."

The bad feeling deepened, darkened. I shifted my weight from one foot to the other. I took a breath. I didn't want to ask the next question, but Chong had made it socially awkward not to. "What's up?"

"I thought you might like to know that Tim has come down with Lymphachela."

A sudden weight squeezed my chest. I couldn't breathe. I

couldn't speak. What I wanted to do was groan, but even that was impossible. Of course, as health professionals, we were always going to be at risk of contracting infections. Our work was innately risky, but somehow it hadn't occurred to me that this virus would strike so close to home. Without realising it, I'd constructed an artificial barrier between the patient and the professional.

Chong must have interpreted my long silence as indifference, for he said, "The Grant I *used* to know would have cared, at least. Now I'm not so sure."

"*What—?*" I managed.

"You heard me."

"I don't know what to say, Chong. I'm sorry..."

Chong, Tim and I had met during O-week and been tight as friends ever since. The shared experience of Med School created a unique bond, but ours—and particularly mine and Chong's—went much deeper. The three of us had been flatmates for a time until Chong discovered black mould in his room and his parents insisted he move back home. We had hung out in student bars together, philosophised together, laughed and cried together. It was Chong who'd helped me pick up the pieces in the years after I lost my mother and probably saved me a small fortune in counselling.

"I always assumed you'd be here, fighting *with* us, if ever something like this came along. We trained together. We knew this was a possibility, right?"

"Yes, but—"

"I never imagined you'd be so quick to turn your back on your old friends..."

"*That's not true!*"

"... You're probably with that Healer now, aren't you? Tim said you weren't staying at your flat. Are you sleeping with her? *Is that it?*"

"*No!*"

"Anyway, the thing that really hurts is that you've been working with this woman, this *Healer*, for a while and you didn't say a word. When I told you about that patient with breast cancer—Fiona Peters—you already knew!"

"Not the details."

"*You bastard!*" In all the years I'd known Chong, I don't think I'd ever heard him swear before. "Well, I told you about Tim, and that was the purpose of my call."

"Can you tell him—"

"No, Grant," Chong interrupted. "You've burnt those bridges with me. If you want to give Tim a message, do it yourself. I suggest you hurry, though. He's pretty sick and I'm not sure if he's going to pull through."

Having dropped that bombshell, Chong hung up on me. I stood there, still holding the phone to my ear. My body was shaking. I felt as though the ground beneath me was opening up and at any moment I would start falling into some bottomless chasm.

Audrey was standing in the lounge doorway. I'm not sure how long she'd been there, or if she'd overheard my conversation with Chong. "I need to go back to the hospital," I said. "My colleagues, my *friends*, are sick with Lymphachela." It wasn't just Tim, of course. There was Jenny too.

"If you go, you'll get it too," Audrey said. "And given what you are, I can guarantee you that the White Coats will make sure you suffer a great deal."

"I can't just sit around here and do nothing. I have skills and they're in great need."

Audrey came into the lounge and approached me. "You *also* have abilities, which are far greater than any of your medical skills, and which we need time to develop."

"You say that, but what are we actually doing to develop my abilities? What's the plan? Right now it seems like all we've been doing is hiding away."

"Sometimes that's the best option." There was a strange smile on her face, an indication, perhaps, that she was half-joking and half-serious.

"No, it isn't," I said.

I understood Audrey was grieving for her son, but we had no more time to delay. Other people were going to die if we didn't take action. Yet for all the pleading I'd done, Audrey seemed unable or unwilling to follow-through with her promise and train me in this, The Healing Art. It was as if she'd withdrawn from the world, to abscond from all her responsibilities, and somehow I had been trapped here with her.

I looked around the cluttered lounge, upon box after box of non-perishables, the evidence of resourcefulness, even if it were buried under a mountain of chaos. I'd seen the way Audrey fought the Seepers in the hospital—she was a fighter, a survivor, and yet it was as if the grief and fear had paralysed her.

There had to be some way to mobilise her into action once more...

I looked across at the bookshelf, and an idea came to me. I edged around the debris, selected the second shelf down, and slid a copy of 'The Healing Art' out. I flicked through the pages, looking for the chapter I was thinking of. Then, finding the right page, I offered it to Audrey. "Here," I said. "What about this? Does this advocate hiding away and doing nothing?"

Audrey took the book and looked at down the open page.

I quoted what I could remember: "'*When the Long Queen breathes her last breath... after two world wars and a brief prosperity...*'"

"'*Once the winter*'," Audrey corrected.

"Sure... anyway, it predicts a 'Great Scourge', right?"

"Yes."

"And you've mentioned the Scourge a couple of times."

"This infection *could* be the Scourge. It's a possibility, at least. But we need to be cautious with prophecy; it's a tricky creature."

"It couldn't be *more* specific. It's pinning it to the Twenty-First Century. It even talks about the 'Outer Islands'. That's got to be Aotearoa New Zealand..."

"You're reading into it what you want to read. Twisting the meaning."

"I don't think so," I said, trying to keep the frustration out of my voice. "I think you'd already reached the same conclusion as me, but now..." I stopped myself before I said too much. What exactly was holding Audrey back? Fear? Perhaps grief? Either way, I doubted pointing out her flaws was going to change her mind. I needed her, needed her buy-in. "What about the next part?" I said, then quoted, "'*Woe to the world if this is let loose*'. To me, that's saying we have to fight this Scourge. We have to fight the White Coats."

"Or maybe it's saying it's time to despair."

"Is that what we're doing? Despairing?"

"No... my point is, our modern sensibilities don't really know what 'woe' in this context looks or feels like. Maybe we're about to get a hard lesson? Perhaps you and I need to lay down our weapons and surrender to the inevitable."

I pulled the book back, leafed through its pages some more, finding another passage that I hoped would sway Audrey. "Alright," I said, finding what I was looking for. "Try this: '*The Student will be a sharp implement, a sword wet with blood'*. You quoted this at me, when you first came to me in the Children's Ward. This is talking about war. If I am the Student, then *teach* me."

Audrey nodded, smiling a sad smile. "'*The Student will surpass the Mentor, for he is born not of fury, but of compassion.*'" She lowered her head, pausing, as if coming to a difficult decision. "Very well. We'll start training tonight. Once it's dark. Think of it as your apprenticeship. We'll go'n hunt some Seepers. And this time you're actually going to do the healing, okay? And when you're up to speed, then we'll go to the hospital and face the White Coats."

"And how long will this training take?"

"That depends on *you*," Audrey said. "But you can speed up your learning by studying 'The Healing Art' further during the day. In particular, read Pim Pusher and Trudy, the Surgeon of Truth. It talks about the *push*. The *push* is the essence of a Healer's power. A Healer doesn't just empathise with those they heal, they are outraged by the existence of disease and the widespread tolerance of its intrusion. The *push* flows from that outrage. While a textbook can't teach you how to *push*, it'll explain the theory."

"I've felt it already," I said. "The *push*. In ICU the other night."

"Great. You should learn quickly then."

"Thank you."

"Don't thank me," she replied. "We may both come to regret this decision."

twenty two

"When coldness reaches a man's soul, silencing even the chambers of his heart, life and death are allotted by touch."

Hyu , page 11, 'The Healing Art'

It was just after 2am on Tuesday morning when we left Audrey's house and headed down the hill into the City Centre.

A sea mist cloaked the place, shrouding the tops of the taller buildings, giving a peculiar, almost ethereal quality to the high-pressure sodium lights and to the darkness itself.

It was bitterly cold. The cold seemed to gnaw at my bones, seeking to feed upon the marrow within. Audrey wore a large black trench coat. I had borrowed a puffer jacket which, while a little on the small side, kept my core warm. I rubbed my palms together. Breath billowed from my nose and mouth, condensing as it met with single digit temperatures.

People ambled along the surrounding pavements, mostly in groups. Short ones, tall ones. All shapes; all sizes. A surprising number of people, given the late hour and the wintery conditions. Most were wrapped in heavy coats or puffed up with multiple layers. Zips were fastened high. There were hats and gloves and scarfs. A smaller number, mostly students, were under-dressed, wearing skimpy dresses or t-shirts with bare arms. Couldn't they feel the cold? Were they so drunk or high that they were impervious to it? They stumbled from pub to pub, from eatery to eatery, laughing, carefree, existing in a world that I had once inhabited, but which now seemed entirely foreign to me. The smell of Kababs, of Asian Cuisine, of something deep fat fried jarred my stomach with unexpected hunger. Music throbbed in the distance; a DJ in a nearby club. The occasional car idled by, its headlights too bright, its exhaust fumes adding to the toxic cocktail already created by cigarettes, Vapes and the skunky, over-ripe smell of weed. Someone jeered. Some couple in their fifties were having a domestic which all nearby pedestrians could hear, if they cared to. Most people didn't seem to care, however, moving to a beat, a rhythm, something sub-audible which the night itself possessed.

There were Seepers out and about too, probably many

more than I realised. Some took human form and were far harder to spot, but there were some that were so outrageously different that I had to remind myself not to stare. One, in particular, had six long tentacles for arms and seemed to slither along the pavement. Another was at least eight feet tall and had impossibly long eyes that were so elongated that they appeared to drip like something out of a Dali painting. Another Seeper resembled the slug/elephant seal-like creature that Audrey had described from her Rest Home days. It was intent on chasing some guy up London Street. The guy puffed and panted with each step, even as he sucked on a cigarette.

The entire array of people and creatures resembled a freak show.

"There," said Audrey, stopping on the pavement where the shadows between street lights were deepest. "Do you see it?"

I suddenly felt nervous.

I followed her gaze to a doorway on the far side of George Street, just beyond the pedestrian area. A young girl was sprawled over the doorstep, looking rather worse for wear, and there was a man stood over her. I wasn't sure if the man was helping her or the cause of her problems.

"Don't stare."

"But didn't you—"

"How many people do you see?"

What an odd question! And I was meant to answer this

without staring? "Two," I said, trying not to frown.

"Technically," said Audrey, "There's just the girl... follow me... and be ready."

So, the man must be a Seeper, but how could she tell at this distance?

"Leave the talking to me," Audrey said. "And look only at the girl. This time we hit the Seeper directly. I'll tell you when it's time to *push*. Got it?" She crossed George Street and walked swiftly towards the doorway, hugging the side of the pavement closest to the shopfronts.

I followed.

The girl stank of booze; it was matted into her hair and it stained her clothes. She was so inebriated, in fact, that after vomiting she had passed out in the doorway of Capers Cafe. The vomit pooled over the step and had soaked into her dress. Not that it was much of a dress, hugging her skinny torso, leaving her arms and legs exposed, shivery and goose bumped. The dress was pretty much all she wore, apart from her underwear, which was on full display. The lacy white bra protruding from the top end and matching, skimpy panties were visible from the bottom, where the dress had ridden up. The girl was a pitiful sight. Her lips were a darkening blue. Her eyes flickered beneath heavily made-up eyelids.

Audrey bent down and prodded her. "Hey! I need you to open your eyes."

The girl murmured like one troubled by nightmares, but didn't open her eyes.

I removed my puffer jacket, draping it over the girl, hoping it would raise her core temperature a little.

I looked from the girl to the creature standing over her. I couldn't help myself. Its face was concealed in shadows. It was dressed in a long trench coat, not dissimilar to Audrey's, and yet it seemed to emanate the cold.

Audrey was still leaning over the girl, but she nudged me —hard—in the leg. "Eyes on *her*."

I tried my best to focus on the girl, but my eyes kept wandering back to the creature. I was curious: What disease process was this creature?

The Seeper turned from the girl to me. It shifted slightly, its face moving out of the shadows. Its eyes were fierce. Ice cold. Its hair was white and spiked. "You see me, don't you?" it asked, a look of perplexity creasing its brow.

Audrey scrambled to her feet and held a defensive posture a couple of steps back.

"Well, yeah," I said. "I see you alright... I'm just wondering what you're going to do to help your girlfriend here."

"Don't speak to it," Audrey said.

The creature smiled. "I've put ice in her veins. And I will wisp away her heat, her energy and, thereafter, her very soul."

"She's probably hypothermic, you know... We'll take her now, and get her to the hospital."

"*The hospital!*" it laughed. "The hospital is Al Nihil's. As for her, she's *mine*."

"I don't think so."

"I don't think we've been properly introduced," the Seeper said, its smile widening. "I have several names, but you can call me Hypothermia."

Suddenly I could see beyond the human guise. Beneath this human face there lurked a shadow... a face behind the face... like a badly exposed X-ray where the edges had blurred. In fact, it reminded me of—

"*Now!*" Audrey yelled.

I lunged forward, intending to contact the creature's torso and *push*, but I must have telegraphed my move. Its icy hands easily flicked me aside. I stumbled away and down and was able to right myself just before hitting the pavement.

"This was *your* mistake!" Audrey told the Seeper, while pointing at the girl. Her voice seemed to carry great strength, great weight. "We'll take her now."

"I don't think so," said Hypothermia.

Audrey took one step forward. Her shoes slapping the pavement. "Really? You think you've got the upper hand? Well, how do you explain that we can both see you?"

This puzzled the Seeper. Its smile faded. It was much taller than Audrey, but suddenly it didn't look so imposing. "What is this girl to you, anyway?" The question was strained, the implication unpalatable.

"Nothing," said Audrey. "She's just a girl. Young, foolish, under-dressed. But we're not going to let you take her." I'd never heard Audrey speak at length with a Seeper; usually she went straight for the kill.

"Will you fight me for her?"

"If we must."

The Seeper looked left and right along George Street, perhaps considering if this was a suitable place to engage in battle. The black mass of Knox Church loomed over us. The mist swirled just above the luminance of the nearest street lights, extending twisted fingers in our direction. The Seeper studied Audrey, looking her up and down. A waver of fear moved deep within its eyes.

But Audrey had done enough talking. She jumped forward in a pre-emptive strike. It proved much more effective than mine. She placed both her hands on the Seeper's face, firmly clenching its cheeks.

Hypothermia howled. It toppled back into the doorway and back into the shadows.

Audrey toppled forward, still clinging to the Seeper's face. Was it my imagination or was the skin of Hypothermia's face, where Audrey had placed her hands, peeling? Was that deeper, more primal face visible as the outer skin melted away?

I didn't know how best to help Audrey. My powers and my knowledge of fighting paled compared to hers.

Audrey and Hypothermia continued to wrestle in the doorway. Audrey huffed and panted, while Hypothermia roared with pain.

Suddenly, Hypothermia swung its arm around, sending Audrey flying. She spilled out onto the hard, wet pavement, landing in an ungainly heap of arms and legs. The tumble seemed to give her pause.

Wasting no time, the Seeper leapt forward and stood over Audrey, large and imposing, its fear gone, the sodium lights revealing a demented look on its face. It would unleash its worst. There was no mercy on that face, only rage and madness.

So, I rushed forward, instinct taking over. I didn't exactly know what I was doing, only that I had to *push*.

Hypothermia anticipated my move. It shot out a hand, the palm open, and pressed it deep into my chest.

This arrested all my momentum. It felt like running into a solid stone wall. The Seeper lifted me a few inches from the ground, and my legs dangled in free space. The coldness spreading from my sternum. A chill so deep that I was certain nothing living could withstand it. It felt like the blood in my vessels and in my heart itself were freezing into red ice. Through the thin cotton of my t-shirt, the chill ran deeper and deeper, spreading wider, causing my entire body to give a convulsive shudder. The end was drawing in on me, a mere seconds away. The cold wrapped around my heart like an icy fist; it sliced through my puny flesh with its absolute indifference. I couldn't stop shivering. My teeth were chattering loudly. I tried to stop myself, but my brain wasn't functioning properly. Bits of me were shutting down little by little. My brain was slowing to a feeble crawl. I even felt myself...

(Dying)

Yes, dying. And I looked up into the Seeper's merciless pupils and they glared back at me: more powerful, filled with great malevolence.

And that might have been my last image...

Except Audrey moved in the periphery of my vision.

She swept the creature's legs from underneath it and it came crashing down onto the pavement.

With Hypothermia's hand removed, the relief was instant. First my chest, and then my whole body, thawed. I lay on my back upon the pavement, panting, watching as my breath billowed up into the damp night. I might have been in pain, but for now, my nerve endings had been temporarily blocked in a blanket of numbness.

Audrey leaned over me. "You okay?" I'd barely registered her concern, let alone articulated a response, when she disappeared again.

The screams and yells from Hypothermia echoed through me and all along this section of George Street, but no one but Audrey and I heard them. If anyone noticed the movement, they did not come to investigate. It was just another scuffle; no more, no less. Eventually, Audrey silenced the Seeper. The final screams were God-awful, and I was glad when it was all over.

I lay there, only vaguely aware of my surroundings: aware

of the small bits of gravel that had embedded themselves into the back of my legs and my arms and the small of my back where my t-shirt had ridden up; aware that a little to my left lay the girl who'd passed out in a pool of her own vomit and wondering if she was still alive; aware of the girl's handbag on the pavement, compact, glittery purple, with its strap broken on the one side.

Audrey stood over me again. "Are you okay?" she repeated.

"Yes," I croaked, "Just c-cold."

Audrey smiled, then looked over at the girl. "Not as cold as her."

I turned my head slowly, carefully. Presumably, everything the creature had done to me was minor compared to the sustained attack it had lorded over this girl. Yet incredibly, she was stirring, rousing from her unconsciousness.

"Do you have your phone on you?" Audrey asked.

"Yeah."

"We need to ring an ambulance. Get her to the hospital."

It was only two blocks to the hospital, but there was no way we could carry her. I wasn't exactly feeling athletic. In fact, I wasn't even sure my fingers possessed enough feeling to operate the touch screen.

"Is the hospital safe? What about Al Nihil? Maybe we shouldn't send her there?"

"Sorry, no choice. If she stays here, she'll die."

I pulled my iPhone from my trouser pocket, but it slipped from my grip and clattered to the floor. "*Damn it!*"

Audrey took the phone instead. She dialled 111 and asked for an ambulance.

I got to my feet slowly, my legs very shaky. I looked down at the dead Seeper. This one hadn't faded like the others. It looked like a man, albeit one with dissolved flesh where its face once was. It had a skull. A tongue. Teeth. Everything. And yet it was a Seeper. Most people, it seemed, couldn't see it at all. Most people, when they walked this section of pavement, would walk right through it, oblivious.

"Why did you talk so much with this Seeper?" I asked Audrey. "Usually, you just kill them."

"This one was strong," she said. "I needed to distract it."

Audrey unbuttoned and removed her own coat. I wondered what she was doing, but my brain was too cold to form or articulate a question. She took the puffer jacket I'd laid across the girl and swapped it with her own coat. Then she rolled the girl into the Recovery Position.

"Here, put this back on," she said, handing the puffer jacket back to me. "You're hypothermic too."

We waited until we could hear the whoop of an approaching siren, then we slipped away into the darkness, leaving the girl in the doorway covered in Audrey's trench coat.

twenty three

"You know how to read the appearance of the sky, but you cannot interpret the signs of the times."
Yeshua of Nazareth, page 81, 'The Healing Art'

It took me a few days to get over my skirmish with Hypothermia. It was one thing to see these creatures, but another entirely to engage them. Most of them, from my experience and from what I've since read, possessed superhuman strength. My chest was painful for days. Every time I expanded my ribcage, it reminded me of the encounter. The chill was the worst part, however. A chill so deep that it seemed to permeate through the marrow of my bones. It was an emotional chill, a psychological chill even, and I couldn't shake it. I thought a lot about my mother's death, and how it might have been avoided if I'd known about Seepers back then. I took several long, hot showers (using too much water for Audrey's liking) but I still couldn't get completely warm.

By Thursday, I was eager to get back into my training. I thought about the things Chong had said. I hated the thought that anyone, especially Chong, was disappointed in me. And, of course, there was Tim. I couldn't sit around Audrey's house while, less than a kilometre down the road, my friend was dying, and I held the potential to heal him.

I approached Audrey. "We need to get to the hospital before it's too late."

"I understand you're impatience," she said. "But you're still not ready. You're blocked. I can't see what the blockage is, but it's severely limiting the flow of your power."

"I'm never going to be ready staying here."

"Baby steps, Grant. You're no good to anyone if you end up dead."

"What have you got in mind, then?"

Audrey sighed. She took a seat on the couch next to me. "We go to South Dunedin. That'll be our second training mission. The people there are poor in spirit. They'll be easier to heal."

"Poor in spirit?"

"It's a biblical phrase," Audrey said. "Meaning: they don't have a hell of a lot and, generally speaking, they don't take their health for granted. In my experience, when people are poor in spirit, they're more open to the possibility of healing."

"But there are people dying in the hospital."

"Yes, I know, but we are not ready to take on the White Coats just yet."

"*What?* So we wait until they've claimed the whole hospital? Then what? We let them take the entire city? They're only going to grow in strength, surely?"

"If this *is* the Scourge, we might already be too late."

"All the more reason to strike now. We've waited long enough, cowering in the shadows."

"It's guerrilla warfare."

"Really? Well, it doesn't sit right with me, not when people I know are dying."

Audrey gestured towards my chest. "How's the injury?"

"It's fine."

"No more hot showers and wasting all my water?"

"Deal."

From the corner of Frederick Street and Great King Street, as we rounded the corner, I saw the cordon. There were guys wearing combat fatigues and holding rifles guarding the main entrance to the hospital. An all-terrain vehicle had been hastily angle-parked, half on the pavement, half on the road.

I froze. Audrey nearly ran into the back of me.

Had things really got this bad?

We crossed the road, taking a route further north along Great King Street, using the trees for cover, effectively circling the hospital but keeping at least a one block distance. Finally, we came to Hanover Street and the fire exit on the south side of the hospital. There was no military presence here. Audrey immediately began prying the door with a flathead screwdriver. I didn't see exactly what she did, but within a few seconds, the door popped open. Simple as that. No alarms blaring. An open door. I wondered what else Audrey hadn't told me about her past. How had she acquired life skills such as these? What sort of nurse had she been?

"Well?" she asked. "Are you coming?" And she slipped inside the building.

I surveyed the surrounding street: the taller buildings still ensnared by the low-lying sea mist and still no sign of the army guys.

I stepped inside.

We were at the bottom of a concrete stairwell. I pulled the emergency exit door closed behind us, hearing it click into place.

The darkness was total.

"Where to?" I asked.

"Anywhere, but the Children's Ward and ICU," she replied. "But first we wait. It takes a little while to get your night vision."

My heart was heavy in my chest. My breathing too. It truly felt like we were committing a crime—breaking and entering, no less—even if our intentions were noble. The hospital was a public building, but this was well outside the areas accessible to the public.

"This way," Audrey said at last, and climbed the steps.

I saw her outline, no more. I followed.

Further up the stairwell, I could see the glow of ambient light marking the sharp corners of the structure we were climbing.

I had to take two steps at a time in order to keep up with Audrey. Soon I felt the pull on my lungs and the pain in my ribs. I wasn't as fit as I used to be. Perhaps not as fit as Audrey, even though she was at least twenty years my senior. During my brief medical career, I'd given little priority to maintaining or improving my fitness. I was simply too busy. How ironic that I had supposed to instruct my patients on matters of health when I didn't actively guard my own. What was the saying? 'Physician Heal Thyself'.

As we climbed, the light improved, until it became a nice, even ambience, the type used throughout most of the areas of the hospital, those which got little foot traffic.

Still, we climbed. Audrey steamed ahead. There was no stopping her, it seemed. I laboured to keep up. Finally, we came to what must have been the seventh or eighth floor. I had lost count. The whole climb, spiralling round and round, was very disorientating, and there were no indications of level on the doors. I guessed few people used these stairs when the lifts were so much more convenient and quicker.

Audrey pushed open the door... then closed it again promptly. A whiff of that oily smell spilled into the stairwell. Audrey turned and looked back at me. "This is a Quarantine Area," she said. "Let's go back."

Might Tim be on this floor? Or Jenny? "Can we... Can we go in?"

"*Absolutely not!* You want to get us both killed?"

"But there's two of us," I said, knowing my argument was weak at best, ignoring the uneasy feeling that welled inside my stomach.

"No. Turn back."

"Where are we going?" I asked.

"I don't know," said Audrey. "We're looking for trouble, but not *too much* trouble."

We descended a few flights of steps, emerging at what I think was the fifth or sixth floor. The walls here appeared to bend inwards. The air felt hard to breathe, thick with toxins, with that oily odour, as if the White Coats had spread their virus throughout the entire hospital and Audrey and I were inhaling it.

We wandered the corridors.

The Snotty-nosed boy appeared around the next corner,

skin, bone, drooped shoulders and wearing only grey rags. This was as we neared the Patient Lifts.

Audrey and I stopped.

"You ought to leave now," he said, his tone resigned and filled with melancholy. "He knows you're here and he'll rip you apart if he catches you."

"Are you trying to scare us?" Audrey asked. I noticed she stepped in front of me, a protective gesture.

"No," said the boy. "I'm trying to help you."

"Why would you help us?"

"I'm sick of being used," said the boy. "He's got a little too powerful and suddenly he's forgotten about those who helped him get where he is today."

"Al Nihil?" Audrey asked.

The boy smiled, but there was no happiness in the smile. "Al Nihil, White Coats, whatever... I wouldn't say that name too loud. You might summon them. They've got ears and eyes everywhere. I suggest we all leave before it's too late." He raised his hand, wiping the flow of snot that ran down from his nose.

Audrey glanced back at me. "For once, I agree with a Seeper."

"*Seeper?*" asked the boy, then coughed. "Who're you calling a Seeper?" He pulled a face of mock horror. A Seeper with a sense of humour.

"That's what you are," Audrey said.

"Suit yourself," said the boy. He shrugged, turned around,

and walked away along an adjacent corridor.

Audrey moved forward as if to pursue the Snotty-nosed boy, but I grabbed her wrist. "Leave him."

It surprised me Audrey didn't offer too much protest. "We need to watch one another's backs," she said finally. "For all we know, this is all a play by the White Coats."

"Agreed."

We came to the entrance of one ward. This was the fifth floor. 5A. It was unclear, however, if this was a Quarantine Ward or not. The Lymphachela Virus may have proliferated the whole hospital by now. There may not be any clean wards; just as there may not be 'trouble, but not too much trouble'.

We entered. Was some nasty surprise waiting inside? The lights were flickering on and off, reminding me of the corridor to the Morgue in my nightmare. Once again, I got that peculiar feeling that the walls weren't quite solid, that they could and would warp, reality itself far from absolute.

Up ahead, the distinctive sound of human suffering—moans; groans; pleas; cries bereft of hope; the occasional scream echoing through the ward, unanswered. Where had all the staff gone? They must have succumbed to this virus or else fled their posts.

We progressed along the corridor towards the Nurse's Station. Audrey slowed, as did I. If this was a ward full of the Lymphachela sick, we might encounter several White Coats too? Was it true what the Snotty-nosed boy had said? Did the White Coats already know we were here?

Suddenly, my idea of coming to the hospital didn't seem so smart. I wasn't ready. I knew it. It had taken me years to train to become a doctor, so why did I imagine that becoming a Healer would happen in a few short days? Suddenly, I was scared and way, way out of my depth.

"*Aaahhhhh....*"

The noise had come from behind the Nurse's Station.

Slowly, carefully, I peered over the top. The dread building inside me.

Someone was curled up on the floor. They wore the tattered remains of a shirt, their arms, their legs, badly swollen with Lymphachela. The face was red and puffy and they fought for breath. I almost didn't recognise them.

"*Aaahhh....*"

Looking closer, looking beyond the swelling and the suffering, it was Chong! My God, *it was Chong!* He'd caught the virus like Tim and here he was, dying on the floor. He didn't even have a bed to lie on and be comfortable in his final hours. "*Chong!*" I rushed around to be at his side.

"Careful!" warned Audrey. She was checking up and down the corridor, looking for signs of imminent danger.

I leaned over Chong. "Can you hear me, Chong?"

Chong's eyes fluttered open. His pupils found mine, and I saw recognition there, albeit temporarily. His mouth opened, but his lips were dry and cracked and the only sound was a croak.

"Don't speak," I said. "We're here to help you."

"No, we're not," said Audrey. She was leaning against the Nurse's Station. "This is far too risky."

I stared at Audrey. "I can't leave him. I *won't* leave him."

Chong's unusually fat hand grabbed my wrist. Was he trying to tell me something? With his other hand, he pointed towards the back of the Nurse's Station. Behind the Nurse's Station was... the Treatment Room. Was there something in the Treatment Room?

Chong's eyes closed and his grip wilted.

I stood. Together, Audrey and I made our way towards the Treatment Room, which was accessible from the corridor.

"We check this room," Audrey said. "And then we get out of here. Seriously, I'm getting some really bad vibes."

I nodded. I was getting bad vibes too. Major ones. My stomach knotted with fear. However, I had no intention of leaving Chong in such a sorry state, but I'd cross that bridge when the time came.

I pushed open the door to the Treatment Room. In the centre of the room was an Examination Table. Dr O'Brien was lying upon it, clearly with advanced symptoms of the Lymphachela Virus. His shirt had been ripped open, buttons popped, his tie missing. Pale, oedematous flesh peaked out.

There was another body on the floor, too, and I recognised him despite the inflictions: it was Tim.

I rushed inside. I went to Tim first. "*Tim! Tim!*" I shook him by the shoulder. His clothes, always the highest in fashion, had become soiled and dishevelled. "Can you hear me?"

Tim opened his eyes. His pupils were dilated. "There are terrible monsters," Tim said, whispering. "I've seen their teeth."

I brushed my palm across Tim's brow. He was feverish and sweaty, yes, but I believed his words and I shuddered.

I checked his pulse and his respiratory rate: both were too fast for my liking. Tim, of course, had got ill before Chong.

"*No*," groaned O'Brien from the table. "Not the darkness again!"

I rose to my feet and went to O'Brien's side. "Dr O'Brien. It's Grant. Can you hear me?"

O'Brien's brow creased. His neck was swollen, the flesh there mottled. He squinted, looking odd without his glasses. "Are you an angel or a devil?"

"Neither."

"Then you shouldn't be in my house," O'Brien said, and chuckled. There was something terrifying about his delirium.

Audrey went to Tim's side, leaning over him. "His disease

is advanced," she said. "I can *push*, but I'm not sure I should. I don't like this. We need to get out of here."

She *pushed* anyway… and immediately Tim's face brightened. His eyes shone with life, the viral load lessened. And perhaps it was my imagination, but was the oedema reducing before my eyes?

Still, a memory came:

The door to Mum's room was slightly ajar. I lingered just outside, unsure. It was dark inside. She'd got the curtains drawn. I pushed the door—just a little. I leaned in. I strained to see my mother in the gloom…

The White Coats converged on Audrey from three directions; one from the corridor, pushing; two rising up from their hiding place behind the Examination Table, pulling her. All of them in human guise. I tried to warn her, to speak up, but it was too late.

Instead, all the air in my lungs escaped.

The three wrestled with Audrey, and she fought back. She freed one of her arms and tried to *push*.

I wanted to help, I really did, but the muscle tone in my legs was gone.

One of the White Coats turned and considered me. "Two Healers together," it snarled. "Isn't that nice?"

The second White Coat held Audrey in a tight grip, its arms locked around her waist and both arms. The more Audrey struggled, the more painful the grip became.

"*Let him go!*" Audrey cried, her face taut with pain. "It's me you want."

"Oh, how noble!" said the third White Coat. "Did you think this was a negotiation? You have no voice here. If we desire to kill you both, or etch lines of suffering through your flesh, so it shall be. This is *our* stronghold."

Audrey broke free from the grip. She spun around and grabbed the second White Coat's face. She scratched furiously... and, for an instant, its face slipped. What lay beneath that human mask was deep, dark and full of alien intent. It was all the suffering I'd witnessed as a doctor over the years, amalgamated into one. The creature recoiled, snarling and hissing, teeth grinding... and then its two companions wrestled Audrey back.

Audrey lashed out at the third White Coat, landing a kick to its thigh and making it stumble backwards.

In retaliation, the first White Coat pushed Audrey so hard that she was driven across the treatment room and crashed into the wall. She hit the wall with such force that I swore I heard bones break.

She didn't get up. She looked unconscious... or dead.

I rushed towards Audrey, but the second White Coat leapt virtually the length of the room and blocked my path. It pushed me back with its long fingers—a small push, comparatively. I skidded back into the examination table, knocking it over, causing O'Brien to fall from it and me to land on top of him.

"Behold, this is what happens to those who oppose us," the creature said, half the skin on its face still hanging loose. The horror underneath was visible. A head-sized tumour rich with blood vessels. Pin-point eyes, sparkling with intent, but otherwise lost in a sea of black.

The other two White Coats gathered around Audrey and began producing this weird popping sound. As far as I could tell, this wasn't a sound produced in the mouth, but seemed to originate somewhere within their heads, some extraneous function of the skull bone, a reminder of how anatomically different these creatures really were.

Pop... p-pop... pop!

Their large hands explored the movement of Audrey's head and neck, their long fingers probing the nasal cavity and the auditory canal; finally, both White Coats combined a string of saliva, letting it bead down into Audrey's ajar mouth.

Audrey couldn't resist. She was completely pliable in their hands.

"*Audrey!*"

"There," the second White Coat said, turning, then fixing its glare on me once more. "You may leave. Run, puny man! But if you attempt to heal her, we will discern it and mete out the same blessings upon your flesh. Behold! What has been done to your Mentor and what is coming to all humankind. Tell them, so that they know whom they should fear."

The White Coats dumped Audrey's body and departed from the Treatment Room.

I went to Audrey's side. I felt for a carotid pulse, not sure if I could trust the beat beneath my fingertips, but then she moved her left arm and her eyes fluttered open. She lifted her head and vomited. She turned her head at the last minute, so the eruption didn't go over me and over her clothes.

She gasped for breath.

"Better?" I asked. "Are you hurt?"

"They've infected me," she said. "Please, take me home. I don't want to die in this place."

"You're not going to die," I said.

Audrey made eye contact with me, just briefly, and although she didn't utter a single word, it was evident that she was under no illusions about her near future.

"Can you walk?"

She nodded.

She got to her feet, despite the obvious pain, the blood and the vomit. With my help, she could hobble towards the door. Things weren't good, though. I could feel the heat radiating from her body as I wrapped my arm around her back to support her. She was burning up. Not only that, but I could see the signs of swelling around the arms and across her neck. This wasn't bruising. This was oedema. She had Lymphachela, minus the Incubation Period. The White

Coats had given Audrey such a large viral load that the disease would quickly overwhelm her.

I wanted to take Tim, Chong and O'Brien with me too, head to the eighth floor and take Jenny too, but I didn't have the time or enough hands. I knew I had to save Audrey. Without Audrey, there was no way to bring healing to anyone else, and my medical colleagues were far beyond the limits of medical help.

I grabbed a wheelchair for Audrey and wheeled her away, taking the elevator down to the ground floor.

The Snotty-nosed boy was in the foyer. He sat upon the Reception Desk, gleefully tearing the pages from the Internal Phone Directory, screwing up the pieces into tight balls and dropping them onto the grey carpet. "Ah," he said, "I see you didn't heed my advice."

I pushed Audrey out of the elevator and across the foyer. I stopped when I rounded the corner and saw the Cordon.

"Is there another way out of here?"

"What's wrong with the front door?" asked the Snotty-nosed boy.

I pointed at the soldiers guarding the exit.

"Oh," he said. "Allow me."

The boy walked out of the main entrance—the doors sliding open automatically—and approached one soldier. There was a brief exchange, although I couldn't hear what they said. The boy coughed. A loud and deliberate cough, aimed right at the soldier's face. Within a couple of seconds, this soldier was keeling over, having some kind of coughing and spluttering fit.

The boy turned to the soldier's buddy and repeated the process. Soon he, too, was doubled over, coughing uncontrollably.

Then the soldiers dropped their weapons and ran.

I couldn't believe it.

The Snotty-nosed boy returned into the foyer. A trace of colour perfused his cheeks. "Two court-martials," he said. "What'd you think?"

"What did you do?" I didn't want to sound ungrateful.

"Don't worry," the boy laughed. "They'll survive." He coughed several times. "Extreme cold symptoms, with a side helping of fear. Man 'flu. You humans are so fragile and so predictable. You, however,"—he stared at me and smiled a strange smile—"*you're* different to most Healer's. Less black and white. I like that."

I'm not sure if this was a compliment or some attempt to flatter me. I didn't have time for games. Either way, I ignored it and wheeled Audrey out in the wheelchair and out into the evening.

twenty four

"I tire of the glorification of the bloodthirsty and the psychopath. Rather, give me the warrior whose heart bleeds, who owns his pain, who sees the suffering of others. The one who cares. He is the real hero."

Sister Winnie Montaghue, page 266, 'The Healing Art'

I got Audrey home, wheeling her up Pitt Street, and I wrestled her into her bed. She slept for two hours. When she woke, sweat soaked her. "Don't leave," she gasped, her breathing sounding awful, that vulnerability clear once more. "I don't want to be on my own."

"Are you in pain?"

"Everywhere aches. My whole body."

I tried to think what analgesia I might have. I had some

ibuprofen and some codeine in my medication bag, but nothing stronger. Then another thought occurred to me. "I can heal you—if you show me how."

"*No.*"

"I'm a Healer, you're a Healer, we can do this—"

"No. You heard the White Coat's warning..."

"Yeah, but—"

"Even if you were strong enough to oppose this virus," Audrey said, "I couldn't allow it. The White Coats... they'd swoop down on *this* house... they'd infect you too..."

"So we fight them. Together."

"Yeah, that went really well in the hospital," she said, grimacing from what appeared to be a pain in her left flank. The remark hurt, mostly because it was true. I'd been useless in the hospital. Guilty as charged. "I need you to promise..." Audrey said. "... you won't attempt t-to... do you promise?"

"Okay."

"And you'll stay?"

I nodded. "I promise."

Audrey's arms and legs had swollen massively. There was no longer any definition in her knee or elbow joints. The fluid shifted beneath her skin, which, in places, took on that transparent appearance. Her face was flushed bright red, as if all the blood had pooled in her head. She was barely recognisable.

Audrey's appearance stirred deep memories for me,

memories I'd mostly repressed, but I'd promised her I'd stay and that's what I was determined I'd do.

She slept for several hours. I sat next to her. Her sleep seemed anything but restful. She tossed and turned on the bed, at one point flinging off her duvet and her sheets and calling out. The words she uttered were mostly incomprehensible. Was it some strange language or fever-driven gibberish?

I dosed on and off in the chair.

At one point, when the night was at its darkest, Audrey awoke in a state of panic. I held her and spoke to her softly. She took a sip of water and a couple of ibuprofen. It was tokenistic, but perhaps it might help with the swelling. She drifted back off into an uneasy sleep.

I couldn't sleep, not after that. I felt panic rising in my gut. It seemed conceivable in those small hours that daylight might never grace us again. These fears proved unfounded, however. Outside the window, as light bled into the day, birds chirped and twittered in a dawn chorus.

Audrey awoke. She was lucid. I checked her temperature: Her fever had broken. "How are you feeling?" I asked.

"Better," she said, a pained smile creasing her fat face. "I had some wicked dreams, although I don't actually remember falling asleep."

"What'd you dream about?"

"I dreamed about Seepers, of course, but Peter and David

were with me, too. I was trying to protect my family, only the Seepers were too numerous, and they were circling us."

"Sounds intense."

"It was. It felt completely wrong on so many levels, not least because I seemed to have feelings for Peter."

She'd brought the topic up, and I was curious. "You *don't* have feelings for Peter any longer?"

She laughed, then she coughed. "No," was all she managed.

I didn't like to pry. I knew enough not to ask for details, so I waited instead. If she wanted to volunteer any details about her ex-husband, that was her choice.

"I've never really spoken about my marriage," she said. "I guess because I felt so let down by what happened. So... betrayed. I'm sure Peter thought he was doing the right thing. In hindsight, I know he was trying his best to protect David. They can't have been easy decisions."

I leaned closer.

Audrey sat up. I adjusted the pillows behind her to make her more comfortable. "A little after David was born, I suffered from post-natal depression. I wanted to love my little boy, but there was this whole chemical imbalance and I... well, I felt nothing. I didn't bond with David, not like I was supposed to. I was disconnected. So all the parental responsibility fell on Peter's shoulders."

"Did you get help?"

"No, I didn't know how to ask. I kept everything inside,

but I wasn't kidding Peter. I remember we had these blazing rows. Anyway, one day it all came to a head, and he signed some papers and got me committed to Cherry Farm."

Cherry Farm was the old psychiatric hospital near Waikouaiti. It was closed now, but I'd heard several horror stories from families I'd dealt with.

"Cherry Farm was hell," Audrey said. "A nightmare. I've tried to block it out completely. I lost weeks and months in that place, doped up on anti-depressants, sedatives and other experimental drugs. They were pretty liberal with the medication back then. And then, when I finally got out, after literally months of my life being taken from me, Peter had been awarded sole custody of David. 'It's about what's best for David,' he tried to explain to me, but I couldn't see past my rage. I felt so betrayed. 'You'll *always* be his mother,' Peter said, 'but what he needs is a stable home: when you're ready to re-integrate, we'll welcome you with open arms.' I said, 'Gee, seems to me you've got everything you want *without* me. You've stolen *my* son. You've taken the place that was for *me*.' I basically lost it, which did very little to reassure Peter that my mental state was much better."

Audrey took a sip of water. "I was in and out of the hospital for the next couple of years, up and down, and I guess Peter and David moved on with their lives. I already felt betrayed by Peter's legal manoeuvres, but then he lodged for divorce and that really sent me reeling."

"How long were you married for?"

"Six years. Not long at all. Of course, becoming ill like I did, I didn't just lose my family—I lost *everything*. I'd just completed my training as a nurse when I fell pregnant, and, of course, I lost my job when I got sick. Eventually, after more years than I'd care to mention, I did a refresher course, and I could pick up the nursing again. But the second stint didn't last very long, either. That's when I saw the Seepers. Eric Bernard Charles. Orabone House. I can't help but wonder if everything I went through, hitting rock bottom, was the reason I saw *them*. It's as close to an explanation as I've got. It makes sense, don't you think? Who better to heal the sick than someone who's experienced vulnerability?"

I nodded. It sounded plausible.

"Anyway, I attempted to contact David over the years. I met him outside school once, which sparked this major security alert and Peter over-reacted. He took a restraining order out against me. It still stands, actually. I'm not meant to go within one hundred metres of my son! Can you imagine?"

I couldn't imagine what that would do to any mother.

"So, you can understand why Peter reacted the way he did on Tuesday in the hospital. His hostility."

I nodded.

"The thing that really hurt me, though, was that Peter could turn David against me, whether intentionally or not. When I realised David was uncomfortable in my presence, uncomfortable when I tried to visit him, I stopped trying. I'd forfeited any rights as the boy's mother, after all."

"I didn't mean to dredge up the past."

"No, it's fine," Audrey said. "It's actually good to tell someone after all these years. I hope you don't mind...?"

I shook my head. "No, not at all."

The exertion of all this storytelling must have tired her. Soon she fell into a deep sleep. I figured I'd let her sleep. It would give her body an opportunity to fight this virus. Sleep was all part of the body's natural defence mechanism.

Later, when she woke again, her fever was back, and she was incapable of stringing even one sentence together. This lasted for nearly six hours. When the fever finally broke, her bed sheets soaked with sweat, I changed them for fresh ones, even as Audrey lay there, sleeping. I achieved this by rolling her carefully in one direction, making sure I didn't roll her off the bed completely, removing the sodden sheets and tucking the new ones under her, and then rolling her in the other direction. I'd seen the nurses use this technique on some of the larger kids on the ward, although admittedly it was probably safer with two people.

At times, Audrey's breathing became very raspy and her respirations fell to less than eight. These were the most worrying. My instinct was to take her back to the hospital, but I had to assume the White Coats had overtaken the place.

On Saturday, I had a brief chat with Audrey about her mother. She was lucid, but very breathless. The swelling, if possible, had got marginally worse. "Mum always said... I was... too skinny," she laughed. "If only she... could see... see me now. Actually, I'm glad she can't! Mum, if you're looking down... on me right now, kindly l-look away!"

Audrey laughed at her own joke, but the laughter only brought pain to her left side and along her back, and then morphed into a coughing fit. "Sorry," she managed at last.

"Don't be sorry," I said. "It sounds like you're very fond of your mother."

"I am. She was the best."

It was lovely to hear Audrey tell some happy stories, to know that while a large majority of her life had entailed heartache and suffering, there had at least been some happy times.

She spoke about healing, and how the healings she'd worked in recent weeks were some of the best she'd ever done. There was really nothing like healing the sick. It gave her a real buzz. It was, without doubt, her life's purpose, and how she regretted not taking more opportunities when they had clearly presented themselves. "I was often too scared," she said. She regretted her reclusive years and the years she'd squandered. "Don't spend your life being afraid, Grant," she said. "Not like... I have. It's a waste."

"Stop talking about your life in the past tense," I said, but she seemed not to hear my remark.

Audrey ate very little. When she got up to go to the toilet, which she needed to do infrequently, she was so weak, so light-headed, that I was worried she would pass out. I hated to think what her blood pressure was, but I didn't have any equipment to check it, nor any means of correcting it, even if I did.

She sipped on water. That was about it.

By Sunday, I was concerned that she was going into multiple organ failure. Her urine output was virtually non-existence. Her pulse was weak and thready. Each breath was laboured. She was sleeping far too much, perhaps as much as eighteen hours out of every twenty-four, and her skin had become reddened around the heels and the elbows. A pressure sore seemed like one indignity too many, but I was one man and I didn't have any experience with these things. I tried positioning her with pillows, so she was lying first on one side and then the other, and mixing things up. I think that helped a little. Maybe. But while it might have been good for the skin, it wasn't so wonderful for her breathing. More and more, I missed the resources that had been so readily available at the hospital.

Sometimes, while Audrey slept, I'd scroll through the news app on my iPhone, looking for any updates on the outbreak. I found a video entitled 'City Under Lockdown' which piqued my interest.

I clicked on it.

A reporter stood on the roadside just north of Waitati, the wind blowing her hair. With such a small screen, I couldn't make out her name, although it appeared briefly on a lower third banner.

"... in breaking news, the situation in Dunedin with the Lymphachela Virus has taken a dramatic turn for the worse. At 11:00hrs this morning, the military detail that had formed a cordon around Dunedin Hospital, which is believed to be the epicentre for this deadly infection, was deployed to three simultaneous locations on the periphery of the city. One unit on the Northern Motorway about half a kilometre from here, in Waitati; one on State Highway 1 near Fairfield; and one on Three Mile Hill Road on the Mosgiel side. The Ministry of Health issued a brief statement: 'The virus is believed to have breached the hospital cordon, and consequently, a much broader cordon has been set up around the entire city. No one is permitted to enter or leave.'"

The video then jumped to a studio in Wellington, where the news anchor said, "*... although information is sparse, the latest figures for the virus show a worrying exponential growth. 'We believe upwards of three hundred people to be infected. To date, the total death toll is one hundred and seventeen...'"*

One hundred and seventeen! I couldn't believe how fast it was spreading. How many of those hundred and seventeen deaths included my friends and colleagues?

I turned up the volume on my phone.

The news anchor continued, "*... joining me now in the studio is Dr Thomas Brienbeer, a microbiologist based at the Southern DHB...*

- Dr Brienbeer, thank you for your time. Now I

understand you are the person who came up with the name of this virus—the Lymphachela Virus?

- *Yes, that's right.*
- *You were the first to discover it?*
- *I identified the virus in what was only a handful of samples, yes. The discovery of a new virus is a career highlight, but I soon realised, looking at this thing under the electron microscope, that it had huge potential for devastation.*
- *Your reaction to today's figures?*
- *Shocking. Any virus has the potential for exponential spread, of course, just because viruses can mutate rapidly. Lymphachela, I believe, may have already mutated several times. Mostly, our immune system is well adapted to manage such existential threats, but in this case...*
- *I understand you're not a fan of the alternative name, Brienbeer's Disease?*
- *(Blushing) I think, given the massive death toll we're seeing, that's a tad insensitive, don't you?*
- *One more question: How come you're not in Dunedin fighting the good fight?*

I didn't wait for Brienbeer's response. I exited the video feed, closed the app, and returned my iPhone to my pocket.

Audrey looked so small in her bed, curled up under her blankets, eyes shut, shivering, occasionally muttering nonsense words. Her breathing was getting shallower and shallower, as little by little her body, all her internal organs, shut down. She was dying. Death, while for many considered a natural state, an inevitable part of living, was senseless and tragic. If there were any redeeming qualities about death, it was perhaps that some people faced it with such dignity. I'd not known many people who'd died, but I'd seen a few during my medical career, each one haunting in its own way. No, it was my mother that mostly came to mind: She had suffered greatly as the pancreatic cancer had eaten her insides… and yet throughout her ordeal she never seemed to think about anyone but me. How was *this* affecting *me*? If she thought of herself, she hid it away from me. I never saw a trace of self-pity. None.

Audrey, it seemed, would face her particular death in a similar fashion.

She didn't really need me anymore; she hadn't been conscious for hours. I was a witness to events, nothing more. Yes, I'd promised I wouldn't leave, but did that really count for much anymore?

Still, what if she did wake and find I'd gone? What then?

I opened Audrey's mouth and examined her tongue. It was coated with thrush. Despite the volume of fluid swishing under her skin, she was very dry. I couldn't bear the thought of her dying from dehydration, not when this was so easily treated with the right equipment. At the hospital, I could liberate some bags of intravenous fluids, some giving sets and some cannulas. I could rehydrate her. She could have a fighting chance. I could do something.

So, I left. Chances are Audrey wouldn't even know I'd gone.

I walked purposefully down Pitt Street. It was late afternoon. The wind had finally pushed the sea mist back out to sea, and the sky was uninterrupted blue. Winter had stripped everything bare; the virus had left the streets deserted. The soldiers were gone, too. I walked straight into the hospital foyer, unchallenged.

No one was there, no people and no Seepers. I didn't like the open space of the foyer, however. I felt too vulnerable there. The White Coat's warning replayed in my head: 'If you're foolish enough to return, we'll mete out the same thing to you.'

I raced to the stairwell. The lights were dimmed, as if the building was operating on reduced power or the back-up generator.

In the gloom, weird shapes appeared before me.

I rubbed my eyes, not believing what they were seeing.

Black shapes filled the corridor, like darkened snowflakes, only they hung there in space, refusing to fall to the floor. Spores! I brushed several of them aside, but they swirled around my hand, regrouping and reclaiming their former space. Otherwise, they all moved together, a sluggish, almost hypnotic drifting motion.

I didn't want to inhale these spores. I switched to nasal breathing.

I reached the first floor. The spores were there too. There were cracks across the linoleum and along the walls too, great fissures in some instances, as if there had been some tectonic shift. From these cracks there issued long, gauzy, dark threads and fibres. These too swayed in gentle unison, like fragments of spider webs caught in the breeze. An oily smell dominated.

I entered the Children's Ward. Beyond, in the patient rooms, I heard an isolated cry. Brief, feeble. Then a second. There were still children alive, it seemed. My chest ached—how could I ignore those cries?—but I knew it would be suicide to investigate.

I moved on. There was only one job I had to do. I forced myself to think only about Audrey. I went to the Drug Dispensary. Inside, there were boxes and boxes of intravenous fluids. I swiped my ID badge.

Be-de-derrr...

My card was declined.

Someone, in all this chaos, had gone to the trouble of taking me off the system.

I smashed my fists into the door, making it shake within its frame. I couldn't stop myself.

Just beyond that door were drugs and medical supplies that could make a real difference to Audrey's last days. Here I was, trained in how to use them, highly skilled, and yet this stupid door barred me!

Access revoked.

Stupid.

Absolutely fucking stupid.

twenty five

"A broken heart, the gush of tears... lift thy head, for these are the currency of the new dawn."

Sophia, The Forgotten Princess and Poet, page 98, 'The Healing Art'

When I arrived back at Audrey's house, I found her curled up in the bed, gasping for air. Blue, parched lips amid a swollen face.

"Audrey...?"

She was unresponsive. She was actively dying. Panic surged through my stomach and my chest. I was the guy who was meant to know what to do, only the rules had changed and now I found myself way, way out of my depth. In my medical career I'd had the misfortune of watching children die (or whatever euphemism you cared to call it), but seeing

Audrey, the Healer, going down the same path was simply bewildering.

I shook her shoulder.

Her bloated flesh wobbled—her arms, her legs, her stomach, her neck. The fluid beneath her skin shifted, its mass having accumulated over days, while Audrey herself, the essential woman, was fading before my eyes.

"Don't leave." I echoed Audrey's words to me. Now it was my turn to beg. "I don't know how to do this without you."

Her breathing was different now. Her respiratory rate had fallen to single digits. I knew this without the need to count. She had the death rattle. Chain-stoking. Worse, now and then, she'd stop breathing entirely, and I'd wonder if I'd just witnessed her last breath.

Her pain, at least, was behind her. If she was still suffering in whatever state of unconsciousness she was in now, there were no visible signs of it. I tried to hold on to this. This, surely, was a good thing.

I touched her face, brushing her fringe aside. Her skin was hot, like all the heat that ought to be in her core was radiating out through her exposed skin. She was no longer sweating. Her body's thermoregulation had failed.

Go in peace, I wanted to say. *I can't heal you, I don't know how, but at least I can wish you a peaceful passage. You have fought a good fight, now rest in peace.*

I couldn't speak any of these things, my lips suddenly dry, but these and other emotions swelled within my chest. I hoped somehow the sentiment might be conveyed through the touch of my fingertips. The words themselves were trite, and better never spoken, but the emotion itself was pure.

She took one breath... then another...

I took her swollen hand and held it, squeezed it.

Deep in her chest, there came a rattling noise, like some inexpressible cough lost in the depths.

A third breath, separated from the others by nearly half a minute....

A fourth. A fifth.

And that was it.

I heard that last breath pass between her lips and flee into that cluttered space, and upon it Audrey's soul passed too. Time of death—I glanced at my watch—was 18:43hrs. Some habits you never lose.

I didn't cry, not at first. For one, a numbness, a flood of unreality, washed over me. How could she be dead? How was it even possible? And if she was dead, why did she *remain* dead? Wasn't *she* the Healer? Wasn't *I* a Healer? What prison could death be when one had the power to heal?

But it was real; and it stayed real.

I sat there holding her hand: puffy, bloated, the warmth slowly ebbing.

And the memory came flooding back, not fragments this time, but everything:

I remembered how quiet the house was. Oh God, it was quiet. I wasn't sure which was worse, the screaming or the sudden silence.

Was it over? Was she dead? Or was it merely one of her lapses, one of many vacant moments, when, for whatever reason, she forgot about the pain she was in?

I waited. I really, really didn't know what to do.

I was supposed to be studying, of course. This was the first year of the Health Sciences course at the University of Otago. I hoped, if I got the grades, to get into Medical School. That was a joke. How could I study when my mother was dying in a room down the hallway?

Dad was at work—as usual. No help there.

I ought to go into Mum's room and check on her, except I didn't want to. More and more, this was how I'd been feeling. I used to sit and hold her hand, that is, until the hand I held, her left, ballooned up. It was known as Lymphoedema. I'd checked it out in one of my pathophysiology text books. It happens when the cancer blocks the lymph nodes, so the lymphatic fluid has nowhere to drain. The swelling began slowly, insipidly. I hadn't noticed at first. Then, one day, Mum had removed her wedding and engagement rings, saying they were too tight. She hadn't worn either since. I doubted if Dad had even noticed, or if he had, he hadn't said anything.

That was just the beginning. Her left hand had grown so big and bloated and there had been all this fluid swishing under the skin, moving about unnaturally, and I didn't want to hold her hand anymore.

Nevertheless, I'd made myself do it. I'd told myself that it wasn't about me, *about* my *feelings, but about being there for Mum and showing her that I loved her. But the longer I held that monstrous hand, the more I was reminded that this disease was going to take her, and I couldn't do a damn thing about it. She was changing. This disease would take her, and it would transform her into something terrible as it did so. Suddenly, I didn't have the stomach for it anymore.*

I hadn't gone into her room that morning like usual. I couldn't. I didn't want to hold her hand, not this brand-new-all-changed hand. I didn't want to witness her pain anymore, or see what changes the cancer had rendered to her appearance overnight. No, enough was enough. And when she had called out to me, I ignored her cries.

I was only eighteen. No eighteen-year-old should have to deal with this shit, for God's sake. It was too fucking hard.

So I sat at my desk, pretending I was studying, doing my damnedest to blank out her cries for help, telling myself that I'd go to her later, perhaps after lunch, if or when I felt stronger. I knew, of course, that I was kidding myself. I didn't want to go into her room. If I could avoid that room for the rest of my life, that would be just fine.

But the silence... well, that'd got me. I'd seen the pattern of her delirium and her pain, I knew how each rose and fell, but to fall silent altogether: that was odd. I really ought to go to her. Just to check. Even if I just peeked my head around the door to check her chest was still rising and falling, just so I knew she was alright.

I really ought *to.*

Of course, if I did that, and she was awake, she'd make me come in and explain why I hadn't come earlier. She'd make me sit at her bedside and hold that damned hand and, I swore, if I had to hold that hand even for one minute more, I'd start screaming!

She wasn't Mum anymore. My Mum was dead already. That was an awful thing to think, sure, but it was as good as true and, in a way, I wished it were *true. At least then her suffering would be over. This disease had stolen my mother, piece by piece, and there was little of her humanity left. I was being totally selfish, I knew. I just couldn't sit around and watch this slow decay and I couldn't stand her suffering anymore.*

Still the silence. It wasn't right.

I got up from my chair, and I moved towards the door. My feet padded over the floor and, not wanting to make a noise, I carefully trod on only the floorboards that I knew didn't creak. I crept down the hall. The door to Mum's room was slightly ajar. I lingered just outside, unsure. It was dark inside. She'd got the curtains drawn. I pushed the door—just a little. I leaned in. I strained to see my mother in the gloom. The duvet on the bed was a mess, and I couldn't see the failing, skeletal figure of Mum for all the darkness inside.

I pushed the door open a bit more and walked into the room. I approached the bed. My heart was racing in my chest, booming, much louder than I thought possible. It was almost as if I already knew what I was about to find, that there was some dark, terrible knowledge I'd perceived in the silence.

I took a deep breath, almost a hiss, and pulled back the duvet.

Mum was there, much smaller in death than when she was

living. All wasted and contracted and, if there was any peace in her current state, then I couldn't see it.

I touched her shoulder. Her nightie now seemed too flimsy, and through it, I felt the coldness of her flesh.

I pulled back my arm. Shocked. Horrified.

She's dead.

There's no coming back from that. None.

At some point, I remembered screaming; I remembered running through the house, lost, confused, then I remembered calling my father at the surgery, and screaming something at him, but so much of the detail will elude me forever...

I had lost *another* mother today.

I pulled Audrey's sheet up and placed it over her face, not because I feared how she looked. I had grown to love that face, even at the end, even in its deformity. Rather, it was an act of respect. Here lay one of the greats, and, although it was tough, I had to let her go.

She didn't deserve to die the way she had.

I had lost my friend and my mentor. My head, my heart, were a mass of conflicting emotions.

I was alone. A lone Healer. A novice at that.

I went digging in my medication bag and brought out a silver strip of medication, searching for something to make me feel better. What did I have to numb the pain?

I stopped.

No.

The pain began as a pin-prick in the very centre of my chest, along my sternum, but quickly blossomed. I couldn't breathe. I tried and... there was nothing. This had to be a heart attack! This was *my* death! I staggered forward. The pain at this point had spread across my whole chest, across my back, up into my shoulders and neck, and down into the depths of my stomach. I tried to scream... but no sound came. It was intolerable. I couldn't understand what was happening to me or why it wasn't happening faster. And then the blockage came from my mouth, a living thing which must have sat in my gut for years. It came out in a rush of vomit and snot; it came out, and I screamed; it came out, and finally one solitary tear slid down my cheek.

A Seeper.

It was about the size of my hand, resembling an oversized maggot with its white, bulbous flesh. It scurried across the bedroom floor on its multitude of legs. A Seeper which was either so small, or had lived so deep inside me, that even Audrey, who had sensed it, hadn't been able to remove it.

I was suddenly full of rage. I would not let it escape into the world. I needed to kill it and know with certainty it was dead.

I stomped on it.

Its body crumbled and green slime oozed over the carpet.

A few more tears streaked down my cheeks. The Seeper

was dead, and yet its death brought no relief to my emotional pain. My rage, at least, had been satisfied and now it dissipated.

I was done masking my pain, hiding it away like some unsightly part, never to be seen. To do so was to dishonour Audrey's memory and, for that matter, my mum's. Maybe there was an unseen truth in this pain which I needed to confront. Why was it I'd never shed a single tear for my mother *until now?*

I went into the bathroom and popped all the pills into the toilet bowl, then I flushed the toilet (even though I knew Audrey would hate it), watching as they were all swept away.

I would *use* my pain. Let it give me momentum; let it give me focus. There was a battle that still needed to be fought...

The tears came thick and fast then, and I let them, only wiping them aside when they blurred my vision too much. And when I thought I was finished, the tears came with fresh vigour and once more I let them. With the tears came exhaustion, and I must have slept, albeit fleetingly, for somehow Sunday night became Monday morning.

twenty six

"Take my hands to the people; for my hands are my Father's hands. Go in resolute faith and free my people from their suffering. The Spirit will guide you, as I promised He would."

Yeshua of Nazareth, page 81, 'The Healing Art'

I left Audrey's house early, pulling the door closed after me. I had to get out. I walked at pace, through the Green Belt, then later, past dairies, past closed fish and chip shops, past houses and apartments. My feet pounded the pavements with its broken pavers, its cracks, its graffiti and its litter. They ached, but I didn't care. I kept walking; I kept moving. I passed roadworks and a cordon of orange cones.

A brisk wind blew in from the Southern Ocean. Grey clouds gathered overhead, barring the promise of the sun's heat. They buffeted up against the existing high pressure system and something was about to give. The air tingled.

I had nowhere to go. I wasn't heading anywhere in particular, but was overwhelmed with the need to escape *everything*. I followed my nose, or my feet, or my instincts. I'm not sure which. Eventually, I found myself at Marlow Park in South Dunedin.

If only I had listened to Audrey...

I rested on a bench, surrounded by the dinosaur-themed playground. The exhibits of this playground were tired and old, their paint fading, but no less loved. A handful of children slid down the neck of a Brontosaurus, but mostly the park was empty at this hour in the morning.

One child, a boy of about eight or nine with dark, curly hair, was limping. When he came closer to the bench, I asked, "What's wrong with your leg?"

He had deep brown eyes, which suddenly grew wide. He giggled, a nervous giggle.

"It's alright," I said. "I'm a doctor. Well, I used to be."

A couple of his mates approached, bolstering his confidence. "You're not a doctor," he said.

"I used to work at the hospital."

"Have you got that virus?" he asked, taking a step back. "My bro says we're all gonna get it. Says we're fucked." He watched me intently, but from a safe distance, to see if his swearing would elicit a reaction.

"No," I said. "But you should stay away from the hospital. It's getting worse."

"I ain't going near the place. I hate hospitals and I don't much like doctors, neither."

"Really?" I liked the boy's honesty. "And what if this doctor had the power to make your leg better?"

"*Bullshit!* No one can do that. It's congenetum."

"*Congenital?*"

"Yeah, that's what I said."

I smiled. "Would you like me to try?"

The boy edged a little closer to the park bench. "Don't try any funny business, mister. I ain't as helpless as I look."

He stood before me. Despite the icy wind, he wore only shorts and a t-shirt, and I could see how his one leg, the left leg, was much weaker than its neighbour, how the bones and joints had become twisted.

His mates stood behind him, looking on with curiosity.

"What's your name?" I asked.

"Ariki."

"Well, Ariki, this isn't going to hurt, but it might give you a bit of a shock, so you might want to brace yourself."

"Oh fuck, mister! You're freaking me out! What're you gonna do?"

"I'm looking for the root cause," I said, which wasn't the best turn of phrase, since one of Ariki's mates whispered how I was going to 'root' Ariki! Ariki wasn't laughing, however. He looked terrified.

I focused my attention on his weaker, deformed leg. I tried to look not only at the leg, but *through* the leg, and when I'd be looking so long that it became awkward, I saw the Seeper. It was a small thing, resembling an overgrown earwig with its pincers and its armoured shell.

"*You!*" I said, challenging the creature directly, the now familiar rage, the same rage I'd felt last night, stirring once more.

Ariki flinched.

"I see you!" I told the Seeper. "What do you think you're doing in this boy's leg?"

And I *pushed.*

Only this time, it was different. *I* was different. The moment I *pushed*, I felt something inside me shift. I felt the power surge along my arms and through my hands, but with it came a change of perspective: I could see *beyond* myself. A part of me moved with the healing power and travelled into this boy. I witnessed the damage the Seeper had rendered to the boy's left leg even before he'd emerged from the womb, how the tendons and muscles had shortened and twisted, how this had thrown his hips and spine out of alignment. I witnessed the pain Ariki had endured, how it often brought him to tears, how he hid his tears away from his friends and, especially, his mother and his auntie.

I drew in a breath.

But there was more: I saw the thing that really frightened Ariki—not the pain, not what he perceived as the humiliation of having this disability, although they were present too. What I saw with absolute clarity was Ariki's fear that he couldn't be the man he wanted to be. Somehow, in his mind, his disability barred him from wielding the mana that was required to reach manhood and to establish his rightful place within his whānau. He would joke and make light of these things, he'd play the fool, but this was him attempting to deflect his fears.

I saw all this and then I saw the Seeper become dislodged from within the boy's knee, dropping onto the concrete. It gave a faint groan, which only I would have heard. It turned to regard me, its dark, crystalline eyes challenging me.

One more touch, one more *push*, and I could have extinguished this Seeper's life. I could do it for my mother, or for Audrey, or all the sick children I'd witnessed over the years, but that changed nothing. My rage had flared, but just as quickly, it had died back down. I didn't have the heart to kill this creature.

The Seeper scuttled off as fast as it could.

I turned to Ariki. "Nothing's stopping you now."

"What did you do?" he asked. He put his full weight on his weak leg, testing it. His eyes and his mouth were wide open. Each time he pressed down on his left leg, it took his weight. "*Jesus!*" he said. "What the fuck did you do?"

"You're welcome."

I stood up. I'd created a spectacle and thought it best to leave the park.

"How'd you do it, mister?" Ariki asked.

"I'm not *just* a doctor," I said. "I'm *also* a Healer." There was an irony in that statement, of course. Some Healer I'd turned out to be. Some doctor too.

"You're awesome!" said Ariki, now jumping up and down. "You wait till I tell my uncle. He's got diabetes. Can you help him too?"

"I'm sorry," I said. "I need to be on my way."

In the distance, ominous clouds were building and building, and they seemed to be localised to one area: the hospital. That was where I needed to be. Since there was no escaping Dunedin with the cordon, eventually, I needed to face my responsibilities.

And if I didn't...

A solitary rumble of thunder rolled over the hill suburbs. "There's a storm coming, boys," I said. "Better get home."

"Not before you heal *me*," said another boy. He was short with blonde, cropped hair and a freckled face. "Can you heal me like you did Ariki?"

"What's your—?" And then I saw it, even through the over-sized sweater he wore to conceal his deformity. The creature was very subtle, but it had somehow attached itself to the boy's spine. A dark entity. From the spine, its shadow had been cast far and wide, infecting even the central nervous system. It was draining his hope and his youthful energy, preying on the boy during his lowest moments, nudging him right to the precipice of despair.

"How long has your back been twisted like that?" I asked.

"You *really* are a Healer!" The boy gasped, presumably because of my diagnostic skills. "It's spondylosis. The doctor told me it'll only get worse and that one day it'll kill me."

"Your doctor's wrong," I said, and I *pushed*.

Further sight came with the *push*. Further understanding. I was operating now in my full power as a Healer. I witnessed the antidepressants the boy's father had forced the boy to take. The criticism. How this criticism had only snowballed and eroded the boy's confidence. How the people who were meant to love and protect him had only made things worse. The boy's growing resentment. His anger. And how he wanted others to hurt just like he did, but he wasn't physically strong, so he picked on the smaller kids in the junior syndicate at school.

"*Leave this boy alone!*" I ordered the Seeper.

As the creature extracted itself, it squeezed the boy's spinal cord. The boy's arms and legs shot out.

"*Freeze!*" I shouted. "Release him *right now*. You've done enough damage."

The creature dropped onto the concrete. It was shaped like a small boy, only it had no real substance, being more shadow. Faceless, lacking in detail. Where once it might have been the same size as its host, now it was curled up, shrivelled and pathetic. It fell before me, pawing at my shoes. "I will serve you, Master."

"How can you serve me?" I asked. "Now *leave!*"

"Yes, yes, of course." The creature retreated towards the bushes on the edge of the playground. "Master is merciful," it croaked. "I will remember."

Meanwhile, the boys were looking at me like I'd lost my mind. "Who're you talking to, mister?" one asked.

"*You did it!*" The blonde-haired boy shouted, and from the way he stretched and flexed and twisted his back, it was obvious to all he was free. "I knew you could! That feels so much better."

"Do me a favour," I said, leaning over the boy and whispering in his ear. "Leave those junior kids alone."

The boy's entire face flushed. "Sure," he nodded.

Meanwhile, the phones came out. The other boys began snapping photos and taking videos of me, texting their mates and God knows who else.

"I need to leave," I said. "But thank you for letting me do my work here. It was good." It was true: with each *push* I got this feeling of elevation, this endorphin rush, but it also came with both physical exhaustion and an emotional burden. I was privy to knowledge that no one, not even a doctor, should know.

"You can't leave now," said Ariki. "We need you here. We got other people coming to get healed."

"*What?*"

"Yeah, the whānau."

"But I—"

"We can't go to the hospital no more," another boy

pointed out.

Soon there was a small, but growing, crowd of both children and adults in the playground in South Dunedin, each one seeking healing. They came with coronary heart disease, with melanomas, with gout, with appendicitis, with gallstones, with scabies, with broken bones, with ascites, with alopecia, with all manner of ailments and conditions. There had been no self-promotion. This was all word of mouth. And I simply let the healings speak for themselves.

And it was a joy.

And it was both emotionally exhausting and strangely energising.

I dislodged almost a hundred Seepers, but I did not kill them. I witnessed it all, great and small. Each triumph. Each miracle. And with each healing, my confidence grew. This was who I was meant to be. *This* was my calling. I could never be just a doctor again. I was finally training as Audrey had intended, and while it couldn't make amends for my failure to stand in solidarity with my medical colleagues, the abandoning of my hospital post, or even being there for Audrey when she needed me most, it was at least a step in the right direction.

I healed for almost two hours until finally I told those who remained that I needed to leave. "There are people dying over there in the hospital," I said, pointing towards the dark clouds and the centre of the storm. "And the longer I leave it, the more blood will be on my hands."

twenty seven

"If you have a sword, you are ready for battle."
Sollimunn, page 144, 'The Healing Art'

Three quarters of an hour later I reached the hospital's Great King Street entrance. The rain fell in heavy droplets. More thunder rumbled overhead. No one barred my entry. The doors slid open, beckoning, a gaping maw, begging the question: Was I foolhardy enough to enter this place filled with White Coats and Lymphachela patients?

I walked in.

I may be a fool, but this needed to be finished.

The air was thick with a cloying, malignant stench. My stomach lurched. My nagging dread was back, and if I stopped to examine these feelings, perhaps I would turn and run from the building, screaming...

Instead, I moved on. I didn't loiter. My shoes creaked as I moved over the great expanse of grey carpet. The lights were out, everywhere cast in shadow. The place strange in its abandonment. Where were the queues at the Dispensary? Where was the receptionist at the main desk? Or the volunteer stood behind the St John's Information Desk? Where were the orderlies moving patients in great, carriage-like wheelchairs? Or Security? Or even those who always sat in or around the Whānau Room.

They had all vanished.

Ghosts now.

The room seemed to flex around me. The ceiling tiles sagged, the walls and pillars warped, the floor rumbled and shifted under my feet. The whole hospital had been re-claimed and re-shaped somehow, a grand apparition that sought to lure me deep within then swallow me in its hungry belly.

The White Coats had left their signature on the walls and elsewhere. Mucus, smeared on every surface they had touched: from brief, possessive caresses to long, lingering gossamer trails swaying in the re-circulated air. Spores were pushed around the building by the back-up generator.

I followed one such trail up the stairs to the first floor. I went past the Dunedin School of Medicine Dean's Office, past the lifts. My footfalls booming through the vacant corridors.

I arrived at the Children's Ward. That seemed

appropriate enough. There was no better place to start this thing. The darkness here was deep and oppressive.

I pushed open the double doors.

A burst of warm, stale air rushed past me, assaulting my nostrils as if with claws. There was the oiliness, the White Coats' smell, but this wasn't the only smell, nor the most dominant. Neglect and death. The acrid tang of vomit, of rivers of bile, unthinkable volumes of incontinence, and, worse still, of flesh left to decay for days in an almost insufferable heat. The stench so ripe, so full-bodied, that it almost took a physical form. The air conditioning wasn't working here.

I faltered.

I drew in a breath, clenched my teeth, and stepped inside. I should have come sooner; much sooner.

The ward, too, had changed beyond recognition, even in just a few days. Mucus dripped from the walls, the desks and chairs. It oozed from door handles and from the bulk of the arrest trolley parked in the corridor. Even the ambient light was less, the shadows subjugating. The spores were more numerous here. The walls were neither straight nor true, but twisted ever so slightly in a manner that was abhorrent. The floor sloped. The heat was oppressive. However, unlike the ground floor, I understood from the coughs and splutters, the moans and groans, the unanswered cries, from the strange interplay of acoustics, that the ward was at full capacity. Not a busyness as before. There was no one rushing from bed to bed or room to room, no one attending the sick, rather the sick had been left to this terrible sickness. Perhaps those who had attended them had succumbed to the virus too? Or maybe they had fled? Moving through the corridor, I wondered what I was about to see.

And where were the orchestrators of all this madness?

A muffled cry came from the first side room. There was no name on the card outside, but I recognised the room: Room 18. It was David Layton's old room.

Did something of David's essence remain here? Were there ghosts dwelling within these walls? And did they look on, consumed by rage? Or maybe they had departed long ago?

The smell was awful, getting inside my throat and lungs. I swallowed, trying to clear the taste, but to no avail.

There was mucus smeared on the handle.

I unbuttoned my shirt sleeve, using it to cover my hand, then pushed open the door.

The room was gloomy. The blinds had been closed, allowing very little natural light to enter. A few spores drifted by. A large figure—almost certainly *not* a child—was huddled under several thick blankets, whimpering.

I approached the patient. I paused. I swallowed. I moved a little closer to the bed. "I've come to heal you," I announced. I extended my trembling hands. My fingers brushing the patient's large, sloping shoulders.

The patient jerked.

Through the blinds, a flash of lightning.

A man's face surfaced from underneath the blankets: eyes wide, sweat slicked skin, unruly hair and coarse stubble. "You're not *him*."

"Who?"

But I knew who.

The man was no longer looking at me. His eyes roamed the room's interior, dancing wildly from wall to ceiling to wall again. "He *knows* you're here. And he'll set you on fire."

"I'm a Healer."

"No."

No? What did that mean? Did the man doubt my abilities, or was he opposed to being healed? The thunder rumbled outside, as if the hospital was the very eye of the storm.

"You don't need to be afraid of the White Coats anymore." This was a ridiculous statement given these Seepers controlled the entire hospital and their virus was everywhere.

The man chuckled. "Sometimes, in the night, he doesn't wear his human face..."

I shuddered.

"And he said that this time there won't be any stuff ups... not like H5N1..."

"Please," I said. "Keep it down." The man's voice was too loud and might draw one of the White Coats. I didn't want to meet them any sooner than was absolutely necessary.

"He already *knows* you're coming..."

"How?"

"He really hates you. And the woman."

"Audrey," I whispered. "Her name was Audrey." Again, I extended my hand to touch the man's shoulder…

The man twitched. "Don't touch me," he said. "You'll only make it worse."

Worse? What could be worse than dying a slow death from Lymphachela?

The man tried to brush my hand away, but I was stronger and held it firm. "I can help you," I said.

"I don't want help. Leave me alone."

"But you'll die."

"Not quickly enough."

I didn't want to hear anymore. I closed my eyes and drew in a long breath… then I *pushed.*

This poor man had not only been infected with the virus, but with a dread so thick that it tainted everything. The dread had, in fact, taken a physical manifestation, and would torment him in the rare moments when sleep brought refuge. The man had lived most of his life afraid, but listening to the White Coat's mutterings night and day had tipped his mind over the edge.

The Lymphachela Virus was the perfect bedfellow: Brienbeer's virus proliferated his flesh and all his internal organs. Hungry mouths snapping and biting, making rapid and devastating progression. Mouths that refused to release, except to burrow deeper. Savaging nerves and obliterating this man's own immune system.

He needed to be released.

The healing went out, travelling along my arm, down into my fingertips and—

Nothing.

The man was blocking me. Blocking my power.

Once again, I focused, breathed in, breathed out, and *pushed*—

The man screamed.

I stepped back from the bed. With all this noise, one of the White Coats would almost certainly come now, if my attempts to heal hadn't already given me away. I thought about making a third attempt, but changed my mind. I'd worked too many years within the bounds of informed consent. Was it right to heal someone who didn't want to be healed? Did this poor man even know his own mind anymore?

"*Get out! Get out! Get out!*"

Another flash of lightning illuminated the room and then plunged it into a relative darkness.

I raised my hands, backing away from the bed. "Okay, okay." I opened the door and slipped out into the dark corridor.

I'd had grand plans of confronting the White Coats and cleansing the hospital of this virus, yet I'd failed to heal the very first person I'd encountered. This was hardly the victory I'd imagined.

Before doubts could take hold, I entered the next room and approached that occupied bed. "Hello?"

A teenage girl lay on the bed. She stirred at my presence, but made no sound. Her eyes flickered beneath their lids, yet remained shut. Suffering was etched upon her face in deep, unnatural lines, lines that did not belong to someone so young. Her neck and her hands had ballooned to at least twice their normal size.

My chest ached. My stomach churned. This was not right.

So, I reached out my hand and let my fingertips dance over the side of her face. She burned with a fever. The heat radiating in wave after wave.

I *pushed*.

This time the healing shot through my bones: humerus, radius, ulna, metacarpals, finally my phalanges, before leaving my body... and finding the girl. All her life she'd been told she was pretty... and now her looks had been ruined by this virus. Her face was huge and unrecognisable, even as her insides rotted away. It wasn't fair. Not only that, but she kept herself fit and healthy—there was the running, the dancing, the skating. She ate clean; always had. None of this was fair. She was far too young to die, and yet death took from her minute by minute. She never imagined that she'd die in this place: unloved, scared, with only the panic cries of other victims for company. Life, she decided, really wasn't fair.

"I'm bringing fair," I whispered.

The power slammed into the virus then, repelling it.

The tiniest smile curled the edge of the girl's lips. A passing acknowledgement before she sank into a deeper, much easier sleep.

That was all. I had healed my first Lymphachela patient. Let her sleep, let her re-gather her strength.

Out of the window: thunder, lightning, sheets of rain.

But where were the White Coats? Surely they would appear now I'd *pushed* their virus out?

My chest felt a little lighter. My fingertips tingled where the healing had exited. It was a win, but what was one patient compared to an entire hospital?

I stood for a moment, watching the girl. Was it a trick of the flashing light or was her neck reducing in size?

I smiled.

I left the room and went to the next, using my shirt sleeve once again to avoid touching the mucus on the door handle. The spores hung in the air like toxic, grey snowflakes that refused to settle on the floor.

The rising smell of faeces pushed me back. Vomit too, the stench reaching down into my throat and making my stomach churn. And fainter, much fainter: the oily smell, all but overwhelmed. I willed myself not to be sick, then continued. The heat inside was stifling. The gloom repressive. There was a sound like grinding teeth, repeating over and over. What was *that* sound? Could it be teeth? Stretched out on the bed, bundled under numerous sheets, the form of a large man. Stirring. Groaning.

Despite the smell, I went to his bedside, careful where I placed my feet, not wanting to slip on unseen bodily fluids. I stretched out my hand—

And the patient reached up and clamped my wrist.

I yelped.

Adrenaline spiked through my body. I tried to pull my hand back, but the grip only became more excruciating, like it might crush the small bones in my wrist.

The figure in the bed rose, the sheets falling away. It was a White Coat. "Newman," it said. "You should not have returned." Its jaw moved from side to side, the teeth grinding once again. It's lips parted slightly. The teeth were no longer perfectly straight, but pointed, with sharp edges glistening in the darkness. It stood upon the mattress, towering over me. "You have not learned the lessons of fear. Did we not say this is our hospital? There will be no more healings."

Suddenly, I was yanked up by my wrist, and my feet were left dangling in the air. The pain in my wrist was like a hot tourniquet.

A low rumble of thunder outside.

How had I ever thought I could defeat these creatures?

Its eyes twinkled. It had the form of a man, yes, but

beneath that, there existed something detestable. A creature that delighted in human suffering.

It threw me across the room.

The lightning flashed.

Even as I flew through the thick, sticky air, my wrist throbbed from the memory of its grip...

Until I struck the cupboard door on the far wall.

The pain lit up my spine, obliterating all other senses. An explosion... and then an equally forceful implosion. The room throbbed and dimmed, throbbed and dimmed. I lay there, slumped, only half awake, my arms and legs useless appendages. There was something wrong with my back! Was it broken?

Far away, as if in some dream, I registered the White Coat leaping from the bed. One moment on the bed... the next on the floor before me, close enough to touch if only my arms would comply.

It stood before me, swaying and grinding its teeth.

Saliva frothed in its mouth. It smeared some upon its fingers, then reached down, its fingers brushing over my lips. *Pop... p-pop...* that weird sound it produced again. While its fingers were coarse, the motion was all the more shocking for its tenderness. This was not an act of compassion, however, but one of artistic mastery.

My lips prickled, like a thousand tiny needles had embedded themselves there.

"How'd you like our virus, puny man?"

A tart, sharp taste spread through my mouth, while my lips felt as if they'd been sunburnt and the upper layers were shedding themselves. I imagined the virus Brienbeer had first shown me under the microscope: millions of those micro-organisms clinging to my lips with their hungry mouths, their tiny barbs designed so they couldn't simply be wiped away, their sole purpose of invading their new host—me!

I *pushed* with all my strength.

And I felt the virus weaken, and then it was expelled. My lips were no longer prickly, and the taste was gone.

Slowly, painfully, I dragged myself along the floor, my back protesting with each protracted movement.

The White Coat walked astride me.

I moved towards the bed, certain at any moment the Seeper would launch a fresh attack. I looked ahead. As my eyes adjusted to the gloom, I noticed there was a woman under the bed. She was naked, shivering, and coiled into a foetal position. Her pale skin was soiled, her limbs bloated and grotesque. Her eyes looked at me with horror. She was lying in a pool of her own urine and vomit.

Little by little, I moved toward her. A warmth swelled in my chest. A resolve. I would not leave her like this.

A vice-like hand wrapped around my left ankle, compressing my bones and ligaments.

The White Coat dragged me back across the laminate floor.

I clawed back towards the bed, towards the woman, but the White Coat was simply too strong.

I was hauled back. The White Coat took my other ankle and then I was lifted and suspended in mid-air.

The room span. I thought I might vomit or pass out. Or both. I squeezed my eyes shut. And I waited. When the spinning subsided, when I opened my eyes again, nothing made sense. I saw shiny black shoes, but they were wrong somehow. Trousered legs: wrong. The lower part of the Seeper's white coat: Wrong, all wrong. And then I understood that the world had been inverted.

The thunder boomed.

The pain—in my back, but mostly in my ankles—focused me.

I extended my neck and sunk my teeth into the White Coat's leg—through the clothing and into its flesh.

The creature roared.

I clenched my jaw and refused to let go.

Suddenly my mouthful was gone... the hands holding my ankles were gone... the White Coat itself was gone... and I was falling, falling, falling...

I was able to tuck in my head before I crumbled in a heap upon the floor, taking most of the fall on my shoulders and upper back.

I screamed as the pain lit up my spine and radiated outwards.

I closed my eyes. I groaned. When the worst of the pain

had passed, I opened my eyes and saw the woman still there under the bed. I rolled over slowly. On hands and knees, I inched towards her. The White Coat would not be gone for long. It would return, and when it did, it would make us suffer.

I made it to the bed, and I crawled under, so that I was hidden and lying next to the woman. The floor was wet. It didn't matter. The smell was so cloying it was a wonder I could breathe at all. She was a mess and her shit was smeared across my hands, but I folded her in my arms, anyway. She was burning with fever. She was hyperventilating.

"Shhhh," I said. "It's okay."

And I *pushed*.

The healing travelled the length of my arms, danced over my skin, then jumped through my clothing and passed into her like electricity. Her body jerked, but she did not resist the power. I witnessed the virus at work, how it had attacked many of her internal organs, especially her kidney, her liver, her gallbladder, and her stomach. Yet for all its destruction, the virus was yet to affect her *where she truly lived*. Her heart still resisted, in a physical sense and in terms of her essence. Here was a person of great strength. When she'd first been admitted to hospital, when the hospital was functional, she had attended to the needs of other patients, even when she had felt so unwell. Here was a person of courage and resolve.

I would not abandon her. "It's okay," I repeated. And it was. For a few precious moments, it was.

Suddenly, one wheel on the bed began to wobble. A squeal of plastic. Soon all the wheels followed suit, a rapid succession of clicks: *Click. Click. Click. Click.* The whole bed was shaking, its metal frame flexed and creaked, the wheels tantruming.

Shit!

The noise stopped... and the whole bed was lifted up, then hurled aside, clattering and smashing against the wall and adjacent window. The mattress slid from the mangled frame. The thunder rumbled. The lightning flashed.

And the White Coat stood before us. Arms raised. Face contorted. Eyes locked upon me.

I tried to protect the woman.

The White Coat laughed. "You cannot defeat us," it said. "But perhaps the Apprentice is a threat, after all. Maybe we'll bless *you* like we blessed *her*."

I tensed. The muscles of my arms and legs rippling. Within my chest, the ache returned, as if a blade had dissected my heart. The pain was acute. *Her*. How dare it speak of Audrey this way?

The White Coat pulled at its own face. The skin came away in its hands; fake, like strips of shredded paper. It's pointed teeth ground together; they at least were real. The rest of its body jerked and twitched as it peeled the last of its disguise away.

And there it stood before us.

I bolted towards the door. I pulled the door, mucus and all, then stumbled out into the corridor. My ankles throbbed. My back screamed. I didn't think I could walk, but I found a way. There was no other choice.

Out into the main corridor, I turned left and ran towards my desk next to the Nurse's Station. I nearly tripped over someone lying on the floor, among the grunge and the shadows. A woman. Her curled-up form, bleating and whimpering.

I scrambled beneath my desk, among the dust and the electrical cables, and I pulled the chair towards me, hoping it might hide me. From there, I could look back along the corridor. I sucked in large lungfuls of air and then had to stifle a cough. I made a concerted effort to control and quieten my breathing.

After a few long seconds, the door from the room I'd just come from was thrown open, its frame shaking, its hinges shuddering.

The White Coat leapt from the room. It's strange black limbs and torso a blur, its speed and agility frightening. No longer resembling anything human, it squatted on the opposite wall, pausing; its neck craning, jaws salivating, teeth grinding, face twisted with what could only be rage. The face was a black mass, filled with eyes, a mouth and those razor-sharp teeth. Blood vessels criss-crossed its flesh and pulsated.

It spring-boarded back onto the floor, covering several metres in one jump.

It sniffed the air. Spores kissing its upturned face.

Suddenly, it pounced upon the woman lying on the floor. I held my breath. I watched it first nuzzle her with what used to be its nose, and then its teeth ripped open her left shoulder.

There was a scream: a long, gargled rattle that filled the corridor.

I saw the woman's face then, for she rolled onto her side: It was Helen Tooms. I had not recognised her at first with the darkness and the ravages of Lymphachela, but now her eyes seemed to look directly into mine, with a sternness I recognised, and that frown line of hers. Perhaps she was looking to me for help, or so it seemed in that moment. I didn't know how to help. I couldn't move. Hell, I was too afraid. For all I knew, she was the appetiser, and I was the main course.

A long tongue unrolled from the White Coat's wide mouth, and it lapped at the Clinical Nurse Manager's blood, which spread across the floor. Then it rose, its head swaying once more. It took another bite, this time out of Tooms' other shoulder.

There were fresh screams, only weaker this time. Her eyes were still locked on me—Could she *really* see me?—but they appeared to lose some of their intensity, some of their focus.

Next, the White Coat formed a seal with its mouth over the latest shoulder wound and drank from her.

Tooms' bloated body twitched for what felt like several minutes, but was probably only thirty seconds. I watched the whole thing, trying to lie still, trying not to breathe.

When her body was thoroughly exsanguinated, the creature cast her aside, lifted its head, and growled.

Would the White Coat smell the fear that oozed from my every pore?

Had it deliberately killed Tooms before me to heighten my fear?

It leapt into the air, taking off suddenly, bouncing off the wall, past my desk and, presumably, further along the corridor.

I waited as long as I could, but perhaps it wasn't long at all. I lay there under my desk; the pain returning to various parts of my body, staring out at the half-eaten cadaver of the woman who used to make my professional life such a hell. My stomach lurched. I closed my eyes, but the nausea only got worse.

Sorry, Tooms, I wish I could have helped you... I wish I—... I wish I wasn't such a coward...

I opened my eyes. I gawped. Even in death, her stare convicted me. I could take no more. Even though there was the risk that the White Coat was poised on top of my desk, knowing full well my hiding place and waiting for me to emerge, I didn't care.

I ran. Gasping. Legs slow and stupid. My aches and pains temporarily anaesthetised. Black spots swirling before my eyes, a strange bloom in an already malignant place. The spores shifting. I ran past the remains of Tooms, all the while waiting for the creature to grab me from behind....

I reached the double doors. I wrestled one door open. And I slipped between the gap, expecting the creature to bear down on me at any moment...

I glanced back; running, still running, surprised to have made it this far.

The White Coat passed through the door: in one instant ethereal, the next corporeal, all teeth and snarls. First the head and then all its terrible black mass egressed from the door.

I ran, and I think maybe I screamed.

The creature's full weight and momentum slammed into me, sending me sprawling, the floor rushing towards me. The pain exploded as every injury in my body was re-ignited.

Then I was scrambling. Arms, legs: scrambling. I regained my feet somehow and sprinted along the corridor. Moving from door to door, trying the handles, finding each one locked. Seeking refuge. Desperate. Hyperventilating. Certain the White Coat would descend upon me any second and put an end to my misery.

Everything slowed. Every movement one of painful exaggeration. I went through another set of double doors, yet it felt like I barely moved at all. Eyes scanning back and forth, back and forth.

But the White Coat did not pursue me through these doors, neither pushing them open nor passing through them.

I ran past the Patient Lifts.

Shape. Movement. I registered both in the corner of my eye, but it was too late—

The Seeper pounced from the recess behind the lifts shafts, where a fifth and sixth lift were located. It took me up. It's long fingers digging in. Pain like a thousand needles piercing my body, illuminating pathways right from my head to my feet, fire dancing over my entire body and igniting my flesh.

Up... then down again. We crashed to the floor.

The White Coat set upon me, its fingernails slicing with wicked speed. Frenzied and vindictive. I raised up my arms, doing my best to protect my head and my torso from the onslaught, but my strength, my hope, my life, were all diminishing.

It had shredded my shirt, and I was bleeding.

Finally, it stopped. Through a mist of red, I saw the creature lean closer. White shreds of a medical coat clung from its vertebrae. The flesh beneath scorched and blackened. Its arms and legs moving with slow precision, sinewy, fibres aquiver. Fingernails and mouth and teeth impossible to comprehend: yet poised, ready. It had tenderised me. Surely now it would go for the kill?

I was pinned to the floor and helpless.

The creature's face loomed before me, huge because of its proximity. Its eyes shifting, but did not blink. The pupils were as black as despair. It lingered there, poised. Its jaw began that side-to-side movement, making its teeth grind loudly.

A second and third White Coat emerged from the wall. They came forward, gathering around me, just as they'd done with Audrey. Each of them produced that popping noise again. They were going to re-infect me.

I drew in a deep breath and *pushed*. I was done with their virus. I was done with *them*, with the suffering they had brought into the world.

All of them recoiled. The one who had me pinned to the ground fell backward, lifting its large hands to its face and making a moaning sound. Its physical bulk diminished considerably.

While they were distracted, I leapt to my feet. On trembling legs, I bounded down the corridor. Past a cleaner's room, a linen chute, the Privacy Officer's room. No time to try any more doors.

I crashed around a corner and slumped to the floor, my back pressed against the wall, panting.

My stomach was throbbing with pain. I ran my fingers across it, and they came away dripping with fresh blood. And with my blood, a little warmth departed too. Was I simply going to bleed out in some anonymous corridor with its shifting surfaces and its mucus-laden artworks?

An ungodly roar bellowed down the corridor.

Looking up, there was a circular mirror attached high on the opposite wall. In its slightly convex surface I saw the White Coats. Two crept along the floor, while the third crept along the wall. Their teeth grinding. They were pissed now.

I regained my feet and moved again. The corridor widened. On either side were display cases filled with medical antiquities. I brushed my fingers over the glass, smearing blood there.

I was shoved from behind by large, callous hands.

I jerked forward. My forehead struck the glass. A flash of pain exploded inside my skull. The glass first buckled, then cracked, releasing the stale air within the case. I slumped forward. The corridor darkened around me.

One of the White Coats roared and yanked me back by my clothing, but my knees folded and I sank to the linoleum.

I didn't stay there, although a part of me wanted to. As if I had no substantial mass, the White Coat raised me all the way from the floor to the ceiling. I was suspended in time and space; lost, slipping into myself. Its fingernails dug into the skin of my left leg and my abdomen. I was held over its head with the same crushing grip. The pain, at least, was a reminder that I was still alive.

Finally, I was released.

I was thrown towards the display case. And when I struck it, I was embraced by an ear-splitting crescendo and a thousand shards of glass. *The pain! Oh God, the pain!* A pain that diminished all the pain I'd ever experienced before then. Shards of glass embedded in my skin. I clenched my teeth, and I gasped. I turned to my side, searching for some sort of comfort, but the display case, its wooden sides boxing me in, was no bed. Uneven objects dug into my back, unwilling to let me rest.

Through a haze of blood and consciousness, I saw—or *thought* I saw—the naked woman dashing through the corridor.

The White Coats—by now they numbered at least five—leapt upon her.

I groaned. I closed my eyes. Part of me simply wanted to die, but I twisted within the case, lifting myself up a little. My left hand stumbled upon a handle and, attached to it, a long blade. I lifted the object. It was the Amputation Knife.

With my right hand, I grabbed the metal lip of the display case and yanked myself up. I climbed over and out, standing upon weak and trembling legs. I transferred the knife to my dominant hand, squeezing the handle. *The Student will be a sharp implement, a sword wet with blood,* according to The Healing Art.

My body hurt in so many places.

I was haemorrhaging.

The White Coats were a great, black mass, their backs to

me, as they poured over and smothered the woman. They did not sense my slow, pained approach—at least, not at first.

I edged closer, knife raised, ready.

I stepped upon a piece of glass. It crunched as it disintegrated beneath my shoe.

One of the White Coats, the closest one, span around. It saw the knife. Its eyes widened. Comprehension darkened its pupils.

I thrust the blade up and into the creature's gut, twisting the handle, allowing the eroded edge to taste fresh meat.

It roared.

The other White Coats turned in our direction, the woman forgotten.

I held the knife firm. How easily it had pierced the creature's leathery exterior. The closeness was intimate; a closeness of death, one way or the other, either mine or the Seeper's. I read its eyes, saw colours where before I'd seen only darkness. Rage, humiliation, passion, determination—I registered each one, or thought perhaps I did—these were replaced with surprise, confusion, before being ultimately swept aside by bitterness, and lastly disappointment.

The creature panted. Ribs rising and falling around the blade. Short, sharp gasps. Rancid breaths issuing from its half-open mouth.

The lines on its face twisting.

Finally, its eyes squeezing shut.

It mewled and, with one last exhale, slid from my blade and slumped down on the floor.

I thought the other White Coats would attack me then, but they didn't; instead, they backed along the corridor or ingressed through the pumice-coloured walls.

My throat tightened. I dropped the knife, no longer possessing the strength to hold it. I closed my eyes, shutting out the horror before me. The darkness was welcome. A few jagged lines appeared, the capillaries that criss-crossed my eyelids. These lines, in turn, gave way to cracks. Then the cracks fragmented. I was broken, emotionally spent, wounded and hurting in so many ways, but I understood this was precisely when the healing power within me was at its utmost. It was strength *through* weakness.

And although I wanted only to lie down and sleep, I knew there was much work to do.

twenty eight

"Revival? This is not a revival. This is not God. If it were, I should see the hospital emptied of their sick and the undertakers twiddling their thumbs. That's the sort of revival I believe in. Show me that."

Attributed to Pastor Craig Johnson of LifeBridge Christian Fellowship, Longmont, Colorado, page 220, 'The Healing Art'

It was a ward round like no other, a Special Ward Round, incorporating the entire hospital.

I dusted myself off and checked my own injuries. I placed my hands on my abdomen, *pushed*, making the bleeding halt immediately. Good. The pain that radiated from my wrists, my leg, my back, ebbed away too. I had many mixed feelings in that moment, too many to contain let alone describe, and so I did what my father had always modelled: I ignored them and got to work.

I went to the naked woman. She was curled on the floor, bruised, battered, her arms and legs shredded. Her eyes were squeezed shut. She fought for each breath, the rising and falling of her rib cage looking decidedly one-sided. I didn't need an X-ray to know she was suffering from a tension pneumothorax. Her heart, the true source of her strength, was showing signs of permanent strain.

I reached for her hand, taking it in mine. "It's okay," I said, "It's over." Was that true? I had killed one of the White Coats, but who knew how many others there were in the hospital?

I *pushed*. "Breathe easy."

Her body jolted once more as the power entered.

On the microscopic level, the armoured tadpoles were all squashed and their teeth ground down into fine dust.

The woman's wounds began rapidly granulating. Her left lung spontaneously re-inflated itself. Her breathing normalised. She opened her eyes, and the faintest smile registered on her face.

She was breathing normally.

I smiled.

Helping her to her feet, we left the Antiquities Corridor and the dead Seeper, walking back towards the Children's Ward. The spores swirled around us. We found a small pile of hospital gowns in the linen cupboard. Although undersized, and certainly not the most dignified garment, she took one and covered herself. I fastened the plastic snaps on her shoulder. She did not speak, though; not even a thank you; there was trauma etched deep in her eyes and her heart, a trauma which even I could not heal. I guided her back out into the corridor and to the stairs. "Go down one floor and exit through the main foyer." I hoped, with the passage of time, full healing would come.

She left, and I returned to the ward.

Outside, the electrical storm was finally receding, moving away from the city and heading north.

I realised then that today was Monday. How appropriate! I understood that this was my last Ward Round. And how fitting that it would start on the Children's Ward...

I went from room to room, healing everyone I met. The ward was no longer dedicated solely to children. Somewhere during the epidemic, this must have changed. Young and old alike, I healed them all, despite saying that I couldn't do adults. I could, and I did. Everyone I met was infected by Lymphachela. There was no one left to look after these people, so many were in a state of terrible neglect, their sheets soiled, physically unable to attend to even their most basic hygiene needs.

The gossamer trails and the spores floated across the rooms and corridors. The smells everywhere were pungent.

I kept moving. I *pushed*. And *pushed*. And *pushed*.

And one by one, the swelling and the ravages of Lymphachela were cast out and people rose from their beds.

On and on and on, my heart swelling with a joy that I'd never felt in all my years as a doctor.

But where were the White Coats? Had they retreated because they feared me, or was it a strategic move? Surely they could sense that I was undoing all the damage they'd done? Should I expect some counter-attack?

I found Charlie O'Loughlin and Lilly Anderson and I healed both of them again. I felt a gush of pride when I saw Lilly helping the younger girl from her bed, holding her hand and leading her out of the ward.

I hoped I wouldn't see either again in a hospital ward.

When I'd healed the entire Children's Ward, I ventured up to the eighth floor, so I could work my way down. None of the lifts were working, so I took the stairs. The first person I encountered on 8Med was a man collapsed en route to the toilet. He was wedged in the toilet doorway. He was covered in his own faeces and vomit and was so weak he couldn't get up or move. He had the telltale symptoms of Lymphachela. His eyes swam in and out of focus as I approached.

I grabbed his hand. "I've come to heal you."

He smiled, but that might have been the delirium. The smile was hidden behind his oedema and general pallor.

I *pushed*.

His whole body jumped as if electrocuted and he hit the door frame. I witnessed the virus retreating. The man was released to a flood of buried memories: warmth; laughter; a handful of loved ones, those most important to him. He blinked repeatedly. His mouth opened. He tried to speak, but no words came, merely a croak. The next thing I knew, there were floods of tears, and I helped him slowly, very slowly, to his feet. His whole body was shaking.

I helped him back to his bed space and to his bedside chair. "Will you be okay?"

He nodded. "Thanks," he croaked.

I went to the side room and found Jenny. Her breathing was shallow. Her pulse was slow and thready. She was barely alive. The oedema was so bad I barely recognised her. I took her hands and *pushed* and the sickness departed.

I saw her real beauty then, the beauty I had always admired in the years I'd known her. I saw her depth. I saw her courage and dedication. I saw how her desire to be a nurse arose from a well-spring of mercy and kindness. I loved this woman. I think I'd loved her practically all these years, so why had I never asked if my feelings were reciprocated? Why omit such an obvious step?

Pink-coloured fingerprints littered Jenny's bed space—on the sheets, on the table and on the bedside cabinet. At first I thought she'd been messing with nail-polish, but this was extremely unlikely given her condition.

Audrey had alluded to another Healer in the hospital, saying that she was immature in her gifting. She'd said something about picking up the "fingerprints". It was the same way Audrey had found me.

Healer's fingerprints.

That Healer was Jenny; Jenny was a Healer *like me*. On some deep level, I think I'd known this, and it perhaps explained my hesitancy.

I helped her up from the bed. She took a few hesitant steps, then threw her arms around me. We embraced for a long time, a little too long for something platonic, and I finally understood that Jenny reciprocated my feelings.

The Healer in her *sensed* the Healer in me, neither of us understanding the power we possessed.

The spores danced around us.

Audrey said, "Grant, there are nightmare creatures in this hospital."

"I know."

She released me, holding me at arm's length. Already the colour was returning to her cheeks. "You've seen them too, haven't you?"

"I've fought them," I said. "My entire career I've fought them, but now I'm doing it with my eyes open."

"I can help you—"

"No," I said. "We can talk about this once you're fully recovered, but right now, I want you out of the hospital."

"Seepers," she said. "They're called Seepers."

"*Who...?* How do you know that name?"

"I'm not sure. I think I dreamed it."

Was there some future where Jenny and I worked together again? Where we healed together? These were questions for another day. Her eyes, her face, her whole body, looked tired. She needed time to regain her strength. "Rest for now," I said, "preferably far from here. I must continue."

I moved on, going to Jenny's neighbour in the next side room. She was a large woman whose age I wouldn't care to estimate. She was extremely large, and I wasn't sure how much was oedema. She lay on her bed, the rising and falling of her chest so shallow I wasn't sure if she was breathing at all. "Are you awake?"

I got no response.

I shook her shoulder gently. She did not stir. I leaned over and listened more intently for breathing. Her lips were blue. I waited for what felt like several impossibly long seconds.

Nothing. She was dead.

My training told me to commence CPR, the response automatic and hard-wired, but I ignored it.

I *pushed* in a different way, using my healing power.

Nothing. I felt nothing.

I *pushed* a second time and a third, running on instinct.

And slowly, very, very slowly, her eyelids fluttered open, and I saw recognition in her eyes. I saw signs not only of life —flavours, colours, passions, art, music—but of wellness springing up from within, and, satisfied, I moved on to the next room.

I found Paul Swartz on 8C and *pushed* Lymphachela from his feverish body. If it was possible, he was more repentant than before. He did not credit his healing to me... but to his God. He was quick in finding his voice. In his thick South African accent, he described his whole stay in hospital as a religious experience. "I've seen the Devil prowling like a hungry lion," he said, "but truly I have been blessed and seen the face of God, not once, but twice! I'm a mere man and shouldn't be alive. Praise be to God!"

It was all going well. Perhaps a little *too* well. I kept waiting for the White Coats to show up again.

When I found Fiona Peters she was at death's door. I offered her my hand and the healing of her sickness. She shook her head. No. She did not want me to touch her, not like the woman had touched her. "Go away," she croaked. "Leave me alone." As much as I wanted to ignore her wishes and heal her anyway, I wasn't sure this was how my power worked. I'd already seen what happened when someone refused my power. I'd seen the same thing with Audrey and Pastor Dixon.

Where was Pastor Dixon now?

"I'm sorry," I said, then closed the door as I left.

I kept moving, conscious that the day was getting on and that there were still many, many people to help in the hospital. I wouldn't allow those who refused to be healed to slow my momentum. There would be time to mourn them later. What I didn't want was to run out of time or energy.

When I got to the fifth floor, I found Tim, Chong and Dr O'Brien exactly where I'd left them. I healed all three, seeing what lay on the inside: Tim's insecurity that he'd never be as brilliant as his older brothers; Chong's constant fear of ageing, of death, and his smouldering resentment towards me. Tim was the hardest to heal. He'd died a few minutes before I arrived. He had, in fact, died in one of his favourite suits, although it looked rather worse for wear. I *pushed* and *pushed* and raised him back to life. The same old Tim, back again. Chong watched. His eyes sparkled with tears of comprehension and I witnessed him letting go of his resentment towards me.

"I came back," I said. "I'm sorry it took me so long..."

Poor O'Brien looked utterly perplexed. While I knew I had evicted the virus from his body, I was worried about his mental state. He was shaken to his core. He was so uncertain, and uncertainty did not bode well with him. For a man who'd built his entire career on certainties, to suddenly be like this terrified him. He scratched his head, further ruffling his already unruly hair. He tried to speak, but words were beyond him. It was true: The old dinosaurs no longer walked the earth, but thoughts of O'Brien's professional extinction saddened me more than I thought it would.

I smiled, and I kept moving.

I stumbled upon Serena Hawkins' parents, although not Serena herself, and while I could heal the girl's mother, the girl's father was a different story. He refused the healing. He blocked all the channels through which my power might flow. He was stubborn and unyielding, even as he struggled for breath. I tried several times to reach him, but in the end, I had to walk away and accept that not everyone could be saved.

One teenage boy had died on his bed.

I *pushed*… and the boy sat up in bed, eyes wide, gasping for breath, alive. The capillaries in his face perfused with blood, as his heart re-started and his circulation re-engaged. Waking in this drab hospital room with its putrid smells and its spores was an epiphany. Life was so… beautiful. He'd missed so much beauty. He wouldn't squander this second chance. His eyes sparkled. Memories, missed opportunities. So many missed opportunities. He took several hurried breaths, then exhaled. He smiled and I couldn't help but smile in reply. His smile seemed to light the whole room.

I finished on the ground floor in the Chapel. I found Pastor Dixon there, slumped in one pew, clinging to one of the kneeling pillows beneath each seat. He was weak and swollen and muttering in some strange language that I couldn't understand.

I *pushed*

… and I hit a wall. Literally, that was how it felt.

I *pushed* again, just to be certain, but just like Audrey had found, my ability to heal was blocked. He did not want my healing. It was not a lack of faith, as Audrey had suggested, but a lack of consent. And just as with Mr Hawkins, I left him to die his defiant, needless death, not from Motor Neurone Disease, but from Lymphachela.

I left the chapel and stood in the foyer, amid spores and those strange, swaying gossamer trials. I had done all I could. I was satisfied that I'd swept every floor, every ward, every bed bay, every corridor, but suddenly I remembered there was one place I needed to visit before I grew too weary.

twenty nine

"A battle, even a war, is the outworking of power. The motion is continuous, back and forth, round and round. There will always be conflict and there is no such thing as the void, not on earth, and not in the Sablosphere."

Kierangilli, page 119, 'The Healing Art'

I took the stairs down to the Lower Ground and followed the long corridor around. There were two boys that I hadn't been able to save...

It had been a long, long day. I felt physically and emotionally exhausted after my marathon healing session. My legs shook with weariness. I twisted the door handle of the Morgue and walked inside.

It was dark inside and warm, putrid air spilling out. The back-up generator had failed. There were no lights and no refrigeration. A stench hung thick in the air, the same stench that I'd smelt on the wards only worse: oil-like.

I pulled my phone out of my pocket and switched on its torch.

The shadows in the room danced away from the light, looking slightly ominous, clinging to the walls and the ceiling. Thankfully, the place wasn't overflowing with bodies like in my nightmare. Faintly, on the far side of the room, I could see an array of large metallic drawers. This is where they kept the cadavers.

I approached cautiously, manoeuvring around the examination table, with its articulating arm and its suction. Here, the dead were cut open and resected. This was not a place of torture, except for the fourth and fifth year medical students who were forced to endure autopsies as part of their studies. And what had we learnt? Had a single dissection ever uncovered the existence of Seepers?

I went to the first drawer, gripping the handle with one hand and keeping the light aimed with the other. I took a deep breath... and then I pulled on the drawer.

The smell poured out and assaulted me. Holding my breath made no difference, for the smell clung to my lips. The body before me was liquifying. The skin of the face was melting, the hair was lifting from the skull; the eyeballs had sunken inside the sockets, dried up and shrivelled. Given the advanced state of decay, it took me a moment to recognise *who* this dead person was. The face was bloated and melted, but those glazed and dull eyes were familiar. The shape of the nose and the jawline were familiar too.

It was Serena Hawkins.

I'd always assumed she'd die of cancer, not Lymphachela, but that, of course, was based on my own assumptions.

I cupped Serena's head in my hands, with its wet hair and melting flesh and

pushed

not knowing if it would work, or even if it *could* work on one who'd been dead for so long, where the skin was eroding from the skeleton and to separate from the muscles and tendons.

Nothing.

I took a shallow breath of foul air, and I tried again. If I couldn't raise Serena, then I wouldn't be able to raise David and Toby, assuming their bodies were held here, too.

I *pushed* and *pushed*.

Suddenly healing power surged through me, breaking down barriers, flowing through my fingertips and into the body of this girl who once was. I witnessed her birth and her death, and all the suffering that was bound by those two dates. I heard screams. I heard pain that couldn't be categorised on a scale from zero to ten. But there was more:

deeper, deeper, I saw the measure of this girl. The potential. I saw the woman she *might be* if she was ever able to break free from her religious shackles and the resentment that festered as a result of unrealistic expectations.

"Come on."

And although my body ached in places I hadn't even felt before, although my mind was fatigued, my heart broken, I kept *pushing*.

And the power flowed...

And that was when Serena Hopkins opened her eyes and sucked in a huge mouthful of air, her first in over a week.

"Don't be alarmed," I said, which was a stupid thing to say! She was disorientated and afraid. She'd woken up in a darkened morgue, inside a body drawer. I defy anyone not to be alarmed. "I'm going to take you to your mother in just a moment."

Her jaw twitched. She was trying to move it, to express herself perhaps, but there simply wasn't enough muscle tone yet.

"It's Grant," I said. "You died, but... but now you're alive again."

Serena raised her hand up towards her face, her fingers probing the skin there. Tears welled in her eyes and dribbled down both cheeks.

I moved to the next drawer. I pulled it open and shone my phone on the body inside. It was Peter Layton. He wasn't as decomposed as Serena and I could raise him with relative ease. Here was a man of simple passions and deep loyalty. Above all, he cared about his family. His divorce had been the most difficult time in his life, leaving a lasting fissure in his heart and soul, leaving bruises in deep places that would never be healed (nor would he *want* them to heal). For David's sake, he'd vowed that he'd never love another woman. In fact, the first word he uttered was, "David..."

David Layton was in the drawer next to his father. Like Serena, David had been dead for quite some time and I had to summon up the energy from deep inside my reserves. I *pushed* and *pushed* and *pushed*, then I thought about Audrey and *pushed* that little extra.

The barrier broke open. That little extra had made the difference. The David I witnessed had been gifted with many great attributes from both his parents; from his father, a steadfastness; from his mother, strength and heart. In the future he would travel the world and would touch many lives.

Right now he stirred, as if from a deep and troubled sleep, and whimpered. The whimper grew and grew, permeating through the darkness and the dead space. I was worried that I'd restored him, but *without* his right mind, and yet I didn't have time to linger and check he was okay.

I would have to trust the power.

I had to find Toby too; I was rapidly running out of steam. I could barely walk. It was difficult to even raise my hands. I was done... but I kept going. The next drawer and the next and the next. And for each body, I lay my hands on the cold, putrefied flesh and I *pushed* life back into carcasses where only death now resided.

Toby was along the bottom row, in one of the last drawers. I raised him, just as I did with David. Toby, with his nightmares of suffocation… Toby, who one day would express this and other fears in writing, and find success as an author… Toby who'd always lived under the shadow of Asthma, although, he was right, all evidence of the disease itself was gone.

I was spent.

Toby coughed and spluttered and almost rolled off the metal drawer. Some of his flesh had sheared away, but it would return; given enough time, it would all regenerate. I grabbed him and steadied him, and I sobbed uncontrollably. It all hit me, overwhelming me. Everything that I'd accomplished on this amazing day, but also the fact that I still didn't have my mother or, indeed, Audrey.

I needed to return to Audrey's house and raise her too, before I was too weak. What if my abilities were never this powerful again? What if, after today, my gifting was spent and I could never heal again?

I was torn between helping those I'd raised and trying to make it all the way to Audrey's house…

A shadow passed behind me. And a second.

I span around.

Several other shadowy figures passed through the

entrance to the Morgue, momentarily blocking the ambient light outside. Many more had assembled in the darkness before me, crowding around me. I lifted my phone, illuminating numerous White Coats, none of them in their human form. There were too many to count. Black and leathery. Long fingers. Mouths. Eyes. They were advancing slowly, their mouths open, their teeth grinding. I might have the strength to battle one, but not this multitude.

A roar filled the room, and they charged.

The sheer forced slammed me into the metal drawers and pummelled me like a giant wave. I was able to *push* against one White Coat, inflicting some kind of wound, but it was too little, too late, the overwhelming momentum doubling me over and trampling me underfoot. I yelped... then I was winded and left mute. My phone was gone. There was absolute darkness. I was swept away into rolling pain. Teeth ripping my skin here, there, seemingly everywhere at once. Panic smothering me. Soon would come a punishing death. There were too many of them. I thought I'd won, but I'd lost, and all my efforts had been for nothing. The White Coats would only reclaim all those people that I'd set free.

The room shook. Perhaps the whole hospital was shaking, I couldn't tell, but I wearily opened my eyes and I saw the cracks in the walls of the Morgue and the green light spilling through.

Suddenly, I was released from my pain. I took a deep breath, surprised that I could breathe.

The White Coats paused.

The walls bowed and warped, flexing impossibly, the green luminosity from beyond gaining more dominance in the room. Suddenly, all around me, a great procession of Seepers were birthed through these cracks and stood before me in the morgue, slick with dark blood and mucus.

I blinked several times, but my eyelids were heavy and it was an effort to even stay awake.

It was the Snotty-nosed boy who approached me. "So, Healer," he said, bowing before me. "Those you have spared swear their loyalty to you. Even those who have heard rumours of you are ready to fight *in your name*. What shall we do to Al Nihil?"

The White Coats had retreated to the back of the Morgue, eyes and teeth glistening in the green glow, bodies taut, muscles flexing.

My throat felt as though it were lined with broken shards of glass. I couldn't speak.

"Will we destroy them?" the Snotty-nosed boy asked, then snickered with laughter.

"No," I croaked, my head spinning, the entire room shifting and whirling around. "*No.*"

"Shall we banish him forever into the Sablosphere?" the boy asked hopefully. His fellow Seepers jeered at this suggestion. They crowded around the Snotty-nosed boy, shadows and forms on the edge of my vision. More and more of them continued to pour from the cracks, that strange light dimming, then flourishing.

The White Coats, meanwhile, huddled together in the far corner, their unsettling *pop, popping* noise becoming a syncopated rhythm.

I only wanted to sleep. I found it hard even to support my weight, to raise myself up from the floor. My eyes were closing of their own volition, as much as I fought the sensation. I knew the Snotty-nosed boy's question was an important question, but it all felt distant and like too much effort. "Yes," I said finally, firmly, my eyes fluttering open. "Send them to the Sablosphere."

The Snotty-nosed boy smiled and retreated.

And then the Seepers, all those who had been banished from the hospital, fell upon the White Coats. They scratched and clawed and bit into the White Coats, and the floor of the Morgue ran dark red with Seeper blood.

I drifted in and out of consciousness, waking now and then to the sounds of anguish and screaming, but then the blackness swept me down again.

I recognised the Seeper from Marlow Park, the faceless Shadow Boy. I saw him—it—riding on the back of a White Coat while attempting to dismantle the creature's spinal cord.

Then I faded out again.

Punctuated with roars of pain, the White Coats were rounded up, then dragged, pushed, even thrown, through the cracks in the walls—into the Sablosphere. I watched with the distant fascination of the truly exhausted, until the very last White Coat disappeared through the cracks, and then the cracks themselves were fused closed and the green light was replaced with darkness.

I closed my eyes and fell into a deep and dreamless sleep.

thirty

"I have reached the end of one career... and the beginning of another."

Tom Grant, M.D., page 281, 'The Healing Art'

A moaning noise woke me.

My eyelids were heavy and opened slowly. All around there was thick darkness. My back was pushed up against a cool metal wall. I rubbed my eyes. More moans and groans came from around me, and someone said, "Hello?". Disorientated, I was afraid to move without knowing where I was.

What was this place?

And then it all came back to me: The Special Ward Round; the Morgue; the defeat of the White Coats.

What an incredible day!

Now I felt weary. I had expelled the pain from my body, the cuts, the bites and the bruises, but the weariness went deeper and remained. I struggled even to get to my feet. The healing power was gone. I had nothing left to give. I could barely push open the door to the Morgue, let alone *push* disease from those who were sick. I was hungover, much like I'd been that morning I awoke in Audrey's house. I was spent.

I stood in the doorway and those still inside the Morgue filed out, shuffling towards the light. These were the dead I'd raised. Many of them looked like I felt. Life had been imbued back to them by some miracle, yes, but the skin of the face and the peripheries, the hair, the nails, would take time to regrow. They were in shock; their hangover worse than mine. They would need time to adjust, peace, quiet, good clean water, wholesome foods, to be re-acquainted with their loved ones… all the things that contributed to people's health. I thought of Chong; Chong would understand.

I helped them from the Morgue. We made our way along the lower ground corridor. The spores were gone. Remnants of gossamer trails clung to some walls and posts, but were fading. There were several cracks along the linoleum and the walls, not some portal into the Sablosphere, but what looked like seismic damage.

We made our way carefully up the stairs and out of the hospital into the late afternoon.

"Thank you," someone said, but her words were lacklustre at best.

A few weak smiles stretched over taut skin.

I left them to find their own way. I had nothing else to offer. I stumbled off down the street. I couldn't tell you how long it took, but somehow I made it up the gradient of Pitt Street, past the spires of Knox Church, past the houses which lined either side of the street, past Herriot Row and finally back to Audrey's house. I let myself in. Apparently, I hadn't locked the door when I left. I crashed through into Audrey's bedroom and found her body there upon her bed, still covered by the blanket.

I pulled back the blanket.

Audrey's entire body was grossly bloated from the virus, but she looked surprisingly serene.

I touched her face—cold.

Her left hand—cold.

I wanted to shake her awake, but she looked so peaceful in death.

I took a deep breath, and I *pushed.*

It wasn't like earlier. There was nothing left. No power. And, of course, there was no response from Audrey. She remained dead. I *pushed* again, again, again. I'm not sure how many times.

I wept. I was so overwhelmed with sorrow, and my tears came so forcefully, that I lowered myself to my knees. My whole body trembled. My eyes blurred. Even my nose was streaming.

She had been a warrior and a mentor. While reluctant at

first, and understandably so, she had brought me into my true life, my *true* calling. I was so grateful for that. She had been a mother... and yet she'd failed totally. At least, this was how she'd viewed things. She was wrong, of course. She was being impossibly hard on herself. If only there was an easy way to heal such deep-seated beliefs...

She talked of God as the 'Old Bastard' when it was abundantly clear, not only to me, but to anyone who took the time to get to know her, that she had cherished the relationship she had had with her God.

She depended on it.

Her death was wrong on so many levels...

No one would get to relate to this incredible woman; no one would experience her tenderness, or her warped humour; no one could gauge just how big her heart really was, where her real strength dwelled. I'd only just scratched the surface. There hadn't been enough time.

Losing Audrey had been like losing my mother all over again.

"Why are you crying?" a voice croaked.

I looked up. *That was Audrey's voice!* I wiped my eyes. She was still lying on the bed, but her eyelids flickered. Her mouth was open. Her voice was raspy. "Is that you David?"

I seized her hand. "No, it's Grant." The relief was enormous. I had nothing left, no healing left, no strength, but still Audrey had been raised.

"Ah, yes. Grant." A smile creased her mouth. "You did it, then."

"I guess so."

Later, I would make us both a meal and fill Audrey in on all the events, as best as I could remember them: from the training session in South Dunedin to the Special Ward Round to the eventual demise of the White Coats. I left the best bit until last: How I'd raised David and how it would be my pleasure to re-introduce her to her son once she was feeling strong enough. She wanted to go to him immediately, of course, but I was able to convince her she'd look and feel much better if she waited a day or two. "Listen to me," I said. "I'm an ex-doctor."

I returned to Dunedin Hospital and found Chong on his old ward, 8C. He sat in the Whānau Room, on a grubby-looking recliner, looking out over the city. At least all those spores had gone. It was obvious from his posture that his fitness had taken a hit from the virus that had nearly killed him, although he looked dramatically better than yesterday.

It was a stunning evening; the sun glinting over the harbour in warm red hues.

"Chong, hey! How're you feeling? I'm glad I found you."

Chong could barely look me in the eye. "I owe you an apology."

"No, you don't."

"Yes, I do," he said, finally turning to look at me. He still looked very pale, like he'd benefit from a couple of units of red cells. "I only accepted you as long as you conformed to the pre-conceived idea I had. I was wrong to take offence."

"It's okay, buddy." I placed my hand on his shoulder. "Really. It doesn't matter."

"I thought you'd turned your back on me, on Tim, that you were a coward of the worst kind, when in reality you saved everyone. I still don't understand how."

"Well," I said, taking the chair next to Chong. The springs squealed under my weight. "Turns out I'm a Healer more than I'm a doctor."

"But doctors *heal*."

"In a fashion, yes, but medicine isn't my calling."

He sighed. "What'll you do?"

"I'm leaving Dunedin, I—"

Chong stared at me, suddenly looking very fragile. His hair had lost much of its shine. "You're leaving?"

"Yeah, that's why I'm glad I got to say goodbye."

"Where will you go?"

"I'm not exactly sure yet," I said. "I'll follow my heart. There's lots of work for me to do elsewhere in New Zealand and maybe overseas too. I can't stay in Dunedin, especially since no one's sick here anymore."

Chong laughed. "Yeah? For how long?"

I thought about all those Seepers that had poured out of

the walls of the Morgue. It wouldn't be too long before they re-established themselves, I was sure. "Don't worry, you'll still have your job."

"Will we see you again?"

"Sure."

"You've got a different path now."

"I found the right one."

"Hey, you know the CEO wants to meet to you. I saw him before in the Clinical Services block. I'm not sure if he wants to give you your old job back with a raise, or if he wants to reinforce your ban from the hospital since you're bad for business."

"I'm not an employee of the Southern DHB anymore," I laughed. "Besides, I don't have time for him."

"When are you leaving?"

"I thought maybe tonight, after I've said goodbye to Tim."

epilogue

FIVE DAYS LATER

It hadn't been Audrey's idea to meet, but the invite pleased her. She'd suggested McDonald's. It felt like neutral ground.

She'd discovered a green dress hidden at the back of her wardrobe to wear, a welcome change from the usual black clothes. She had tied her hair back from her face. She'd even gone to the trouble of putting on a basic foundation, lipstick and mascara, all she had in the way of make-up. It had been a painfully long time since she'd worried about her appearance.

"Hello, Audrey," said Peter.

"Hi, Mum," said David.

They ordered their meals on the touchscreen menu—she went for McNuggets, fries and a strawberry milkshake—and they took their seats. Peter had offered to pay for her meal. She'd smiled and accepted.

"Thank you both for this," Audrey said. "Especially with the Restraining Order still active."

Peter blushed.

She continued, "It means a lot to get this second chance."

"It seems like the least we could do after... after..."

Audrey nodded. "I know. It's weird. I was dead for less than twelve hours and the truth is I'm still getting my head around things. It's going to take a bit of time."

Peter wore black jeans and a navy blue short-sleeved shirt. While he'd never been one to make much of an effort with his appearance, today, it seemed, he had. He'd even run a comb through his hair and styled it with gel. "We don't have to talk about... *that*..."

She sucked on the straw, drinking more milkshake. "No, Peter," she said, correcting him but trying to do so with kindness. "If there's one thing I've learnt, it's the importance of talking things through. I think—for us—it's long overdue." She gazed at her son and then back at her ex-husband. "I just don't know if either of you will hear me out."

"Of course we will, Mum."

She smiled. She turned to Peter, who hadn't been so quick to reply. "Peter?"

He leaned against the Formica table and shifted on the high-density foam seat. The colour scheme was cheap and garish, although better than what she remembered. "I can't promise we can make this work," he said. "Not after so long, but I *will* listen. I owe you that much."

"Thank you."

"So, what'd you wanna say?" he asked.

She looked directly at her ex-husband. He had aged in the intervening years, had his own fair share of lines and blemishes, but his eyes were a soft blue and sparkled with kindness. He was a good-looking man. "I haven't been well mentally for quite some time, and the truth is, that's why our marriage failed."

He nodded. "Water under the bridge."

"The thing is," she said, slurping on her milkshake again. "I've spent more years than I'd like hiding from the world, trying to pretend that the gifts I had and the reality I saw weren't real. I hurt myself and, I'm sorry to say, I hurt both of you. Sorry..." She swallowed hard, keeping her emotions in check. "Well, I'm done hiding. And with Grant (I mean Dr Newman) embracing the Art, I... well, I see myself as semi-retired... and I've got more time for... you know... I'd..."

"What?" Peter asked, leaning forward.

"Social skills!" she said suddenly, realising that she'd said too much, changing tack. "I really need to work on my social skills."

"You were about to say something else," Peter observed, smiling, and, for an instant, she fancied she saw understanding, perhaps even yearning, in his eyes.

"Maybe," she said, the colour blossoming in her cheeks. "But not on a first date."

David's eyes brightened. Was it her use of the word 'date' or that she'd refer to it as the 'first'? Maybe it was the combination. He had grown into such a handsome and well-balanced boy despite the many obstacles life had thrown in his path. Despite the obstacles *she* had put in his path. It was impossible to describe how much she loved him. How proud she felt of her boy.

"David and I may be able to help with your... er... social skills."

"Thanks," she said. "Don't worry. I'm under no illusions that this will be easy, nor do I come with huge expectations."

"Baby steps," Peter Layton said finally, taking a sip from his Coke.

She smiled. She'd said that exact phrase to Grant a few days prior, although it felt like a long, long time ago. She and Peter had this shared vocabulary. Even in the brief years they'd been together, a bond had formed, and maybe it was more durable than even she knew. "That's all we can do," she agreed. "That, and trust God."

THREE WEEKS LATER

Serena Hawkins stood next to her mother on a cold August afternoon, wrapped in her thick woollen coat. They stood next to the iron fencing, where a multitude of wreaths and personal messages had been affixed. Beyond the fence, a bulldozer and a crane with its wrecking ball rested. It was a Sunday, after all. A day of rest. Of reflection. Against the grey sky, the mangled remains of the hospital loomed high. Steel bars protruded from solid blocks of concrete, the remnants of one of the wards exposed to the elements. The seismic damage to the old hospital was simply too great. So, it was out with the old and in with the new.

The tapu-removal ceremony for the old hospital was conducted by a local pastor and Kaumatua. He was a young man, tall, slender, his brown eyes sparkled with fire.

"We remember all those we lost in this place," he said, his voice boomed from the PA system and battled against the howling wind. "For although God did a great miracle in this place, not everyone is here today to testify. It is only right as we decommission this place that we remember *them.*"

Her mother squeezed her hand. Serena glanced up. They both thought about her father, although neither spoke. He was many things, her father, a man of fierce and uncompromising faith, but when all was said and done, he'd been right at her side until the very end. She couldn't fault him on that. Serena gazed out at the ruins of the old hospital. Her eyesight, like her skin, had not made a complete recovery. The flawless beauty of childhood was lost forever, but she was living and breathing and surely she ought to be grateful for that much? The old hospital was the place she'd always assumed she'd die. And yet here she was alive, and it was her father who had perished there. God's plans were a mystery. Why had the doctor healed everyone else, even raised the dead, but not her father?

She didn't understand.

"We must not let the memories of those who died in this place go unspoken," the pastor continued, his voice slow, measured. "For our Lord knows each and everyone's name. We bless them and pray for safe passage to Hawaii-A-Nui. Join with me please as we pray..."

Serena lowered her head and closed her eyes.

The pastor spoke well, with genuine passion, and it reminded her of the hospital chaplain, for he too had been a man of great faith. Yet he, like her father, had been among the small number who never walked from the old hospital, but were carried out by others in body bags. Faith, it seemed, was overrated.

She released her mother's hand and stuck both her hands deep into her pockets. While her mother, passive fool that she was, recited the pastor's prayer, Serena refused to.

God—*if* He existed at all—wasn't listening and certainly didn't care.

SIX MONTHS LATER

Everyone was talking about what had scared the student nurse, but for Jenny Epp that was mere diversion.

The talk in the changing room was of CNM Tooms'

return, although, for most staff, they hadn't worked with Tooms and knew her only by reputation. Was it possible that Helen Tooms had returned from the grave to terrorise a young woman on her transitional placement?

"I think it's Paula's over-active imagination," said Hilda. Hilda had only worked on the new Children's ward for two months. "She's far too sensitive."

"I'm not so sure," said Sandy. "I've seen stuff on nights. Stuff I can't explain."

"You been helping yourself to the CDs?"

There was laughter.

Sandy ignored it. "Or it might be the Grey Lady."

Jenny knew it *was* Helen Tooms. She'd seen the Clinical Nurse Manager frequently on nights, usually around 4am. The old manager had always liked to target the weakest. Nothing had changed there.

"Don't be stupid," she heard one nurse rebuke another. This was a little later, as Jenny was passing the sluice room. If the old sluice room had been flash, the new one was next level. The metallic surface still shone, yet to fade with the repeated stains of bodily fluids. "This hospital's too new to be haunted. There's isn't enough unrest or bad blood."

Ghosts, like Seepers, liked to congregate where the people were. The fact that Helen Tooms was brutally murdered in the old hospital site didn't seem to limit her movement around the new hospital.

Paula Kerrigan, the student in question, had encountered

Helen Tooms' ghost in the early hours of Tuesday morning, and had not returned to the ward since. By all accounts, she had been assigned to check obs on the sickest children. To minimise the sleep disturbance, the lights were kept low and Paula walked around with a pen torch. She had just finished her rounds and was walking along the back corridor when she suddenly felt cold. It was freezing... and yet the ward had a state-of-the-art temperature-regulated air conditioning system. A thin, bony finger tapped Paula on the shoulder and when she turned around to see who was there, by all accounts, a slender woman in a dark power suit was standing before her. Half the woman's face had been torn off, but what remained was smothered in layers of foundation, prominent eyeliner, and garish lipstick. The Clinical Nurse Manager smiled. Paula dropped the obs gear and ran screaming from the ward.

However, Jenny wasn't bothered by Helen Tooms' ghost. She was harmless enough. It was the other *things* she'd caught glimpses of that were the real issue. The new ward had only been commissioned two months ago, the paint barely dry, when the sick children returned. A slow trickle soon became a fast-flowing river. Suddenly, all those childhood illnesses were back, and the ward was full. And with the children came all these creatures.

She never saw them directly. They lurked on the edge of her vision, and when she turned her head, they'd disappear. Yet these creatures—these Seepers—were responsible for the children's suffering, and she didn't know what to do about it. She dared not mention them to anyone. They'd have her sectioned under the Mental Health Act.

If only Grant were still here...

Nearly everything Grant had achieved on that special day six months ago had been undone, except, of course, that the Lymphachela Virus had been eradicated. Grant who, it turned out, had been much more than a doctor. She missed him. The ward was not the same without his frequent visits. Her feelings for Grant had not faded over time; in fact, the opposite was true: they'd grown stronger and more persistent. There was much she wished she could talk to him about. He had promised her an explanation, of course. He would understand what the Seepers were. And then there was that hug they had shared six months ago, a hug so simply intoxicating that it lingered in her senses after all this time.

So, she did her best: she nursed the children and tried never to react to the things in her peripheral vision. Some of them, it had to be said, were quite horrific. She missed Grant and wondered where he might be, but she tried not to dwell on such things.

Jenny sat at the computer, typing up her notes for the shift. When she was done, she clicked on Outlook and checked her emails. There were the usual DHB All Staff notifications; a message from Michael Fontaine, the CEO; a reminder that a couple of mandatory training modules were overdue. Delete, delete, delete. And she might have cleared the entire Inbox, but she noticed a different email, a personal message from an external email.

She clicked on it.

To: Jenny.Epp@southerndhb.govt.nz
From: grant478@gmail.com

Hi Jenny, sorry it's taken me so long, but I thought it was time for that chat. We need to talk about this Sensitivity you have and what it means. Email me.

Best wishes, Grant.

Yes, it was time. It was well overdue. She hit the reply button and typed.

Andy Evans
March 2017 - November 2022
Dunedin, New Zealand

acknowledgements

I'd like to acknowledge a number of people who, in various ways, have made this novel possible. To my wife and children, who accept and understand my passion for story and my need to write most days. Thank you. I love you.

To my colleagues and fellow health professionals who've helped on this story. Thank you Mark, Edith, Scott, Margie, Rowena and Ben. Thanks for letting me bend your ears and ask my weird, hypothetical questions.

A huge thanks to my beta readers—Angela, Wendy, Mike, Mark, Edith, and Karen. Thank you for giving generously of your time and, of course, for your feedback. I hope you approve of the changes I've made. This story is stronger for your support.

To Simon Hainsworth (Simon@vertexdesign.co.uk) for the cover image. You've managed to capture the dark tone of this story perfectly. Thank you.

To my parents, for *always* being there, even when we're separated by such a vast distance (a distance only made worse with this pandemic). Mom, thanks for the taking on the proofreading. Dad, thanks for volunteering her. I love you both.

And finally, thank you to you, Dear Reader, for reading this book out of so many other choices. May I ask one more favour? If you enjoyed this book (or even if you didn't), please leave a review through whichever marketplace or store you purchased it. If you were given a copy, or even if you stole it, please tell your friends what you thought. It makes the world of difference to an indie author.

Thank you.

also by andy evans

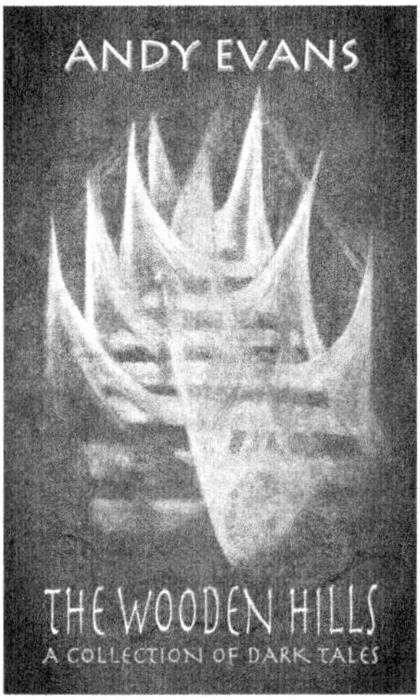

The Wooden Hills: A Collection of Dark Tales (2014)

about the author

Andy Evans is a Registered Nurse with aspirations to be a full-time professional writer. He loves good stories. He especially loves stories within the horror genre. This love was fostered when, as a teenager, he discovered giants of the genre—authors such as Stephen King, Clive Barker, and James Herbert.

Andy has had his work published in print and online. In 2014 he published *The Wooden Hills: A Collection of Dark Tales*.

He lives in Dunedin, New Zealand, with his wife and three children.

For more information

www.andyevansfiction.com

Printed in Great Britain
by Amazon

12781252R00253